War, I

A novel

By
Bogdan Kotnis

Contents

PROLOGUE

The second half of the eighteenth century was critical to two great nations, the Commonwealth of Poland-Lithuania and the United States of America. It began shaping the balance of power in the world as we know it today.

After 800 years of impressive growth and expansion, Poland was crumbling under her weight and weakening. Russia opportunistically stabbed Poland in the back and eventually morphed like a supernova into a significant worldwide power. Meanwhile, the United States challenged the empire of Great Britain for the domination of the American colonies and, ultimately, the world.

Through fifteen years of struggle, 1764-1779, which shook the entire world, the nations of Poland and the United States were intimately connected through one person. A hero of both countries, Kazimierz Michał Władysław Wiktor Pułaski (1745-1779), a noble person of Ślepowron coat-of-arms, who fought with expertise, bravery, honor, and distinction for both Poland and the United States.

He was a mortal enemy to the most powerful monarchs and a dear friend to others. Love and betrayal were subtly used as weapons among European royals and reached Kaz. His story helps to better understand the complexity of the global geopolitical tensions of today's world. Let us follow Kazimierz (Casimir) for these fifteen eventful years. We will call him Kaz.

PART ONE: POLAND

CHAPTER 1
Buffalo Hunt (1763)

Encounter

Kaz was riding his horse Zefir along the northeastern portion of his family's estates. After two days in the saddle, he felt like one with his horse and the steppe. Rolling waves of tall grass swayed in the breeze as Zefir pushed his torso up and down through the shimmering blades. Kaz saw an eagle hanging over the grassland high in the sky. Suddenly, the eagle pulled its wings close to the body and plunged into the sea of green, tightening a surprised hare into his claws.

Kaz, a youth of eighteen years, spent almost every day in the saddle, and Zefir was his steed of choice whenever he stayed at his father's eastern estates. At first, they came to accept, then trust and rely on each other in almost all long-ride decisions. Zefir became an extension of Kaz, who felt every puddle of water, a pebble, or a hole in the ground under Zefir's hoofs as if the rider and the mount shared information through an invisible network of neurons. Kaz could interpret the behavior of Zefir and read what Zefir sensed.

Over time, as he became aware of this subliminal exchange of feelings and premonitions, Kaz's awareness and ability to feel what Zefir sensed expanded. When in the saddle, Kaz continued direct dialogue with Zefir – an exchange of understanding, operating at the

3

core of hardly conscious attention. This unique connection receded when someone approached and spoke a word, though, even if interrupted, the link was never broken. With the return of quiet, the horse and horse master would again begin to blur into one another.

It was a late sunny summer morning, a time when the steppe pulsated with life. In the solitude of the plain, Kaz felt his mind expanding out beyond the horizon. He felt the gentle strokes of tall grass on his legs and the sun's heat on his cheek as he rode through the vast expanse of the grassland. The light painted the sky azure blue with white wisps of high cirrus clouds and dark bluish grasses swaying gently in the background. The kaleidoscope of color and blossoming fields invigorated each cell of his body, imbuing him with boundless energy. He was simultaneously aware of what the eagle saw when it folded its wings and how focused the hare was feeding off the grasses. The symphony of light, sound, touch, and smell harmoniously evolved in front, behind, and around him, with Kaz as a spectator and first seat in the orchestra of creation. Kaz closed his eyes to take in the green and yellow lights behind his lids. Submerged in this instant of being, in his momentary eternity, he pushed his left foot in front and his right heel behind Zefir's sides. Zefir changed direction to the right, moving the horse and rider as one, the lord of the prairie.

Kaz opened his eyes, recognizing a presence in the southeast. Although out of sight or smell, Kaz felt a tremendous sense of being. Kaz and Zefir instantly focused on the newly perceived element in the equation of signals and threats. A dark brown mound appeared out of an incline. Three to four feet high grasses changed to smaller vegetation fields, where the bison was feeding on dry bluish-green grass, not paying any attention to Kaz. As the rider approached, the animal's attitude changed. The bull turned to him, and though half a mile away, Kaz knew he was recognized and acknowledged as an intruder. The beast would take this as a challenge and pick up the gauntlet with the same ferocity as his forebears.

[Polish bison]

The bull began moving towards Kaz. With each step, it gained momentum. In an instant, the distance between Kaz and the bull melted in half. Although Kaz turned around and began riding west away from the bull, the bull followed. Kaz had to push Zefir into a full gallop to keep a hundred yards distance. Constantly changing direction, Kaz was able to slow the bull down. When Kaz began ascending a small hill, the bull lost interest and decelerated, only to stop halfway up the hill. Kaz did not look back and continued down the incline in a gallop. The wind was rushing through his ears; the tall blades were whipping him and Zefir as they strove further west. The grass waned shorter, and trees emerged on the horizon in huddled clumps.

To the right of a nearby copse, several tents crouched in a semicircle with long sticks protruding from their tops like rooster's combs against the cyan sky. Kaz was dashing close to the left of the tents. Men dressed in pointed leather hats appeared in front of the tents' flaps in plain view no more than a hundred yards away. These men were the Tatars who belonged to the security detail of the manor hired by Kaz's father. They bowed as Kaz galloped past them. Zefir could feel his stable just minutes away and picked up his pace. One final hill and the manor house roof appeared through a cluster of trees. Zefir rushed by the open gate and clattered to a stop in the middle of the courtyard.

Kaz yelled to one of the servants working around the stables, "Buffalo, buffalo! I've seen a buffalo!" A man who wore a white linen shirt with sleeves rolled halfway up his muscular sun-tanned forearms looked at Kaz.

"When? How far away?"

"Over those hills, Tom, less than an hour ago. It's a bull!"

"Let's get ready," Tom decided. He was in his mid-thirties with intense, penetrating blue eyes, which always seemed to look beyond the horizon.

Kaz and Tom ran to the stables and started preparing for the hunt. They took lances and bows while the grooms tended to the horses.

"Witek, Witek!" Kaz shouted. "Wipe Zefir dry and give him some water but not too much. He needs to be ready for a hunt."

"Yes, Sir, Zefir will be dry, clean, and ready in no time," answered a blond, not more than 18-year-old boy taking the saddle off Zefir's back. He brought some hay and brushes and put them on a rough, long table standing by the stable wall. Witek started drying Zefir's skin with long, gentle downward strokes, loosening sheets of sweat and mud. He followed the grooming routine by cleaning Zefir's hooves from heel to toe with a metal hoof pick, paying meticulous attention to the cleft around the frog. Then, he took a stiff brush and brushed away the remaining dirt and chaff.

Everyone around the estate knew their jobs well and was ready for immediate action. In an emergency, speed and efficiency could mean life and death in Podole (Podolia), the Wild East – the eastern regions of Poland. Although the times were less uncertain now, everyone here remembered the brutal attacks of Tatar or Muscovite soldiers. It had become second nature to scan the horizon to the east for threats.

Kaz and Tom knew exactly what to do and were quickly ready.

"Is he alone?" Tom asked.

"I haven't noticed any others," Kaz responded, checking the tip of his lance with his thumb.

"It looks like he should be your first one. You are ready."

Kaz was of a short and compact build. With his long legs and arms, he had the body of a perfect rider. Extensive training had made his movements decisive, balanced, and confident, while hardship had sown confidence in his broad chest. He had exceptional eyesight and excellent hand-eye coordination. At a gallop or stock still, Kaz placed arrows or lead shots as carefully at twenty paces as he did at a saber's length. Shooting an arrow or a pistol while riding a horse at full speed came to Kaz naturally. He gloried in the hunt. The hours spent breathing, listening, and allowing himself to exist as a creature of the steppe. He enjoyed the thrill of pursuit and had remarkable patience for long hours of waiting without motion if the situation required.

Tom had taught him the open steppe of Podole, the features of her face, and her temperamental habits. The open country would provide anything to the industrious man who respected her secrets but would not coddle fools. In the far reaches of Podole, the unwary rarely survived their first mistake, where a man had to be ready for any surprise if he wanted to succeed or even merely survive the challenges of an open frontier. An unpleasant reality was a constant threat of an unexpected swift attack by a band of Tatars bent on stealing some horses or kidnapping people. Looking for enslaved people and horseflesh, they struck without warning and carried off survivors to be sold, murdered, or even worse. In winter, a sudden wind shift could bring a blizzard or a pack of hungry wolves. The wolves of Podole were considerably larger than their western kin and were known to stalk a rider for days.

This time, the task was clearly defined for Kaz and Tom. They were to follow the buffalo, which Kaz had spotted, and Kaz was to hunt it down using a bow, arrows, and a spear. They did not intend to use pistols or muskets. Such a hunt was a rare occasion to test a warrior's prowess. Because Polish żubr preferred wooded areas, spotting a lone bull in an open steppe was quite rare.

They took off from the courtyard and, in a few moments, were passing by the security detail's Tatar tents. Tom rode first, and Kaz followed due east. Once the tents disappeared over the horizon, they picked up the pace. Kaz's two twelve-foot lances, tied to the saddle, dragged through tall grasses. Soon Tom found a fresh trail.

"He is behind this hill," Tom said as they slowed down an incline.

"He knows that you are coming. Remember, don't miss with the arrows, don't let him gore you with his horns, and finish him off with the lance."

Kaz nodded his head, asking, "Any other tips?"

"No, just don't get gored; your father would be furious with me. I would never hear the end of his complaining. Also, don't miss. Neither of us could live with the embarrassment."

"The master huntsman is wise," Kaz said with a smile and slight bow as he rode off. Tom followed to the top of the hill to watch his disciple's performance.

The bull was feeding on the grass and watching Kaz approach slowly downhill. It was apparent that the bull had chased Kaz, knowing that he would return. There was no hesitation on either side. Both Kaz and the bull knew what to expect. Kaz sensed that the bull had much deeper energy and consciousness than Zefir. The bull had the gravitas of a patriarch and the calm, steady gaze of a long life scanning the brim of the prairie. If this lord of the steppe spoke to Kaz on some ancient level, the young hunter could not listen, nor could he understand. It appeared as if the ocean waves stirred by a storm of fate pushed Kaz while the buffalo observed him from the deep, the cradle of existence.

Kaz spurred Zefir to full speed downhill and loosed two arrows as he rode past the beast's right. The bull seemed surprised and annoyed by the arrows. He lowered his head and prepared to charge the horse. Kaz put his bow away and reached for his lance as the left side of Zefir faced the bull. Both looked at one another briefly, and the bull began to charge. With each step, the bull gained speed and momentum until he reached the peak of his power and fury. Kaz turned Zefir towards the bull, charging slightly to the right past the approaching animal. The bull, at full speed, seemed to slow touch and turned to the left, aiming straight at Zefir's chest. Kaz quickly moved his horse to the left to avoid the horns, but he did so late that nothing seemed to save him from the strike. A cloud of dust surrounded both the rider and the bull. Tom was watching from the hill, waiting for the dust to settle. A slight breeze swayed the grasses and rose the dust like a curtain.

Still on his horse, the rider circled and prepared his second lance. The strength seemed to leave his body as the bull stood with the arrows and a lance stuck in his brown mass. He lowered his head, not being able to hold it up anymore. Kaz approached in a gallop and threw his second lance by the bull's left leg, aiming for the heart. The bull stiffened and began to breathe heavily. As Kaz turned Zefir around and approached the bull, Tom leaned forward, squeezing his horse with his feet, and began descending the hill.

With each turn, the bull was panting heavily and moved its head to the left and right as it got lower to the grassy soil. Finally, the bull's legs began to tremble. Then, his front legs gave way, and his head hit the ground. The bull's colossal mass dropped to the grassland carpet, breaking one lance. He was still heaving laboriously, and the arrows were trembling on his back. When Kaz and Tom reached the bull, his body lay still, with the lance pinning him down to the ground like a gigantic butterfly on display.

"It was too close," Tom remarked. "You should have given yourself a little more room," Tom said, riding around the carcass and carefully inspecting the minute details of the scene.

"I knew what I was doing. The risk was acceptable," Kaz retorted, still breathing heavily.

Tom looked at Kaz and said slowly, "No matter what, don't get killed because then it's all over. You don't get a second chance and never do it for show. You do it to survive. If he had gotten you in the groin with his horn and I had not been around, you might have bled to

11

death before anyone would find you. Don't get killed but also don't get injured because, at the end of the day, it's the same thing."

Tom put his hand on Kaz's shoulder, saying, "That said, you did well, my boy. I am glad I saw it; otherwise, nobody would believe you helped, and Zefir would get all the credit." Kaz shoved Tom's shoulder playfully in protest, and they both grinned. "Let's head back."

As they rode back to the estate, Kaz suddenly felt a strong sense of the bull or what he represented. It seemed that it was a call from the depth of being, the awareness of the storms to come that would push Kaz on the waves of events and stir the waters of life deep to the core of existence.

Saber Skills

A few days later, the bull's head was ready to be mounted on a wall. Kaz decided to display it above the fireplace in the main hall next to the heads of a 14-point deer and a wild boar. Going along the hallway decorated with pictures of his ancestors, he felt a sense of accomplishment, hoping his father and brothers would be proud of him. He wanted to surprise his father, brothers, and sisters with the bull's head already mounted when they arrived in a few days.

Tom and Kaz were admiring the trophy and reminiscing about the hunt. Tom walked towards a set of sabers hanging on the wall to the right and said, "I am delighted that I was able to witness this hunt. Important events in one's lifetime happen so quickly that it is easy to miss them. They pass us, never to return." There was a modest arsenal of blades belonging to the members of the Pułaski family on display; each one had saved a family member's life on at least a dozen occasions. Some still carried notches in the steel from the day their owners fell. Each was always kept oiled and ready for use.

Tom walked over to the table in the middle of the room set up with food. A loaf of freshly baked bread was among platters with meats, cheese, and fruit. Tom took his saber from its sheath and pushed the blade into the brown crust of the bread. The bread caved in, but the crust jumped up when Tom lifted the weapon, and the loaf looked like nothing touched it.

Tom looked at Kaz and said, "The same is with human flesh. Bread is softer, obviously, but the principle is the same. If you keep the blade sharp enough, it hardly matters anyway. See what happens when you slice it?" Tom said as he cut across the bread. "It has taken some time to figure out which blade shape is the best in a battle. Some prefer straight, heavy, or long weapons. I think that the Polish saber is the best. You can poke with it, hit with it, but most importantly, you can slice with it through almost anything. I have seen men twice your size hefting two-handers as tall as your horse, weighing half a stone. I have seen those men cut two to three times before they could lift steel to defend themselves. Some say you can't thrust with a Polish saber, but I could introduce those people to some corpses I've met."

Kaz watched and listened, knowing that the lesson had only just started. Tom stepped outside and turned toward the orchard of apple and cherry trees next to the manor. He walked between the trees and suddenly pulled out his saber. In an instant, he cut off a heavy branch.

Kaz took Tom's saber and gave a similar branch a heavy hit. Unfortunately, rather than a clean cut, the saber got stuck halfway through the width of the branch. Kaz tried to wrestle the saber of the tree, but the blade was frozen solid in the fresh wood.

"Make sure you don't break the blade," Tom said as he came over. He bent the branch to open the cut and released the weapon.

"It's tricky. You need strength and speed, but you need timing to know how much to chop and how much to slice. There is only one right way. If you chop too much, it is no good, but it is as bad if you slice too much – chop and slice simultaneously. Don't overthink it; swing and follow through; let the weight of the steel do the work. Use the momentum, and follow through. What you need is practice. Here, try it again."

Kaz took the saber and went around the orchard, cutting the branches off various trees with little success. Finally, when the saber got stuck, Kaz bent the branch and released the blade as Tom had demonstrated. Tom watched Kaz for quite a while and then came over slowly.

"Watch," Tom said as he cut off a thin branch.

Kaz looked at him with questioning eyes.

"Slice with the grain; remember, use the weight of the steel; you have the most power at the apex of your cut." Tom let his blade loose like a falconer releasing a raptor and pruned another branch with as little effort and then a third, each as thick as Kaz's wrist. Tom drew the edge close and indicated a point a third down the blade from the tip. "That's power," Tom said. "Remember, the weight of the steel, cut with the sweet spot a third of the way down the blade, hit at the apex of your swing, and follow through with momentum. Be ready for the next cut. He can't cut you if you've cut him twice already." Kaz nodded sagely to give the impression of complete understanding. Although Tom did not totally believe him.

"Measure your strength and skill to what you can accomplish," Tom observed. "See, I've been doing it so long, but I've never even tried to cut the trunk off. It is too thick for me."

Over time, Tom would make a rare swordsman of Kaz, strong in the fundamentals of fencing and possessed of both confidence and boldness, which fed into one another in a steadfast cycle leading to mastery.

Zazulińce

The House of Pułaski owned extensive land holdings, with Zazulińce (now Zozulyntsi, Ukraine) being one of them. The seat of the house, where the family would usually congregate, was in Winiary, a few leagues outside Warszawa. It was Winiary where the family would usually gather. Kaz spent vacation time in Zazulińce while his brothers would serve various family interests across the Commonwealth or abroad.

Zazulińce was a typical manor house like thousands of similar country estates dispersed throughout the vast central and eastern reaches of the biggest country in Europe, the Commonwealth of

Poland-Lithuania. It was located on the left bank of the Dniestr River (now Dniester, Ukraine), about thirty miles from Kamieniec Podolski (now Kamianets Podilskyi, Ukraine), surrounded by a ten-foot-high wooden palisade. The entrance was a sizable double-hung doorway. The house faced 11:00, meaning the sun's rays hit the front gates at eleven a.m. Three giant steps led to an expansive porch with two white columns supporting the triangular pediment. Wide double doors served as the main entrance, carved with an elaborate geometric pattern arranged into a floral design. Intricately contrived triangles and squares tessellated into recognizable flora of the Commonwealth.

Through these gates lay a spacious central hall. Wooden benches with backrests were placed around the walls, all carved of soft linden boards and painted green. Each bore a pattern of swaying lines and spirals carved into the sides and backrests, reminding one of the swirling grasses of the steppe and lending the otherwise austere hall a lively touch and some much-needed seating. Hangers of various sizes and shapes pegged clothes, tools, and weapons to every available space. Three doors, one on each hall wall, lead to the master wing on the right, the servant quarters on the left, and the fireplace dining and entertainment room across the main entrance. The center of the wall opposite the main entrance was decorated with the Ślepowron coat of arms and portraits of venerated ancestors in gilded frames.

[Ślepowron coat of arms, Pułaski family crest]

The door leading to the great hall lay to the right side opposite the entrance and was framed by the mounted heads of two wild boars underlined by a pair of crossed battle axes. At night, they were lit by bronze sconces framing a mirror. An assortment of lances, sabers, pistols, and rifles was arranged on the walls for decoration and immediate use. An almost life-size portrait of a hussar was on the right wall next to the door leading to the master's chambers.

[Polish hussar]

The painting dominated the room. It reminded all how strong the proud tradition of Polish cavalry was to the owner and the inhabitants of this manor house. The hussar, dressed in red pants and characteristic yellow boots, was seated on a glamorous white Arabian stallion of perfect proportion. His leopard cloak was tied over plates of steel, which shone like silver fringed with gold. White eagle feathers attached to a wooden frame fastened to the rider's back added an extra dimension, not to mention height. They made a fearful noise during a charge and imbued the devout riders with the impression they were angels descending holy wrath upon a terrified enemy. He looked as if standing at the 1500 feet tall Kahlenberg Mountain between his hussar Lord Brothers minutes before their famous final attack on the Turkish Kara Mustafa troops surrounding Vienna in 1683. The "winged" lancers quickly gained an enduring reputation with friends and foes.

The fireplace chamber was surprisingly large, with a high ceiling decorated with wooden cassettes. Each wall had a door, which seemed small compared to the room's size. The left door led to the servants' quarters, the right one to the master wing, and the back to additional rooms starting with the antechamber.

To the right of the manor house was the stable with wide double doors in the front and back and double rows of horse stalls. The arrangement was large enough to drive a coach through the stables. It had sixty stalls, thirty on each side. In heavy winter, two horses could squeeze in one booth. Next to the stables was a carriage house full of wagons, coaches, and the equipment to serve any transportation need.

The back of the carriage house was dedicated to the distillery, which produced alcohol for consumption and sanitary purposes. To the left of the house were a shed for cattle and a barn for straw, hay, and grain, with a room for various food supplies. It housed large amounts of oats, mainly for animal feed. A deep stone well covered with a cedar-staved roof was between the stables and the manor house.

In case of a raid, the people from the surrounding villages would find shelter in the manor house. They would man the raisers around the fortification. The main gate was protected with a heavy oak beam placed across on solid metal hangers. If the palisade were breached, the windows would be locked with thick boards, with narrow vertical openings to shoot arrows or guns at the attackers. The defenders would congregate in the main hall, able to withstand any attack for weeks, if not longer.

An anteroom stored small cannons, cannonballs, extra bullets, shot powder, and rifles, accessed through the back door to the great hall. It was where barrels of food and water were also stored. It was also equipped with a hand quern and a wooden cheese press. It had a concealed hatch leading to a narrow tunnel, which could lead secret escapees to an opening by the stream. The quern had two round stones. One was set in motion by a wooden peg inserted in a hole by the rim of the stone, while another concave bottom stone was grooved so that the ground flour would end up in a sack placed to the side of the quern.

The cheese press was a set of two oblong wooden boards arranged as a slight incline connected by two large wooden screws attached to the bottom board. A linen sack of freshly made soft cheese would be placed in this vice and screwed tight by wooden bolts. Each day, the bolts would be turned to maintain pressure. At the end of the process, a hard block of cheese was ready for storage or consumption.

The roof of the manor house was double the height of the main elevation. It was used for extra storage and sleeping quarters for guests. It had a hatch between two chimneys, which could be used to pour water on the roof if any attacker decided to set the house on fire.

The Starosta (Sheriff)

After his morning routine of riding around some parts of the Zazulińce estate, Kaz returned to the manor house and had Witek fix him a tub of hot water to wash the dust off his face and hands. As Kaz was drying his face, Tom showed up and said, "Kaz, we have visitors awaiting you in the hall."

"Who are they?" Kaz asked.

"You must go there and see," Tom answered. Kaz was surprised by this response because Tom usually would be straightforward and always did what Kaz told him. He would answer any question from Kaz directly and without hesitation. Kaz smiled and gave the towel to Witek.

"Interesting; let us see these mysterious guests," Kaz said, walking through the main hall into the fireplace chamber. He was pleased to see his father Józef and his brothers Frank and Anthony seated around the table. He came over to his father and kissed him on the hand. Józef stood up and embraced his son.

"My dear boy. As you see, I also can visit you. You look so mature. My father's heart soars to see you and your brothers. You make me a happy man," Józef said, walking from son to son.

"How can you visit me if this is your estate?" Kaz asked, laughing, thinking that he had caught his father on an illogical statement. To seize his father on any inconsistency was quite uncommon. Józef practiced law for years. Thus, carefully choosing his words was a trained skill, which had become his second nature.

"Yes, you would be right, my son, if not for this document," Józef answered, amused, and produced a roll of paper tied with a ribbon. "Check this affidavit, and you will understand," Józef continued, handing the scroll to Kaz.

Kaz looked at his brothers, who were sampling some mead and observing him with amusement. He understood that all three of them knew what the document entailed. He could judge from their smiles that they were sure it would make quite an impression on Kaz and were waiting for his reaction. Kaz was expecting some practical joke, which his brothers never spared him. The problem was that his father was rarely in on their pranks.

"The answer is in the text; I better read it," Kaz said, unrolling the scroll. As he began reading, his face changed from guarded caution to disbelief and stunned satisfaction. He looked at his father and then his brothers.

"Do you mean it? Do you really mean it? Isn't it too early?" Kaz asked.

"The time is right. Over the last few years, you have proven that you take your studies and duties seriously. I am convinced that you will be a great starosta. Now, all of you three have your duties, Francis the starosta of Augustów, Anthony of Czeresz, and Kazimierz of Zazulińce. Kaz, it is time for you to immerse yourself in all aspects of our family activities," answered his father.

Frank came over and slapped him on the shoulder, saying, "Yes, my little brother, you are officially the Starosta of Zazulińce. Not a single peasant in any of the villages within the estate could scratch his back without your permission from now on. You will sign all the documents releasing grain or cattle for trade. After hugging our mom when visiting Winiary, you will have to report on what wonders you have achieved here. I am expecting healthy revenue growth. Unfortunately, you are still my little brother and have yet to ever beat me in a race, and neither of those things will ever change," Frank said, laughing as he tousled Kaz's hair.

"Now, as the starosta, you can pour me a glass of your mead," Anthony chimed in.

"Pour us all a glass so we may toast the new starosta," Józef asked.

Kaz reached into the cupboard and pulled a greenish oblong bottle covered with dust. He cleaned it with a cloth and spoke, "You know that I don't know too much about drinking, but I know that some of these bottles on the bottom shelf have been stored for a special occasion. I want to use it to thank you, father, and you guys for your trust. Honestly, I did not expect such an honor for quite a while." He poured a heavy amber liquid into the glasses. "Toast to you."

Józef got up and raised his glass, turning to his sons, "Kaz, hard times are coming to our beloved country and our house. We might be called to action, and we must protect our holdings from the enemies within and without. It is no time to be careless or inattentive. You all are ready for anything that might be thrown our way. The biggest strength and value we all share is our love and trust in one another. Let us drink to our House of Pułaski and the Commonwealth."

"To the Pułaskis, to the Commonwealth," his sons responded.

Józef took his seat at the head of the table and spoke.

"As you all know, the function of the starosta is assigned to a person for life. If you do well, a chance is that you could pass it on to your sons and heirs. I procured all the necessary documents. It makes me proud that all three of you have been officially appointed the starosta of your respective holdings. If we coordinate our efforts, we should continue growing our family assets. As of today, we own 108 villages and 14 towns. We mostly focus on protecting the lands from any attack, raising grain, cattle, and horses. I am convinced that you Kaz know enough about horses and the military. You must now learn more about grain and cattle production from your brothers.

"The cattleman cannot survive on the steppe without the cavalryman, and the cavalryman cannot survive without the produce of the cattleman. Our territories are vast, my sons, and so is our economic base. None of this can be taken for granted; none of this was simply 'given' to us. Generations of Pułaskis look to us now to steward our people because if we do not look out for them, no one will." The old man cleared his throat with a ragged cough before speaking again.

"Taxes collected on transporting grain and cattle are beginning to get out of control. Crown privileges state that we, as szlachta, the noblemen of Poland, do not pay taxes. Through the years, however, various roads and bridges have been granted the right to collect tolls. It seems every year, the owners of these turnpikes and bridges become more affluent, and the Crown becomes poorer. These tolls, my sons, to put it simply, are ruinous, and I do not predict this situation to resolve itself in the near term.

"The Prussians maneuvered themselves into the position of tax collectors on the Wisła (Vistula River). They successfully changed their political identity from a religious order of Roman Catholic Teutonic knights into a secular kingdom of Prussia. Poland allowed this transformation, and King Sigismund 'the Old' officially accepted the Prussian homage in 1525. Over two hundred years, step by step, they were able to put their foot in the door of our revenues. Now they dictate terms to the Commonwealth, robbing us szlachta blind. Soon, their Wisła riverbank outpost in Kwidzyń will demand tolls on our grain barges passing by on the way to Gdańsk, cutting us off from all the markets of Europe as they please. They will tax us not as agents of the Crown of Poland but for themselves. Unless we stop them, we will have to pay whatever they ask, or else we can forget selling anything overseas again."

Anthony looked at his father and said, "It reminds me of the pressure our ancestors felt from them before the war against the

Teutonic Knights three hundred years ago. Today we have the same problem of their control over the Commonwealth's access to overseas trade. Either they will back down, or it will end in violence. Ever since Konrad, the Duke of Mazovia, invited them from Jerusalem in 1226 to fight pagan Prussians, we have had nothing but trouble with them. These Germans have overstayed their welcome by some centuries now; enough is enough."

"It is complicated," Józef responded, motioning to Kaz to pour another round. "I have spent years debating these issues with Brühl and various King Augustus III court administrators," the assembled crossed themselves at the mention of the King's name.

"Heinrich, Count von Brühl, the statesman at the court of Saxony and the Polish-Lithuanian Commonwealth, was the most influential representative of the Polish King Augustus III, the second Saxon of the House of Wettin on the Polish throne," Józef recited.

The old man smiled at his youngest son Anthony and continued, "I will keep on getting involved, but in the meantime, we might be forced to re-route our transport through Królewiec (now Kaliningrad, Russia) or Ryga (now Riga, Latvia]). That's why I sent Kaz to serve as a page at the court of King Augustus' son, Carl Christian Joseph, in Mitawa (now Jelgava, Latvia). Kaz, any chance that we might get a better deal in Courland or Semigallia?"

"I can only repeat what you said, Father," Kaz replied. "It is complicated. The Wettins have lost their position there. I saw Russian soldiers swarming all over the place. Even if we get some promises, I don't know how reliable they will be or how they will turn out in practice. It is a mess, but I will keep on trying."

"It was so much easier in the old times," Frank added. "We would get our swords and be done with them."

Józef nodded and said, "It always looks simple from a distance. I have been looking at it all my whole life, and the older I get, the more convinced I am that it has always been the same. Thieves do everything to confuse their victims. If you listen to them and do not focus on what they stole from you, they will try it again. If you are friendly and look for compromise, they treat you like a fool and get even bolder than before.

"Brühl insists that we should be tolerant and all-inclusive. We are losing money while he is getting kickbacks from the Prussians. He doesn't care for Poland or the Commonwealth, just his coin purse. He talks of more religious tolerance for the Protestants while avoiding talk of tax collection or import duties. Religious wars are not about theology but money and the source of power. If you look carefully, you will always find that the winner in these grand theological debates was the one with more money or soldiers."

Kaz got up from his chair and started pacing around the room, from the fireplace to the windows and back to the table. His father and brothers knew he could not stay seated for too long, and they did not mind following him with their eyes all over the great hall.

He looked at his father and added, "Through my studies, I noticed how the Germans used the Roman Catholic religion to gain support for their genocide of Prussians in the 13th century. And, of course, you could not call them Germans. They were the Teutonic Brothers. Forget that they spoke German and sent gold to their families in various German lands. Once they killed all Prussians and loaded their pockets with the blood money, they did not want the Vatican to pry into their affairs or count their spoils. They turned their state into a non-religious enterprise and called it Prussia. What audacity! Then, they converted to Protestantism, which gave them the right to rob all Roman Catholic churches they could reach, much the same way they robbed the pagan Prussians. Now they are fighting for the rights of Protestant theology; all this in the name of religious freedom and tolerance, of course. If we let them continue, they will rob all Roman Catholic churches in Poland in the name of progress and justice."

"Religion and politics are a combustible mixture, my son," Józef continued his argument. "Moral and ethical judgments are the best way to confuse and control anyone who falls into distraction over them. If you are not cautious when playing with the vagaries of truth and dogma, you might forget what's real. Never argue with liars, boys, as you will always be correct, but always lose; often while the liar's friends are picking your pocket or rustling your horses."

Frank nodded in agreement and said, "With so many multi-generational cases languishing on the court's docket these days, we cannot expect a lawsuit over these toll rights to change anything, any time soon. Last year, when I accompanied Father at the capitol, half of every day in court was devoted to cases from two generations ago." He lifted two fingers. "Cases arguing over the rights of long-dead grandfathers. So, no, those sycophants would never lift a finger over these ridiculous toll privileges." Frank crossed his arms over his chest and glowered into the fireplace as he finished speaking.

"In the meantime," Józef observed, "Brühl gets richer by the minute under our noses. We all know about it but are powerless to intervene. The crooked Count bribes and extorts whoever he needs to buy to protect his ill-gotten gains. Empress Catherine pretends to fight for religious freedom while her troops harass Roman Catholics. She is pushing for the rights of the Orthodox Church, which she controls. We support the Wettins, but the deal is getting sourer by the minute. Rather than us controlling Brühl, he seems to be the one to run circles around us."

"It all is pretty depressing. I hope you will not quit on us, brother, and resign your starosta title," Anthony observed, shoving Kaz's shoulder playfully as he passed on the way to the window.

"You are right; enough of politics and economy. We need some fresh air. Show us the horses, Kaz," Józef suggested.

Zazulińce had a large stud of carefully bred horses arranged into three groups for various functions. One was kept wild; the other was used for domestic needs, and the third was trained as war horses. If a szlachcic (nobleman) were lucky enough to purchase a Zazulińce mount, he would gain a long-term investment. Such a horse could be put out to stud after a long life, siring generations of the proudest mounts.

"Witek!" Kaz shouted. "Witek! Witek, here on the double! Where are you!?"

Kaz needed Witek to arrange the trip to the herds, but they could not find the boy anywhere. It was strange. Witek never left the manor house without asking for permission first. All personnel of the house started looking for Witek to no avail. Eventually, Kaz and Tom ended up in the back of the carriage house. As they were rummaging through piles of saddles and strips of leather used to make or repair harness elements, they heard some bubbling and faint snoring.

In the corner of the carriage house, Surma, an old Cossack companion of Józef who settled in Zazulińce, ran a distillery where he was manufacturing Zazulińce vodka for various uses. Witek was lying on a straw mat with his head resting on the mash pot. In his hand was a brown mug. Kaz picked up the empty cup; the sour smell of the unfinished brew was unmistakable. Witek imbibed on Surma's concoction and was sleeping off the effects.

Surma was a Cossack with years of experience on the warpath. For decades, he switched alliances and followed various leaders. He tried his luck in Turkey and Russia, fighting both against and alongside several Tatar bands. His graying hair and long mustaches drooping over his narrow lips and reaching his lower jaw made him look like a tried-and-true frontier man.

It was never fully explained what he had to do with Józef Pułaski, but they shared the unimaginable. Such was the case of men who went through battles and wars. Stories they knew stayed with them only to be heard at times deep at night when they started screaming for no reason. When asked what happened, they would say they had a bad dream, never with any further explanation. You would never find out more if you insisted or even tortured them. You could not threaten these battle-tested warriors. They were afraid of nothing because they lived through all imaginable and unimaginable nightmares, pain, and terror. Long familiarity with danger had inured them to fear. It was impossible to threaten such men, having long since come to terms with mortality. One winter, Surma stopped by Zazulińce, and he had been there ever since.

He was the keeper of the moonshine who knew all the recipes and tastes. He could make a grain or a potato vodka or produce 160-proof alcohol from plums, cherries, apples, or honey. Supplies of Surma's draughts were used to entertain, disinfect, or warm up during long winter treks through the howling wind and deep snow. This time Surma's liquor put Witek to sleep. The problem was that it was in the middle of a busy day.

"See what you can do. I want him to go with us," Kaz said, looking at Tom, who was standing over Witek and shaking his head.

Surma and Tom lifted Witek and carried him to the well. They placed him in a wooden trough and started pouring bucket after bucket of cold water on his sleepy head. With the first bucket, Witek jumped up, but Surma kept him in the trough while Tom was spilling the next load. Two stable boys were turning the well crank as fast as they could. When the boys pulled a bucket full of cold water, an empty bucket descended into the well. Witek did not even try to fight too much. He was sitting in the trough as bucket after bucket of ice-cold water was landing on his head. After at least ten buckets, Tom decided to terminate the therapy.

"If you want to drink, you must know how and when. Your timing was bad, and you have much to learn about how to do it. Get dressed. We are going to check the herds," Tom said.

Witek sprang out of the trough and ran toward the servants' quarters, where grooms were prepping the mounts. Soon a party of six was ready to leave the manor house compound with Kaz and Witek at the front. Tom brought up the rear. They rode to the nearest corral, paces from the manor's main gate. In the middle of the fenced-off space, as if on display, one of the local herdsmen put a bay bronco through the paces. The stable boy rode the bronco in tight eights, growing ever tighter as the young horse gained confidence. As they rode past, they watched three colts no older than three with sacks of grain tied across their saddles in another adjoining enclosure. The bags reached mid-way past the young horses' ribs.

Among the six colts, a trained eye would notice three mature mounts. Warhorses were ridden once they reached the age of four. Before a man would mount them, they were trained to carry a saddle and grain sacks for at least a year. Mature horses were with the young to help them cope with the trauma of saddles and sacks. The pressure of bags on their ribs made it easier for them to tolerate a rider when the time came.

[The herd of horses]

Kaz was eager to show off his recent investments and expansions to the stables and surrounding workshops. The proudest of his recent purchases, Kaz knew, was sure to interest his father and brothers.

One could buy a horse for fifty to a hundred złotych, while exceptional horses were worth a thousand or more. There was also a famous stallion bought in Istanbul by Count Franciszek Ksawery Branicki for twenty thousand. Kaz pulled the trigger and bought a Turkish Palomino stallion for one thousand złotych. It was a magnificent four-year-old Arabian one with a hint of Persian blood. It stood on large blackish hoofs, which supported high ergot and long sinewy legs. His broad breast held a long neck and an elongated head with small ears. His large nostrils, tight muzzle, and big intelligent black eyes made him stand out in a herd. Even when standing, his flat croup, high withers, and long torso promised speed. The concern was that he might have been poorly trained, but from the first days in Zazulińce, he was ready for all routines and was coming along handsomely. Kaz decided to name him Bystry, which meant fast.

Witek brought the group to a little valley where a herd of around five hundred horses ran wild. They stayed in the steppe all year round. From the wild herd, the horses were selected for domestic or war duties. Once a leader of such a pack decided that strangers challenged him, he could attack them with the help of some lead stallions. A black stallion who seemed to be the herd leader recognized Witek and Tom. They could ride close by without worrying that they might be attacked. The horses were nibbling on the grasses. In perfect condition, horses continuously ate small amounts of grass and moved over considerable distances in search of food. Herders oversaw where the herd was and ensured it stayed within the bounds of the Zazulińce lands.

Bystry was in a smaller group of a few warhorses running long patterns today. One of the objectives was riding through bushes with boys hiding in the thicket with drums, pipes, and horns. They were spooking the horses while their handlers were to calm them down. If done correctly, a horse would rely on his handler to decide whether a given noise was a threat. It was one of the critical skills of a seasoned warhorse. Soon, they heard a high pitch of pipes, and a few riders appeared. You could recognize Bystry even if you had little to do with horses. His Palomino hue was of intense gold. He reacted to his handler and ignored the clamors, which did not impact him much. The visitors saw Bystry run stop-and-go patterns while the horns blared, and the drums banged. One of the drills was for Bystry to stay calm as riders were jumping from the bushes and running past him in front and back. An untrained horse would not remain peaceful in such a melee. Bystry passed the test with flying colors.

Józef, visibly happy with his son's accomplishment, said, "You are doing a great job with the herd, Kaz. I congratulate you on Bystry. It looks like you struck gold with him. He might be a horse of legends if he continues this way."

"Make sure that Witek does not teach Bystry how to drink Surma's vodka, and he should do just fine," Frank joked.

Witek was embarrassed with his molt sampling experiment and did not mind the cold shower and wet clothes. Kaz did not say a word about the incident, which was probably the harshest punishment. He knew that he deserved every bit of it. Now, it was time to show through his work that he was sorry and would do everything to regain the trust of Kaz and Tom.

The final demonstration started when a rider working with Bystry rode half a mile away and chased him out using a straw mat. Bystry took off in a full gallop and disappeared between the bushes at the horizon's edge. The rider returned and stood by Witek, who got off his mount and put both hands' middle and index fingers in his mouth. He blew a high-pitch modulating whistle, reminiscent of an eagle peal call. Some believed that this call was a signal for action. Although hawk screech seemed stronger, nobody knew how animals received these high-pitched sounds.

After Witek's third attempt, a drop of gold appeared on the horizon and got closer and more prominent. Soon, everyone recognized Bystry and his long stride, which made him look like a gold bolt of lightning crossing the steppe. When Bystry approached Witek, the boy patted Bystry on his crest and caressed his muzzle. Then, he gave him a lump of sugar on his flat, extended left hand. Bystry had already been trained not to accept anything from the right hand.

Robert

When Józef gifted Zazulińce to Kaz and appointed him the starosta, he assigned one of the soldiers he had hired quite a while ago to its security detail. He was an immigrant from Scotland named Robert Frost. Robert was a tough and rugged kind with deep blue eyes and black curly hair, always ready to smile and tell a joke. However, when there was any danger, Robert turned into a ferocious warrior. He was one of those you would call on first in case of trouble. You could trust Robert with your life. You would not have to look back when you chose him to protect your rear. If he lived, he would be there. It is almost sure that even if he were killed, he would still be there for as long as you needed him. He was an invincible force, a trusted companion, and a welcome partner who could brighten up any group of the sad or depressed. He always found a way to cheer you up, even if you did not want to be cheered up.

Once Kaz moved to Zazulińce as the starosta, he spent most of his time in the company of Tom and Robert. Kaz spoke Polish, Latin, French, German, and a little Turkish. He welcomed a word or two of English from Robert.

"I know that fighting for land is the highest honor," said Robert once during these long hours after sunset. The great hall was lit by a few candles and a big fireplace. The three were sitting around the hearth, looking into the smoldering logs. "The knight's lot is what saves the rest. Some trade, others plow, and others write or pray. The knight keeps all these actions possible with his blood. I am honored that you gave me the privilege of risking my blood for this land."

"Why don't you fight in Scotland?" Kaz asked.

"Sometimes your enemy is too strong. Anytime I fight someone here, in my mind, I am fighting an Englishman. One day, if not me, maybe my son will have a chance to fight them directly. What you carry in your heart is what matters. Time and space do not change what is in your soul. When I am at the steppe and close my eyes, I often think that I am on a glen and see it with my mind's eye."

"What do you see?"

"Oh, it is lush green, and there are hills, wonderful hills. The eye is not bored like here with a flat horizon. There is always something new up, down, or around. And then, we have water, plenty of water, wind, and boats."

"We are glad you are with us, Robert. These Englishmen can wait. There always will be some Tatar or Russian to keep you entertained," Tom said, pouring some more mead into his and Robert's glass. Kaz preferred water with a hint of wine at times.

"I'll give you that, Tom. Nobody in England can ride like a Tatar. Thank God for their outfit camped in the tents, which your father has invited to Zazulińce. They stay to themselves, and I never know if they are not here to spy on us. Still, there were a few times when they gave us a good warning ahead of time. Why would they do it?" Robert asked, reaching for his glass and waving his hand towards Tom and Kaz.

Tom looked at the glowing embers and said, "It is tough for them. They must obey. To their higher-ups, they are dogs. They are to serve the khan or die. They have a better life with us. They are fed and warm, and their life does not hang by a thread every minute. Still, when the time comes, they will obey the khan. It is not only their lives but the lives of everyone in their clan which is at stake if they do not follow the khan's orders. Let's hope they won't be forced to betray us."

"If they are out there, how can they know about an upcoming raid?" Kaz asked.

"Oh, they have their ways. The news travels fast across the steppe. They are always on the lookout. Sometimes, I hear from them about what happened in the wild fields days before the news travels through our official channels," Tom said, stretching his long legs towards the fire.

"Any news lately?" Robert asked.

Tom emptied his glass, slowly swishing the mead around in his mouth and enjoying a deeply sophisticated tart and sweet blend. The flavor of honey and alcohol enhanced with hints of ginger and clover reached all taste buds augmenting the taste palate. He answered Robert's question, "They say that Muscovites are on the move. They have seen some cattle killed and the cleaned-up bones lying by the fire. The tracks were obvious. There were about a dozen Russians. They were not in a big hurry, but still, they were pushing west." He put his glass back on the table and continued, "Didn't you say that you were reading interesting stories about them in your college in Warszawa, Kaz?"

"Yes, I was reading the Bielski Chronicles. Marcin Bielski started it, and his son Joachim continued after his father's death."

"When did they live?"

"I remember it well. Marcin started writing his chronicle in 1550, over two hundred years ago. It describes the history of Poland from the beginning, starting with Adam and Eve. When Marcin died, Joachim was already a secretary to King Sigismund III Vasa and continued his father's work.

"Marcin was on the warpath against Tatars and Muscovy. He describes a story of a Polish envoy who joined a march of the Porte army against the Muscovites. Because Poland did not let them pass through our lands, tens of thousands of Turks took a big detour along the Volga River. This Polish envoy joined the Sultan's army and hardly survived.

"Tatar guides were leading them astray, stealing their supplies and horses one by one. Turks would die of hunger and thirst. Eventually, they accepted that small units, which separated from the main army, would be found dead killed by the Tatar arrows. They never made it to fight the Russians, and only a few returned to tell the story.

"Tatars are a formidable opponent surviving between Mongols, Turks, Poles, and Muscovites for centuries and moving across the vast expanses of Asia and Europe. They behave like a well-run pack of wolves if they are on your trail. They attack, withdraw, incircle, send a decoy, and disperse, but they never let go. Day by day, devoid of sleep, you lose your strength and focus being on constant alert. If you let your guard down for a moment, they would come at night and cut your throat."

The conversation of these three frontier men was starkly different from the chatter of the elites in Warszawa. It seemed crude and brutal with no hint of refined exaltation, yet they were the defenders of those seated in gilded armchairs and sipping coffee from Meissen porcelain cups.

"Let us talk to our Tatars tomorrow and learn more about the Russians. Have a good night, gentlemen. I see that you still didn't finish your mead," Kaz remarked and pointed to a bottle on the table. He got up and left the room, heading to his bedroom.

CHAPTER 2

The Trespassers (1764)

The Eastern Flank

For centuries, the Wild East of Poland was a place where the threat of sudden attack was constantly imminent. Out of nowhere, a band of Tatars might appear on the horizon. They would steal whatever they could carry while killing, burning, and destroying everything in their reach. They would sell captured people on the slave markets of the Ottoman Empire. Children suffered the worst fate. Some would be sold to training camps where they would be conditioned into brutal and heartless weapons - assassins able to be used without any concern of doubt or remorse. Imagine the horror when in one of the terrorists, you would recognize your son.

With the raid came the killing of everyone they could not take with them. Often the victims were too weak and too terrified to seek help. However, despite vast expanses of the steppe and low population density, a threat remained that if Tatar terrorists left a survivor, the story of their raid could reach others. When the information was recent, the neighbors or a military commander in the area would organize a posse and chase the terrorists. If the attackers murdered everyone, no one would ever discover their presence in time to react.

Therefore, when attacking a homestead, the order was to kill all able-bodied defenders and capture saleable humans. It was the first step in the preparation of human transport. After a successful raid, the Tatars had to escort the captives for weeks or months while avoiding capture before presenting them to a buyer in Caffa (now Feodosia, Crimea) or Balaclava (now Sevastopol, Crimea). A strong prisoner in a transport, able to use weapons well, was a constant threat. He could try and attack the escort at any time. The ideal transport group consisted of women, children, and men unable to challenge the bodyguards.

There was no time to hesitate when a Tatar with a characteristic leather cone-shaped pointy hat appeared on the horizon. His companions might have already lain in ambush. If a defender did not have a weapon with him, he might not have had time to run to his house and get one. The raiders' objective was not to talk, ask, bargain, or threaten. They went straight for the kill. The best way for a Tatar was to grab the victim from behind by their hair and cut his throat with a kindjal, a slightly curved double-edged long knife.

Tatars employed terror, a recognized tool used by the Mongols since time immemorial. They executed devastating attacks on Europe in the 13th century in the same way. Small numbers of Mongolian riders sowed terror and destruction. Mongols substituted terror for their lack of human resources to exert administrative control. Once they showed up, the local population was terrified into believing that they would die if they did not follow orders. A usual way to greet a Mongol was to fall to the ground face down and not raise your eyes.

If you did, you could be summarily executed. In such a way, all possible opponents were butchered then and there.

This reign of Mongolian terror destroyed the burgeoning civilization of Kyivan Rus. Muscovy, a small outpost hidden in her swamps at the outskirts of the Mongolian Empire, survived. The Muscovites paid their dues and, terrified, followed all orders without hesitation. They began to prosper when they convinced the Mongols to let them enforce Mongol tax collection on nearby cities. Eventually, Moscow gained strength and influence over her neighbors while the Mongolian Empire collapsed. They built their strength not on collaboration or cooperation but on division, cunning, and deceit. The key to their power was manipulation and brute force. The symbols of their power were chains and whips.

In the meantime, Poland grew in strength and developed into a wealthy and prosperous Commonwealth of Poland-Lithuania. However, she did not have unlimited manpower to continue successful expansion to the east of her political system. Even if the buffer territories tried to join the Commonwealth, the answer was often "no," as the politicians in Kraków and later Warszawa knew they could not effectively police these vast land expanses or protect the borders from the incursions.

The territories to the east beyond the effective control of the Commonwealth were called "the wild fields," the place where law and security were but a furtive dream. Some of them were within the boundaries of the Commonwealth, but the effectiveness of Commonwealth administration and law there was dubious. These were the terrains where a deserter soldier could meet a peasant, a Cossack, a Tatar, or an adventurer bored with predictable stability. You survived there if you acted fast and had the support of your neighbors who were determined to drop anything in case of an emergency, stand with you, and fight like hell.

The preferred language of Muscovy elites in the 17th century was Polish. They were hoping that it was only a matter of time before they would be allowed to join the Commonwealth. Some enterprising Poles, usurping the privilege to represent the Crown, traveled to Moscow, hatching all kinds of scenarios of the imminent union. Whenever these activities reached Warszawa, they were mostly rejected as ill-conceived and premature. The debates in the Polish Sejm on accepting Muscovy to the Commonwealth regularly concluded that the Crown could not guarantee safety and adequate support of an administrative network to afford such a union.

In the seventeenth century, these "sad times," as the Muscovites called them, of knocking on the door of the Commonwealth were put to an end by the rule of Peter the Great. He had a vision, determination, and perseverance to chart a more optimistic outlook on what the Muscovites could and should do. Empress Catherine continued the main course of Peter's plan. The Muscovites started calling themselves Russians and were claiming to represent all Rus. It was ironic for most Poles because Kijów (now Kyiv, Ukraine), the seat of ancient Rus, was a Polish territory. Also, quite recently, Muscovy boyars (Russian noblemen) were looking to join the Commonwealth of Poland-Lithuania. Theoretically, on paper, Russia was no match to the military potential of Poland. However, Poland lacked the critical ingredients from a long list of necessary elements of power – focus and resolve.

During Kaz's lifetime, marauding Russians, more often called Muscovites, became an imminent and unpredictable threat like the bands of Tatars. They often pretended to be on peaceful missions supporting the Polish King or searching for fugitive Russian peasants.

The facts on the ground in the Wild East were far from what the politicians in Warszawa chose to admit. Groups of Russian soldiers on the move fed off the land. They did not attack like Tatars but used maskirovka, the strategy of hiding their intentions and pretending to be friendly. Muscovites would demand supplies, claiming they were soldiers sent to protect the Commonwealth. Often, it was enough. If this ruse did not work, the officers encouraged or accepted any violence as long as nobody saw the crimes and could testify. If they were caught stealing or some witness complained, the Muscovites would try to talk themselves out of trouble using elaborate lies rather than kill everyone the Mongolian way.

The Tatars

The next day, after the morning chores, which included fighting drills and dispositions to the supervisors of various villages belonging to Zazulińce, Kaz and Tom drove over to a group of yurts spread to the northeast of the manor house just beyond the horizon.

It was a location where around thirty men lived with their women, children, and horses. It was difficult to know how many there were at any given moment. They were free to move around or do what they wanted and worship whatever God or Spirit they chose. There were fifty of them at times. Other times only three or six were left. They could move from Crimea to Kijów, Moscow, or Warszawa. They would never go directly to Moscow or Warszawa, but they could camp by a river without lighting a fire in a few hours distance to the city out of sight of any sentry. They had their ways of communicating and executing orders.

The Pułaskis did not investigate their ways. It was a relationship of convenience for a given moment in time, which could extend for months or years but was not a permanent association. Tom knew just a few of them by name. The others would come and go keeping to their anonymous ways. Kaz knew Alim, who was the leader of the group. Kaz knew that Alim meant "wise." He was past his thirties, but the upper limit of his age was hard to guess. He could be forty or even older. There was a timeless extension to his physical presence. If you talked and looked at Alim long enough, you would sense that he hardly belonged to the here and now. He was an entity of a vast continental mass where people, countries, and civilizations came and went. He belonged to the deep core of existence beyond the turbulence of current affairs.

Usually, when Kaz or Tom approached the yurts, someone would come out and talk to them and then bring them to Alim. This year, the men around Alim, who Tom and Kaz knew, were Aydar, Damir, and Ilgiz. They did not realize that Aydar meant "the settler," Damir "the persistent," and Ilgiz "the traveler."

46

"Praise be to Allah who is bringing us such esteemed visitors," said Aydar, who bent over, almost touching the ground with his head.

"Be with God, Aydar," said Kaz, who stopped Zefir feet away from Aydar. "I hope you stay safe and fed. I also hope that Alim is doing well."

"Oh, Alim is a rock of health. May he live one hundred years."

"Yes, indeed," Kaz repeated. "May we see him?"

"Let me take you to his yurt. We will take care of Zefir and Lord Tom's mount," said Aydar looking at Zefir with admiration. There was no need for Aydar to shout any commands. Everyone in the group knew their place. Alim was already in front of his yurt, waiting for Kaz and Tom. When they dismounted, young boys ran over to the horses and took them to the field.

Alim bowed his head low and showed the guests in with a broad arm wave.

"Praise be to Allah. I thank him for such honorable guests. Please, come in and have some kumis. My women just brought a fresh batch."

Tom and Kaz did not like the taste of this potent drink made of mare's milk, but they would never think of refusing such a generous offer.

"Congratulations on your father's decision. You are now our new Master, Lord," said Alim looking at Kaz respectfully. "We are your faithful dogs ready to serve you."

It was just a titular phrase, which did not mean much. First, Alim was his own master, and he did as he pleased, but within the limits of the tenuous freedom he gained here for himself and his men. Second, he would do only as much as he had to. It might include fighting bravely for Kaz with all his unquestionable skill and cunning. It could also mean that he would leave this place with as many horses as he could take from Kaz, including Zefir, first, if possible, and never return. Kaz and Tom knew this reality well and accepted it as a norm of frontier life. There were no hard feelings but rather cautious interest. Kaz wanted to learn as much as possible about Tatars. However, he did not want to risk anything close to what the envoy described by Marcin Bielski in his chronicle endured when he joined the Porte march on Moscow.

Kaz and Tom sat on a rug beside Alim and tasted his kumis. Kaz sampled sip after sip and smacked his lips.

"This is the best I have tasted in my young life. I hope I can grow old drinking your kumis," said Kaz, putting the clay pot away.

Alim bowed his head. He appreciated the patience of this young boy with whom he must establish a reasonable relationship. Tom looked around and spotted a new bow hanging on the wall.

"Alim, is this a new bow?" Tom asked.

"Oh yes, my Lord. The khan gifted it to me. May he live long," answered Alim, visibly pleased. He went over to the wall, and handed the bow to Tom, who got up, accepted it carefully, and admired the handiwork.

"Is it bamboo inside? Tom asked, surprised.

"Yes, it is, my Lord," Alim answered.

"I see hornbeam and ash glued together as well. The wrapping is birch."

"You know it all, Tom. And you see it all."

"I also see a silver ring on your thumb."

"Yes, it goes well with the new bow."

"You know, Kaz," Tom turned to Kaz, handing him the bow. "The thumb ring is used to draw the bow. I was never able to do it right," Tom continued.

"Can I see how it works?" Kaz asked, thinking he might have moved too quickly.

"Let's go out and try," Alim answered, who did not mind Kaz's interest.

They went outside while two warriors carried additional equipment, including various arrows. Alim took a long 40-inch shaft with a bone blade. He handed the arrow to Tom.

"It is a whistling birch arrow for a deer. What distance can it hit the target?" Tom asked, giving the arrow to Kaz for inspection. "This arrow has an eagle fletching from the tail. They whistle so that an animal stops looking where the strange sound is coming from, and the archer has time to shoot another arrow; pretty ingenious," he explained.

One of the warriors jumped on a mount and carried a straw target about 1,000 feet away. Nobody made a comment when Alim took his bow and the deer arrow. He used his thumb with the silver ring to draw the sinew string. He moved his head from left to right, slightly checking the wind direction and velocity, steadied his position, and let loose. The arrow whistling traveled through the air and hit the target. It was hard to see exactly, but the warrior galloped over and retrieved the straw mat. The arrow was in the middle of a two by three feet rectangle.

"Amazing," Kaz whispered, not able to control himself.

Alim looked at Kaz and said, "I hear you are quite an archer, but I have never seen you shoot. Would you like to try?" Alim asked.

Kaz was delighted. Alim chose a shorter, about 30-inch-long arrow with a crane fletching and waved at one of the warriors. In a moment, the warrior returned with Zefir. The target was placed about 500 feet away. Kaz was supposed to shoot the arrow in full gallop, riding along a rail about fifty feet from the target. A rider did not aim but had to rely on muscle memory of thousands of arrows shot over many years of practice. Kaz knew it was quite a challenge, but he didn't mind. He was ready to prove himself.

Kaz let go of the reins and squeezed Zefir's ribs. The mount knew precisely what to do and stretched out in full gallop, almost touching the rail. The arrow whizzed in the air and hit the target. Kaz turned Zefir on a dime and galloped over to Alim. He motioned his head, asking for one more arrow. Alim obliged. Kaz darted straight at the target, ignoring the rail. But rather than shooting from the saddle, he leaned down and shot the arrow underneath Zefir's neck.

The air filled with wild screams and shrieks. The audience, observing the scene discreetly from a distance, knew very well how difficult a shot it was. This moment would stay with everyone watching forever. These warriors have been trained to draw and shoot since they could walk. If ever Kaz were to fight with them at his side, they would die for him, considering it an honor.

When Kaz returned to Alim and Tom, both seasoned soldiers were thrilled. They appreciated the skill.

"Lord," said Alim, bowing his head to the ground. "I am yours any time you wave your hand." This time, he might have meant it to a certain extent.

"If so, why don't you help us track the Russian soldiers?" Kaz inquired.

"When do you want to ride?" Alim asked.

"We will be here before dawn tomorrow," Kaz answered. He jumped off his mount and handed the bow over to Alim.

"It was a thrill. Thank you for sharing your dearest prize with me. I do appreciate your gesture," Kaz said.

"It is time for us to go back and get ready for tomorrow," Tom said. They bid Alim farewell. The warriors brought Tom's mount, and they left the camp.

The Russians

The next day when the steppe took a short breath between night and day, Kaz, Tom, and Robert approached the Tatar encampment. They could hardly make the shapes of the yurts when a single line of riders appeared. Ilgiz was at the front, followed by Alim, Aydar, Damir, and a dozen more. Kaz, Tom, and Robert lined up behind Alim, and the column moved swiftly and quietly.

All of them were seasoned warriors. Now was the time to focus and be on alert at all times. Every move and every step were performed with total concentration. They did not exert any unnecessary effort, and still, they were moving at the maximum allowable speed. Ilgiz led the group and relied on Aydar for consultation, rarely stopping or slowing down. Around noon, they reached a small creek and let the horses take a break. The Tatars were squatting in a circle munching on some biscuits. Kaz, Tom, and Robert joined the group and shared the meal with their slanted-eyed companions.

"I am thinking about how long we have been working together chasing the Muscovites or Turks around our lands. Did you know that

Polish kings relied on Tatar help almost immediately after Subatai left Europe?" Kaz asked, breaking a biscuit piece.

"We remember," Alim said. "It was Dzalal-al-din, the ninth generation straight from Genghis Khan, who brought two thousand warriors to help King Jagiełło in the great battle of Grunwald. They all fought with Allah-u-Akbar on their lips. I am here to serve you, Lord. It is in a way the same," said Alim, squeezing history into a quantum essence.

"It was in 1410, over three hundred years ago. How did you know?" Kaz asked, surprised.

"We know," stated Alim, standing up to stretch his bowed legs from squatting.

"Wherever we are, no matter how far we look back, there is always someone to fight. We promise ourselves that once this enemy is vanquished, we will enjoy our peace. When will it all end?" Robert asked.

"It never ends," Alim replied. "It is the nature of things in this world. If we see that the war is over, it is only because we are blinded by winning a battle. War is ceaselessly upon us," Alim again collapsed many experiences and feelings in one summative phrase.

"The horses are rested. It is time to move on. We should make contact with them tomorrow after daybreak," Ilgiz said. Alim nodded, and Ilgiz turned to the rest of the warriors. They were all on the move in a quarter of an hour.

The next day with the Sun midway up the horizon, they passed through a large orchard when they spotted an old Jew sitting under an apple tree. They stopped and let the horses loose on the grass. Tom, Kaz, and Alim walked over to the Jew sitting on a stool and swaying back and forth gently.

"What are you doing here alone, Asher?" Tom asked.

"Not much, waiting for devekut (adhesion to God); I sit under my apple tree, the gift of peace from Lord Pułaski, waiting for Shekinah. She will come to me. It is the third new moon. She is coming."

"Have you seen any riders today?"

"You mean the Russian soldiers, the little green men? Yes, they are snooping around."

"Did they talk to you?"

"No, they were talking to the chicken they stole."

"How is life treating you here? What about your community?"

"We are doing fine, Lord. Ever since Besht, I mean Israel ben Eliezer anchored us here. We found peace and focus. Let us hope that these Muscovites don't destroy it for all of us."

"What else do you know?"

"My knowledge is in these apples. I have no knowledge you are seeking."

"Stay safe, Asher," Kaz said, motioning his head to the others that it was time to move on.

As they were walking to their horses, Kaz reminisced of his experience in the apple orchard with Tom, teaching him how to use a saber. He felt gratitude for these trees, the orchard, and the tranquility they were bringing. It reminded him of Jan Kochanowski and his poem about the linden tree. Kochanowski described his pleasurable experience when relaxing under a linden tree in his orchard and feeling invited as a guest to enjoy the shade and tranquility that the hospitable tree offered. Trees were the mute witnesses of human strife. Kaz noticed how the horses, with their lips, were carefully picking apples strewn under the trees and adding them to their diet of grass.

"Who is this Shekinah?" Kaz asked Alim.

"She is not of this world," the Tatar answered.

"How do you know?"

"I know," Alim said. "We call her Sakinah. She brings gifts to the blessed. She brings tranquility and peace."

"Rather than wait for her here with Asher, we must move on," Tom said.

Soon, they formed a single line again and headed northwest. The trail was obvious. The Muscovites were not in a big hurry.

Ilgiz, leading the train, pointed to a firepit they were passing by. Chicken feathers were swaying in the air on the grass. They did not stop but rode by slowly, each looking carefully at the leftovers of the Russian feast.

"We can make contact with them any time, Lord," Alim said. "What is your bidding?"

"Let us get in front of them and get ready. I will ride alone and meet them in a place where you will lie in the ambush. Depending on what happens, I will signal you what to do," Kaz answered.

Ilgiz brought his mount to full gallop, and they followed swiftly in a large circle positioning themselves in front of the Russian unit. Eventually, Ilgiz slowed down at a slight incline, pointing to tall grasses and some bushes.

"Yes, it is a perfect place," Kaz decided. "You hide here, and I will get ready to meet the Russians as they come."

The Tatars, Tom, and Robert spread around in an instant. Some made their horses lie down in the tall grass with the riders in their saddles. Others stayed behind the bushes around fifty feet from where Kaz was to meet the Muscovites. They were all ready for what Kaz had planned without any more commands. There was no need to explain that they should maintain total silence and refrain from unnecessary movement.

The Ambush

Kaz was leisurely riding Zefir down the incline when the Muscovites appeared on the opposite side. They were dressed in green coats and black trousers, looking like little green men from a distance. Their leader stopped momentarily, but the two-column green caterpillar continued its slow descent into the valley. Kaz was moving towards them at the same steady pace. Soon, he could see their fur hats and yellow epaulets. The Muscovites stopped in front of Kaz with their officer facing him and his green men fanning slowly around in a semicircle.

The officer, seated erect on his mount, looked at Kaz and bit his little mustache.

"What are you doing here away from home, riding alone across this empty countryside, my boy?" the officer asked.

"I am not riding away. I am home. It is my land. What are you doing here on my lands, and who are you?" Kaz retorted, watching the soldiers inching to his left and right. The officer was looking at Kaz, not moving a muscle while his narrow, slightly slanted eyes were scanning the boy up and down. He noticed Kaz's saber and the pistols around his saddle.

"I am Captain Valery Riazin on a mission from the House of Czartoryski. They asked Empress Catherine to provide security assistance in the election of your king in Warszawa," Riazin answered.

"I don't know what the Czartoryskis want, but I know that I am unaware of any of this. I also know that you are trespassing. I am the Starosta of Zazulińce, and this is my land," Kaz answered.

Riazin moved closer to Kaz and said, "The matters of the Crown are more important than your local private concerns. You better be on your way and don't interfere with state affairs," Riazin added through his clenched teeth, continuing to bite on his mustache and coming feet away from Kaz.

Kaz moved Zefir forward so that the two horses were head-to-head. Neither of the two stepped back an inch. Kaz looked the Russian officer straight into his dark, squinty eyes and retorted, "Listen, Riazin, you will not tell me what I should or should not do on my lands. If you have deals with the Czartoryskis, handle them on their lands. Don't tell me what you would do on behalf of the Polish king. We still have the interregnum."

"Step aside, boy or…." Riazin continued showing his long, razor-sharp K9 teeth.

"I am not a boy," Kaz interrupted. "I am Count Pułaski, and if you don't turn around and start riding east this instant, there will be blood."

Riazin looked around to check where his soldiers were stationed, ready to surround Kaz and use force if he had to. His mistake was that he took his eyes from Kaz, who motioned his left hand slightly, and the Tatars rose from the tall grasses seated on their horses with their sabers drawn, encircling the Russian soldiers. Riazin started scanning the new situation, biting his mustache when Kaz drew his saber and cut him across his left arm.

The situation was dire for Riazin, and he had no suitable option. His military training took over, and he did not flinch a muscle. At the same time, Robert and Tom appeared from behind the bushes. Blood started trickling down Riazin's arm.

"I would have this arm looked after," Tom said. "What do you want us to do, Count?" Tom asked, looking at Riazin and Kaz, ready to react instantly.

"You don't have to do anything," Kaz answered. "You, Riazin, turn your horse around and start riding. I don't want my men to spot you or your soldiers on my lands in two days."

Riazin was still assessing his position. It was evident that rather than about attack, he thought about getting out of this trap without losing any of his men. Ever so slightly, he turned his horse to the right and away from Kaz but did not break eye contact.

"By the way, Riazin, you don't have to pay me for the chicken you stole. You can tell the Czartoryskis that it is my treat."

Riazin turned his horse around and headed back with his soldiers riding gingerly between the Tatars until they gained a safe distance. Once in the clear, they formed two columns and followed their commander. None of Kaz's men moved until the Russians disappeared behind the horizon.

"What now?" Tom asked.

"We should scout around to see what else these Muscovites did and then ride straight back. We must let my father know what happened here before the Muscovites reach their units."

"Lord, let Damir contact your father," Alim proposed.

"Good idea, Alim," Kaz said, nodding his head. Alim called Damir, and in a few minutes, Damir hit his mount hard. The horse jumped into a full gallop, and Damir disappeared behind the bushes.

"Spread around and look for any sign of more Russian groups or any damage they might have caused. I will see you here before sunset," Kaz instructed his men, tsking off southward with Robert. Alim waved his hand, and the Tatars were gone. Tom turned his mount northward.

The steppe received the men and their actions into its fold. Only a trained eye could see what unfolded here in this tiny spot sheltered by soft mounds, tall grasses, and clusters of bushes. A drop of blood and a few broken twigs were all that was left of the incident. It was hard to imagine how many more significant or lesser confrontations happened across the vast expanse of the eastern Polish frontier on that day. Animals, birds, and vegetation continued their existence without paying much attention to the men, who left an insignificant imprint of their drama on life as it had evolved over millennia across the steppe.

They all returned to the incline as the Sun touched the grass with its fiery red disk. It appeared that there could have been a few more groups of Muscovites moving through the Pułaski's lands in Podole.

There wasn't any significant damage, except for some theft of food and drink. Kaz moved his unit back through the night.

At dawn, they reached the apple orchard where they had met Asher. They drove to a spot where the Jew had been sitting on his stool before. The seat was still under the tree, but they did not see Asher from a distance. Kaz planned to find out more about the Russians from him. As he rode over to the stool, he noticed an oblong shape in the grass.

It was Asher lying with his face down, arms stretched, his right leg bent at the knee, and twisted grotesquely away from the torso. Kaz jumped off his mount and leaned over Asher. He turned him around to find his mouth and eyes opened wide, surprised with what fate had brought onto him. His neck and robe were cut, leaving open wounds while the blood must have soaked into the ground. All around him were apples squashed into the grass, trampled by hoofs and boots.

Zosia

Kaz moved his group quickly. There was no time to waste. He wanted to be in Zazulińce in case his father decided to take decisive action. They trotted and galloped as often as possible with short breaks for the horses. The Sun was hitting them in the eyes when they spotted a farm girl walking erratically in the emptiness of the steppe. She was staggering from left to right. Her white dress was stained with blood. When Tom, Kaz, and Robert dismounted and approached the girl, they realized she was in shock, unable to recognize them. She finally stopped and stared ahead with wild eyes and arms raised halfway. Her hands were facing front as if expecting a heavy load. Tom took a canteen and poured some water on a scarf. He pressed the scarf against the girl's forehead. Then, he poured more water and rubbed the back of her neck and face.

"What happened to you?" Tom asked calmly, but the girl did not respond. Alim walked over to Kaz and Robert, standing a few paces behind.

"They raped her. There must have been many of them. She would not look like this after one," Alim whispered. "Take her to her village. We cannot do it."

Tom sat the girl in front of his mount sideways. She was not able to sit across the saddle. He looked around and rode off toward the tip of a church steeple visible on the horizon. Robert approached Kaz and put his hand on his shoulder, saying, "No, not now, Kaz. We must push on. There will be time to look for vengeance or justice, but not now."

Kaz was sitting erect with his eyes closed and tears oozing out from behind his lids. He swiped the moisture off his face and mounted Zefir.

"Let's ride on," he said, pointing towards Zazulińce with his forefinger.

When they reached the Tatars' camp, a file of rides peeled off and disappeared between the yurts. Alim stayed with Kaz, who slowed down and, looking at the manor house, said, "Thank you, Alim. You can stay here as long as I am the Starosta."

"Thank you, my Lord. I am your faithful dog any time you need me. Praised be Allah," Alim bowed deeply from his saddle and followed his men.

Zazulińce was buzzing with activity. Kaz saw his brother, Anthony, in the doorway. He ran towards Kaz, and they embraced with a firm hug, which would break the ribs of less athletic men. Anthony started pounding Kaz on his back.

"Brother, I haven't seen you in a while. You are getting stronger and stronger. Let me look at you," said Anthony smiling and pushing Kaz at arm's length.

"Do you know what happened?" Kaz asked.

"Yes, I know it all. Damir was here. We have bigger things at stake now," answered Anthony as he was dragging Kaz into the house. "Our father wants us in Warszawa. The date for the Convocation Diet has been set." They walked across the rooms into the main hall. "It does not look good for Duke Carl Christian Joseph. We will probably support Great Crown Hetman (military commander) Jan Klemens Branicki. In the meantime, Russians are coming to help the Czartoryskis. It can be quite a mess."

They sat around the table set for a big hearty meal. Kaz took a seat opposite the fireplace wall facing the head of the buffalo he had hunted. He looked at the mount and felt the deep primordial presence emanating from the wall, an almost audible hum of the source of life.

"Your żubr," Anthony remarked. "Quite a find here and quite a hunt from what Tom told me."

"Where is Tom? When did he arrive?" Kaz asked.

"He's been here for a few hours. He should join us with Robert soon. Go ahead, eat, drink. We have a long ride ahead of us."

Just when Anthony finished his sentence, Tom and Robert appeared. They took their seats around the table.

"Go ahead, gentlemen," Anthony said. "Get your nourishment. God knows when we will have a chance to sit together around the table, share a meal, and enjoy our company. Robert, you will ride to Warszawa with us. Tom, you stay and keep an eye on everything here." Tom and Robert nodded and started helping themselves to the food on the table.

"Tom," Kaz asked. "What happened to the girl?"

"I took her to the rectory. The priest was overwhelmed, but luckily, he had a visitor. It was Carmelite friar, Father Marek. He seems always to be present when you need him. He took the initiative."

"Was it Father Jandołowicz?" Anthony asked.

"Yes, exactly," Tom replied. "The girl was tending to some cattle in the fields when the Muscovites showed up. One of them grabbed her and rode away. Others whipped the children who were with her and followed the kidnapper. No one has seen the girl since then. The priest knew everything because her parents went to the church asking for prayer on her behalf."

"Riazin. I will remember that name. I hope I will see him in Warszawa," Kaz exclaimed.

"Who is Riazin, brother?"

"He is the officer leading the group we had a problem with, Valery Riazin. I cut his left arm deep. I should have cut his right arm," Kaz continued. "What is the girl's name, Tom?"

"Zosia. Her name is Zosia. What a sweet little thing. She opened up when she saw her mother. She ran to her and cried matulu (Mommy). It was difficult to look at," Tom said. "The hard part is that Zosia's parents ran away from Russia looking for freedom. They were so happy to work in the village. Her father said that he felt blessed to escape the whip of his Russian masters. And here we are."

"What a mess we are getting ourselves into," Kaz commented. "We are supposed to protect these lands and people from Tatar raids, but we cannot stop Russians from raping, murdering, and stealing. They are using the name of Czartoryski as an excuse. It has gone too far. When Riazin said that Czartoryskis invited them to our lands for protection, I waited for a blizzard to strike him from the blue sky, but nothing happened. It has gone too far, brother, and we should stop it now. Either we are honest and direct, or we will all pay dearly for our doubt and hesitation."

"We must first consult our Father. You know that he will insist on following the rule of law," Anthony observed.

"With the law, there should be enforcement," Kaz continued. "Law without enforcement is a miserable farce. I would expect the Czartoryskis to enforce the law. They should punish Riazin and his men when they find out what happened. Better yet, let's ride and find Riazin and his vermin. I am the Starosta of these lands, and they challenged me directly. They committed robbery, rape, and murder. They must not get away with it."

"Riazin is on his way to Warszawa. We will meet him there," Anthony calmed down his brother. "We must go to Winiary, meet the father, and decide what to do next. I expect that Riazin will answer for his crimes in front of the full majesty of the Commonwealth. It will be a warning to other Riazins. I also hope the Czartoryskis will open their eyes and see how much they endanger our freedom and security with their insatiable political ambitions."

In a typical Zazulińce fashion, all preparations for a trip to Warka were complete in a few hours. Kaz, Anthony, and Robert were ready, seated on their mounts in the courtyard. Tom wished them safe travel and promised to watch everything around the estate. There was no time to tarry any longer. They would rest in their saddles as they set off for Winiary.

CHAPTER 3

The Election (1764)

(See appendix for historical background)

Warka

Kaz, Anthony, and Robert made it to Warka, the seat of the Pułaski family. It was situated thirty-five miles south of Warszawa, a few miles from where the Pilica River flows into the Wisła River, a convenient location for Józef Pułaski, who spent most of his time in Warszawa as an attorney of the Crown Court. Here, in Warka, decisions were made about all family assets and how they generated income. A strong economy of the Commonwealth based on the export of food products and raw materials, supported by successful legal practice, guaranteed sizable profits for the Pułaskis. Their cattle and grain from Podole reached the markets of German principalities, Sweden, France, and England. Trade with the southeast reached Turkey and, through the Black Sea, Venice. Legal work on behalf of the Crown added strength to the impressive fortune of the house.

[The Pułaski residence and current museum in Warka]

The residence of the Pułaskis at Warka was designed differently than the Zazulińce manor house. Rather than being defensive in nature, Warka was a place of leisure and status. Its classical design was beautified with later baroque additions to the interior.

The palace had two multistory wings built of brick and plastered white, connected by a single-story pavilion. The right-wing was the main entrance to the estate. It opened into the vestibule, which led into the grand reception room to the left and other parts of the palace to the right. They included a small reception room, the library, and the study of the master of the house.

The palace was situated in the middle of about a forty-acre park on an escarpment overlooking the Pilica River Valley. A straight avenue ran from the town of Warka into the palace. Other roads curved around the park leading to two ponds and a picturesque cluster of chestnut trees. A chapel of the Virgin Mary was placed in a cave built into the slope of the ridge. The park's composition enhanced the terrain's attributes with a combination of meticulously manicured lawns and wild landscapes by the escarpment resembling the typical English garden. Ancient oaks and giant linden trees along the alleys attracted visitors and created a pleasing variety of esthetic experiences. The foliage of carefully selected elm, larch, maple, and poplar trees invited leisurely strolls.

The estate welcomed everyone with spacious accommodations. Józef Pułaski purchased the "white" palace, constructed in 1678 for Stanisław Szczuka, a Lithuanian Deputy of the Commonwealth. Although born into a middle-class szlachta family, Szczuka advanced through hard work and political talent. He was the secretary of King Jan III Sobieski and an advisor to King Augustus II. The effectiveness and strength of the Commonwealth allowed yet another middle-class szlachcic, Józef Pułaski, to afford such a palace on the power of his legal talent and work ethic.

The royal election was a rare occasion for the whole family reunion. Besides his two brothers and father, Kaz enjoyed meeting his mother, Maryann, and his six sisters, Wiktoria, Joanna, Józefa, Monika, Paulina, and Małgorzata. Frank, born in 1743, was the oldest of three brothers. Kaz was born in 1745 and the youngest, Anthony, in 1747.

Rather than revel in his status and enjoy the art and parties in Warszawa, Józef continued the systematic work to benefit the country and his family. He treated the royal election as an essential step in the continuous effort to keep the status of the Commonwealth as the top country in Europe. His sons shared their father's dedication to patriotic principles and shunned the decadent life of Warszawa crowds. The choice of a royal candidate was severely skewed in favor of the Familia, the House of Czartoryski. It did not mean that Józef intended to give up the fight for his candidates: Carl Christian Joseph, the son of the deceased King, or Jan Klemens Branicki, the Great Crown Hetman.

For 800 years, since the country's baptism on the Holy Saturday of 14 April 966, Poland prospered and grew due to the effort and wisdom of voters who chose consecutive Polish kings. Good or bad, these kings preserved the autonomy of Poland by supplying the country with essential leadership and growth. Until the last election of 1764, the process had been a sacred ritual. Poles believed that once chosen, the King was anointed by divine intervention, and regicide was out of the question, regarded as a grave crime and an affront to God.

Often, the election brought miraculously successful leaders to the seat of power, as if gifted by divine providence. Sometimes, the kings made decisions in error, which was then interpreted as a warning from the Almighty that the country needed to reform and improve. The key was to fight for your candidate and accept the outcome by recognizing the victorious one.

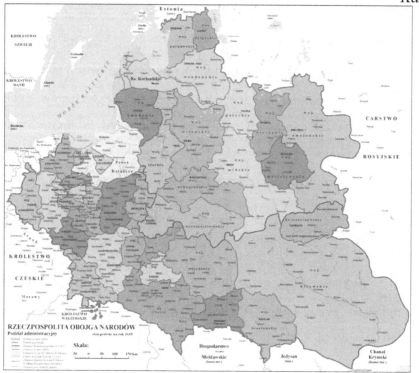

[Pre-partition Poland]

In the mid-14th century, Poles risked much by offering the Polish Crown to a pagan Lithuanian prince who sometimes fought Poles, Muscovites, and German Teutonic Knights. The bargain paid off handsomely; Jagiełło was an intelligent, hardworking, devout, and focused leader. He convinced the Lithuanians that joining Poland would give them a chance to be a part of a system that secured their lands from the west, the north, and the east while allowing them to earn fortunes beyond their wildest dreams.

The first official document signed to unite the two was the Union of Krewo (now Krevo, Belarus).

[Union of Krewo, 14 August 1385]

After careful negotiation between Polish and Lithuanian nobles, they agreed that the lands of Lithuania and Rus would be attached (Latin *applicare)* to the Crown of Poland. The treaty of Krewo was followed by the documents of the Union of Horodło on 2 October 1417. Here, the word "attached" was extended into "incorporate, inviscerate, appropriate, conjoin, adjoin, confederate, and perpetually annex" (*Latin: incorporamus, invisceramus, appropriamus, coniungimus, adiungimus, confoederamus, et perpetue anectimus*). The purpose of added verbs was to avoid any misunderstanding or misrepresentation of the essential intent of the union, as well as to constrain any creative readings by future jurists.

Almost two hundred years later, the Union of Lublin was signed on the 1st of July, 1569. It created one single state, the Commonwealth of Poland and Lithuania. A single elected monarch who was the King of Poland and the Grand Duke of Lithuania ruled the Commonwealth.

[Union of Lublin, 1 July 1569]

The official creation of the union was needed because the last of the male line of the House of Jagiełło, Sigismund II Augustus (1520-1572), remained without a legally recognized, legitimate son. He became the first King of the Commonwealth of Poland-Lithuania in 1569, the largest multicultural and multireligious country in Europe, enjoying religious tolerance. The capital and the seat of power was Kraków. The language used by over 80% of the citizens was Polish.

With Russian interference after the final partition of the Commonwealth in 1795, there were endless debates about how strong the union of Poland and Lithuania was. It was like the union of

England and Wales, to make it clear. Welsh is still a recognized language, but there is little doubt about the relevance of English and Welsh in today's Great Britain.

It shows how critical the heredity rights and the election process were. Unfortunately, the importance of the process was beyond the grasp of the penultimate King of Poland, Augustus III the Fat. Although he had sixteen legitimate children with his wife, Maria Josepha, he could not secure the position for the House of Wettin on the Polish throne after his death.

Neminem Captivabimus

Józef Pułaski brought two cases with him to Warszawa from Winiary for the Crown court to consider. One was Marcin Konicki, a szlachcic captured by the Russians and charged with the alleged killing of a Russian officer in Podole. The second was the case of Captain Valery Riazin and his crimes.

In the first case, Józef was prepared to argue that Marcin should have never been captured and should immediately be released based on the "Neminem Captivabimus" law. It stated that a szlachcic could not be imprisoned without due process, which required that the proof be presented in court and approved by a judge before capture. The law dated back to King Jagiełło, who in 1430 signed this privilege in Jedlna. The full Latin privilege stated: *neminem captivabimus nisi iure victim* (We shall not arrest anyone without a court verdict).

The Russians argued that the Russian soldiers were invited to Poland by the Familia, the House of Czartoryski, to protect the election process. In broad daylight, this Polish rascal Konicki killed a Russian officer performing his duties. They neglected to mention that the Muscovites were burning one of Marcin Konicki's villages and stealing his cattle, food supplies, and drinks. When Marcin demanded that they leave, they said that the peasants refused to give them needed provisions in the service of the Czartoryskis, and for that, they must be duly punished. The village was not even on Czartoryski's land.

Allowing Russians to decide on matters of the law in the Commonwealth was a dangerous precedent. It would mean that while the King could not imprison any szlachcic without a proper court order, the Muscovites could. It was a deliberate mockery of Polish law. If Polish courts did not address the Konicki case, it would mean they had no jurisdiction over a group of Russian soldiers on the territory of the Commonwealth. It would emphasize that it was the Russians who enforced their justice on Polish lands. It was not a case of just one person's right but a test of the constitutional protections for the citizens of the Commonwealth. If tolerated, it would adversely impact one million szlachta.

[Polish nobleman, by Rembrandt, 1637]

The title of the szlachcic of the Commonwealth had been bestowed on the nobility of Poland, Grand Duchy of Lithuania, Royal Prussia, and Ruthenian lands for over two hundred years. A lengthy legal procedure of accepting the nobility beyond historic Poland proper as equal to the original Polish szlachta started in the 14th century. In 1569, after the Union of Lublin, a lengthy and complicated process was completed to serve in perpetuity. All legal challenges, remedies, and decisions were duly documented and addressed. With a continuous process of confirming old and adding new rights and privileges by a king during the election process, the Commonwealth szlachcic enjoyed unprecedented power and freedom.

When addressing one another, the szlachta community used Panie Bracie (Lord Brother), an old honorific. "Lord Brother" carried an aura of honor, tradition, and respect honed by centuries of proud service to the Motherland. The bond of the noble fraternity was repeatedly tested on the battlefield. The szlachcic defended and served the Motherland with blood, if need be, but would not compromise ethical and moral principles. It was unthinkable to break the accepted code of conduct. Robbery or rape would automatically defame a szlachcic.

The second case was Captain Valery Riazin, a Russian military officer who trespassed with a group of his soldiers on the Pułaski estate in Zazulińce. While trespassing, his soldiers committed robbery, rape, and murder. Riazin claimed that the Czartoryskis asked him to protect the election. The case involved Riazin, his soldiers, any Russian soldier or group of them, and the Czartoryskis usurping the right to ignore the state borders for their personal benefit. If true, the Czartoryskis would be guilty of usurping the right to act as if they had already won the election. It was apparent to everyone that even the King had no right to bring foreign armies into the territory of the Commonwealth. Quite the opposite; he was charged with protecting the sovereignty of the Commonwealth from any foreign meddling.

As Crown Attorney, Józef was aware that rather than quick enforcement, thorough documentation and proper record keeping of these cases were much more critical. It was a way to ensure that such crimes would not be swept under the carpet of interregnum chaos. The opposing side would try everything in its power to stop the filing process and any legal action. Józef decided to seek an audience with Primate Władysław Łubieński, who served as the Interrex, and present both cases for consideration.

Pułaskis in Warszawa

Kaz came to Warszawa at the last moment before the election process started at the Wola plain, three miles west of Warszawa. The Convocation Diet in May was to select viable candidates for the elections. In September, the Election Diet was to choose the King. Previously, the elections in Warszawa had been held east of the King's palace across the Wisła River. For the last hundred years, however, they took place in the village of Wielka Wola, west of the castle and away from the river.

[The election field at Wola]

The election field was surrounded by a moat and a rampart, measuring 140 x 68 meters (460 by 223 feet). There were three gates leading into the election field. The east gate was for Lithuania, the west for Great Poland, and the south for Little Poland, which the voters from the terrains of Ukraine and Volhynia also used. The north side was the location of the senators' pavilion and two senators' gates, one to the east and one to the west. Szlachta was organized by voivodeships (provinces) and concentrated in the middle to the south of the senators' pavilion in the circle section.

Russian-Prussian Pact

After years of preparation and changes of fortune, the positions of Russia and Prussia were coming close on the issue of who they would support in case of the royal election in Poland. To formalize the agreement, Catherine sent an emissary to Prussia.

As he approached King Frederick, seated by his large oak desk in front of a window of his royal chamber, the Russian envoy said, bowing, "Your Royal Highness, we have agreed on all terms. There is nothing left for you but to sign this secret agreement."

On 11 April 1764, Russia and Prussia signed a secret pact in which both sides pledged to promote Poniatowski to the throne. He was the least popular of the candidates and Catherine's former lover, so he would be easily controlled and manipulated. Even if he were to start acting independently, it would be relatively easy to overpower him since he had little support except for those he could buy from his royal coffer. Since he entered the race deep in debt, there was little chance that he would ever have any funds to influence politics or the administration of the Commonwealth against the wishes of the courts of Russia and Prussia.

Catherine rejected the candidate proposed by the Familia, Prince Adam Kazimierz Czartoryski. He would be too strong and too independent. Adam Kazimierz yielded to Catherine's pressure and surrendered his seat to Stanisław Anthony Poniatowski. Prince Adam decided that Catherine would not send promised gold and soldiers if he insisted. During the election, the Russian party bought votes and threatened the electors to ensure a smooth victory for Stanisław Anthony. Russian soldiers surrounded Wola demonstrating Catherine's power. They made sure that Poniatowski won the election without any open dissent and that everybody knew that Poniatowski was Catherine's client and not an independent politician.

Political Debate

As all critical figures assembled in Warszawa, Polish Roman Catholic Primate Władysław Alexander Łubieński invited them to his palace. The Pułaskis arrived at their residence and found an invitation ticket waiting for Józef. The Primate invited Józef and one more person of his choosing. Józef decided it was an excellent opportunity to introduce young Kaz to the bevy of personalities who would impact his future life for good or evil. The caliber of the guests guaranteed fierce political debate.

After the death of Augustus III, Primate Łubieński assumed the role of the Interrex, who served as the interim executive power. With his spiritual and temporal authority, he oversaw the turbulent times of the interregnum. Among the power brokers of the Commonwealth who were already in Warszawa for the Convocation Diet, the Primate invited Prince Adam Kazimierz Czartoryski, Stanisław Anthony Poniatowski, Great Crown Hetman Jan Klemens Branicki, Karol Stanisław Radziwiłł, and Józef Poniatowski. The significant absentee was Carl Christian Joseph of Saxony from the House of Wettin, the Duke of Courland, and Semigallia, the son of the deceased King Augustus III. He was kept up north under the escort of Russian soldiers in his palace in Mitawa, Courland, at the coast of the Baltic Sea.

The guests assembled in the palace's great hall and enjoyed superb food and music. During elaborate festivities, the key guests were discreetly invited into the library. They sat around a large, exquisite walnut and mahogany table with delicate gold ornaments and rosewood marquetry.

Prince Adam Czartoryski, Primate Łubieński, and Stanisław Anthony Poniatowki represented the Familia, a coterie lavishly supported by Russian gold and soldiers. Crown Hetman Branicki, Karol Stanisław Radziwiłł, Voivode of Vilnius and Master Swordbearer of Lithuania, as well as the Pułaskis, were Republicans. Czartoryski, Branicki, and Radziwiłł belonged to the wealthiest families of the Commonwealth and Europe. As the senior of the Familia, Prince Czartoryski welcomed the assembled guests, "Gentlemen, we are here to talk. It is a great occasion to share our thoughts freely without any foreigner listening to each word and using our wisdom to weaken our resolve. Regardless of the outcome, I hope you will take this conversation with you as a lesson and a message which will benefit our common treasure, Poland." He looked around and welcomed each guest with a slight nod. He continued turning towards the Interrex, "Your Excellency, lead us with prayer so that we direct our attention beyond mere physical concerns."

Primate Łubieński stood up and folded his hands on his chest, saying, "In the name of the Lord, Son, and the Holy Spirit. We are, first of all, the servants of our Lord God, and we should pray that he, through the Holy Spirit, will bless us with clear thought. Lord Jesus, help us free ourselves from the shadow of personal interest, which often clouds our judgment, and make us see our Motherland's light shining upon us like a beacon in the stormy seas of this interregnum. As faithful children of the Blessed Virgin Mary, we pray that she protects us from the sins of greed and shortsightedness. Let us pray."

All heads bent to their chests. The lords got up from their chairs and knelt on the floor, as they all did in their respective Roman Catholic, Lutheran, and Orthodox churches since they learned how to talk, from Poznań to Kijów, from Gdańsk and Mitawa to Kamieniec and Bracław through Kraków, Lwów, Warszawa, and Vilnius they joined in a choir of supplication:

Our Father, who art in heaven,
Hallowed be thy name.
Thy kingdom come,
Thy will be done on earth,
as it is in heaven.
Give us this day our daily bread.
And forgive us our debts,

as we forgive our debtors.
And lead us not into temptation,
but deliver us from evil:
For thine is the kingdom,
and the power, and the glory,
forever. Amen."

They slowly got up and took their seats. A long silence followed while all focused intently on why they came here. Indeed, they all had their motives, agendas, circle of influence, and interest at hand. To put all these aside and think intently about their serene republic, Poland in the Commonwealth with Lithuania, was quite a leap.

To start, what was Poland? What was the Commonwealth? The boundaries had blurred, and their individual interests often weighed more. What about Rus and their requests to join the union as recognized partners? They had been waiting and fighting for their rights within the Commonwealth. What about the neighbors – Turkey, Sweden, the German countries, Saxony, Austria, and Prussia? And, of course, the elephant in the neighborhood, Russia. Yes, the Muscovites grew into a powerhouse and could impose their will. It was impossible to treat them as a small, insignificant city concealed in the swamps, hiding from the Mongols, Swedes, Poles, and Turks. The Russian troops surrounded the election field at Wola and threatened the vote directly. It was Catherine who was pushing her candidate onto the throne.

And what about their immediate families? They all had experienced a great run. With it came endless complications. They had to worry about French governesses for their daughters, Italian architects, porcelain from Meissen, transport of goods to the Baltic

Sea, and maintaining the position of influence so that their wealth would be safe, especially from the competition within the Commonwealth.

The Crown Hetman broke the silence and said, "It was a good idea to meet. Indeed, there are so many issues, and we have so little time. We must try to speak honestly and directly. It is not easy, even if we try. I feel that organizing our thoughts and agreeing on terms will be a challenge. But first, what should we focus on?"

Prince Czartoryski proposed, "We need to elect the King, but it is a secondary challenge. We must agree on the reforms, on what we are trying to achieve, and then choose a candidate best suited to accomplish this task. If we continue to let it go, just eat, drink, and loosen our belts, we will have no strong army and no adequate administration to govern Poland. We will squander our wealth through mismanagement. We must think about how to strengthen the center."

Karol Radziwiłł, Darling Dear, earned his nickname by using his favorite phrase, "darling dear," with everyone from kings to servants, from enemies to friends. He took a big swig of wine standing before him and proclaimed, "We are the island of the blessed, and we should stay that way. We should pray to our Lord God for the blessings he has bestowed upon us and revel in our freedoms. No other country enjoys the wealth and splendor we have accumulated. Believe me, darling dear, I have been around, and with each visit abroad, I see how fortunate we are in Poland. Let us enjoy the fruits of our labor and let others get into their wars and armies."

"It is impossible to think only about us," Józef Pułaski remarked. "We need to build coalitions with our neighbors, and we must also decide which alliance is best for us. Historically, we tried all sides south, east, north, and west. We united with the Czechs, the Lithuanians, the Swedes, and the Saxons. One could say that we did well twice and not that well on the other two occasions. I'm not too fond of this upcoming deal with Russia, which is pushing Poniatowski. It might cost us even more than the unions with the Swedes or the Saxons.

"The southern alliance with Bohemia gave us the blessing of Christianity and stopped the German threat from the west in the 10th century. Four hundred years later, the pivot to the east and north gave us our Commonwealth of Poland-Lithuania. We see now that our northern experiment gave us nothing but trouble. The Swedes behaved like they always do. While we were counting on mutual benefits, they prepared their biggest plunder yet. They robbed us blind. In the war, we lost forty percent of our population and enormous treasures, which they took up north. They were right in thinking that we would not have the resolve and focus on raiding them between their cold rocks and getting our property back. We let it go."

Prince Adam interjected, knowing that Józef was standing behind the House of Wettin and would not criticize the Saxons, observed, "Let us not forget that the Saxons are here to grow fat on our prosperity and nothing more. They squandered their opportunity. Rather than create a new value matching the vision of the Jagiellons, they grew on our wealth enough to provoke the Prussians and the

Austrians but not strong enough to handle the pressure exerted from them."

Crown Hetman Branicki moved in his chair, nodded, grunted, and remarked, "We can decide on an outside partner, but our strength is within. Let's be honest. We are still unconcerned much with our neighbors, believing we can field necessary armies and handle any serious outside threat in an emergency. The key is we do not want either of us to grow too strong within because then our power will suffer. Individually, we have grown too strong to our detriment. Our wealth and strength come from being Polish or Lithuanian in the first place. If we do not protect and strengthen the Commonwealth, we will be picked one by one, and we will all lose in the end. It will not happen overnight, but our power and wealth will diminish yearly. I suggest we pick a Pole, one of us who will lead like Sobieski, meaning that we must address all military threats now before it is too late."

Primate Łubieński summed up by saying, "Gentlemen. Thank you all for coming. We must meet more often and work together to improve the condition of our serene republic. It is but the first step to opening the possibility of dialogue, which will enable us to exchange our views and hammer out a way to a bright future in the crucible of opposing views. God bless our dedicated efforts."

As the guests started milling around, Józef Pułaski introduced Kaz to Adam Stanisław Krasiński of Ślepowron coat of arms, bishop of Kamieniec, Great Crown Secretary, and the President of the Crown Tribunal.

"Your Excellency, let me introduce my son, Kazimierz."

"Ślepowron produces fine gentlemen," said Krasiński, looking at Kaz warmly and benevolently. "I hear that you served in Mitawa at the court of Prince Karl Christian Joseph. What did you learn there?"

"I learned to listen and blend with the tapestries," Kaz answered, bowing to the bishop. "I also learned that the Baltic Sea is the door to the world, which we should keep well-oiled and ready to be opened or closed when we see fit."

"You also spent some time at Theatines College in Warszawa. It looks like you are growing into a promising diplomat. What can you tell me about various countries, and how do you see them? What if you were to be sent as an emissary?"

"I read Krzysztof Warszewicki, which helped me understand the traits of various nations. It influenced my way of perceiving different countries. The key is not so much what I want but rather knowing how to reach them and make them understand and accept my point of view. In the end, I need to find out what they want first and only then think about my intended goals."

"Well said. How are then the various nations different? What of Turkey, for example?"

"From what I understand, if sent to Turkey, you must be forthright and brave. They will challenge and threaten you upfront to test your resolve. Also, in Turkey, you need deep coffers because before you reach the Sultan, you must have gifts for court dignitaries of various levels. If you cannot afford lavish gifts for them, you are deemed unworthy of His Highness's attention."

"What about France?"

"There, you must show versatility and speed of intellect. They will test your education, wit, manners, and culture. The way you dress and flirt with women is also important."

"Ha, ha, there you have it in a pill. And what about Moscow?"

"Between their Mongolian brutality and faith stemming from Greek orthodoxy, you must be ready for lengthy disputes and cunning. Only a man with a strong head for drinking will succeed because they use vodka as a truth serum. When drunk, you might reveal the deepest secrets."

Józef used this informal opportunity and approached the Primate, who graciously extended his hand and allowed it to be kissed on the ring.

"Your Excellency, I have matters of primary importance to address with the royal court. If neglected, they might turn into quite a controversy or even physical confrontation, which might spill beyond Warszawa."

"Dear Count, my door is always open for you. Why don't you come tomorrow around ten?" the Primate answered.

Józef bowed and retreated while Prince Adam approached the Primate. The intention of the Primate for this meeting was not to come to a mutual agreement with his guests but rather to gauge the opponents. His motivation as a member of the Familia was to clear a path for Stanisław Anthony to take the Crown. After the meeting, the Primate and Prince Adam agreed that the Crown Hetman was still a sizable threat. Rather than challenge him directly, they decided to use procedural intrigue to eliminate him from the list of contenders. If it worked, the road for Stanisław Anthony would be opened. Regarding the input from Stanisław Anthony himself, he was not in league with others to be asked for advice. Once the deal makers made up their minds, they would simply inform Stan of the next steps using all manners of etiquette and courtesy.

The Churches

Despite political commitments, voters sought weekly spiritual atonement, focus, and guidance. Most frequented were Roman Catholic churches. Many voters, especially from the eastern reaches of the Commonwealth, attended masses at the Orthodox churches, whereas some followed Lutheran and Calvinist denominations.

[Religions in the 18th century Commonwealth]

The Pułaskis decided to celebrate Sunday mass in a relatively new Church of the Nativity of the Blessed Virgin Mary. It was opened adjacent to a Carmelite convent in 1682 by the Provincial of the Carmelite Order Father Doctor Marcin Bohema, who purchased the land for 2,000 złotych. Among other formalities, permission to build was given by the co-owner of Leszno Rafał Leszczyński, the father of the future King Stanisław Leszczyński. The main altar of the church housed an icon of the Holy Mother.

Father Marek Jandołowicz, the Carmelite friar, who helped Zosia with her trauma after her violation by the Muscovites around Zazulińce, asked Kaz to pray there for the girl in front of the holy icon.

[Our Lady of Białynicze]

This icon was a copy of a famous Białynicze Hodegetria, hidden from the Mongolian hordes during their attack on Kijów in 1240. It was believed that divine intervention protected the Lachowicze fortress from 30,000 Russians during their three-month-long siege in 1660. The blockade of Lachowicze, the heartland in the middle of the Commonwealth, ended when Hetman Jan Paweł Sapieha and Hetman Stefan Czarniecki brought their armies to the rescue. This miraculous intervention was as famous as the one in the southwest of the Commonwealth. There, the divine intervention of the Blessed Black Madonna helped protect the fortress of Częstochowa from the Swedish month-long siege in 1665.

Kaz knelt in his pew and focused on Zosia and her family. He prayed intensely, asking for her peace of mind and the strength to endure. Her family was one of tens of thousands of Russian serfs seeking shelter in the Commonwealth from the whips of their Muscovite lords. He promised to watch her and her parents through the upcoming years. Father Marek was God-sent succor in their hour of need. He had been known for his enormous spiritual focus and strength honed through years of fasting and prayer. As a Discalced Carmelite, he started his day with two hours of silent prayer before dawn. His vows followed the teachings of the foundress Saint Teresa of Ávila and the co-founder Saint John of the Cross. It combined the mendicant eremitic tradition with the service to the secular society. A friar had to find the strength and dedication to do both. It included personal solitary communion with God and interacting with and providing spiritual service to the community.

When Kaz was getting ready to receive his communion, he noticed a young woman lining up to receive the holy sacrament. The light from the stained-glass window cast a hue on her profile and surrounded her in an aura of luminescence. She seemed intensely focused on her thoughts and oblivious to her surroundings. Her long slender neck bowed in supplication, and her hands clasped in prayer on her chest glowed in a perfect harmony of color and form. This image was instantly etched in Kaz's mind. He wanted to know who she was and what made her focus so profoundly and passionately.

When he tried to concentrate on Zosia, his thoughts wandered to the image of the unknown lady he saw. Before, he was pushed away from women, unsure what to expect. He usually felt the double play and insincerity of intentions and attitude. This time, he did not sense negative emotions but was attracted by a genuine passion and beauty.

After the service, the Pułaskis visited the rectory, where they left a substantial donation. Among a few persons they met there, they were introduced to Count Franciszek Wielopolski. He, in turn, presented his niece, Helena Szafraniec, who accompanied him to the Sunday service. She was the mysterious lady Kaz noticed in the church. There was no opportunity to interact much except for cursory looks and bows. Kaz promised himself he would find out more about Helena and meet her at the first opportunity.

Canaletto

As the Pułaskis were riding over to the election field at Wola, among groups of riders, carriages, and wagons, they noticed an imposing figure standing on an elevated platform surrounded by three-legged stands and some open wooden chests. Kaz decided to ride over and see what he was doing up close. Kaz saw a large canvas stretched on a wooden frame propped on one of the easels. In front of it stood an imposing man in a long white wig of curls with an impressive beer belly holding a large palette with a rainbow of pigments in his left hand.

"Who is that person?" Kaz asked a man sitting on a wagon filled with a tent, pillows, and a featherbed. He looked like a poor szlachcic who could not afford to stay in the city but was willing to attend the election as his civic duty dictated.

"Lord Brother, don't you know? He is a famous Canaletto, an Italian artist who came here to paint the election at Wola. Czartoryskis paid him handsomely to memorialize Warszawa for posterity. I hear that Stanisław Anthony wants to keep him with us longer if he wins the election," answered the szlachcic pulling the flaps of his gray coat over his knees.

[Stanisław II August election at Wola, painting by Canaletto]

"Are you going to sign the election documents for Stanisław Anthony?" Kaz inquired.

"Who else is left? Besides, look at my boots. I was in a tavern yesterday, and one of my companions there gave me these handsome yellow boots saying I could keep them if I voted for Poniatowski. What do I have to lose? He will win anyway. Nobody knows what the future will bring, but I will at least have solid boots to show for as a profit."

"The boots look great. I wish you all the best, Lord Brother," said Kaz, tipping his hat to the footwear profiteer.

They were inching west, observing various colorful uniforms of soldiers belonging to security details of prominent citizens. Besides Polish and Lithuanian outfits, there were Cossacks, Scots, Hungarians, Prussians, Silesians, Swedes, and Tatars. They noticed a company of about two hundred Hessians with their characteristic pointed hats adorned with triangular front golden plates shining in the Sun. They belonged to the entourage of over two thousand troops brought to Warszawa by the Master Swordbearer of the Grand Duchy of Lithuania, Karol Stanisław Radziwiłł, Darling Dear.

Riazin

Unexpectedly, an urgent dispatch was forcing his way through the colorful maze of voters, servants, and onlookers, pushing his mount blindly through the crowd. As Kaz pulled Zefir to the side to give this insistent madman some room, he spotted a group of Russian soldiers spread around. It brought his blood to a boil. Here they were in broad daylight, defying the sanctity of the electoral process of the Commonwealth. Their presence was a sobering sign of who was in charge and the consequences of opposing Stanisław Anthony.

Among them, he noticed an officer sitting astride his mount as straight as a broomstick. He looked like a sculpture cut out of a piece of wood, not moving a muscle. Yes, only one man held himself this rigid on a horse. It was Captain Valery Riazin. He was still quite far away, but riding the steppes, Kaz was used to recognizing a rider before he could see the features or details of his dress. Riazin did not know that his Wild East adversary was that close. Kaz decided to confront Riazin right here before the crowds of onlookers. He started riding straight at him. Fortunately, his brothers, Anthony and Frank, instantly read his intention and chased him down. They caught up with Kaz and pushed into Zefir's ribs from left and right.

"Kaz, it is not the way to handle Riazin now. Our father is serving papers through the court while you are challenging him here in the field," shouted Anthony, grabbing Zefir's reins.

"Leave me alone. I am the Starosta of Zazulińce, and this man is my responsibility," Kaz retorted.

"It makes no sense, Kaz. Calm down. We have a bigger fish to fry here, which we must settle once and for all," Anthony continued as the horses were slowing down to a trot.

"Kaz, listen to Anthony. Don't let these Muscovites provoke you. They would love for you even to kill Riazin. It would eliminate you and our family from any political consideration," Frank added.

"Let us work together with our father and the Republicans. Don't give Catherine any presents. She has already gotten enough by being able to push her Stanisław Anthony to the throne," said Anthony as they were turning away.

Kaz accepted the intervention of his brothers, but still, he was turning his head back now and then, watching Riazin, who seemed planted in a group of Russian soldiers like a scarecrow in a wheatfield. With each turn, Riazin's figure was getting smaller. However, although unsure of the sudden commotion, one could still see that he positioned his mount towards the Pułaskis, ready to face any potential threat. Ultimately, it looked like Riazin did not recognize Kaz in these heavy crowds, each trying to work their way towards their destination.

"All right, I promise I will work with you and Father," Kaz exclaimed, visibly fighting to control his urge. "I should have dealt with him then and there. It is my fault that he is still alive."

The fact that Riazin was there pretending to protect law and order was a lot for Kaz to endure. He saw Zosia spreading her hands in her blood-stained white linen dress of innocence. Kaz remembered Asher swinging back and forth on his stool under an apple tree, waiting for Shekinah. He failed them. He felt that as matters were developing now, here in Warszawa, he would not be able to protect Zazulińce from trespassers manipulating facts and twisting the notion of safety and justice into a monstrous farce.

Then, he pondered the legitimacy of the electoral process. Trying to address legal infringements, the citizens of the Commonwealth were overwhelmed by the sheer number of Russian manipulations. Once one was handled, they came with ten more. They did not care if Poles won or lost a complaint to a single violation. They showered the Commonwealth with an avalanche of troubles sewing confusion and distrust.

Catherine did not compete with other candidates through an open challenge or a debate but handled them using innuendo and a set of well-orchestrated lies, maskirovka, a camouflaged deception. The Commonwealth drowned in these lies like in a stinky swamp. You wanted to escape the mud, but the more you tried, the deeper you were enveloped by smothering muck.

After the Convocation Diet, even Kaz's father, Karol Stanisław Radziwiłł, and the Great Crown Hetman Jan Klemens Branicki gave up without a challenge. During the Election Diet, they all signed the election of Stanisław II August Poniatowski as the King of Poland and the Duke of Lithuania, treating it as the lesser evil.

The Great Crown Hetman Jan Klemens Branicki explained, "How can we call it a free and legitimate election? Most of the szlachta, disgusted with the manipulations, did not even show up in Warszawa. Rather than having 50,000 to 100,000 out of over one million eligible voters here today, we have a little over 5,000."

Stanisław Anthony was elected with no opposing candidates. Of four worthy rivals, Duke Carl Christian Joseph, Prince Adam Kazimierz Czartoryski, Prince Michał Kazimierz Ogiński, and Hetman Jan Klemens Branicki, none were on the election field as approved candidates. In the 1696 election, King August II Strong faced seven rivals. In 1668, King Michał Korybut Wiśniowiecki competed with fourteen. Everyone in 1764 knew that Catherine the Great was running a sham of an election, and no one could oppose it, entangled in a web of lies and innuendos. It was a fake election, which Stanisław Anthony did not win honestly. Catherine placed Stan on the electoral chess board, moving him around to focus viable candidates on immediate internal conflicts rather than the long-term welfare of the Commonwealth of Poland-Lithuania. As a result, potential 100,000 disappointed voters stayed home disgusted with the flawed process, pointing fingers at various domestic contenders while Catherine remained in the shade, away from the immediate scrutiny. Having her pawn Stan as the King of Poland was an ideal way to confuse the voters who would lose the election and eventually the country.

Russians were fighting the Commonwealth below the threshold of open war but still inflicting heavy blows and weakening her structures. It looked like packs of rabid wolves surrounded the eastern provinces and the wild fields, always on the prowl, ready to strike at any moment of weakness or lack of vigilance, destroying peace. With every attack or even the threat of one, they were straining the inhabitants' resources and cohesion. Kaz realized that what he witnessed at Zazulińce transpired across the eastern wall. The deliberate, cold-blooded attack on the integrity and independence of Poland was in full swing.

Kaz and Helena

Kaz told his father that he had to take a ride or go mad in Warszawa. There were so many things happening at the same time. He thought about Neminem Captivabimus law and his decision to fight the Russians on his estate. How could he protect the borderlands, the eastern flank, if he couldn't even protect his lands? The Muscovites might attack Zazulińce, burn it to the ground, and bring his corpse as proof that he had committed a crime.

Zefir was brought to the courtyard, and Kaz left, heading towards the river. Soon, Zefir would run in a full gallop along the bank of the Wisła. Both Kaz and Zefir needed this run. They left a busy embankment full of passersby, horses, and boats on the river. The track had a river on the left and clumps of trees on the right. He noticed a rider strolling along the same path. He looked closer and recognized Helena, the lady he had seen in the church. Kaz decided to stop and talk to her. He slowed down, matched the pace of Helena's ride, and closed to within a few feet.

"Hello Helena, I hope I am not disturbing you and you can tolerate my company. I am Kazimierz Pułaski. Do you remember me?" Kaz inquired.

"Of course, I do. You were so deep in prayer. I felt that whatever you were praying for reached Lord God directly," answered Helena with an honest, inviting smile.

"I felt exactly the same when I saw you," Kaz echoed. Then, he continued after a pause, "This city is too much for me. I feel trapped in its walls. Sometimes I don't know if it's the walls or the people. But I am glad that I've met you." He realized that he probably never said that much to a woman before, and so honestly.

"No, not at all," Helena replied. "I feel the same way," she continued glancing at Kaz with her blue, penetrating eyes.

"Where is your escort? Kaz asked.

"Oh, that. I sneaked out of the palace. Before they start looking for me, I will be back."

"If anyone finds out, we will have everyone looking for you in no time."

"I know. I wouldn't say I like the way women are treated. My uncle has no option but to tolerate my protests. He will probably wait first before he starts the chase if he finds out. Then I will hear yet another lecture on how I should behave."

"I understand. Good luck with your adventure," Kaz commented.

He rarely paid attention to women. Most of them outside his family estates were refined representatives of various courts and the nobility. He was never sure what they meant. They seemed to be experts at the game of pretense and intrigue. There was always a second bottom to their interactions, some ulterior motive, which had to be divined despite their apparent actions. To make sense of their intentions, one had to know their background, including complicated family relationships and social connections. Their main occupation outside their family circles seemed to be the game of trapping a suitable man or being trapped by one. Even if they tried to be sincere and trustworthy, there was always a hint of the power struggle of the sexes, making Kaz uncomfortable.

He preferred honest and straightforward people like Tom and Robert. He felt at ease with his father, brothers, and sisters. At the other end of the spectrum were the courtiers at Mitawa. The whole life there, sophisticated and elegant, was covered by an ominous specter of Russian influence. It was not visible and apparent. Still, it penetrated every aspect of the court. Only if one were to do the unthinkable, the Russian soldiers would appear out of nowhere to enforce the ultimate rules of the game. Any time Kaz met women, all these confusing emotions rushed to his head, and he preferred not to get engaged with seemingly innocent exchanges of platitudes or flirting.

For most men his age, whom he knew from his college, relationships with women were at the forefront. They would talk endlessly about what beauty they met or wanted to meet, what the girls said, how they were dressed, when they would see them, or how to avoid their parents. Sometimes they would say, "You are such a bore, Kaz. We know honor, Motherland, protection of the borders, and your family. Don't you want to do something for fun, live a little?"

Kaz didn't want to "live a little." He wanted to live to the fullest and embraced all life's fascinations and mysteries. There was so much he wanted to experience and learn. However, the court intrigue was like a rotten decay on the nation's flesh. He wanted to be far removed from its suffocating effect. The games he saw between men and women at court were part of this smothering ritual aimed at snaring a victim. It started with putting your true personality and honest feelings aside, hiding them well so that one seemed to forget who he was. Women, for him, were not sincere and genuine but always concealed behind the veil of half-truths and hidden agendas powdered by fake smiles. They seemed on constant guard not to reveal their true nature. They were trained to move, talk and dress according to sophisticated rules and expectations, which stifled authenticity and honesty.

What a refreshing difference Helena was for Kaz. He was attracted by her eyes and small lips with a chain of pearly teeth. Her small, thin nose pointing slightly upwards made her look like a perfect rendition of the canons of beauty. He would love to walk with her and wrap his arm around her thin waist. He felt that he could share with her his dreams and ambitions. He would love to have her by his side and watch her in a garden full of fragrant flowers or between low-hanging fruits of some apple or cherry orchard. He already knew that she honestly liked natural surroundings and was sensitive to the beauty of what nature had to offer in all its various forms, smells, and textures.

"This city," Helena continued. "People are so cramped together that I feel they cannot function or think as independent spirits. My awareness shrinks, overwhelmed by these crowds and their demands. They do not ask me what I want or would like to do. They want me to go where they like, eat what they like, dress, and move how they like. They bow, dance, smile, and talk in a pre-arranged scenario. I do not feel like a human here but more like a puppet in an ugly play pulled by the strings of an invisible master. I am always in defense mode, protecting my genuine personality. They treat me more like a piece of wood to be carved into a statue of their liking. I hate every moment of this freak show.

"Only these horse rides remind me that there is still life beyond the crowds who participate in a play directed by a cruel puppet master with no heart. Looking at a tree or a flower gives me hope that real life and beauty still exist."

"I never looked at life from your perspective, but I must say that you make a lot of sense," Kaz commented.

"Look at this countryside, flat as a pancake," continued Helena getting off her horse and walking along the bank of the Wisła River with Kaz by her side. "This dull river has no life in it. Where I come from, rivers are sparkling with energy, and the Earth is formed into rocks, hills, and mountains. Thank God for the forest and the meadows here, willow trees and birds. Otherwise, it would be a nightmare of the countryside.

"I came here to honor the centuries-old tradition of the free election of our Polish King, but I don't see much honor here. I am of Starykoń coat-of-arms, but since all male descendants of my line are gone, I do not count. I am Helena Szafraniec, but I came here with my uncle Kazimierz Wielopolski, also of Starykoń coat-of-arms. What a silly tradition. The line is extinguished because there are no more males in the queue. I wonder who brought all these males to life. Entrusting your lines to patrimony is a sad joke. And this Stanisław Anthony. I don't know. My uncle supports him, but I do not like the Russian soldiers who are his escort and protection. Where are his Polish knights?

"What about you, Kazimierz? Who do you support?" Helena asked, looking at Kaz with her deep blue eyes rimmed with a hint of black around the iris. Kaz knew she wanted an honest answer, not a mere exchange of elegant platitudes.

"I am here with my father and brothers. We supported the Saxon candidate, but he didn't have enough votes, so he did not even come. My father says he has endorsed Stanisław Anthony to avoid unnecessary fights and brawls. Our job will then be to look at his rule carefully, support him in good deeds, and oppose if he blunders."

They both realized their quick horse ride out of the city took much longer than planned. Kaz handed Helena his reins and went down towards the river. He returned quickly with a bouquet of blue cornflowers and blue bottles adorned with a yellow daffodil.

"Here, take these to the city. They should remind you that beauty still exists and waits for you here."

"Oh, thank you, Kazimierz. You give me hope. You should visit me one day and see real beauty down south," said Helena mounting her horse. "We should hurry back before the Russian soldiers catch us and deliver us to this awful ball arranged by my uncle." They urged their horses into a full gallop and lowered their heads close to their crests.

Kaz thought about his mother's words, "Don't worry about girls. When the time comes, you will know. Love will overwhelm you like an avalanche of cravings and urges, demanding immediate attention. It will not be subtle or confusing. It will grab you by your heart and squeeze it like a sponge. There will be no hesitation." Kaz had just felt this firm squeeze. He would love for them to ride fast to Podole rather than return to Warszawa.

King Stan and Empress Catherine

King Stanisław II August Poniatowski had known Empress Catherine for quite some time before his election to the Polish throne in 1764. They met in 1755 when a presentable, young, and dashing Stan worked in Saint Petersburg as the secretary to the British Ambassador Sir Charles Hanbury Williams, KB, MP. The latter was the envoy extraordinary to Russia. Sir Williams was a Welch diplomat and a member of the Parliament of the United Kingdom. Letters MP stood for the Member of the Parliament, and KB denoted the Knight of the most honorable order of the Bath.

KB was founded by King George I on 18 May 1725 as a regular Military Order. It was a select group of 36 hand-picked noblemen who were the executive arm of the King. He had 24 knights of the Garter and 16 of the Thistle at his disposal, but they were appointed mainly by heredity and were not blindly loyal to the King. They could not be entrusted with the monarch's most secret and daring enterprises. On the other hand, the 36 KB knights were a specially selected elite group sent worldwide as the King's eyes, ears, and arms.

[Knight of the most honorable order of the Bath, Latin text around the three crowns, *tria juncta in uno,* means "three joined in one."]

[Princess Sophie of Anhalt-Zerbst, future Catherine the Great]

Serving as secretary to Sir Williams meant that Stanisław Anthony was on the topmost level of diplomatic intrigue spanning the whole known world. When Sir Williams decided to place a 22-year-old Stanisław in the chamber and then in the bed of a 26-year-old Sophie, he used Stanisław as a sophisticated, dangerous, and brutal weapon of politics.

At that time, Catherine was married to then-Grand Duke Pyotr Fyodorovich for some ten years. It might be shocking to the uninitiated, but the reality of the courts was that Catherine was contracted to breed a male who would then be in line to take over as the Czar of Russia after his Father, Peter, now waiting in line for the title, would die.

The person running the family affairs at the highest level of the Russian court was Elizabeth Petrovna, future Empress Elizabeth, Peter's aunt. She wanted Peter's son to continue the line of Peter the Great. When Elizabeth became the Empress of Russia, she brought Peter from Germany. His parents were deceased then, and Elizabeth, whose mother was Polish, positioned this German nephew in line for the Russian throne. In 1739, Peter's father died, and he became Duke of Holstein-Gottorp as Charles Peter Ulrich (German: Karl Peter Ulrich) at the age of eleven. When he made it to Russia in 1742, Elizabeth made Peter her heir presumptive. Since then, Peter has always been called "the Grandson of Peter the Great." Forgetting to use this formula would cost one untold trouble in the Russian court. Everyone got used to it with practice, and it was inconceivable to think otherwise.

Since Catherine did not produce a son for Peter in ten years, the doors to her chamber were discreetly opened for potential lovers. If she were to be impregnated with a male offspring, the sperm donor would most probably be assassinated. The fruit of this genetic engineering would be made a legitimate son to Peter, waiting in line for the Crown.

The future Catherine II was Sophie of Anhalt-Zerbst, born on 2 May 1729 in the then-Prussian town of Stettin by the Baltic Sea. As a fifteen-year-old girl, she was sent to Russia and met the brutal realities of a power struggle from the first day. It was a miracle that she survived the ordeal. She despised her husband, who was a simpleton and a brute. He treated her horribly. Probably Peter and Empress Elizabeth caused Catherine to turn away from their scheming and, as the antidote, get closer to Russians at court. She started studying the Russian language and culture. After Stan left St. Petersburg, Catherine began developing her Russian identity earnestly. Rather than listening to naïve prospects of pure love and marriage proposals presented by

Stan, she relied on her noble Russian favorites and lovers, most notably Count Grigori Orlov and Grigori Potemkin. She was assisted by highly successful generals such as Alexander Suvorov and Piotr Rumyantsev and admirals such as Samuel Greig and Fyodor Ushakov.

When Catherine met Stan for the first time in 1755, she was already a sophisticated, well-educated, and tried by combat participant in the royal game of thrones, with several deep emotional scars. Stan was related to Catherine through King Christian I of Denmark. On the maternal side, Stan was a Scottish House of Steward descendant. Stan's and Catherine's relationship's forbidden fruit was a girl named Anna Petrovna, born in December 1757. Stan was not around when his daughter was born. In 1757, he was ordered to serve in the British Army during the Seven Years' War, thus severing a close emotional relationship with Catherine. When the frail Grand Duchess died on 8 March 1795, Catherine kissed the child on the forehead following the Russian Orthodox Church rites and buried her in the Alexander Nevsky Monastery.

In 1764, Catherine, already the empress of Russia, spent a staggering 2.5 million rubles to aid Stan's election. She deployed regular Russian army units in the election fields of Wola and used a formidable group of people for special operations all over Europe to support Stan's victory. Some organized the uprising of peasants in Ukraine to terrorize the prospective voters and destroy eventual support for the Bar Confederates there. She paid Voltaire in France to criticize Poland and spread lies about the Bar Confederation, a military opposition to Stan's disastrous policy. He published a fake

Confederate Oath, including manipulated lines claiming they swore to assassinate the King.

Stan hoped that Catherine would marry him and rule Russia and Poland together. Some said that Crown Prince Wilhelm of Prussia warned Catherine that he would go to war if she were to marry Stan. Turkey would also be pushed into war against Russia if they were to get married. Catherine, however, did not intend to marry Stan. She used him as a pawn in her maneuvers to strengthen Russia. Stan was one of many who used love as a political tool to influence and hopefully control Catherine. He was one of the monsters of politics who whipped Catherine into the most formidable player on the global chessboard. His plans to control Catherine had the opposite effect. Catherine handled Stan and played him as a pawn in her game.

For a sophisticated, intelligent, and surrounded by the web of intrigue Catherine, Stan was a disappointing episode. Even if she accepted some early vows or expressions of love, it was quickly apparent that he was just a mere servant in the hands of others. He was clearly below her level of refinement. He could have promised her the sky only to follow his master once Sir Williams yanked the chain. Stan left his lover and their daughter in the pit of vipers to follow orders wherever they would send him. He must have been a letdown to her in many ways and no match for her obvious intelligence and political talents.

Even his coterie, the House of Czartoryski, did not see him as their runner-up for the throne of Poland. Their obvious choice was Prince Adam Kazimierz Czartoryski, but Catherine opposed his candidacy.

Prince Adam was forced to resign as a contender, and the Czartoryski family agreed to Catherine's demand that Stan runs for the job. If they had opposed Catherine's bidding, no Russian military would have roamed Poland to threaten any competition to the Familia. There would not have been Catherine's gold either.

Secret Visit

Catherine summoned Repnin to finalize her strategy for Poland.

"Look at Stan. He is a perfect tool that can be used by playing on his passions and weaknesses. I am so lucky he is unlike George III, King of Great Britain. George genuinely loved Lady Sarah Lennox but dropped his feelings for the Crown's sake. Although, God knows whether it didn't cost him his sanity. I don't think Stan would drop any of his mistresses for something so sublimely abstract as Poland. He loves Poland, art, and intelligent debates, but none beats the pleasure of a beautiful woman in his bed. I know that I can play him like a piano. He will sing for me any time I hit the right key. You, Repnin, will be one of the keys I will use to make Stan dance for me."

"I am here to be whatever you desire. Let us destroy Poland, this elephant in the European China store. How do you want me to hurt them?"

"We will not attack them directly. They are too powerful for us to risk a confrontation. Poland is so great that we will use her greatness to hurt herself.

We cannot win an open war with Poland. We need to maneuver this giant and divide it into factions. They are great fighters. Let us use their skills to fight one another."

While supporting Stan's candidacy for the Polish throne, Catherine refused his request to visit her in St. Petersburg. She did not want to see him for personal reasons, but what was even more important, politically, it would have been a mistake. King Frederick II of Prussia made it clear that he would go to war if she were to marry Stan and unite Poland with Russia. Merely showing him in St. Petersburg would bring an avalanche of domestic and foreign consequences.

Officially, Catherine did not want to allow Stan a visit, but eventually, she decided to spend a night with him. She planned to set him straight and gauge if she should have any concerns that he might try to maneuver himself into independence.

The news broke throughout Warszawa that Stan was sick. He would stay in bed until the doctors decided it was safe for him to venture out. In the meantime, Repnin arranged for a coach run with Stan as a passenger. It was a gruesome three-day nonstop day and night ride one way. Even when he needed to go to the bathroom, Stan was forced to use a potty.

Horses pulling the carriage were replaced every six hours. When they pulled over for a change, a ready double pair was waiting at the roadside. The procedure took less than five minutes, and the coach was on its way. At the end of the trip, Stan was exhausted, and it looked like he might get genuinely sick.

They arrived late at night. Catherine received Stan in her private love chamber. It was a room that enforced the feeling of decadent perversion. The table had legs in the shape of phalluses. The central theme of the paintings on the walls was the vagina. Multiple strategically placed mirrors enabled Catherine to watch the sexual performance of guests from any imaginable angle.

Catherine experienced an extensive list of lovers and male sex toys through the years. The first on the long list of her St. Petersburg flings was Count Sergei Vasilievich Saltykov, even before Stan. She implied in her memoirs that he was the father of her son, Paul I of Russia. A favorite of Catherine's Russian lovers was Alexander Petrovich Yermolov. First, he was tested in bed by Countess Anna Stepanovna Protasova, the confidant of Catherine, and only then did Catherine decide to give him a try. He was great in bed, but he made one strategic mistake. He collaborated with the enemies of Prince Grigori Aleksandrovich Potemkin-Tauricheski. The same Prince Grigori who introduced Alexander Petrovich to Catherine and frequented her bed before Alexander Petrovich. Alexander spent the rest of his life in Schloss Frohsdorf in lower Austria for that mistake.

There was also Count Alexander Matveyevich Dmitriev-Mamonov. He was promoted to colonel, major general, and chamberlain for his prowess. A suite of apartments was assigned to him in the Winter Palace. The most important of them all was Prince Grigori Grigorievich Orlov. He led the coup that overthrew Catherine's husband, Peter III of Russia, and installed Catherine as empress. For some years, he was a virtual co-ruler with her. We must also mention Ivan Nikolajevich Rimsky-Korsakov, Count Pyotr Zavadovsky, lieutenant-general and count of the Holy Roman Empire, Semyon Zorich, born in Serbia, and probably her last lover, Prince Platon Alexandrovich Zubov.

When Stan appeared in Catherine's boudoir, she was reclining on a sofa with a horsewhip in her hand. As Stan approached her, attempting to kiss her hand, she pushed him away from the couch with the whip. Stan stumbled a few steps backward.

"My love. I missed you so much," he implored. "It was torture not being able to see you all these years."

"Stan, save it. You were never a good actor," replied Catherine getting up from her sofa.

"Your Highness," squealed Stan bowing low with a trained curtsy extending his arms to the sides, "life without you is such a depressing affair. I am glad we can meet again."

"You forgot to tell me how beautiful I am. Need I remind you how to talk to a woman?" commented Catherine looking at him with a hint of contempt.

"I am blessed to admire your loveliness yet again. You are the mother of my beloved child; may she rest in peace," whispered Stan trying to get closer to Catherine.

"You were not interested in her, or me for that matter, when I was giving birth to her," responded Catherine, giving Stan such a look that he froze mid-step.

"I cannot ever forgive myself for that negligence. If not for honor and duty, I would have been by your bed day and night."

"No, you wouldn't. You are too used to luxury and comfort. You would not last a full day. Still, what a brave assertion," Catherine protested as she started pacing around the room, holding her horsewhip in her hands folded on her back.

"What a lovely dress. You have always had great taste. Who is your dressmaker these days?"

"Stan, we don't have time to go over my skirts, shoes, and stockings. You must be back in your coach in an hour to get back to Warszawa unnoticed."

"Won't we have time to enjoy ourselves a bit longer?"

"No, we won't. This visit is long enough for me to decide if I want to continue spending money and my political capital on you."

"Rest assured, with my experience from Dresden to London and Paris to Vienna, I can be very political."

"I am more concerned if you are strong enough to follow my directions. You don't have to worry about being political. You must be smart and obedient."

"You know that I love you and will do anything for you."

"You don't have to love me. I want you to be true to your only love, the love of yourself. If you only love yourself, you will do fine."

"But, Your Highness, you judge me so harshly," Stan tried his feeble defense one more time.

"No, Stan. I like you, and I don't want you to end up like those who disappoint me. Think about my dear husband, Peter. What a horrible death. I know that you are more afraid of poverty than death. If you play along, you will not be short of money."

Stan resigned, trying to match Catherine in this conversation. He sat in an armchair with two phallic legs of Catherine's table behind him. They aptly framed his current position.

"Money, yes. It is a problem in Poland. The treasury is empty, and the needs are great."

"You will have enough to meet all your needs. Stay close to Repnin, and don't get too adventurous. He can be crude at times, but he is effective, darn effective. Even if you do not understand his actions, do not think about crossing him. You might ask him for explanations, but for the love of God, do not stand in his way."

"You are right. He is clumsy and primitive, which earns him lots of enemies in Poland."

"He can handle his enemies. I am playing a big game, which involves the whole of Europe. I don't want you to be a casualty, especially if it could be avoided by just following Repnin."

"I will try to do my best, Your Highness, but it won't be easy."

"I won't promise you 'easy.' I promise you money and security. Don't confuse your priorities, and you will do just fine." Catherine rang the bell, and Countess Anna Stepanova appeared. Catherine smiled and said, "Dear Countess, I had a lovely chat with my friend, the King of Poland Stanisław Stanisławowicz. Make sure that he makes it to his coach undetected. "

"Rest assured, Your Highness," curtsied the countess looking at Stan and the boudoir through her inquisitive hazelnut eyes for any hint of what had transpired between the two. She was a beauty in her own right and did not engage in sex adventures only because of her sense of duty to the empire. Her long neck and full lips seductively opened in a charming smile were enough for most men at court to lose their heads. She led Stan through the dark hallways out through a side gate. In a few moments, Stan opened the doors to his coach, almost stepping into the potty when the coach jerked violently and was on its way back to Warszawa.

Catherine concluded that Stan was impoverished and isolated from any meaningful power base. He used Repnin as his source of income, which gave Catherine absolute control over Stan. The web of intrigue and control had been set. Catherine could proceed to suck

Poland out of any energy, and Stan would be the main conduit leading to the ultimate digestion of the serene republic.

CHAPTER 4

The Bar Confederation (1768)

King Stan's Rule

Catherine the Great was not satisfied with the progress of her plans regarding Poland. King Stan was weaker than she had predicted and could not stand up to Polish senators. They made him approve reforms that would strengthen Poland. If Poland increased its army and focused on new tax revenues, Russia would lose the window of opportunity to topple the Commonwealth.

Before King Stan for over 800 years, Poland skillfully adjusted to the challenges brought by geopolitical pressures. After times of trouble, the kingdom always came renewed and strengthened. Poland had been free to venture south, east, north, and west with her ideas of inclusion based on mutual interest and respect for different cultures, ethnicities, and religions.

The venture south was accomplished by the marriage of Mieszko, the pagan prince of Poland, to a Roman Catholic Bohemian princess and the adoption of Christianity in 966. It brought Poland into the Pan-European Latin culture, which shared the same religion and language. Latin was the language political and religious elites shared from Italy to England and Spain to Poland.

119

The venture east and north sought a risky alliance with pagan Lithuania in the 14th century. It paid off handsomely. The Jagiełło dynasty brought impressive improvements and unprecedented decades of stability and growth to both the Kingdom of Poland and the Duchy of Lithuania. A Polish student could travel to Germany, Spain, or Rome and listen to lectures in Latin as he would have in a Polish university.

The third critical expansion attempt was the offer of a Polish Crown to the Swedish Vasa dynasty. On 19 August 1587, Sigismund III Vasa was elected the King of the Commonwealth. His mother was from the House of Jagiełło, and there was no legal male Jagiellon to take the throne. By God's grace, King Sigismund III was the King of Poland, Grand Duke of Lithuania, Ruthenia, Prussia, Mazovia, Samogitia, Livonia, and the hereditary King of Swedes, Goths, and Vandals. It turned out to be a strategic mistake with colossal consequences. The Swedes waited for three generations of Vasa kings before striking Poland hard, true to their Viking blood. They killed 40% of the Polish population and looted almost every palace, castle, and manor of the wealth they knew everything about, watching tax collection for the Vasa kings.

The fourth direction of the expansion attempt was westward. Here, the Saxon House of Wettin was a choice. Unfortunately, the Wettins did not have the intelligence or vision to understand Poland's potential for growth and wealth. They degenerated Polish prowess into the excessive indulgence of consumption and lust, which led to their disappointing end. During the reign of Augustus III, the saying went:

za króla Sasa jedz, pij i popuszczaj pasa (during Saxon Reign, eat, drink, and loosen your belt). The balloon of their greatness lost all hot air, and what was left was a sad, crumpled shell of what could have been.

The Crown did not carefully analyze what the neighbors of Poland were doing and neglected to protect the Commonwealth from their potential greed and attacks. Most szlachta followed the example from the top and enjoyed life, spending extraordinary amounts of money on trinkets and enjoyment. It was acceptable to bring foreign cooks, artists, architects, soldiers, and servants hailing mainly from Italy, France, or Germany. Money flowed like a river from a well-designed and administered food production system. When some warned of possible danger from such irresponsible behavior, the accepted response was *Polska nierządem stoi* (Poland is strong through her lack of governance). The argument was that if they were peaceful and militarily weak, they would not be a threat to anyone, and they would leave us be. All foreign powers who wanted Poland to remain vulnerable supported and reinforced this self-defeating argument. Competing between themselves, the neighbors of Poland were united in one aspect; they all wanted a weak Poland.

In 1762, Kaz spent time as a page at the court of the son of King Augustus III, Carl Christian Joseph of Saxony, Duke of Courland, and Semigallia in Mitawa. Rather than fight for the Polish Crown when his father passed, Carl Christian enjoyed a lavish lifestyle at his palace but could not move. Russian soldiers surrounded the palace and stopped him from challenging Stanisław Anthony Poniatowski to the

Polish Crown. Carl Christian's position and status were a furtive illusory dream. He was a toy in the hands of powerful despots.

His father, King Augustus III, was a letdown. He was more interested in ease and pleasure than in the affairs of the state. He covered his political impotence with a pretense of lavish accouterments, spending more time in Dresden than in Warszawa. In 1733, the composer Johann Sebastian Bach dedicated the Kyrie–Gloria Mass in B minor to Augustus. He famously asked his plenipotentiary and a de facto viceroy of Poland: "Brühl, do I have money?" During the Seven Year War, he allowed Saxony to be bled by Prussia and could not use the formidable resources he had at his disposal as the King of Poland. His son never had a chance to be a challenger for the Polish Crown, mainly due to his father's negligence.

There was no real competition between the abilities of the rulers of Poland and Russia. Catherine II earned her nickname "the Great" many times over. Russians had ambitions of becoming a great power, but these were primarily dreams before her rule. Catherine turned this long-term vision whispered in the hallways of the Kremlin into reality. She moved from win to win during her reign, leaving the foreign competition in the dust.

In 1764, the time was ripe to place a Russian puppet on the Polish throne, with Catherine as the ultimate puppet master. Ambassador Repnin showed up in Warszawa to steer the Polish marionette, King Stan, into whatever Catherine thought was good for Russia and bad for Poland.

The rule of King Stan was a series of disasters. He was constantly scheming, planning, and meeting with groups of supporters, but the outcomes of these continuous conferences were a sad farce. His grand visions and ideas were pleasant daydreaming fantasies but had little practical connection to the reality of political life in the Commonwealth and abroad. Catherine tightened the noose around the Commonwealth while Repnin could do anything he wanted in Warszawa. He yelled at those in court or Sejm who did not follow his orders fast enough. Still, the King would ignore his unacceptable behavior and discuss grand improvement visions. The actual position of King Stan was like that of Carl Christian Joseph in Mitawa, where he was posing as the Duke of Semigallia. Poland was about to fiddle away, disappearing from the realm of politics. Much the same way, the Wettins lost their chance of positively impacting the Commonwealth and Europe.

Kidnapping

Repnin was increasingly obvious and crude with his demands on the Commonwealth decision-makers. When yelling did not work, he would push and kick some parliamentarians. During a heated exchange with Kaz's father, Józef Pułaski, Repnin threatened to bring 15,000 more troops and be done with this pathetic opposition, which blocked Russian demands to approve of the laws dictated by Catherine. Józef answered, "You may even bring 100,000. It will be your undoing. Watch what you wish for, ambassador."

On 13 October 1767, Repnin called Józef's bluff and stepped up the escalation ladder. This time, it was not robbery, murder, or rape in the Wild East borderlands of Poland but direct violence in the center of Polish power, Warszawa. He kidnapped two bishops and two senators in the middle of Warszawa and took them to prison in Kaługa, Russia, where they spent five years in exile. Bishops Józef Andrzej Załuski and Kajetan Sołtyk, hetman Wacław Rzewuski and his son Seweryn were leading the opposition against the Polish-Russian treaty of friendship pushed by Repnin. All of them were members of the Senate of Poland.

Józef Andrzej Załuski, the sixty-five-year-old Senator and Bishop of Kijów, educated at the Sorbonne University in Paris and the Jagiellonian University in Kraków, was internationally respected for the opening of the Załuski Library. He had amassed one of the finest collections of prints and manuscripts recognized globally, with over 400,000 volumes, which Catherine eventually plundered during the partitions of Poland. He earned respect and reverence as a bishop and as an intellectual giant. Repnin humiliated the bishop publicly and showed how powerless he was in the face of Russian might. Four soldiers grabbed the bishop in the middle of the night and put heavy chains on his hands and ankles. He lost his wig as they held the chain and dragged him down the stairs to a black coach.

Wacław Piotr Rzewuski was a sixty-one-year-old Senator, a Grand Hetman of the Crown. He was a recognized dramatist and poet, the great-grandfather of Ewelina Hańska, wife of French writer Honoré de Balzac. Because he put up a fight, the Russians clapped the chains on his hands behind his back. It took a little more effort and a few more blows to the head to drag him out of the house. Ultimately,

Riazin gave him a final push, and the Senator ended up in a black coach, like Bishop Załuski.

Kajetan Ignacy Sołtyk, a fifty-two-year-old Senator, was the Bishop of Kraków, educated both in Poland and Rome. He shared the same fate as Bishop Załuski. The fourth senator was Wacław Rzewuski's son, Seweryn Rzewuski. Seweryn was a writer, a poet, the general of the Royal Army, and a field Hetman of the Crown. He returned to Poland after his exile in 1773 and, in 1775, received restitution from King Stan with the orders of St. Stanislaus and the White Eagle. Still, he never forgave King Stan and blamed him as the key instigator of Repnin's kidnappings.

The rest of the intimidated senators postponed the Sejm until February 1768. They were supposed to vote on the final draft of the Polish-Russian treaty of friendship, which would render the Commonwealth a Russian protectorate. The blundering King was giving Poland's sovereignty away day by day. Even this act of violence would not make him decide on any effective countermeasures. On 27 February 1768, during the Silent Sejm, the Cardinal Laws and the Polish-Russian treaty, which Russia guaranteed, were signed into law. It indicated that Russia was sovereign over Poland, and any change to these agreements would be possible only if approved by Catherine.

Józef Pułaski felt that filing motions through the court, pointing to mistakes and blunders, was not changing facts on the ground. The open kidnapping of Polish senators and bishops for refusing to follow Repnin's dictates was a de facto coup with passive approval from the

King of Poland. Instead of immediately arresting Repnin or expelling him out of the Commonwealth, King Stan called yet another assembly to discuss the next steps.

Time for Action

The senators gathered at the palace with the King seated on his throne, sporting a perfectly coiffured white wig, a white linen shirt with frills covered with a light-yellow silk vest, and a knee-long blue coat. He wore long silk stockings and low-heeled blue leather shoes with pointed toes on his legs. The King looked around, smiled faintly, and began by declaring how unfortunate it was that some assembled were acting irresponsibly. He started his speech cautiously, unsure how the assembly would receive it. With every word, King Stan felt more comfortable. Finally, he continued with poise and conviction, almost believing his words.

King Stan explained to the assembly that he had everything under control, but the situation was challenging and complicated. It required the most sophisticated brinkmanship of diplomacy, while the unnecessary outbursts of crude emotions might bring disastrous results. He asked for more meetings in various subcommittees to settle outstanding issues of import. He agreed with everyone but did not decide on anything.

"Gentlemen," continued King Stan. "It is with the utmost pleasure and satisfaction that I attend meetings of this august body. We all hold the welfare of our serene republic deeply in our hearts. The complexities of political expediency demand that we ponder deeply and act responsibly. Any rash reaction or immature decision might have grave and unforeseen consequences exceeding our darkest nightmares."

Józef Pułaski exploded, "Enough is enough. Stop talking, you bumbling fool. You don't have the slightest idea what you are getting all of us into by your indecision and cowardice. If we continue doing nothing but talk, we will lose any pretense of independence."

"Józef, offending the majesty of the King of the Commonwealth is not a way to address serious matters of the state," reacted King Stan, casting his glances at the crowd to check who was with Józef.

"You do not understand what 'serious' means," Józef interjected. "You are a joke of a king. You think it is a love affair with a girl from St. Petersburg. Rather than being the King, you think about romance. You have had enough courtesans. Take a few more if you need to but stop treating Empress Catherine as your lover."

"It is outrageous!" exclaimed King Stan. "I never had sex with that woman Catherine. Besides, she is not merely a woman. She represents the majesty and strength of all of Russia. We must be careful when addressing matters of that caliber."

"You should not flirt with Catherine. You think you are playing a love game with a woman, but you gamble Poland. What about your majesty as the King of the Commonwealth?"

"I repeat again; I did not touch that woman, Catherine. She is the Czarina first and a woman second. You are taking your liberties too far. Anywhere you look, you see nothing but scheming and conspiracy theories. Besides Pułaski, you are here to advise what we should do and not what I should not do."

"Sire, you endanger our way of life and eventually the very existence of the Commonwealth," Joseph implored the King. Stan looked at Józef haughtily and leaned on the ornate arm of the throne.

"I am used to being offended by some, but it is not the time for brawling. I wonder how you can protect us from the Tatars at your frontier estates, Sir Joseph, if you are so afraid of everything. Being a man of limited imagination, you fear that Poland might be endangered, especially by Russia," said King Stan looking around the chamber for support and laughter, but none was forthcoming.

"It is you, King Stanisław, who has limited imagination thinking that Poland might not be in danger," Józef replied. "Russian soldiers roam the Commonwealth and do as they please without any reaction from the Crown."

"Poland is as safe with me as I, her King, am safe here in this chamber," retorted King Stan, visibly pleased that he found such a decisive response.

Józef could not take this pitiful grandstanding anymore. He thought that maybe Kaz was right when he called for decisive action to enforce the law. Perhaps he was too old, believing that reasoning and well-crafted arguments would win the day. The decision having been taken, his feet carried him to the Royal Presence, stepping gingerly onto the platform, padded with damask rugs where the throne of the Kingdom of Poland sat. There he leaned down over the sitting King and struck him on the cheek with all the force of the flat of his hand. King Stan covered his face. When he lowered his arm, the powder from his face was partially gone, and his white wig tilted sideways. There was a red mark with a noticeable sign of Józef's fingers on his left cheek.

Nobody moved. Everyone was watching what King Stan would do. He fluttered his hand in agony, visibly shaken. The guards were waiting for a signal to arrest Józef, but there was nothing. King Stan was more focused on his burning cheek than the majesty of the Crown he represented. He started waving his hand erratically as if chasing a stubborn fly grimacing his handsome face in pain, which visibly he was not used to. In the meantime, Józef turned around and left the chambers.

There was no time to spare. Józef knew that he would be chased and arrested in a matter of minutes. Blood was pumping throughout his veins, making him feel decades younger. He woke up the slumbering energy he had been trying to control through decades of legal training and practice at the Crown Court. He thought about his sons and how to coordinate the opposition to the King.

He had the legalities of contention prepared as one of the options discussed among the Republicans. It was only a matter of inserting the date, location, and names of the participants to have the Articles of Confederation ready to be filed. The challenge was moving from a tedious legal battle below the threshold of open rebellion into a decisive fight. Still, duly registering the actions as a legal remedy supported by the Constitution of the Commonwealth was a must for Józef.

As the crown court attorney, he treated the law with all due reverence. The proceedings of the royal court were adjusted during the Sejm action in 1578 when King Batory ceded his right of a supreme judge to the Crown Tribunal. It was continually reaffirmed by duly elected kings ever since.

The chamber was still in a state of shock. It was evident that King Stan would not act in the open but instead use his preferred operating methods behind the scenes through various proxies and innuendo. The guards were hardly controlling themselves but would only dare take the initiative with the King's direction. If they did, it would show the obvious; that the King lacked the resolve to be an effective commander-in-chief. This delay gave Józef time to leave the palace and hop into his carriage. Since Kaz was in Warszawa on the Zazulińce business, Józef decided to see him.

Once the carriage arrived at Kaz's residence, Józef almost ran inside, pushing the servants out of his way.

"What are you doing here, Father? I thought you would be at a meeting in the palace," spoke surprised Kaz walking away from his desk full of documents. "I need your help checking all the paperwork for the shipment of grain through Gdańsk, but it could wait."

Józef staggered over to an armchair and collapsed into it. He was catching his breath like a fish out of water. Kaz was looking at his father more and more surprised.

"Our Mitawa connection to export grain with Russians controlling Courland makes less and less sense," Kaz continued, increasingly concerned with his father's behavior. "What is it, Father? Talk to me," Kaz said, leaning over his dear and venerated ancestor.

Józef ripped a scarf from around his neck and muttered: "I did it."

"I did it," he repeated, shrieking.

"What, what did you do?"

"I slapped King Stan. I slapped him in front of everyone in the chambers," Józef exclaimed for the first time, able to take a full breath of air.

"You did what?" Kaz burst out in disbelief.

"I did it. It is time to act. I should have listened to you a long time ago."

"Wow, even I would not move that far. Good for you. And they didn't arrest you?" Kaz inquired and started pacing to the window and back.

"It all happened so quickly. I think they are all still sitting there in a state of shock."

"What do you want to do now? It changes everything."

"We must officially start a confederacy. I have all the paperwork prepared. We need to serve it through the Crown Court."

"Not now, Father. Now, we must get out of Warszawa, far enough so that the Muscovites do not send us like the Rzewuskis to their jail somewhere in Kaługa."

Kaz thundered, "Witek! Get in here on the double!"

Witek's head appeared in an instant.

"How may I be of service, Lord?" he asked, glancing around and stopping when he saw the disturbed Józef with his legs stretched out in a pose Witek had never seen the old master before.

"Get the horses and the coach ready. We are getting out of here now! We must ride back to Zazulińce before the Russians come. They can be here any minute!"

"Yes, Lord," Witek yelled and was gone. Tom and Kaz personally selected and trained all Kaz's servants. They knew exactly what it meant to act quickly and decisively. Any manner of emergency was practiced and engrained in their actions in Zazulińce. Kaz gave his father a glass of water.

"Here. Take a sip, Sir. The next glass you will have will be in Podole. We are leaving now!"

He pulled his father up from the armchair and walked him out of the room. Down in the courtyard, there was organized chaos. People were running back and forth. Someone was bringing chests and tying them up to the backbench of the coach. Others were carrying rifles and pistols. Kaz placed his father into the coach and closed the door. Witek was prepping a small field cannon. The horses were lined up behind the coach. Kaz ran towards Zefir, putting on his saber. He checked the girth and hopped into the saddle. He gave a hand signal, and about fifteen riders mounted their horses. One more hand motion and two columns of seven headed by Robert appeared out of nowhere, ready for action. Kaz nodded and yelled to the coachman, "Follow me!" They left the courtyard with a few surprised servants standing around, unsure of what had just happened.

Kaz didn't want to use a ferry and cross the Wisła River in the city, knowing that the Russians had their patrols all over and would be able to mount a chase. Since the Wisła did not freeze yet this year, the coach would have to stay on the west bank. On the other hand, it was rather obvious where they would go. Riding around to confuse the chase would merely slow their progress. There was only one option left. Drive straight along the river and fight their way through if need be. Ultimately, Kaz sent the coach south, upriver with Robert riding on Lublin and Lwów. He took seven men and headed across the Wisła. After confusing the chasers, he wanted to cross the Wisła back and reunite with his father and Robert's group.

A pontoon bridge was built across the river in 1764 to ease election voters' passage from the east. It was destroyed the same year by high water and ships with grain, which the current pushed on the bridge. The Crown calculated that a permanent stone bridge would cost 655,000 ducats, around 11,790,000 Polish złotych. It was too much for the Crown to afford. It was another dream of King Stan, who controlled a mere 5 million złotych out of the total Crown budget of about 30 million.

Kaz was right. There were a few Russian and Crown soldiers positioned by the river. He decided to commandeer a ferry and get across. As he was rushing through on deck, two Russians rode over, trying to stop him and his men. He didn't think twice. He drove Zefir into one horse, pushing the rider into the water and cutting the other Russian across a shoulder. A Crown soldier recognized Kaz, and rather than engaging him, he grinned and touched his hat in a discrete salute.

Kaz hopped on the ferry with his seven following close by. Some sentries on the other side noticed the commotion. Kaz saw a few riders fanning around the ferry slip. He turned around and flashed a pistol to his men. They all were ready with their guns drawn. Kaz and his men shot a volley into the group when the ferry touched the shore. Two of them fell from their destriers. As Kaz rode between them with his saber up high, there was no serious attempt to engage him. A few overzealous soldiers drew their sabers, but they were no match for Kaz and his men. In seconds, they separated themselves from the confused sentries and turned right along the river, riding at full speed.

At the edge of his line of sight, about a half-mile away from the river, Kaz noticed another group of riders. They were moving around, unsure of what had just happened and how to react. He drove past them, not slowing down, and veered away from the river heading into the surrounding bushes and trees. He wasn't sure, but it seemed that one of the riders he had just passed was Riazin.

Once in the woods, Kaz pumped his left hand with his fingers spread three times. The riders behind him disappeared like a spell had been cast upon them. In a few hours, they all reappeared a few miles downriver.

"Anyone had any problems losing the chase?" asked Kaz. They all shook their heads left and right.

"Good. Let us continue till dusk, and then we will ford the river back on the west side."

At sunrise, they met the group led by Robert. Kaz opened the door to the coach and found his father sleeping soundly with his legs across on the opposite seat and a few pillows under his head. He smiled and carefully closed the door. They continued together on their way south.

Family Commitment

The carriage with Józef Pułaski arrived at the main entrance to the Winiary castle, followed by the entourage of fourteen riders. The attendants pulled the steps and opened the door to the couch. Józef stepped down energetically and looked at Kaz, who jumped off his horse. There was no hesitation in Józef's posture and moves. He marched across a graveled carriageway, followed by his son. He embraced his wife, who ran into the vestibule and headed straight into the main reception room. Soon, his sons Frank and Anthony dressed for combat and joined Józef and Kaz. Carmelite monk, Marek

135

Jandołowicz, appeared with his hands folded in supplication over his chest.

Józef took a saber belonging to his father, Jakub, from a wall. This weapon accompanied Jakub's body from the battlefield where he died defending King Leszczyński, the last King of the Piast dynasty, the oldest Polish royal family dating back to the tenth century.

Józef rose the saber over his head, solemnly proclaiming, "I worked hard to build the fortunes of our house, but today I pledge it all on the altar of Poland. You boys have made me proud so far. Join me and pledge that you will raise your arms and not lie them down until Poland is free of the Muscovites or die fighting."

The sons drew their sabers and crossed them with their father's weapons. They fervently swore to sacrifice their future and lives, if need be, to defend the country. A light breeze moved fluffy cumulus clouds and cleared a pathway for the Sun to shine its winter rays upon the scene. Out in the park, the leaves of ancient trees rustled. Listening attentively, one could hear a whisper, "We bear witness." Polished steel over the heads of the Pułaski family braves glimmered like a beacon of hope and resolve. They all kneeled on the floor, and Father Mark placed his hand over each head, making the cross sign with his thumb on their foreheads.

"God bless you, noble knights, on your holy quest. May God and our Virgin Mary protect you and give you strength to endure in your venerated effort no matter how long, perilous, and far your path leads you." All of them fought until death in the country's service and faith from this moment on. The weapons raised on that winter day by the banks of the Pilica River led the way for generations of Polish patriots. They never accepted the onslaught of Muscovy from the east, no matter what name the invaders used to disguise their colonization effort.

The preparations for the confederation had been in motion for some time. Most of those opposing the King were convinced continuing his reign meant losing the independence of the Commonwealth. After Józef's demonstration in the palace chambers, messengers were sent across the country. The decision was made that the location of the confederation would be Bar in Podole, far enough from Warszawa, and Russian troops operating between Warszawa and St. Petersburg.

The location was close to Kamieniec, where Bishop Adam Stanisław Krasiński was one of the key supporters of the confederation.

[Kamieniec, now Ukraine]

He signed the declaration stating that the Convocation Diet was illegal, during which all candidates for the King except Stanisław August were disqualified. Much like Józef Pułaski, he signed the decision of the Election Diet to elect Stanisław August but opposed most of his actions. He was the one who contacted the Ottoman Empire and traveled to France to seek support against King Stan. King Louis XV promised him political assistance and donated 40,000 ducats in gold to the Bar Confederation. The Turks started a war with Russia on 25 September 1768 when the Russians crossed their border chasing after the Bar Confederates. On 31 October 1769, Krasiński met with Emperor Joseph II and was promised the support of Austria as well. In 1770, he took over military leadership after Józef Pułaski's death and became the head of the General Command of the Bar Confederation.

[Marshal of the Bar Confederation Michał Krasiński receives an Ottoman dignitary. Painting by January Suchodolski]

CHAPTER 5

Częstochowa (1770)

Bold Attack

The General Command of the Confederation ordered Kaz to join the French advisor to the Confederation, Charles-François du Périer Dumouriez, in his idea to attack Lanckorona. Kaz opposed the plan, thinking they needed a solid base of operations rather than a quick victory in a less prominent location, which would not secure a strong defensive posture, even if they won the battle. The Confederation had no time or resources to blunder. It could not afford any mistakes. When the General Command opposed Kaz's suggestions, he acted on his own and showed what made sense through action. Ultimately, Dumouriez's plan failed while Pułaski persevered with his efforts.

[Bar Confederates skirmish with the Russians]

140

In September 1770, Kaz had command of over 2,500 confederates, with Robert as one among his officers. They were in Kraków with Józef Zaremba, a commander of the Bar Confederation, when a dispatch came to inform them of Russian troop movements.

"General Drevitz is chasing you, but he sent some troops to take Częstochowa," an officer reported.

"If they conquer the monastery, they will have a powerful base of operations, and it would be almost impossible to dislodge them from such a formidable fort," Zaremba remarked.

"I hear rumors that your friend Riazin is leading one of the groups on the way to Częstochowa," Robert said.

"You don't need me here in Kraków, Michał." decided Kaz, jumping up to his feet. "We must beat Drewitz in his effort to occupy Częstochowa. If we succeed, we could build a powerful base of operations on the Kraków-Częstochowa axis. It is time for me to beat Riazin yet again."

Kaz was ready to ride with about two hundred troops in a matter of hours. They moved through Jerzmanowice, Olkusz, and Klucze, heading straight for Częstochowa. In excellent condition after weeks of pampering in Kraków, the horses could be pushed hard. They approached the walls of Częstochowa after a forced overnight ride.

On 8 September 1770, Kaz took about twenty of his men and rode up to the Lubomirski Gate of the monastery. Some Crown troops stationed there were no match for Kaz's soldiers. The Confederates were waving a signal flag from the bastions in an hour, and the rest of Kaz's troops entered the hallowed grounds. They left their mounts and passed the Jagiellonian Gate of the shrine with their hats in their hands. They followed the hallway to the right, leading to the Assumption Church, and turned left at the pulpit before reaching the main altar. An exquisitely wrought-iron grille welcomed the knights into the Gothic Chapel of Our Lady. The holiest Byzantine icon of the Black Madonna, the spiritual queen of Poland, was displayed there on the wall, protected by a shiny silver cover. They all fell to their knees, gave thanks to the Blessed Virgin, and only then continued with military necessities.

[Pauline Monastery at Jasna Góra]

Within minutes, Kaz was led into the intellectual heart of the monastery, the library, where he met Pauline General Paweł Esterhazy and prior Pafnucy Michał Brzeziński. General Esterhazy belonged to a noble family of the largest landowners in Hungary with roots in the Middle Ages. Prior Brzeziński was a famous preacher who delivered sermons in Kraków and Warszawa. He assumed his duties on Jasna Góra in 1768, the same year the Bar Confederation was formed. The Pauline brothers, the monks of St Paul, the First Hermit, had been unceasingly praying, meditating, and studying behind these walls since 1382 when they were brought to Poland from Hungary. They were led by a continuous chain of leaders they called generals.

"Your Eminence, we are here to defend our queen, the Blessed Virgin, against the Muscovites much like she was defended against the Swedes a hundred years ago," Kaz announced.

Esterhazy made a sign of the cross, laid his hand on Kaz's shoulder, and said, "We will pray for you, my son. We dwell in the spiritual realm and leave the corporal matters to you. However, I am personally pleased to host the defender of the Blessed Virgin rather than a hungry bunch of Muscovites who are open enemies of the faith and our serene republic. Godspeed."

[The Bar Confederation swore an oath to defend Polish
independence on 4 March 1768]

The dispatches were sent immediately, and the number of
defenders swelled to over a thousand in a few days. Kaz was
pleasantly surprised to find 140 combat-ready cannons, large supplies
of cannonballs, and ample stock of explosives ready for action. The
monastery was a modern fortification, which gave any military force
in Southern Poland a robust strategic base of operations. Once inside
the sanctuary, Kaz could defend it against overwhelming odds.

After the Swedish attack of Jasna Góra in 1655 and the heroic
defense, the monastery walls were reinforced. It was an elevated
compact rectangle of defensive walls with four bastions at the corners.
A deep moat surrounded the monastery, and high ramparts were
reinforced with a wall of sharp logs. A swampy terrain enveloped it
beneath the hill.

When Riazin showed up with his troops, he was disgusted to find out that he could not take over the command of Jasna Góra fortress as Drevitz had planned. Rather than a few Crown forces, he saw the Confederates and their guns. He positioned himself across the main field by the trees northeast of the Potocki Bastion and decided his next move.

Kaz was at the walls and spotted Riazin much the same way he had spotted him on the election field at Wola. He sent an emissary and requested that Riazin ride over to the walls. Once they were within hearing distance, Kaz showed himself and yelled:

"Riazin, you never learn. Didn't I tell you to go back to St. Petersburg? How many more times do I need to repeat the same for you to get the message? Poland is not to be raped by you anymore. Take your goons and leave."

Riazin did not say a word. He scanned the walls with quick squinty eyes while biting his mustache and turned his horse around. There was no need to talk. They both knew that Kaz would never give up the fortress, and Riazin would not quit his siege unless ordered by Drevitz, who would not give up the assault because his future depended on his success. Repnin and Suvorov did not have any use for Drevitz blundering his assignment, which was to be done with Pułaski for good. Once Pułaski was defeated, captured, or killed, the Bar Confederation would practically be over. The die was cast. There was nothing left but an all-out battle to the bitter end.

Riazin began with the expected course of action. He launched a few probing attacks and started digging trenches. The attacks were to gauge the strength and tactics of the defenders. The dugouts were a standard procedure during sieges, which would get the attackers closer to the walls and eventually start excavating a tunnel under the walls. He did not know precisely what Drevitz would decide, but digging would not hurt. Kaz could fend off Riazin's attempts and launched a few counterattacks of his own.

Kaz often visited the chapel with the revered Byzantine icon of the Blessed Mary to pay homage and pray. One night, he decided to spend more time there. The holy picture was protected with the heavy silver cover mounted in 1673 with a Latin inscription:

Ascend mortals to this mountain top,
For here through Mary all shall obtain salvation.

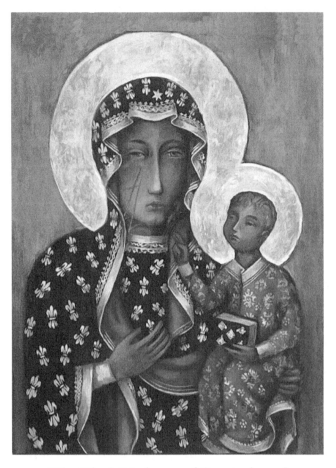

[The Black Madonna of Częstochowa]

The monks lifted the cover for Kaz. He knelt and looked at the dark oblong face of the Holy Mother, resembling burned wheat. She looked back at Kaz with solemnity, majesty, and sanctity through her elongated, drooping, and profoundly pondering eyes. There were two large parallel scars across her right cheek, which widened down her neck to fade softly under her dress. The third scar cut through and across the other two near the base of her nose. The wounds were caused by the attackers who tried to steal the icon. The legend goes that when they loaded the holy picture on the cart, it would not move as if held by Divine force. The frustrated attacker slashed the icon and left it while fleeing with looted treasures.

She held baby Jesus in her left arm, who was presented as Christ-Emmanuel. He held the Book of Life in his left hand while his right hand was raised with two bent fingers in the gesture of blessing. His tilted head with curly black hair raised slightly looked full of wisdom and maturity despite his tender age.

The Council of Ephesus defined the divine motherhood of the Virgin Mary in 431. Her virginity was continually mentioned throughout the centuries, including during the Second Council of Constantinople in 553. The Black Madonna of Częstochowa spanned the faith beyond the east and west schism of 1054 when Patriarch of Constantinople Michael Cerularius was excommunicated. This started the "Great Schism," which created Eastern and Western sections, the Roman Catholic Church, and the Eastern Orthodox Church.

The icon was believed to be the 5th-century Hodegetria lost during the Ottoman siege of Constantinople in 1453. It was then that Sultan Mehmed II defeated Emperor Constantine XI Palaeologus. The importance of this story was that Catherine continued the claim that Moscow was the Third Rome, a new house of the Palaeologus Dynasty. The Grand Prince of Moscow, Ivan III, married Sophia Palaeologus in 1472, which started that claim. Many believed that if the Black Madonna was in Częstochowa, Poland was destined to reconcile the Western and Eastern sections of the Church through the religious tolerance of the Commonwealth.

Kaz lay face downward, touching the cold marble with his burning forehead and hands extended outwards. He prayed for the Commonwealth, his family, the Church, and Helena. He prayed that he would get rid of Riazin and others like him swarming Poland. He prayed that Stanisław August would be removed from the throne and a suitable candidate would be found to lead Poland out of her predicaments. He prayed for Zazulińce and Warka, his father and brothers, Jan, Robert, and Alim, with his Tatars. Kaz prayed that Asher would meet his Shekinah. He prayed for Zosia and the healing mercy of time, which would help her cope. He prayed for tranquility and peace.

Most of all, Kaz prayed for the souls of his father, Józef, and his older brother Frank. They both gave their lives in 1769, defending Poland from the Russian onslaught and the treachery of King Stan. On April 20, Józef Pułaski died of smallpox in Kopanka by the Dniestr River after his imprisonment in Jassy, Turkey. On September 15, Frank, the confederate Marshall of Przemyśl, died killed in action. Kaz prayed for strength to continue fighting until all Russians were chased from the Commonwealth, including their marionette, King Stan.

Heavy Cannons

Drevitz assessed the situation and concluded he had little chance of removing Kaz from Częstochowa. The only hope he saw was transporting large cannons that the Prussians offered. With the firepower of these cannons, he might be able to crack the walls and create a rift needed for an all-out attack. Since the secret Russian-

Prussian pact, it was only a question of time when these cannons would find their way to the feet of the holy shrine, the bulwark of Polish faith and the unshakable foundation of Poland's independence.

On 31 December 1770, the cannons were ready to pound the monastery. On January 3, the bombardment began. Each powerful explosion was a nail to the coffin of the defenders. As an enormous cannonball hit the wall, the whole hill shattered. The elaborate stained-glass windows of the churches fell on the marble floors and splintered into thousands of forlorn rainbows. Candles were tumbling down, dislodged from the candelabras.

In a secret correspondence, Drevitz informed his superiors that after taking Jasna Góra, he would send the defending troops in small groups to the interior of Russia. In the meantime, he sent emissaries to Kaz promising free passage to the defenders if they surrendered. Kaz responded that the Russians might lay their weapons in front of the monastery, and he would guarantee them free passage to St. Petersburg.

The Pauline monks continued with their rituals during all mayhem and imminent death. A daily procession around the fortress walls followed the Stations of the Cross, a 14-step Catholic devotion that commemorated Jesus Christ's last day on Earth as a man. The monks walked on top of the walls on bitterly frigid winter days with freezing snow while deadly cannonballs were raining destruction and death on the shrine. Each station was where the faithful stopped and prayed in utter concentration on the pain and suffering of the savior. It reminded them that Jesus was condemned and forced to carry his cross, on which he was martyred. He fell three times on the way, and Veronica wiped his face from sweat and blood. During the tragic walk, he met his mother, and Simon of Cyrene helped him carry the cross. Eventually, Jesus was nailed to the cross and died. The 14th station reminded them that his body was laid in the tomb. Miraculously, none of the monks was injured during these holy processions.

On January 4, after sunset, the defenders assembled in the Chapel of our Lady. There must have been over a thousand of them standing squeezed in supplication, praying to the most sacred icon of Poland. The silver cover was lifted as the bells were struck. Unexpectedly, first one, then a dozen, and eventually all joined in the singing of Bogurodzica (Mother of God).

[Notes and words to Bogurodzica]

This medieval Roman Catholic tune, composed in Poland around the 10th century, evolved from religious to war hymn and a battle cry. Polish and Lithuanian knights sang it during the Battle of Grunwald in 1410 and all-important battles afterward. No other song would better ignite a fire under the cauldron of patriotic devotion and zeal. With every stanza, the determination to fight grew.

Virgin, Mother of God, God-famed Mary
Ask Thy Son, our Lord, God-named Mary,
To have mercy upon us and hand it over to us!

152

Kyrie eleison!!
Son of God, for Thy Baptist's sake,
Hear the voices, fulfill the pleas we make!
Listen to the prayer we say,
For what we ask, give us today:
Life on earth free of vice;
After life: paradise!
Kyrie eleison!

Despite the humiliating election of King Stan and the disastrous rule of the Saxon dynasty before, the Polish fighting spirit was legendary. They always responded with unbelievable feats of courage and perseverance if pushed to the wall. When everything seemed hopeless and lost, they discovered a hidden reservoir of bravery and tremendous strength to continue struggling.

True to this character trait, Kaz had no intention of giving up. On the contrary, he devised a plan to take the fight to the Russians. The next night, together with five select companions, including Witek, they lowered themselves down to the ground along the wall of the northeast Szaniawski bastion of the fort closest to the trees. They wanted to avoid opening any gates or using the main entrance, which Russian sentries could notice.

The plan was to take as much gunpowder as they could and blow up the heavy cannons transported with such an effort from Prussia. If they were to succeed, the Russians would not have any weapons to break the monastery's walls. Once they blew up the cannons, they would try to get back to the foot of the bastion and climb up the walls. If they failed, they would gladly die trying.

The monks used the cloth from their white robes to prepare long, sturdy sacks and filled them with gunpowder. Each of the commandos carried twenty pounds of explosives, which gave a total of one hundred twenty pounds. If they shoved the explosive concoction down the cannon barrel and blocked the opening, the explosions should rapture the ominous, destruction-bearing pipes.

The cannons were positioned in the middle of the camp on a ten-foot-high redoubt. Kaz knew from intelligence reports that the crew stood at the artillery base with sentries at the top of the redoubt. They did not carefully watch the steep side facing the shrine and treated it as a direct line of fire. Anyone approaching from that direction would be visible from the top. The challenge was moving along the tree line in a wide semicircle to the right, not venturing too deep into the woods swarming with Russian units.

Everyone selected group member was deadly with a knife, especially Lech and Zak, while Bartek and Wiktor were excellent archers. If they had to eliminate anyone on the way, the best way was to gain physical contact and use a knife. Shooting someone from a distance was dangerous because you never knew if he had no partners around who you would not be able to see. If anyone used a pistol or a rifle, their mission would be over because the noise would bring overwhelming numbers of Russians to their position.

They quickly covered the semicircle's first half, scurrying from tree to tree or crawling on their bellies. They had to sneak around a few groups of soldiers sitting by the fires, but they were never seriously threatened. Any further movement, however, seemed almost impossible. There were hundreds of Russians in groups of about a dozen each. They tried venturing in various directions, but there was no chance for all of them to get through. Even if one tried his luck, the possibility of covering the whole distance was slim. Trying to climb the redoubt and stuffing the gunpowder sacks into the cannon nozzle seemed questionable.

Witek, Kaz's servant, decided to save the day. He produced a secret weapon, which he intended to use. These were three precious bottles, which he carried with him, not telling anyone. They were bottles of vodka.

Witek crouched low to the ground and whispered, "We have to hit them where they are most vulnerable. I will go with Lord Kazimierz. Lech and Zak will follow. Bartek and Wiktor will keep behind with their bows and clear the way in case of trouble.

"Here, Lech and Zak, take the sacks from us. You must carry them to the cannons and load them up while Kaz and I lead the way." They all nodded in agreement. None of them had any better idea. Actually, they had no single idea to challenge Witek. He hid two bottles and had one in his hand. Lech and Zak were tying extra sacks around their waists. When they were done, Witek and Kaz staggered into the light of the first fireplace as if drunk. About ten soldiers were squatting and standing around the fire. Witek dragged Kaz in front of the first trooper.

"Cold. Damn cold. Not as cold as where I come from, but I have here something better than fire to warm you up, friend," said Witek

155

laughing and showing the bottle to the Russian soldier. "Here, give it a try and say if I am wrong." The Russian got up, confused, and looked at the soldiers in his unit. They were unsure what to make of it but started nodding and nudging each other with the elbows, saying, "strange, but it wouldn't hurt to try."

"What's your name?" Witek asked.

"Vitia, that is Viktor," replied the Russian, grinning.

"Vitia, here you go. It will make you feel like you are at home sitting on the stove."

"Ha, ha, ha," responded Vitia's comrades. Soon all of them were passing the bottle around and checking the veracity of Witek's assertions. Yes, this vodka filled their bellies with a potion that spread soothingly around their freezing bodies.

"No, no, my friends; take it easy. Don't drink it all. I must hand it to my cousin, Ivan, freezing his ass around the big cannons. Today is his birthday. He probably forgot about it in this cold. But that's why I am here, his dear cousin, to make his day. Who can lead me to Ivan? It is so dark. I cannot find my way. What about you, Vitia?" asked Witek.

"You better take Vova. He is a sergeant. Everybody knows Vova," Vitia answered.

"Oh, Vova," Witek exclaimed. "Here you go, take an extra swig, Vova. Can you take me to my cousin Ivan?"

"I don't see why not," Vova said. "It is not every day that you have a birthday and such a good bottle to top it up," Vova laughed. He took the bottle in his hand and used it as a compass to lead the way. The story of Ivan's birthday spread around like wildfire. The three companions, Witek, Vova, and Kaz, were all staggering their way through between the campfires. Vova was pointing with the bottle to where the big cannons stood.

"Ivan, Ivan, we are coming. We will not let you freeze tonight," Vova yelled.

"Give way. They are going to see Ivan," added voices by the fires. "Make way. Here are the good friends with presents for Ivan. Make way!"

And there they were, enormous barrels glistening in the light of campfires, looking like menacing dragons ready any moment to blaze lethal flames of destruction.

"Ivan! Where are you? Your cousin is coming," Vova yelled. It was about to end quickly when two officers started approaching from the direction of the redoubt. One was already ten feet from them when Witek whacked Vova on the back.

"And I have another bottle for Ivan. Here, look and see," laughed Witek and flashed a new bottle in front of Vova's eyes. At the same time, the first officer staggered with an arrow deep in his neck. Kaz lunged with his knife at the second officer. In a moment, Kaz shoved both into the bushes. Vova was still looking at the second bottle, mesmerized.

"One more bottle. One more bottle," he repeated as if enchanted.

"Yes, one more bottle. Here, you can finish the first one, Vova. You earned it," Witek said. "What a friend you are. Ivan will be so pleased."

Vova didn't have to be told twice. He took the first bottle, tilted his head back, and started dancing around.

"What a good vodka. I have never tasted anything better. We must find Ivan," Vova decided. They all climbed up and stood between the cannoneers.

"Which of you is Ivan?" Vova asked. The cannoneers looked surprised. They heard the commotion but did not know the details.

"Are you Ivan?" Witek asked one of them.

"No, I am not," the cannoneer responded with astonishment.

"Yes, you are," Witek insisted. "At least tonight you are. "Look what I brought you," said Witek laughing. "I brought it for my cousin Ivan, but he is not here. Well, it is his loss and your gain. Happy Birthday, Ivan. Here is to your health," Witek grinned. He took a big swig from the bottle and passed it to the surprised cannoneer. "Drink, be happy, and don't forget about your friends!"

In the meantime, two commandos, Lech and Zak, were loading the cannons with their deadly meal. Kaz looked around and found the store of cannon fuses. He cut three long pieces and tossed them down to Lech and Zak. They were moving quickly. They stuffed the cannons with tree branches and hammered them tight with special wedges they brought with them.

"You know what, you have your fun here, but I must find Ivan," Witek said. "No, no, keep the bottle. It is his fault that he is not here. Come on, Vova, help me find Ivan." Vova was not too happy, but he changed his mind when Witek came over, put his arm on his neck, and let him see the third bottle.

"Aaaa? Can you help me?" Witek squealed. Vova did not have to be told twice. He started yelling earnestly, "Ivan, where are you, Ivan? Damn it, has anyone seen Ivan?"

The three companions staggered down the redoubt, retracting their steps from fire to fire.

At the same time, Lech and Zak lit the fuses. One of the cannoneers noticed the sparks and got up to check. Unexpectedly, he fell down the steep wall with the arrow through his neck. Two more tried, but they also ended with the arrows, which stopped their curiosity.

Suddenly, the Earth shook, and the redoubt burst into flames with pieces of metal from destroyed cannons flying all over. Simultaneously, Witek, Kaz, Lech, Zak, and the two archers ran along the tree line in the opposite direction. Nobody was paying much attention to them as their eyes were directed toward the exploding rampart. Our six covered the distance back to the bastion in record time. They whistled an agreed signal, and the ropes were lowered for them. Soon, all healthy and sound were sitting on the stone floor of the rampart, breathing heavily. Witek pulled the third bottle and started passing it around.

"What? You never know when you will need one," Witek explained. They all started laughing heartily and taking long swigs. Kaz did not miss his round this time. Drevitz again had to accept that he had not yet broken the walls or the defenders' will.

Pieskowa Skała

Kaz decided to do the unthinkable yet again and look for help in the hornet's nest. King Kazimierz the Great built a chain of castles near Kraków in the 14th century, which served as a network of sentries protecting Poland from any incursion from the south. One of the castles was Pieskowa Skała (the Dog's Rock), currently owned by Count Franciszek Wielopolski. He took the castle over from the Szafraniec family after the male line of Szafraniec was extinguished. Both families, like the Pułaskis, shared the same coat of arms, Starykoń. Helena Szafraniec, whom Kaz met in Warszawa, lived in the castle under the protection of her uncle Count Franciszek, Frank.

It was a challenging and risky mission. Count Wielopolski was in a group that requested additional Russian military support when the Bar Confederation was proclaimed. Being in the vicinity, Kaz decided it was worth talking to Count Wielopolski face to face and arguing about the need to oppose King Stan. Kaz wanted Frank to listen and, if not directly, maybe help the confederates by being passive. For Kaz, Poland trumped any political division, and arguing on her behalf with any Pole was a worthy endeavor.

Kaz rode to Kraków first to spend a day with Zaremba. He was stopped on the way by a cattle drive. Herds of cattle were moved from Podole through Poland to the west of Europe. This one was a five thousand herd on the way to Silesia. Luckily, almost half was sold to the merchants in Kraków, so the herd size was dramatically reduced.

The next day before dawn, Kaz was on the road heading northwest towards Jerzmanowice across a hilly terrain dotted with picturesque white lime rock formations. The land was covered with farms interrupted by church steeples, the spiritual beacons for the faithful. The sound of bells covered all farmlands when the congregations were reminded daily during canonical hours to turn their souls to Lord God. Every hill and valley were either planted with wheat, oats, and barley or covered with lush orchards full of apple, pear, cherry, or plum trees. Before reaching Jerzmanowice, Kaz turned slightly right and descended into a valley hidden to a stranger by a thicket of trees and the undulation of the terrain.

[Entrance to the Prądnik Valley]

You could miss the entrance riding a few hundred feet away if you did not know it was there. Once on the descending trail, Kaz entered a hidden world of vertical lime rocks and a valley half a mile across with a clean brook to the side. The meadow covered by lush grass and a rainbow of fragrant wildflowers looked like a magic carpet woven by an expert oriental artist. The air filled with the balsamic scent of pine tree resin mixed with the smell of oak and ash trees felt invigorating, like refreshing nectar. After an hour of the leisurely ride, Kaz spotted a white limestone pillar about a hundred feet high to the right. He knew that the castle was minutes away. He also knew that the locals called the rock the Cudgel of Hercules.

[The Cudgel of Hercules]

When Kaz rode through the main gate, he saw a few riders leaving the upper courtyard. Among them, he recognized Riazin, the same Riazin who Kaz fought at Zazulińce, kidnapped Senator Rzewuski and challenged Kaz at the walls of Jasna Góra. Yet again, Kaz had to restrain himself not to charge at him. It was too late for Kaz to turn back and hide. He was ready to fight his way through if need be. Riazin recognized Kaz but did not react in any way. He and his two assistants glowed at Kaz but rode past him and out of the castle. Count Wielopolski was too much of an authority for Riazin to challenge.

Kaz announced himself to the guards and was asked to continue to the upper courtyard. Once there, he was met by Count Franciszek Wielopolski himself.

"Welcome, dear Kazimierz. I am glad we met, "said Wielopolski. It was a breach of etiquette. Typically, a visitor like Kaz would be welcomed by servants and brought into the chambers for an audience. This time, Kaz and Frank were walking side by side.

"I noticed Captain Riazin on my way in. I am surprised that he didn't stop me. Drevitz would give a lot to catch me," Kaz observed.

"Yes, Riazin, he would not dare," countered Wielopolski as they were entering his study. "We are political enemies, Kaz, but we are still Polish patriots first. Riazin would have to go through me to get to you. I cannot guarantee that he would not chase you to Częstochowa on your way back, but this is a completely different matter. You are under my roof as a guest."

"I had a fight with his unit on my lands in Podole. I wounded him. Later after they left, I found out that his soldiers raped one of my peasant girls and killed a Jew. Had I known it when I met him, I would have killed him together with his soldiers."

"Dear Kaz, our country needs wise strategy and not rash actions. The fights and wars between us only weaken our determination. We must reform the country, or we will perish. Russians and Germans are serious opponents, which have gained too much strength lately. They will not stop trying to depower us. The King is doing everything in his capacity to reform the government and bring the needed changes."

"The King brought foreign armies to Poland and is following Empress Catherine's bidding. He should be tried for treason first, and then we may talk. As regards his power, he has none. I don't see how we can stop the Confederation before we accomplish its mission of dethroning him."

"You are right, Kaz. You don't see. You should go to Warszawa and find out what is happening in detail. It is six years after the election, and much has been done. It would help if you had patience and time. We need you on the side of Poland and not scheming with a group of old-timers trying to protect what is already gone."

"I will give all I have left to fight for Poland!" Kaz burst out.

"You don't have much left. The revenue from your estates is shrinking, and if you continue this way, you might lose it all."

"I already lost it all. My father died after being released from a Turkish jail like a common criminal sentenced by some basha. Frank buried him in foreign lands in a barrow somewhere on the road to Mohylew near the Dniestr River. I cannot even bring his remains to Warka. Where is Poland to fight for her honor and her citizens? When will she respect her servants? Empress Catherine must approve of any decision King Stan makes. Russian Ambassador Repnin stays in Warszawa and yells at Polish heads of state. We started the Bar Confederation because the Russians were kidnapping Polish senators and bishops in broad daylight with the consent of our King. You want me to support such Poland?"

"I am so sorry for the loss of your father. He was a beacon of justice and honor, said Count Wielopolski, tapping his hand on an exquisitely encrusted oak table. "Kaz, I am empowered to offer you money, a serious amount of money, and the return of total revenue from all your estates. Give it time to recoup your family losses. It would help if you gained your strength back as a Pułaski. We need people like you to fight for what is right in Poland but fight so that you might win. Weigh your strength and your ambitions. I see that you have expanded all the strength you used to have, but you still have not adjusted your ambitions. It will lead you to a disaster and certainly not help Poland."

"I need something from you, Count. You know that we are protecting the Monastery at Jasna Góra from General Drevitz's troops. They had already burned the town of Częstochowa to the ground. They do not give quarters, even to women or children. Once they breach the monastery walls, nothing will be left standing. The sacred picture of our Holy Mother, which protected us for 400 years, might be destroyed. Please help us with needed supplies."

"I cannot offer you any help, Kaz. I have offered you advice; my offer stands any time you change your mind."

"It is good that we are talking. Thank you for your hospitality. I understand that you have received me thinking about the welfare of our serene republic in the first place. My offer to you stands as well.

Any time you open your eyes and see how dangerous King Stan is for Poland, I will accept you in Częstochowa with open arms," said Kaz, getting up and bowing with reverence. The Count rang a gold bell standing on his desk, and a servant appeared at the door. As Kaz was about to leave the chambers, he turned to Count Wielopolski and added: "Good luck in dealing with the Russians. I am certain that Riazin came here with demands and not to offer his services."

"Dear Kazimierz, I will always have sentiment for you and your youthful vigor. Grow up, mature, slow down, and think strategically. I hope that we will meet again."

Kaz left the chambers and followed a series of luxury rooms filled with stunning art and sophisticated furniture. He knew that Helena was there somewhere, but he did not think searching for her would be a good idea. He did not ask anyone about her either. Kaz did not want to embarrass or cause her any problems because of their acquaintance. Once he left the upper courtyard, Zefir was brought to him. Kaz went through the main gate, knowing that Riazin might be waiting for him somewhere in the valley. Rather than take a route back, he turned right and started looking for a trail that would allow him to summit the valley walls. There was no way out, so Kaz decided to get close to the canyon walls and hide in the foliage dotted with ancient chestnut and oak trees. He waited for the Sun to set before venturing into the main path.

Hiding in the thicket, Kaz could not stop thinking about Helena. She was so close and yet unreachable. He knew she would be glad to see him, but he did not want to take unnecessary risks. If he were to meet her today, he would tell her that her beauty forced him to seek her out. She attracted him the instant he laid his eyes on her in the church in Warszawa. He could not even imagine how he could miss an opportunity to see her again. The ride they shared in Warszawa was the happiest moment in his life. He felt like her presence was a soothing gift healing his soul. He knew Riazin was searching for him, but he didn't care. He would not focus on anything else without seeing her and would probably stumble on Riazin.

Kaz and Helena

The dusk set early in the narrow valley surrounded by thick woods with ancient trees remembering the first builders of the castle who toiled here over four hundred years before. Long shadows started covering the valley like a veil of protective secrecy. Kaz estimated that he would move in these shadows without being detected by Riazin or his men if they were looking for him. Rather than continue down the valley, Kaz turned back and led Zefir through the bushes toward the castle. He found a secure place and left Zefir there.

Instead of leaving undetected, he decided to call on Helena. The urge was more potent than years of training and continuous focus on every detail to avoid numerous traps set for him by his enemies. He knew that she lived in the central tower. He decided to climb the wall at dusk and knock on her window. It was a silly move, but reason had little to do with Kaz's actions.

Kaz took a rope with a triple hook at the end from his saddlebags and climbed a steep hill covered with slippery grass and wildflowers towards the high palace wall. As he moved along the lower section that separated the palace gardens from the valley floor, he spotted a white lily flower growing among other plants. He picked it up but could not carry it and climb simultaneously. Eventually, he put the flower between his teeth and threw his grappling hook to the top of the wall.

This part of the climb was relatively easy. Once on the wall, Kaz balanced along the top until he reached the tower's base. He aimed at the first window up and to the wall's right. There were two more high stories of windows, but these were beyond Kaz's reach. Knowing how Helena liked nature, Kaz hoped she would be as close to the gardens as possible.

Now, the trick was to throw the rope so the anchor would hook up to the window ledge. Military training came in handy again. Kaz was lucky on the second attempt. He pulled on the rope, and it looked like it should hold to his relief. If it slipped, Kaz would die at the bottom of the tower. It was the least of his concerns.

He wrapped the rope around his waist and traversed the tower wall to the right until he was right under the window. He pulled himself up inch by inch, placing his feet against the rocks of the tower wall.

[Pieskowa Skała Castle]

He peeped inside cautiously, and to his delight, he saw Helena reclining on a loveseat with a book in her hand. Kaz knocked gingerly on the window, but Helena was too absorbed in her book to hear his signal. He started beating on the windowpane louder and louder. When he became concerned that he might break the glass, she finally looked up. She did not see Kaz outside in the dark, but the noise made her put the book down on the ormolu-mounted parquetry lowboy and go over to the window.

She looked at him with her eyes open wide. Most women in her situation would probably freeze or scream for help, but Helena acted decidedly. She grabbed the lever in the window and opened it. They looked at one another with surprise and delight. After an awkward moment, Helena took the initiative and said, "You kept your word.

You came down south to see me. I would rather that you came through the door, announced."

"I am a rebel opposing the King and your uncle, chased by the Russians."

"I know. People talk. There is no church service where someone would not approach me and hint something about you."

"Anything good?"

"More good than bad. Rather than describing all the details, let me tell you that we have only one minute if you do not want to get caught. I am expecting a visitor to take me to dinner."

"Can we meet tomorrow outside the castle walls?"

"It can be arranged. I will take a ride after breakfast. Wait for me by the Ojców castle," whispered Helena looking at Kaz attentively. "Is that for me?" she asked, taking the lily flower from Kaz's mouth. He did not realize that he was talking with the lily stem between his teeth all this time.

"I'll be there," said Kaz as Helena secured the latch. The moment she turned away from the window, her door opened wide.

The Ojców castle was an eagle nest fortress carved out of the lime rock of the valley. It was only a short ride from Pieskowa Skała.

[Ojców Castle, Alamy files]

The next day, hiding in the thicket to the side of the valley walls, Kaz recognized Helena from afar. She was an excellent rider, one with her mount. Still having the picture of her riding along the Wisła River near Warszawa, Kaz would recognize her in a crowd of riders.

"I see that Riazin missed you again," Helena called out, showing her pearly white teeth.

"He will have his chance, but not today," Kaz smiled back. He was delighted to see her, and nothing could spoil his mood, even a dozen Riazins. Their horses were trotting briskly just feet away.

"You give me flowers every time we meet. Let me give you something," Helena said and waved at Kaz to follow. She rode into the bushes and stopped by an old oak tree in a few short moments. All around in front of her, there were blueberry fields. She jumped off her mount and started gathering the berries. Kaz watched her and felt how his heart was melting. It was exactly how he imagined her in his dreams, tending to flowers or other plants with satisfaction and delight.

She was back with a handful of blueberries in no time and waved at Kaz to get off his mount. When he did, she served him a handful right into his mouth. He felt that her hand tasted sweeter than the berries. He wished that this moment would last forever. Helena watched him swallow the fruit and laughed heartily, worry-free. Some dark blueberries fell on his shirt and left blue smudges.

Kaz looked at her and said with a note of admiration and astonishment in his voice, "I have never been happier in my life. I feel that with you, I could do anything. You have the power to chase all my worries away." Kaz smiled and looked back instinctively. Yes, there were some riders he saw between the trees. Kaz recognized Riazin right away. He turned around and looked at Helena with a troubled gaze.

"What is it, Kaz?" Helena asked.

"It is Riazin and his men. They have not given up or are coming back to trouble your uncle."

"They will not spoil our day. Forget it," Helena declared. "Follow me, Kaz!" she said, jumping on her mount. They rode through the scrub for a while, and then Helena dashed into the open road and pushed her horse into a full gallop. It seemed that Riazin and his men did not see them, but Helena was riding as fast as her mount could anyway.

Eventually, they got out through the main entrance to the valley and continued south-southwest. Helena slowed down when she found an uphill trail. After a short climb, they reached access to a cave.

"They will not find us here," Helena said. "Do you know what it is?"

"A cave," Kaz ventured a guess.

"Yes, a cave, but what cave?"

"I have no idea," answered Kaz puzzled.

"It is the Łokietek's cave. It is the cave where our King Łokietek was hiding from King Wacław of Bohemia in the 14th century. Do you know how Wacław missed him?"

"Go ahead, tell me."

"King Wacław's men found the entrance to the cave, but a spider's web covered it. They concluded nobody could have gotten in if the spiderweb covered the entrance. It is how a spider saved our King."

[King Łokietek's cave]

They left the horses by the entrance and ventured inside.

"Try to be quiet here," Helena whispered. "You do not want to wake up Łokietek's knights. They are sleeping here in the cave and will wake up when Poland needs them."

Kaz took Helena by her hand, and they wandered around the giant boulders strewn across the cave's floor. Helena thought that if Łokietek could unite divided Poland four hundred years ago, her Kaz could do it now. She caught herself that she called him "her Kaz." Yes, she felt that this was the man of her dreams. The knight in a shining blueberry-stained shirt, her Blueberry Knight. Helena had never kissed a man before, but now she wanted Kaz to be the one.

This moment should last forever, but it was time to go their separate ways. She had to return to the castle, and Kaz had to return to Częstochowa. They strolled out of the cave hand in hand. Helena stopped and squeezed Kaz's hand. He looked into her deep blue eyes and felt as if he was being drawn into a pool of mountain spring water. He put his arms around her thin waist and saw how her eyelashes closed the entrance to her soul, much like Łokietek's spider sealed the cave with his magic web. They kissed for the first time in their young lives. The world took a deep breath and stopped for a moment like a steppe near Zazulińce just before sunrise.

Nowy Targ

Kaz used Częstochowa as the base of operations and ventured deep into various parts of Poland and Lithuania to seek support and supplies. One such raid was south of Kraków near Nowy Targ (New Trading Post), at the foot of the high peaks of the Tatra Mountains. He decided it was perfect timing to show the Polish mountains to Robert. He wondered if this terrain would remind his Scottish friend of the glens he missed so much.

One early morning, Kaz opened the door to his bedroom and yelled, "Witek!" It was enough to have Witek appear as if conjured up by a wizard's wand. After the vodka adventure at Zazulińce, Witek took it as a point of honor never to be late when Kaz needed him. "Get a dozen ready and let Robert know we are leaving on a foraging raid."

"Where is it going to be this time?" Witek asked.

"We will look around Nowy Targ. I have news that there are great people there who are willing to help our cause."

As always, the execution of orders in Kaz's unit was done with utmost diligence. It was a matter of fact that Kaz's troops knew precisely what to do and were competing between themselves to please Kaz. They were always ready to show him he could consistently count on them. The main reason for such dedication was that Kaz led by example, and would not allow himself to get lazy, disorganized, or condescending to his troops. In Częstochowa, they felt the presence of the divine and were even more motivated.

They were all mounted and waiting for Kaz by the Jagiellonian gate in two hours. He appeared with Pauline General Esterhazy, who blessed them with the sign of the cross. Kaz knelt in front of Esterhazy in spiritual reverence and crossed himself. He then jumped on his mount, ready for action.

"We will be moving swiftly for three days. Be on the lookout at all times. Drevitz has been sending his troops trying to catch us. We must stay a step ahead of them."

This time Robert, Witek, and Surma were among the riders. At every estate they stopped for a break, they were welcomed as saviors of the Commonwealth. According to the traditions, each landholder expected the guests to stay for at least two to three days of continuous wining and dining. The challenge was to limit the stays to a necessary minimum.

Kaz decided to swing west and south of Kraków this time. They moved through Ogrodzieniec, Olkusz, and Wadowice towards Rabka. From there, it was hours to Nowy Targ. The hilly terrain was more pronounced once they passed Wadowice and moved closer to Rabka. They left the flat vistas of the countryside around Częstochowa and Ogrodzieniec with its imposing castle, where the eye could reach for miles until the horizon met the sky. The trail was winding between hills and mountains covered with dense pine, fir, oak, and linden trees. They were often riding up or down with brief respites along flat valleys.

Robert would ride uphill ahead of others and stop at the top, admiring the view and muttering, "This is what God intended when he was creating land. The flat areas are where he gave himself a break. Look at these magnificent mountains. There are hundreds of them, and each promises a valley where the local clans live." When riding along a valley floor covered with grassy meadows, he saw the first herd of sheep. He could not restrain himself and cried, "I am home!"

Soon, they were riding between the herd of hundreds who were passing the valley. It seemed as if they were moving between the clouds. Looking down, they saw a white and gray mass of woolly shapes dotted with patches of black. The figures were moving as if blown by stellar winds. At the outskirts of the herd, they could notice white silhouettes moving like lightning and shaping the cloudy mass into a cohesive form. These were the mountain shepherd dogs. They were the leading conductors of the dramatic, colorful display of shapes and textures performed at the level of horses' knees.

The riders were moving slowly ahead across the river of wool. At the end of the herd, a quarter mile up the valley, around half-a-dozen men were descending briskly. You could see their white woolen trousers decorated at the front with intricate floral patterns from the waist halfway down their thighs. They wore white linen shirts and black vests with colorful red, yellow, and green embroidery. They were wearing at least ten inches wide leather belts with small hatchets on three feet long handles stuck behind them. Their round black felt hats had a distinct white or red narrowband adorned with small shells.

[Polish Highlanders]

Robert was thrilled. He waved at the men, and they waved back. One of them took his hatchet and raised it above his head, shaking it vigorously.

"They are not afraid of us. Do they know who we are?" Robert asked.

"Of course, they do," Witek answered. "We have made enough noise and more around the southern parts of Poland for them not to know. They can recognize any rider who lives around here. We are strangers, but I think some of them recognize Zefir as well. There are legends about Kaz but also about his mount."

"I would not be surprised if it turned out that they were the Scottish MacGregors or Camerons," Robert added.

"We are just riding through their lands while they have been in these valleys for centuries. People like us pass by now and then, but they remain. They are the salt of these mountains." Kaz explained.

"Yes, you are right. It is exactly how we have it in Scotland. I bet you that they were also fighting the Kings of Poland."

"Actually, the Kings have recognized their unique position. They have special privileges and are treated as the protectors of mountain passes. If we can convince them to join the Confederation, we will have our backs secured."

They left Rabka to the left and were moving further south. Leaving narrow winding valleys, they entered a vast plain framed by the high snow-covered peaks of the Tatra Mountains. Nowy Targ was just ahead, obstructed by a hazy fog when two riders approached them at full speed. They were dressed in highlanders' outfits with the lapels of their white woolen gowns flapping in the wind.

"Count Pułaski," yelled one of them, waving his hand. "The Russians are burning Nowy Targ. You better turn back. They have been looking for you. Hundreds of them are swarming the countryside, looting, and raping."

Kaz stopped his men and asked, "Who are you, and who sent you here?"

"I am Klimek, and this is Bronek," the taller of the two answered. He was an imposing figure with a pronounced eagle nose, deep blue piercing eyes, and long black hair falling on the standing collar of his white coat. "We were sent by those who wish you well. We are the guardians of the mountain passes."

It was now evident to Kaz that the fog was the smoke rising from the town buildings on fire.

"Thank you for your service to the motherland. When did the Russians show up?" Kaz asked.

"Just a few days ago. Their general Drevitz talked to one of the House of Radziwiłł in the market square in front of the whole town. Drevitz ordered that they let him know when you arrive, but Radziwiłł answered that he should not dare to give orders to a free citizen of the Commonwealth. Drevitz was not too pleased. But when Radziwiłł said you are a member of a legally formed Confederation, Drevitz went mad. He ordered his men to burn a newly built town hall.

"The soldiers started burning, stealing, and going crazy. You could hear horrible screams of women who they degraded in front of

181

their children and husbands. They would grab a husband, keep him with his hands tied behind his back and then start raping his wife. Often after they were done, they would cut the man's throat.

"The Muscovites said that it was all your fault. You made them do it because you tried to kill the King, and they had to stop you. Anyone who would not swear to fight you would be killed."

Continuing their way was sheer madness. Drevitz obliterated Kaz's plans of having Nowy Targ as one of the centers of the Confederation. It was an important hub at the foothills of Poland's high mountains, which had been the doorway to the passes leading to Hungary and Bohemia for centuries. Nowy Targ, which meant a new trading post, was a Crown town founded in 1346 by King Kazimierz the Great. In 1586, the town's role was strengthened when the customs chamber moved here from Myślenice.

Taxes collected from the goods passing Nowy Targ boosted Crown coffers and financed buildings in Kraków and some palaces in Warszawa. Currently, the political control of the lands south of the high mountains and across the Dunajec River was in the Austrian Habsburgs' hands. Seeing Russians plundering this Polish stronghold was an abomination.

Kaz decided to turn east and get to the Niedzica castle, the last stop on his wide swing across the southern reaches of Poland. Klimek and Bronek volunteered to lead the party straight up the Turbacz Mountain and then descend on the castle. It would give Kaz a chance to scout the terrain from up high rather than wind his way along the valley floor and approach, not knowing the situation on the ground.

[Niedzica Castle]

They moved along highlanders' pastures and valleys, getting higher up the mountain every mile. When they thought they were about to reach the peak, another range appeared in front of them and led to a higher crest, revealing yet another path uphill. Whenever someone asked Klimek or Bronek how much farther it was, they received the identical answer, "It's almost there, just behind that ridge."

After one of the crests, they saw a valley covered with snow. The cold wind made them hunker down and button up their coats. One more crest and the next meadow led them gently down. The snow disappeared after a few more pastures, and they began their descent. The highlanders stopped by an abandoned chalet.

"Here is where we will stop for the night, and tomorrow, we will be in the castle if the Russians have not already taken control over it in the name of King Stan," Klimek said.

Bronek, with his springy step, moved quickly around the pasture. He returned with a bundle of dry branches and started preparing a bonfire. He was a young, around twenty-year-old burly, and energetic man.

"This is a chalet we use when we are grazing our sheep," Bronek explained. "Nobody will find us here. You can rest safely. We have plenty of hay for your horses behind the chalet and freshwater down there in the creek."

The highlanders prepared food for all, bread, smoked meat, and tasty smoked goat cheese in light and dark brown round conical spheres decorated with embossed patterns. They all gathered around a large blaze and enjoyed the starry night.

[Oscypki, Polish highlanders' cheese]

Kaz came to the fire and threw down a handful of firewood. He looked at the highlanders and said, "It warms my heart anywhere I go to see how many dedicated and committed citizens we have, from the coast of the Baltic Sea to these beautiful mountains. If only spending time with you and sharing the toils and dangers is worth the fight. Often, we forget how many of us there are and how much we are willing to sacrifice to protect our motherland. We have not seen many men passing through these winding valleys, and I did not expect to meet you. I am grateful for your help."

"Oh, we are here. We have been here forever and served Polish Kings whenever they needed us," Klimek responded.

"I know. I heard how grateful King Jan Kazimierz was when you saved him from the Swedes here."

"Yes, it was not far from where we are now, in a gully beneath the Three Crowns Mountain. Do you know that King Jan Kazimierz carried a copy of the icon of Our Lady of Częstochowa with him during his travels? He donated this unique copy to the town of Żywiec in 1669 in gratitude for our services. We built a church and placed this holy picture in the town of Rajcza in 1674. Any time I pass by, I make sure I find time to go to that church and pray," Klimek said.

[Virgin Mary of Rajcza]

"I didn't know about the Virgin Mary of Rajcza. Thank you for sharing this story," Kaz answered, surprised.

"Yes, and you are the defender of the Most Holy Virgin Maiden of Częstochowa. Thousands of us will fight with you. My father walked on a pilgrimage to the Jasna Góra Monastery. I hope I will have a chance to do the same one day," Klimek continued.

"I don't see how the Russians can conquer a country full of fighters like you," Robert added. "I know that the English tried to get to the mountain passes back in my country, but they never succeeded.

186

Even if they took a town or two, our pastures and glens remained in our clans' hands. They never succeeded in breaking our spirit."

"The same is here," Klimek echoed. "Russians have no idea of most of us and our dwellings. We see them from up high, and we can strike like eagles. But like eagles, we do not venture down. We do not know how to spread our wings there in the valleys."

Kaz sat beside Surma and asked, "Did you spend nights like this with my father?"

"Not in the mountains, but the steppe; yes, we did," Surma answered.

"Why did you not follow the Cossacks but decide to stay at Zazulińce?" Kaz continued with his questions.

"There were thousands of us working with the Commonwealth until the Muscovites showed up. Then, we had mostly two choices, join them or die. Any of us who believed in the Polish cause ended up dead if he was lucky. Often, he was tortured first," Surma explained.

"Why didn't you then join the Commonwealth for good?"

Surma threw a few branches into the fire and continued, "It's easier said than done. We were stuck between the Tatars, the Turks, and the Muscovites. Most of us wanted to join Poland and Lithuania in the union of three equal nations, but neither Poles nor Lithuanians agreed. They allowed us to participate as registered Cossacks in times of war but were stalling forever on the formal union with all the privileges enjoyed by the szlachta of the Commonwealth. Warszawa was too short-sighted to see us in the Wild East.

"Some of us got tired of waiting and decided to force a Polish hand. They united with the Muscovites, who promised eternal friendship. Once they penetrated our towns and villages, they never left. We ended up serving the Czar like the Turkish Janissaries served the Sultan. This meant absolute rule and heavy punishment for disobedience. Our golden freedom was over. Muscovite whips and chains shackled us to the Empire. Many of us hate the Commonwealth for their blindness and pride."

Surma checked the fire and poked it with a stick. The sparks flew into the sky as if his departed comrades were trying to say, "You are right, Surma."

"I don't dwell on it. It hurts too much. I fight what is in front of me and don't look beyond the tip of my saber," the old warrior concluded.

In the meantime, Witek was poking around the bags attached to his saddle. He produced a bottle and went over to Kaz, saying, "Lord, we all deserve a drink to keep us warm up here in the mountains."

"Where did you get this bottle?" Robert asked. "I thought you would stay away from alcohol after your experiment with Surma's moonshine."

Kaz nodded in approval, and Witek passed the bottle to Robert.

"Oh, I learned my lesson," Witek said. "Vodka kicks you like a wild stallion. I never drink more than a swig, but I also know that it makes sense to have a bottle, just in case. It can save you from infection but also infect you with good humor and optimism in dark hours."

They all imbibed with pleasure. Bronek picked up his clay ocarina and started playing a lively tune. They were surrounded by the enchanted circle of light created by the bonfire. The sparks were jumping in the air, mixing with the steady glow of the stars, covering them with the canopy of celestial illumination. It seemed that up here in the clouds, they were forever protected from any threats or harm for as long as they decided not to go down.

One by one, they placed their heads on the saddles and descended into the realm of their hopes, desires, and dreams. The early morning chill let them know it was time to get up and continue on their way. Klimek and Bartek lead them down from glen to glen, surrounded by tree-covered hills. Far in the distance, they could see snow-covered peaks of the High Tatras.

Passing midday, they could see the winding Dunajec River and the ramparts of the Niedzica castle. Klimek and Bronek stopped the group by a creek running fresh, sparkly water down the pasture.

"This is the last stop before we descend," Klimek said. "Take a break here. We will go down and look around. We should be back soon after the horses have had time to feed on the grass and have plenty of water."

The travelers admired a breathtaking view spreading below. A winding silvery path cut through the mountains by swift currents of the Dunajec River, which looked like a decorative trim separating one hill from another. The deep greens of the forests were adorned with white limestone shapes of the Pieniny Mountains. You could see village buildings hugging the banks of the Dunajec, which looked the same on both sides, although the river was a borderline between the two countries for centuries. Most of that time, the country on the south side was Hungary. Recently the Habsburgs decided to rebrand the land across Dunajec into their Austrian Empire. The Dunajec River began at Nowy Targ and flew east until it eventually took a sharp turn north. It left the border behind, venturing into Poland and pouring its waters into the Wisła River.

Klimek and Bronek did not have good news upon their return.

"Niedzica castle is swarming with Russians," Klimek said. "They have patrols asking for you all along the border. We must turn left before the castle and move due east. Our posts will be on the lookout so that, hopefully, we will be able to escort you safely out of trouble."

It seemed the only possible way. Turning west towards Nowy Targ would box Kaz in a narrow valley between the forces around Nowy Targ and those stationed in Niedzica. As they rode along the Dunajec, they kept close to the tree line at the foothills of two Lubań peaks to the north in the Gorce Range. Now and then, either a rock was thrown or an owl shriek would be an obvious sign to Klimek and Bronek. They immediately led the group into the thickets and watched as a patrol passed them. It would happen almost every hour, which meant that Russian sentries were tasked with a specific mission of policing the area.

Because the road straight between the Gorce and Pieniny ranges was blocked by the patrols, they turned southeast, hugging the Dunajec River. Soon, they were passing by the Three Crowns Mountain, but there was no time to stop and marvel at this imposing white rocky crown. It seemed it was placed on the green foundation of trees looming under the blue sky as a symbol marking the entrance to the Kingdom of Poland from the south.

[The Three Crowns Mountain]

Suddenly, a large Russian outfit appeared from behind and started chasing them. Klimek led Kaz into the Homole gorge, the same place where the Swedes confronted King Jan Kazimierz a hundred years before. Half a mile from the entrance to the canyon, another group of

Russians emerged from the gorge. Kaz and his men were boxed by Russians upfront and in the back. Their right flank was blocked by the Dunajec and the left by the Three Crowns Mountain.

Klimek picked up his hatchet and pointed straight at the gorge. Kaz raised his saber, and the unit picked up speed heading at the Russians, blocking the entrance to the Homole. It was a do-or-die decision. They would burst through the Russian defenses regardless of the costs. When they could already see the whites of the Russian eyes, a rain of rocks started falling on the Russian heads. It was followed by heavy logs hurled at them from the canyon walls. A few Russians fell from their horses. Others started circling their mounts in confusion, anticipating the next wave of rocks and logs.

Surma was at the group's lead and hacked his way into the valley, with Kaz and Robert at his flanks. They were able to obliterate any resistance and disappeared between the limestone boulders. Muscovites were on their heels, ready to give chase, but they were met by an avalanche of heavy boulders and large tree trunks. Venturing into the valley was sheer suicide.

Following Klimek and Bronek, Kaz's group was moving quickly along the riverbed of a creek. The highlanders knew precisely when to ride along or across the riverbed and circle the red and white boulders scattered around this narrow gorge. They reached the Dunajec River again, which veered sharply to the north, leaving the border of the Commonwealth and Austria.

"You are safe here. There are no more Russians. Thank God they do not have enough troops to police the whole country," Klimek said.

Kaz drove over to him and shook his hand, saying, "And yet again, you were here in the hour of need. Thank you from the bottom of my heart, Klimek."

"We are the guardians of the mountain passes. We will be here when needed. We will always stay with the knight of Our Virgin Mary," Klimek answered.

It took them some handshakes and pats on the shoulders to say their thankyous and goodbyes without dismounting. After a few hands in the air waved in gratitude, Klimek and Bronek stayed behind alone. Soon, they disappeared into the underbrush and the pine trees of the Tree Crowns foothills. It would take a trained pathfinder to discover any traces of them on the round river rocks of the Dunajec bank, which witnessed the efforts of men yet again. The rapid water observed the events carrying the memory with the swift current until it joined the Wisła River and drifted across Poland to the city of Gdańsk and the Baltic Sea.

Although Kaz could not establish a Confederate stronghold in Nowy Targ, his venture rallied southern borderlands. It sent a signal that King Stan did not control south Poland. There was a chance to anchor the Confederation on a power base extending from Częstochowa and Kraków to Lwów. It would be a shield protecting the Confederation, a power base to rally the Commonwealth on their terms.

When Kaz met Joseph II, Holy Roman Emperor, in Preszów on 9 June 1770, the ruler of Austria congratulated Kaz on his achievements. Now, Kaz felt that his control of Częstochowa and Kraków gave even more reasons for optimism. The longer the Confederation lasted, the weaker King Stan became, and the better were the prospects of increased support by France, Turkey, and Austria.

CHAPTER 6

The Capture of King Stan (1771)

Repnin's Secret Visit

In 1771, after three years of fighting, King Stan and the Russians could not squash the Bar Confederation. With Pułaski in Częstochowa and the Confederates occupying Kraków, Little Poland, the cradle of the Polish nation, was in the hands of the forces opposing the marionette government of King Stan and his Russian masters. General Drevitz was chasing Pułaski all around southern Poland, but Kaz was always a step ahead, maneuvering his troops in and out of Drevitz's hands.

In Poland, Kraków was the seat of kings, the historic cradle. At the same time, Warszawa was an administrative center of convenience, helping to facilitate communication between Sweden and Poland during the reign of the Swedish Vasa dynasty. With years passing by, Warszawa became the accepted capital.

The Russians were losing on international fronts, concerned that their league with Prussia and England could collapse if the French, Turks, and Austrians actively assisted the Confederates. There was also a religious battle where Protestant Prussia, Orthodox Russia, and Anglican Britain challenged the power of the Roman Catholic Church, which dominated Poland, France, Italy, and Spain. It brought the Vatican on the side of the Confederates as well.

Catherine decided to have secret talks with her envoy to Poland, Prince Nikolai Vasilyevich Repnin, who was running Poland with a brutal grip. He was an ideal tool of intimidation, steering cowardly King Stan and his supporters but did not impress the Confederates and Kaz in particular. Repnin met Catherine in St. Petersburg.

"My dear Prince," she said. "I am delighted how you keep on frying Stan like a fish on a skewer. He is wiggling and weaving, but eventually, you make him do all our bidding."

"Thank you, Your Highness. I am just a simple tool in your able hands. Although to be honest, I feel I am pushing too hard at times." Repnin replied, bowing deeply.

"It is what I am expecting of you. Poles hate you so much that they come to me and complain. I look like a benevolent supporter of their silly Commonwealth. You help me look good in the international eyes as well. I am pretending that your rude and rough tactics are beyond my control. Some even believe this pack of lies. Keep on wielding your stick and shaking the purse."

"I am concerned that we stretched the string so tight it can snap."

"You are doing a marvelous job. They all seem overpowered by your tactics. Rather than plan something effective to their advantage, they wait for your initiative and succumb to all your threats. Wonderful," said Catherine looking at Repnin and realizing he was getting older. Even the best-applied makeup could not account for his sagging eyes and tired lips.

"Our problem is the Confederates, and especially Pułaski. He does not drink. He is not interested in women. Rather than taking bribes, he is losing his own money. To sum it up, he is a total nuisance. We must come up with a way to handle him."

"Drevitz has been chasing him, and there were times when he almost got him. I hope it is only a question of time," Repnin replied.

"Yes, time. It is what we lack. I'm not fond of Louis XV of France openly supporting the confederates. I sent Suvorov to fight in Turkey. He is our most able commander. Unfortunately, we have only one Suvorov, and I cannot have him on all fronts. Squandering our gold with other balls in the air costs too much and has not yet brought the desired results. If we lost our investment in Poland, it would bankrupt us."

"I heard that Drevitz was successful in bribing some Austrian soldiers who let him cross their border and surprise Pułaski. Drevitz almost caught him there by the Dunajec River. Maybe we should increase our pressure on the Austrians?"

"Even if we catch Count Pułaski, he has grown too popular around Europe. He is treated like a hero. Also, the Wettins in Dresden, after the death of Polish King Augustus III, are not thoroughly eliminated from the big game. He is meeting with them, and it does not bode well. We must kill his fame first. We must maneuver him into a trap where he would lose his reputation and good name. We should make it so that no respected European monarch would want to deal with him."

"It's a grand idea. The minor challenge is how to accomplish such a feat," Repnin whimpered.

"Dear Repnin, don't give up on me so soon. I value your instinct for mischief too much to believe you would not come up with something. Think. How can we reach these Poles who value honor, silly morals, and their boring, most serene Republic? How can we use their conviction and their strength against them?"

"You are right, Your Highness. They always talk about how they respect the Republic and how they respect the office of the King. Many see King Stan as a pathetic coward worrying about his pleasure and safety first, but they would not dare challenge him, the anointed one. They wait and hope that his rule will be brief. In the meantime, however, nobody would challenge the majesty of the Crown but the Confederates."

"So, we must make Kaz commit this sacrilege and disrespect the King."

"Yes, I got it. I have an idea. I hope you will find it mischievous enough."

"Go on, Prince, make my day, make my week, make Count Kazimierz Pułaski go away into the catacombs of disgrace."

"What if we kidnapped King Stan, abused him a little, and blamed it on Kaz?"

"What if we attempted to assassinate the King and blame it on Kaz?" Catherine prodded further.

"It is too much. It is our way, but no Pole in his right mind would commit a regicide. I don't believe they would believe in a story like that."

"I don't care if they believe it. I want other kings to believe. I want the international opinion to turn away from the Confederates and Kaz as if he had leprosy. I want to stop any help to him from Turkey, Austria, or France. They may doubt this scheme in Poland. They may even like Kaz and sing songs about him if they do it with our chains on their hands." Catherine was delighted with Nikolai Vasilyevich. This secret meeting exceeded her expectations.

"Dear Repnin. I adore how your twisted mind works. It is perfectly disgusting. Try to find the assassins who would pass as the Confederates and work out the details. I think this will be the garlic, the aspen stick through his heart. We will get rid of this monster for good."

Strawiński

Stanisław Strawiński traveled to Częstochowa and announced himself as an emissary of the General Command of the Confederation to Kaz with a critical proposition. The fortress was in the middle of preparations against the imminent Russian attack. Teams were working on reinforcing the walls, setting up the distribution of cannonballs and gunpowder to the cannons placed on the bastions and the walls, organizing provisions, and checking each musket and barrel with hot water, stones, or tar. The faithful gathered in the monastery for hourly prayers. Monks were circling quietly around, beholding their vows of silence. Strawiński waited two days, but he could not meet with Kaz directly. He conveyed his urgent message and promised to return shortly to receive the response.

On his second trip, Kaz received Strawiński pacing around the table in the library. He turned toward him when Strawiński appeared and asked, "I understand that you are Stanisław Strawiński, sent by the General Command. We have a lot of work here and little time for talks. What is on your mind, Sir?"

Strawiński bowed curtly and said, "Thank you for finding time to meet me in your busy schedule. I will get right to the point, Sir. General Command believes that since we fight the King, we should attack him directly in Warszawa. I think that we will be able to get to him in Warszawa and end this war."

"It is a great plan. How are you going to carry it out?" Kaz inquired.

"We will kill or kidnap him, which should end the war," Strawiński explained.

Kaz shook his head in disagreement and said, "We do not fight the King. We fight the offender of the Commonwealth. For almost 800 years since Mieszko, we never desecrated the majesty of the Crown with regicide. Besides, our power center is here. Between our ancient capital of Krakow and the shrine of Poland in Jasna Góra, we occupy the high point. We should focus our efforts here and build enough strength to march on Warszawa when ready. I don't think we are ready yet. It is Drevitz who is attacking us here. I don't see him attacking General Command in Warszawa."

"The Confederation is not only you and what you want. Many of the Confederates thought that focusing our forces here was a mistake. We are far removed from Warszawa, the real center of power," Strawiński remarked.

Kaz grimaced slightly and retorted, "I know you all have one new idea a day. Besides talking and brainstorming, we need action. Where would we be if I did not decide to go to Lithuania and bring 4,000 soldiers? Where would we be if I did not ignore Dumouriez and attacked Lanckorona with him? Now we have the attention of Paris, Vienna, and Istanbul. Our enemies' power is not the person of the King, who, in fact, has no power.

"I cannot lose focus and squander what we have gained here. I cannot get involved in any plans of assassination. You do what you must, but I am needed here with all my ability and attention. If we lose Kraków and Częstochowa, we are done. It is not the time to weaken our power base and venture into unpredictable adventures in Warszawa."

"But Warszawa is the main focus, and all-important persons are there," Strawiński insisted.

"Yes, but what power do they have? What resolve? They sit and talk while the Russians roam the country, doing whatever they want. No one in Warszawa has stopped a single Russian soldier," Kaz responded, still unconvinced.

"We have moved too far in our plans, and we are not stopping. If we kidnap the King, can we bring him here to Częstochowa?" Strawiński asked.

"If you pull it through and bring him, the hell will unleash on us here. But if we want to put up a fight, there is no better place to concentrate our forces. You bring him here, and I will do everything in my power to keep him under lock and key until he resigns the Crown or is tried for treason," Kaz decided.

When Strawiński left, Kaz ran from the basement, where they secured the explosives to the cannons that faced Riazin. He wanted to see with his own eyes how the defenders moved this dangerous load. He ordered some sacks to be removed from the stairs to clear the passage and decided to select a dedicated group of Confederates in charge of carrying the precious cargo.

Suddenly, Witek stood before him and said, "Lord, you must come with me now. There is something that cannot wait."

"What is it?" Kaz asked.

"You will see, sir," Witek answered. Kaz knew better than to argue with Witek. The boy could be stubborn sometimes, and it made more sense to follow him than to differ. Kaz nodded, and soon they ended up in the dining room.

Kaz noticed a silver food dome placed on a laced scarf. He looked at Witek with questioning eyes. The boy motioned to Kaz to sit in the armchair in front of the food dome.

"What kind of a joke is this, Witek? I don't have time for this nonsense," Kaz insisted. Still, Witek did not give up. Resigned, Kaz took his seat while Witek lifted the food dome. Kaz saw a large porcelain bowl decorated with green flower garlands, red berries, and a delicate golden rim full of raspberries and blueberries smothered in heavy cream with a gold spoon to the side. Witek handed Kaz a letter that read:

To my darling Blueberry Knight
Helena

Kaz placed his elbows on the table and buried his face in his hands. He touched his eyebrows with the tips of his fingers and rubbed them gently as the tension of the day diminished, and the only clear thought was that of Helena and this thoughtful gift. He took the spoon in his hand, studied the handiwork for a moment, and dipped it in the fruit bowl. Witek bowed and discreetly left the dining hall.

During his third visit to the monastery, Strawiński presented all details of the scheme, saying, "We have everything planned. Some say we should kill the King on the spot and be done with him."

Kaz opposed the project, saying, "I am a soldier, the knight of Poland, and not a murderer," Kaz answered, disgusted with the idea of regicide. "I will fight King Stan in an open field but will not agree to an assassination attempt. I have been fighting Muscovy for three years now in an open field. I will not spare a soldier to go to Warszawa and corner the King in a dark alley. We are duly registered confederates and not a bunch of lawless rebels."

"I only report to you what others consider," Strawiński responded.

"That's a silly and dangerous idea. I do not condone regicide. The majesty of Poland does not deserve such rushed action. Also, we would probably lose all support from France, Turkey, and Austria if we acted so irresponsibly," Kaz said.

"Let me make sure. You agree that if we were to kidnap King Stan, we may bring him here and count on your cooperation?" Strawiński verified.

"Yes, I am not going anywhere. I have enough trouble with General Drevitz all the time. He will keep me busy," Kaz repeated.

Strawiński bowed deeply with a sigh of relief and said, "Thank you, Count Pułaski. We will kidnap him, put him in a coach and bring him here to Częstochowa. It all should be done in two weeks."

Concurrently, on 13 October 1770, the declaration of Preszów written by Ignacy Bohusz was signed by most confederates. Bohusz wrote:

"The clamor of arms; the slaughter of citizens; the whole country filled with foreign troops fed from our estates; breaking of the most solemn treaties; freedom dying at the feet of tyranny; old cardinal rights trampled; new laws written to protect crimes and subjugate us to the might of Moscow; the Holy Roman Catholic religion despised; new treaties to protect the throne forced under arms; tyrants and perpetrators guarded by the Crown and foreign weapons; senators and envoys torn from their seats by sacrilegious hand; all in despair; the provinces of the Republic (as is the case of Courland and Ukraine) surrendered to Moscow; all country set ablaze; crying, poverty, devastation, murders, rape, captivity, shackles, chains, sentencing lists, daggers, stakes, hooks and various kinds of cruelty. These are the true and essential hallmarks of Stanisław Poniatowski, the intruder, and usurper on the Polish throne!"

Kidnapping King Stan

Late at night on 3 November 1771, the King, with a small escort, was returning from a visit to his sick relative, Chancellor Michał Fryderyk Czartoryski. Three groups led by Stanisław Strawiński, Walenty Łukawski, and Tom Kuźma charged the King's guards on Miodowa Street between Senatorska and Kozia Streets. Some shots were fired, and the carriage driver was shot dead. The Confederates charged at the Kings' guards, who ran away after a short brawl.

The kidnappers noticed that the King escaped in the melee and ran down the street. They chased him down and caught up with him when he was knocking on the gate of the Czartoryski castle. Nobody appeared at the gate. Kuźma shot at the King but only grazed him, leaving a red mark. Łukawski and Strawiński hit him repeatedly with their flat sabers. The King was cut slightly on the back of the head and then forced to mount a horse. In the skirmish, he lost one of his boots.

205

[King Stan's boot on display at the National Museum in Kraków]

Shortly, all three groups raced downriver to reach the forested undulating terrain of the Bielany woods. The King was with Kuźma's group. As they were crossing a moat, the King's horse slipped and broke his leg. In the dark of the night, the kidnappers got lost. The King ended up alone with Kuźma, who offered him his boot.

Eventually, Kuźma did not reach the coach waiting to carry the King to Częstochowa. Instead, he took the King to a miller's house in Marymont by the Wisła River. From there, the miller's apprentice was dispatched to the King's palace with a letter from the King. In the morning, the King's guards arrived and escorted King Stan to the safety of the royal court.

Once in the palace, King Stan announced that he was to be executed on the orders of the most inhuman and blood-thirsty rebel, Count Kazimierz Pułaski. The King was saved through God's grace combined with his exceptional eloquence and bravery. His magnetic charisma made Kuźma change his mind. King Stan was a hero who escaped certain death, while Kaz became a wanted criminal, despised by law-abiding citizens. King Stan presented the boot he lost during the kidnapping and a pair of used gloves as evidence of the regicide. Illustrating the ultimate proof of Kaz's crime, King Stan tried the gloves in court. They fit his hands, which he claimed confirmed the alleged regicide beyond any reasonable doubt.

Rather than defenders of the Commonwealth, the Bar Confederates overnight started being portrayed as the obtuse and confused group of old-timers out of touch with the demands of modern times. King Stan published his account of events in his newspaper with wide distribution. Ribbons, bowties, saddles, and banners with the slogan "King with the nation, a nation with the King" were distributed throughout the Commonwealth.

Conveniently for the King, the only lethal victim of the kidnapping was the coach driver, who happened to have a beautiful wife. She, in turn, was one of King Stan's courtesans. The King solved yet one more problem that frightful night: a jealous husband's challenge. By the way, nobody seemed to wonder why a select group of dedicated bodyguards sworn to protect the majesty of the King with their lives simply ran away.

The Russians immediately picked up the King's story and advertised it in all courts of Europe. One by one, the promoters of the Bar Confederation and Kaz personally decided to pull their support. Confederates were left alone in the face of an ever-increasing number of Russian soldiers chasing them all over Poland. It was impossible to rally any fresh troops or find passive supporters of the Confederate cause.

When Repnin came to pay King Stan a visit to the palace, Stan said, "This kidnapping is the best thing that could have happened. We couldn't stop the Confederates for years. Now, the support they built in the country and abroad is crumbling. We must use the kidnapping as a weapon to frame Pułaski and destroy the Confederates for good."

Repnin seemed concerned about King Stan's health. When he found out that no harm came to His Majesty, he sighed with relief and bowed with rare reverence saying,

"Your Majesty is a consummate politician. We need to find a mouthpiece that will reduce Poland and the Confederates to the level of savages of Europe they are."

"Wouldn't it weaken my position as the King of such an undesirable country?" asked King Stan with a note of concern.

"Don't worry, Your Excellency. We gave you the Crown. We saved you from the rebels. We will protect you from France, Turkey, Prussia, and Austria if need be," said Repnin, smiling reassuringly.

"Isn't it a bit too much of a challenge?"

"With complete control over Poland, we will grow into the key player in Europe. Before they realize it, the Germans and the French will follow our dictates. Rather than executing their plans, they will be reduced to reacting to what we would decide. Soon, they will be happy that we did not attack them and will agree to our terms, whatever they may be. You, my dear Stan, will be one of the best-fed chickens in our chicken coop. "

Prophecy

The news of Strawiński's betrayal reached Pułaski at Jasna Góra. His options for a continuation of the fight were rapidly closing. He was blamed for the attempted regicide and could not raise fresh troops or seek support for the Confederation in the country or abroad. If he decided to visit Count Wielopolski at Pieskowa Skała again, the Count would undoubtedly have him arrested and delivered to Drevitz.

Kaz met prior Pafnucy Brzeziński, whom he found kneeling deep in prayer before the venerated picture of the Virgin Mary. Paulin spoke without turning his head, "tell me what troubles you, my son. It is time to let go of all your sorrows and be happy that we still have faith to carry us forward."

"I have given it all to the cause of a free Poland and our serene republic," Kaz said, kneeling next to prior Brzeziński. "All hopes are lost. They have stabbed me with a lie, and I cannot even defend myself. The rumors are spreading. I am standing here at a loss, powerless. There is nothing left for me but to leave the country and be chased away as a banned leftover of betrayed honor, glory, and hope."

"Do not despair, my son. Like countless others, our families have defended Poland for centuries. One dirty trick will not extinguish the everlasting flame of our motherland. We will endure. Remember, Jesus was betrayed and died on the cross, yet his cause never died;

209

indeed, it was reborn and grew ever stronger," Paulin said. He stood up and continued with a voice that gained conviction and strength. Finally, it seemed like he was a conduit of spiritual energy whispering through the ages, materializing to deliver a message.

"A bunch of power-hungry Muscovites, even if united with the Germans, cannot destroy what has been flourishing here in our hearts for over 800 years. You are a messenger of Poland charged with a holy quest to carry her torch far beyond the walls of this church, this country, or the boundaries of our physical life. Remember that Judas betrayed Jesus, but the Son of God still carried on. It looks like Strawiński is your Judas. Take your cross and have faith. Take solace in the lesson Lord Jesus left for us. You will be reborn."

Looking at Virgin Mary, Kaz said, "Do not compare me to our Lord Jesus. The Lord and the church do not know me."

"The Lord works in mysterious ways. Men cannot penetrate God's judgment. The Almighty has his own purposes, and we all are just a flock of our Lord's sheep. If he so chooses, he might even make a Pole the Pope who will lead the way if the need arises."

Pauline placed his hand on Kaz's head and pronounced, "Time will come that your fight and your message will gain strength. It will endure transcending political borders and generations of men. It will indeed become timeless, without boundaries, and it will call to arms eons of knights who, when the time comes, will carry the flame of freedom and justice worldwide. Their call to action will be Pułaski and the response Poland."

Kaz Leaves Częstochowa

The situation was indeed hopeless. The confederates were losing battles on many fronts. There was still a chance to plead for mercy and protect the estates of some of them, but Kaz was beyond saving. Charged with the regicide in absentia, Kaz was to be captured or killed on sight. Anyone helping him as an accomplice would lose all protections of the law. Not willing to risk the lives of his comrades, Kaz decided to leave the country.

On 31 May 1772, dressed as a merchant, Pułaski left Częstochowa. His letter to those remaining in the monastery said:

"I have picked up a weapon for the public good, and for it, I must lay it down. The union of three powerful states takes away all our defenses, and the case in which I am involved would make it difficult for me to work the surrender terms for you, linking you to my misfortune ... I know your zeal and your courage, and I am sure that when the circumstances for serving the motherland luckily come to pass, you will be the same as you were with me."

[General Kazimierz Pułaski by Tom Styka]

Kaz ordered Witek to leave the fortress and save himself for better days, but the boy refused. The only thing he promised Kaz was that he would not do anything "stupid" and obey the terms of surrender. When Kaz was leaving in his disguise, Witek followed him at a distance, dressed as a peasant.

The cart with a hooded merchant was passing Russian units close to the three large cannons with obliterated barrels. Their twisted steel fragments looked like sculptures symbolizing a mute accusation of barbaric sacrilege. One of the officers stood out from the group. He sat astride a noble Palomino steed with a hint of Persian blood, which shone like a drop of gold against the background of bushes and trees. Only one Russian officer could have such a rigidly upright posture. By some devilish chain of events, Captain Riazin was sitting on top of Bystry.

When Kaz noticed Bystry, he almost jumped out of the cart, ready to charge Riazin with bare hands. Suddenly, Kaz heard a modulated high pitch whistle, which sounded like a peel call of an eagle. Riazin had to restrain Bystry, who wanted to follow the sound. At the third call, Bystry jumped up and stood on his hind legs, trying to get rid of Riazin. Kaz followed Bystry's struggle turning his head towards the clash, but he did not get out of the cart. He remained seated on the bench, his body twisted to the left and his head facing backward. A tree obstructed his line of sight, and then more trees and bushes drew the curtain down on the confrontation between the rider and his mount.

Saddled and bridled, Bystry calmed down. Two parallel red horizontal streaks on the gold horsehair covering his ribs and a few drops of blood drying on the grass were the signs of Riazin's stirrups. The double slashes vaguely reminded the cuts on the reverend face of the Black Madonna of Częstochowa.

On 28 April 1772, Wawel Castle in Krakow surrendered. On July 13, the Tyniec monastery near Krakow fell. On August 18, the monastery fortress at Czestochowa capitulated. The last bastion of the Confederacy, the monastery at Zagórz, gave up on 28 November 1772.

[Ruins of the monastery at Zagórz]

Voltaire

The war with the Bar Confederates was more challenging than Catherine had predicted. Fortunately for Catherine, the lie about Kaz's intention to murder King Stan was the right move, which devastated carefully built Confederate alliances. It weakened the support for the Confederate cause in Poland and froze burgeoning cooperation with France, Austria, and Turkey. Catherine needed to ensure that the world at large would be given a story of what had happened in Poland in a way that would remove any suspicion of wrongdoing by Russians or Prussians.

They selected a suitable man for such a propaganda campaign in France. He was François-Marie Arouet, known under his pen nickname Voltaire. He was a recognized critic of all at the core of Polish strength: tradition and the Roman Catholic Church. The truth that Poland was a tolerant multireligious, multicultural, and multilingual country was not a problem. Voltaire could write anything. In his lifetime, he produced 20,000 letters and 2,000 books and pamphlets. The content of his writing depended more on the money a sponsor was willing to expend than on the truth or his beliefs.

In the age of relativism, when noblemen switched religions and love was based more on practicality than ethics or morals, it took little convincing for Voltaire to write whatever Catherine suggested. Once he decided to take the job, he became more compelling with every new word of his epistolary magic. The Russians and Prussians invested even more money to ensure that his word reached all countries of the civilized world. The lavish financing Catherine secured for Voltaire outweighed the hardships of censorship from the French monarchy. He was admired as a brave dissident fighting the Roman Catholic Church while loading his pockets with money from

Catherine, the Orthodox Christian convert, and Frederic, the Protestant.

The world could not be more appreciative of Voltaire. The only threat he was risking was that the money sent from Catherine would run out. On one beautiful afternoon, when Voltaire weighed the pros and cons of his direct attack on everything Poland stood for, the emissary was announced in his chambers. He came in with an air of camaraderie and an ounce of arrogance, saying, "Here is the money for your trouble, Francois. To make it easier, make sure that you include this manifesto and an oath written by the Confederates." He continued, handing Voltaire a roll of paper tied with a red ribbon.

Voltaire moved over to a window and unfolded the bundle. Putting the document closer to the light, he started reading. He was interrupting his lecture with glances at the messenger, admiring the paintings on the wall.

"It says here that they swear to kill the King. Isn't it a stretch? You told me we should frame Pułaski for the attempted regicide, but now you want to implicate them all."

"Dear Voltaire, truth. The concept of truth is but a mere intellectual exercise. Let Thomas Aquinas argue the truth. You, my dear friend, look at these doubloons. This is real gold. How can you argue what some people in Warszawa think or do against these juicy chunks of gold? Let us be pragmatic. Truth, if it were so powerful, should defend herself. She does not need you. Besides, how much does the truth pay you?"

"I have my principles."

"Where did you have your principles when you took Frederick's money and protection in Prussia? You stabbed France in the back following his bidding, and now you want to tell me that your principles stop you from giving Poland a little stab of your pen? Winter is coming, and Russians have great pelts. Sitting by the fire in a warm sable robe while pondering justice would be nice. You are a man of reason. Be reasonable."

Secret Pact

In February 1772, Russia, Prussia, and Austria signed a secret pact in Vienna.

They all agreed to seize parts of Poland's territory. On 5 August 1772, the First Partition of Poland was officially announced to the world, and the troops entered the annexed lands. Poland lost thirty percent of its territory and four million citizens, almost half its depleted population. Prussia instantly gained eighty percent of Poland's trade. Adding to the total humiliation, the partitioning powers demanded that Poland ratify the annexation of land and people. On 18 September 1772, the invading armies forced the Sejm to assemble and officially confirm partition articles. King Stan earnestly and dutifully signed all necessary documents. When Poland was extinguished after the third partition of 1795, King Stanisław II August Poniatowski signed all the required documents and retired in St. Petersburg, drawing a well-earned pension from his de facto employer, Catherine the Great.

PART TWO: THE UNITED STATES

CHAPTER 7

On the Way to Boston (1772)

France (1773)

Kaz left Poland for Silesia and then for France. Since he was charged with regicide, his funds were blocked. He was not used to being penniless. For the first time in his life, he had to ask for money. Till now, Kaz could afford anything he wanted. He was raised to appreciate human labor and money, but if he decided to get something, money was not an issue, whether he wanted to buy a horse or a unit of soldiers. He could dress and feed his men, providing them with dashing uniforms, first-rate horses, and weapons.

At first, his name was enough to get him any credit he wanted. But the correspondence from his sister was alarming. He, a well-to-do nobleman of Poland, was robbed by King Stan. The Bar Confederation was a lawfully registered opposition to the King according to Polish law and the customs of most of Europe at that time.

Usually, the Confederates either won or resigned after a fair fight for succession, which was treated like a duel between free men struggling for the country's future. The King would negotiate the terms of surrender and would pardon the Confederates. They were perceived as a group of honorable citizens taking risks and, at times, sacrificing their lives for what they believed was right, which gave them the respect of szlachta.

The understanding was that sometimes it was not enough to complain verbally. If you meant what you were saying, you would have to fight for your rights with arms in your hand, risking your life, your money, and your position with the monarch.

The Regicide Trial

Back in Poland, the court proceedings regarding the alleged involvement of Kaz in the regicide attempt were carried out in full force, officially beginning on 7 June 1773. The main witness was King Stan himself. Nobody opposed when the testimony of Kuźma and Strawiński was presented in writing only while they stayed abroad. King Stan awarded Kuźma with the title of szlachcic and the right to use the name Kosiński, adding a substantial annuity of 400 ducats. He lived in Italy and returned to Poland after the third and final partition of the Commonwealth. Strawiński lived under the protection of Empress Catherine. He delivered his written testimony on 9 April 1773, a year-and-a-half after the kidnapping. In it, with exquisite detail, he described the events claiming that Kaz ordered him to kill King Stan.

On 30 June 1773, Kaz wrote to the court denying any attempt on King's life and requesting that he retain a defense attorney. The Senate decided that Kaz would be permitted legal representation only if he appeared in Warszawa in person. Some senators tried to oppose such an unjust decision, but their addresses were drowned by loud clapping.

Eventually, King Stan said, "It is your choice. However, if we do not sentence those guilty of regicide, there will be no pardon for those participating in the Bar uprising. My advice is to choose a lesser evil."

As the only witness to the kidnapping, King Stan once again described how he outmaneuvered the cold-blooded killers sent by Kaz. Without giving any other cause for the regicide, Kaz's pure hatred of King Stan was the reason for the abduction. In his testimony, the King further claimed that Kaz ordered to quarter the King's body, burn it, and blow the ashes around, but leave the arms cut off by the elbows to display on the pikes by a public roadside and confiscate all King's wealth. Kaz was found guilty of the alleged crimes. This ruling was one more embarrassing example of how low the country's political elites descended.

The verdict was vacated in 1792 when, for a moment, Russians lost their tight grip over Poland. Still, until today many historians, who do not bother to study Polish sources carefully, quote the manipulated verdict and claim that the regicide was the most significant political mistake of the Confederation. They further follow that the botched regicide attempt proves how naïve and unrealistic the movement was.

Turkey (1774)

With financial assistance from Prince Karol Radziwiłł, Darling Dear, and Paweł Mostowski, Kaz tried one more time to look for international support for the Confederation. After Karol Radziwiłł resigned from challenging Stanisław Anthony Poniatowski as the prospective candidate to the Crown of Poland in 1764 and left the election field at Wola with his entourage of 2000 soldiers, he continued his lavish lifestyle. With the passing years, he realized how dangerous its new King Stanisław II August was for Poland's safety. In 1768, Prince Karol was one of the first who joined the Bar Confederation. Since Empress Catherine or King Stan did not freeze all his assets, he could finance Kaz's trip from France to Turkey. Kaz took an entourage of a few trusted officers and sailed through Venice, Italy, to Dubrovnik (now Croatia) and then traveled through Nis (now Serbia) and Sofia (now Bulgaria) to Shumen near Varna (now Bulgaria) in the Ottoman Empire.

They all knew that Varna, at the coast of the Black Sea, was a place of historical and symbolic significance to Poles and Turks. Here in 1444, Polish King Władysław III earned his nickname Warneńczyk. This twenty-year-old King of Poland, the Grand Duke of Lithuania, the King of Hungary, and Croatia led his army to end the Muslim threat to Poland. The campaign ended with his premature death on the battlefield, stopping Polish expansion to the south. He was the oldest son of the famous Jagiełło, the King of Poland and the Grand Duke of Lithuania, who in 1410 beat the Teutonic Knights at Grunwald in the largest battle of the Middle Ages. This battle broke the backbone of the German expansion to the east for over three hundred years.

Rather than fight the Turks, Kaz was there to arrange the alliance against Russia, which turned out to be the most dangerous and deadly enemy for Turkey and Poland. Turks were the last hope for an ally strong enough to make a difference and bring the fight to the Russians.

Kaz realized that with his funds blocked by King Stan and the Russians, he did not have enough money to buy the necessary gifts for all levels of the Ottoman bureaucracy. He knew, however, that Turks understood the threat the Russians posed. They challenged Catherine when she brought her military forces into Poland to help King Stan win the election. They declared war against Russia right after the Bar Confederation started. It was the Turks who looked like the last hope for the Confederation.

The attempt was daring and risky, but it was not the first time that Kaz was putting everything on the line to force a win. With Catherine's campaign trumping around the world how brutal the Bar Confederates and especially Kaz were, a diplomatic support mission was even more challenging. He remembered how dangerous Ottoman chambers of power were to so many Poles. His father was imprisoned by the Basha of Khotyn (now Ukraine) in Jassy (now Romania), which led to his death on 12 April 1769.

[Khotyn fortress]

Kaz reached the encampment of the Grand Vizier in Shumen after the Turks lost their battle with the Russians on 20 June 1774 at Kozludzha (now Suvorovo, Bulgaria). This battle effectively ended the Russo-Turkish war, which started in 1768 after the Bar Confederation was launched. At Kozludzha, 40,000 Turks led by General Abdul-Rezak Pasha lost to 8,000 Russians under the command of General Suvorov. After seven years of fighting, the Turks were demoralized by numerous defeats. The Sultan's coffers were empty, and the soldiers were unpaid for over a year.

The Ottoman Empire calculated that helping the Bar Confederates would bring Poland on its side in its power struggle with Russia. A pro-Russian King, Stan was their natural enemy. The defeat of the Bar Confederation accelerated the Turkish loss of the seven-year-long war. Turks had to sign a treaty of Kuchuk-Kainarji on 21 July 1774, which gave Russia control over Crimea and ports at the Black Sea. It also gave the Russians the right to use the Dardanelles and Bosporus Straits when sailing to the Mediterranean Sea. It ended the period of the Black Sea being the Ottoman Lake, which started when Sultan Mehmed II built forts on both sides of the Bosporus, finishing the Rumeli fortress in 1452. These forts opened Constantinople to the Ottoman attack of 1453, after which it was renamed Istanbul and served as the capital city of the Porte.

[Rumelihisarı as seen from the Bosporus Strait]

Kaz offered his services to the Turks to continue fighting the Russians. The first condition was that he converted to Islam, which Kaz, of course, could not accept. He almost shared the fate of his father and hardly escaped Turkey. Finally, Kaz got on a ship and sailed to Marseille, France.

Franklin

The boat was carrying Kaz away from the Orient and back to France. The hopes of any serious challenge to the Russians were slim. Kaz was returning as the representative of a losing cause, with most former supporters turning away from the Confederation.

Benjamin Franklin served as the American ambassador to France from 1776 to 1785 with great success. He convinced the French to join the fight against the British and concluded the Treaty of Paris in 1783, ending the Revolutionary War. From the beginning of his mission in France, he scouted for skilled military officers able to help the American cause. When Franklin heard about Kaz, he was not convinced he should consider a controversial young Pole charged with regicide as a prospective American military commander. They did not need troublemakers in the United States' precarious international position. The more he hesitated, the more French supporters of the American cause insisted that Kaz was precisely what the United States needed; a battle-hardened cavalry commander able to fight but, more importantly, organize groups of volunteers into a combat-ready strike force. They ensured that Kaz was a man of honor. If he denied the charge of regicide, the accusation was undoubtedly false. Besides, if the British and Russians wanted Kaz dead, it was reason enough to at least talk to the man.

In the spring of 1777, Kaz met with Franklin and Lafayette, urged by Kaz's friend Claude Carloman de Rulhière. In 1762, Rulhière was in Russia and witnessed the coup, during which Catherine killed her husband and ascended the throne. He also visited Poland in 1776. Catherine's power reached so far that Rulhière's book about Catherine's coup had to wait until her death to be published.

After the first meeting with Franklin, Kaz returned to his humble apartment, pondering whether to apply for the US military. He did not want to leave Europe. He had just returned from Turkey, where he did not achieve anything. Still, he was considering Austria or France as the countries where he could try and rally some support. It was a daunting challenge, but for Kaz, nothing was impossible until he tried.

He was deep in his thoughts when he was interrupted by incessant knocking.

"Open the door," said Kaz, only to realize he did not have a servant. He got up and went to meet the visitor. A grinning face with a lush mane of curly black hair greeted him as he opened the door. It was Robert, his officer from Zazulińce.

"Robert, how did you find me here?" Kaz asked, embracing his friend.

Robert pushed Kaz away at the length of his long arms to give him a careful look. As always, his grin never lost his face.

"Did you think that you would go to fight the English without me?"

"How do you know that? I don't even know that."

"Your sister sent me here with some letters. Once in France, I found out through my Scottish friends that you talked with Benjamin Franklin. You did not talk with him about the latest fashion in wig design or where to order a new outfit for a ball, did you?"

"I am not sure, Robert; it is so far away, and what does their fight have to do with Poland?"

"Remember?" asked Robert. "I told you that I was fighting English in Poland. Countries are all connected into one web of family intrigue across Europe. Powerful families think primarily about themselves first and often treat countries instrumentally as tools to dominate other strongmen of the world. This network connects all of them into one disgusting web of deception.

"George and Catherine are the same kinds of evil. They are made into godlike figures representing their nations and religions, reinforcing their invincible image. You are to trust, obey, and love them, even die for them if they so wish. You are not to question them or oppose their decisions. It is ridiculous. They are only people but act like demigods with crowns on their heads.

"If the Continentals win in America, it will weaken Catherine's grip over Poland in a way. More people in Poland will understand that neither Empress Catherine nor King Stan was sent from heaven. If they make mistakes or work against the national interest, they should be opposed and, if need be, removed from power by force.

"And now, you are here charged with regicide, unable to use your money. I hear that the British are also interested in you. They know that you talked with Franklin. They would hate for you to go to America and help the rebels. With your experience of success in the field and international connections, you can become a formidable political weapon."

"I don't know. It all is too much too quick."

"Hear me out, Kaz. I don't know all the reasons, but I know this much. England is gaining from the collapse of Poland. With your steady grain production, nobody in Europe thought much about where all this food was coming from. Now that you are entangled with wars, and the Prussians are choking your grain trade, guess who benefits?"

"I don't even know what you are talking about," Kaz answered.

"Listen, British colonies used to produce grain primarily for their consumption at first. Now, their ships are exporting it to Europe and the West Indies. They are taking over Polish markets. The British don't have to worry about the Danes or the Dutch, who move your grain and control the passages from the Baltic Sea to the Atlantic Ocean. They load their ships with grain in America and bring them to Europe while Poland's grain trade suffers, and your profits shrink by a minute!

"Do you want to tell me that you are getting tired? Do you want to slow down? What is this world coming to? Come on, Kaz, open your eyes. Who always told me that you must give it all, all the time? Wasn't it you?"

Rather than pacing around his apartment, Kaz was sitting at the table, visibly disheartened and overwhelmed. He looked at Robert sadly and said, "Look where it brought me. My father died after his release from a Turkish prison. Frank buried him in the steppe by the Dniestr River on the way to Mohylew, only to be killed in action a few months later. I am chased away like a criminal, and you want me to get into more trouble."

"Looks like trouble is looking for you, my friend," Robert remarked. "Your options are to face it or to give up. You will not give up if you live. I know you too well."

"Muscovites are not English. I do not have any reason to fight the King of Great Britain."

"You have more reasons than you think. They are a lot like Muscovites. The English and the Russians both pretend to be masters of the world, but in truth, they have a slave mentality. The English were Roman slaves. Then the Vikings, the Danes, and the French invaded their lands. It all rotted their souls to the core. I sense fear, hatred, and resentment in them all the time. They do not treat others as equals or as possible partners. They want to control and conquer it all. They are like locusts. Once they get on their boats, there is no stopping them.

"Muscovy is the same. They are gobbling lands like the Mongols used to do. Being slaves to the Mongols, they know fear and humiliation. They will not stop until they have it all. On the other hand, you Poles experienced continuous growth for so long that even after the betrayal by the Swedes and Germans, you are still looking for partnership and cooperation. What you did together with the Lithuanians is impressive.

"I have never been treated with superiority or scorn in Poland. I felt honesty and virtue. I think the American Continentals are fighting for the same. They want freedom and honor the Polish way, willing to die for it. Their revolution is the threat to the absolute monarchs like King George or Empress Catherine."

Robert poured himself a glass of wine from a bottle on the cupboard. He looked at the goblet, brought it to light, and swirled the content. For a while, he was focused on the ruby-colored liquid, which moved around like blood on the battlefield. He put the glass on the table and looked at Kaz with new intensity.

"You know a lot about various Polish, German, or Russian noble families, but you never focused much on England," he said in a changed voice. "I know them as well as you know the Wettins. They think about their family first. It does not matter what country they are supposed to rule if they hold power. They rule a particular country or a group of people with a firm grip. The story explaining why they have the right to that rule is secondary. It is only a nicely spun tale for the naïve and the uninformed.

"How did Catherine become the Empress of Russia? Wasn't she just a Prussian princess and not precisely from any top shelf of the nobility pool? What if I told you that she was in touch with the British Ambassador, Sir Charles Hanbury Williams, before she killed her husband, the Czar of Russia? What if I told you that she wrote him a letter explaining in detail how she was planning to take power in Russia into her hands? What if I told you that not only Sir Williams read this letter?

"Sir Charles was the Ambassador of Britain in Dresden at the time when your Polish King Augustus III spent more time there than in

Warszawa. You served as the page to Carl Christian Joseph in Mitawa, Courland, so you must know something about it. Sir Charles met Stanisław Antoni Poniatowski in Berlin while Stan was there under medical treatment. Yes, Antoni, because as you remember, King Stan changed his second name from Antoni to Augustus only after he won the Polish Crown.

"Stan went to Saint Petersburg as the personal secretary to Sir Williams. Charles introduced Stan to the Russian Grand Duchess Catherine Alexeyevna in Saint Petersburg in 1755, which led to their famous romance. And only then she became the future Catherine the Great, Empress of Russia. Isn't Catherine the one who benefitted the most from Stan's kidnapping in Warszawa?

"She had a big problem with the Bar Confederation and you personally, one of the most successful commanders in the field recognized from Paris and Vienna to Rome and Istanbul. The Confederation lost all international support only after she blamed you for attempting to murder King Stan. Now you sit here with no money, no power, and little respect. King George is your sworn enemy. Look, some people want to fight George in America. You should join their cause."

CHAPTER 8
In the USA (1777)

Boston

On 23 July 1777, Kaz landed in Marblehead near Boston. Robert Frost and Jan Zieliński accompanied him on this trip. Robert was no longer a mercenary hired by Kaz's father but a dear friend who shared the last years of a losing battle against the Russians and King Stan, their essential ally. Jan was Kaz's cousin and a former Bar Confederate. Robert and Jan decided to join Kaz in his American adventure.

Kaz had a letter of recommendation from Benjamin Franklin to George Washington and wanted to stand in front of the commander of the Continental Army without delay. Robert was instrumental in these first days with his English language skills and several Scottish acquaintances in the colonies.

The three-masted schooner Massachusetts moored at a busy harbor, and the three friends landed on American soil. Robert maneuvered between the crowds of opportunists whose job was to make sure that the newcomers spent the first money on goods or errands they offered. Almost, as a rule, the cost of these services far exceeded their value. Often the value of the services equaled zero. Kaz and Jan knew enough to watch their purses and a few valuables they had brought.

They moved down the pier briskly and hopped on a cart selected by Robert, which took them to a hotel. Robert chose a room with three beds and suggested that Kaz and Jan wait for him as he looked around to find the quickest way to contact General Washington. He brought them to the hotel restaurant and said, "Try some local cuisine, and I should be back before you finish your steaks. Kaz, I know you don't like alcohol, but you must have a pint of beer."

Robert was right. As Kaz and Jan were halfway through their juicy steaks, he returned. He ordered another round of beer and a steak for himself.

"We must do some shopping before we hit the road to General Washington's encampment at Neshaminy Falls. Let us start with a tailor shop. We should not buy anything from the shelf because the Continentals are boycotting clothes from England. If we met the colonial military, they might not be pleased if we did not follow the nonimportation agreement, which was expected of all supporters of the United States in the colonies. It will take a day or two to have our breeches and coats made for us," Robert explained.

"What is the nonimportation agreement?" Jan asked.

"It is the agreement to boycott British yard goods, ready-mades, and other luxury items from England," Robert answered.

A man sitting at the adjacent table with a friend looked at Robert and asked, "It looks like you are new; straight from England, I guess?"

"Yes, we have just arrived, only not from England but from France. We need to purchase some supplies to get going."

"Where are you headed?"

"Philadelphia, I guess. Where can we find a good tailor shop where they know what they are doing and are quick? We also need a stable where we can buy some good horses."

"You are just a block away from a good tailor. He will get you whatever you need. He is Carlin, the cousin of the famous William Carlin, who makes clothes for Washington and Franklin in Virginia. You cannot get better than that; turn right, and see a large store window.

"The livery, the livery, let me think. For this, I would look at the outskirts of the city. There are some decent stables. Ask for Johnson, and you should be happy. He always has a few dozen choice animals. If you stay longer, I would like to hear news from France. Is there any chance they will help us beat the British here?"

"You never know. We might be back, but now we must hurry and see Carlin. "Thank you for your advice, Sir," Robert answered, gifting the stranger with his big smile and a nod.

The stranger was right. Just around the corner, by a large window, they spotted a big sign CARLIN over a double-hung glass door. As they crossed the threshold, the doorbell rang, and an energetic young man with a small triangular chin and a hint of a mustache greeted them with an inviting smile.

"I am Jonah, and I will gladly help you meet any clothing needs. How may I be of service, gentlemen?"

"We have just arrived from France and need some clothes to look presentable in Philadelphia. Rather than buy clothes off the rack, I hear we should invest in something you could make for us. What would you recommend?" Robert asked.

"It looks like you know all you need to know, Sir. It is my job to do the rest."

They were standing next to an excited boy dressed in a long gown and someone who looked like his father. The boy was jumping, hardly able to contain himself.

"What is it with your son?" Robert asked. "I assume he is your son. I see quite a resemblance."

"Oh yes, he is my son Timothy. It is a big day for him. He will just receive his first set of man's clothes. He is seven years old, and I think it is time for young Tim to be dressed like a man and not like a baby boy," explained the father, who was almost as giddy as his son.

"Yes, Father," Timothy said. "I am ready."

At this time, a thin, long-legged assistant hopped to the floor. He had been sitting cross-legged among about a half dozen men on a large, long table by the enormous window. They were busy cutting and sewing various articles of clothing. He picked up a pair of breeches, a shirt, and a coat and approached Timothy.

"Here you go, Timmy. I have just finished. Let us go in the back, and you will return as the man you are. Come on," the tailor encouraged Timmy, who did not need much convincing. He was ready to step into the grown-up world, skipping in his first set of men's clothes.

Just as Timmy and the tailor disappeared behind a curtain, a broad-shouldered man wearing a tight coat and a black triangular hat rang the doorbell as he crossed the threshold with a stack of o papers. He started handing them over to everyone inside. It was a wanted man poster stating that:

A young negro man named Joe, about 20 years of age, about five feet seven inches high, well made, has a round face full of bumps, and a mole on his neck, ran away from his rightful owner. He had an osnaburg shirt and trousers. He can read and write. There is a suspicion that Joe wants to enlist as a free man. Whoever catches this negro and brings him to his rightful owner shall receive a reward of $20 and all reasonable expenses reimbursed.

Signed,
Charles Smith, the owner

When Kaz took the poster and read it, he turned to Robert with a questioning look, asking, "What does it mean?"

"It is an ugly reality. Some people own slaves and treat them like any other property."

Kaz advanced to the distributor of the posters and asked, "Why would you distribute your pamphlets here? Do you think that Joe would come to this store?"

"Indeed, I do. He will most certainly try to get some clothes and get rid of his osnaburg outfit."

"Do you think that they would sell him clothes here?" Kaz continued his investigation.

"Why not? Money is money. Joe is a strong nigger. It would not be difficult for him to find a job and earn enough to buy any outfit he desires. On top of that, he is smart. He can read and write. It is the trouble Mr. Smith has. It is difficult to keep your property up north when so many don't mind hiring blacks and don't bother to check if they are someone's property."

Kaz turned to Robert and, shaking his head with disgust, said, "If I found this Joe, I would give him the $20 to keep him away from Charles Smith."

At this time, young Tim showed up dressed in his new breeches, shirt, and coat. He was not skipping anymore. He walked straight with an aura of youthful dignity.

"Here you are, my little man, properly breeched," said his father proudly.

Tom looked at his father and at his jacket, twisting his head around, saying, "I saw myself in a mirror, Father. I am not a baby boy anymore. I am a grown-up man."

"See what a new garment can do to a man," a tailor announced, admiring his handiwork.

Tim's father proclaimed to his son and all in the store who cared to listen, "Son, remember, you are not a baby boy but a free man from now on. Nobody but me will tell you what to do or make you pay taxes you don't want to pay. If any king or some other wants your money, he will have to work for you to earn it. If he doesn't, we will fight him and keep our money for ourselves. That's God's honest truth."

As the happy father finished his proclamation, Jonah approached Robert and asked, "Have you decided on anything in particular?"

"We all need breeches and coats to match," Robert answered.

"I expect these will be clothes for gentlemen. You see, we serve all kinds of needs. Today, I had an attorney, a bricklayer, a carpenter, a farmer, and a clergyman."

"Is this the store for gentlemen or laborers? Jan asked.

"Here in the colonies, it doesn't matter. Maybe George Washington does not have to spend as much from his income on clothes, but any laborer can earn enough in a month to afford the same item of clothes. If he does not have enough money on hand, but his job is steady, Mr. Carlin will gladly give him credit so that he can afford the exact coat or breeches as Mr. Washington.

"We need something that will feel comfortable on a horse and will be acceptable in a respectable living room," Kaz explained.

"I know what you have in mind," Jonah smiled. "It will be something to emulate what the local gentry finds attractive and practical. I think about three pairs of breeches and shirts for three shillings each and three waistcoats at twelve shillings each. Our breeches with fitted waistbands are especially comfortable if you ride a horse. Follow me, please."

Jonah took a strip of paper and started taking measurements from Jan. With practiced quick motions, he placed the ribbon across the chest, waist, shoulders, and back. He followed by measuring arms and legs. Each time, he marked the strip of paper with his scissors. He then followed with a new strip of paper, measuring Robert and Kaz.

"One more thing, and we are done. We need them ready for tomorrow," Robert said.

"I am sorry, but it will take a week. This work requires time to be done right," Jonah shook his head.

"What can you do with this extra dollar for your effort?" Robert asked.

"I wish I could have them done for tomorrow, but we need daylight to work. Therefore Mr. Carlin spent all this money on the largest store window in town. But with this dollar, your order can be completed in two days. I will come before sunrise and work the moment I can see my needle."

"You have yourself a deal, Jonah," Robert answered, and they left the store looking for Johnson's stables.

Kaz felt excited when the three arrived at Johnson's stables. They saw some horses in the stalls and about twenty in the corral. As they approached the fence, Kaz's mood sank. These were not warhorses or anything that Kaz would call a mount. They were domestic animals not fit to be reliable rides.

"We must find some other place. I don't believe they do not have a better choice somewhere around here. I have heard so much about the quality of horses on the new continent, but not even one in this stable deserves to be called a decent horse," Kaz complained.

"Let's get inside and ask around. Maybe they know a better place," Robert suggested.

A stable attendant in his mid-thirties with a rope in his hand ambled over from the stable, clinging with his stirrups, and asked, "What are you looking for, gents?"

"We were looking for some riding horses, but I don't see you have any. Is there any place where we could buy a decent mount?" Robert asked.

"These are ten-dollar horses. It looks like you are looking for at least a twenty-dollar horse," the attendant answered.

"We are looking for three riding horses to take us to Virginia and back. If you have anything of that quality, we can talk about the price then."

"We have all kinds of horses, destriers, mounts, war horses, Arabian, English, Indian ponies, or Mexican beauties."

"Show us three solid mounts."

"How much do you want to spend?"

"We don't want to spend a dollar, but we will pay what needs to be paid for a decent horse."

"Do you want to look, or do you want to buy?"

"Listen, my man. We don't want to talk. We want to buy three mounts and three saddles, and we want to ride them out of here today if you have what we need," Kaz said.

"No need to get impatient. It is that there are so many people who I take to our choice horses, and then we come back here, and they select a horse from this corral or go home."

"I cannot guarantee I will buy what you show me, but if it is a decent horse, we will talk money today," Kaz said.

"Follow me then, but do not expect to find anything for less than twenty dollars there," said the attendant, leading them a few blocks to a larger corral on the outskirts of town.

The choice was much better there, and Kaz felt he could select three decent rides. Kaz pointed to two sorrel American Quarter horses with small, refined heads and muscular bodies.

"Twenty dollars each," said the attendant and looked at Robert, trying to guess if our company had enough money to afford horses at that price. He sighed with relief. It seemed to him they should be able to afford them. His boss repeatedly yelled at him for wasting time and wandering around showing customers horses they could not afford. And then he saw Kaz pointing to a black Arabian horse, and he knew that he was in trouble.

"Forty dollars; I cannot go even a dollar less," he said with resignation.

"Great," said Tom. Let us see the saddles.

"You don't want to try them? And the price is right?" he asked, not believing that he had just sold three horses. It would be the quickest sale of his two-year-long career if true.

"If he says these are the horses, then these are the horses," Robert assured the attendant pointing to Kaz.

Kaz did not need much to spot a quality animal. He had seen and ridden thousands of them back in Poland. Kaz scanned the horses from the bottom to the top and learned everything he needed to know from their posture and how they moved around the corral. He could have played a game of checking the hoofs, running his hand down their legs, and giving them a spin around. Once they were brought to him, he studied their teeth and looked into their eyes. He was convinced they would be adequate for the tasks ahead.

The black Arabian stallion was worth much more than forty dollars in Kaz's eyes. It was a horse that a Polish szlachcic would not mind calling his own. It had his characteristic long thin neck and high tail carriage. He belonged to a good-natured, quick to learn, and willing to please breed. It had been a horse used in war all over the world. If he missed something in training, Kaz knew that he could bring him up to speed with time.

"What is the name of this horse?" Kaz asked.

"He is a horse. We don't give them names. We sell them. You can call him whatever you want," the attendant answered honestly, expecting the best day at work. Larger purchases were made through the owner, and he never had a dime out of these sales. Here, he could count on a nice commission.

They selected three American saddles. Kaz was impressed with them because they seemed to protect the horses' backs, withers, and loins, which could hurt a horse if neglected. He knew that riders often focused on themselves, forgetting that the horse takes most of the abuse during a ride. The key to a good cavalry saddle is that it protects your mount during days of forced marches as well as abrupt runs and stops.

Grain Trade

Our three newcomers rode back to the hotel on their mounts, sporting new American saddles. They left the horses with the hotel attendants and decided to finish the day at a hotel restaurant. Once they were seated, their morning acquaintance, standing at the bar, approached their table.

"You are back, gentlemen; remember, you promised me your report on France. I am Patrick Ferris, a local landowner," Patrick said, obviously pleased to see them and interested in their account of the possible ally of the United States."

"Join us, please, Patrick. Your information on the tailor and the stable was most helpful. Let us see if we can repay you in kind," Kaz said.

Patrick went back to the bar and returned with a glass of beer. He sat the glass on the table and pulled up a chair. He looked like an honest, thoughtful person seeking information and not merely drinking companions. He had short curly blond hair with a small bald spot at the top.

"How long was your voyage? How long is an average trip from the old continent here?" Patrick asked.

Robert assumed the role of the primary source of information. He started with his broad smile and a wave of the hand. When the waiter came over, Robert said, "Give us a pitcher of beer and glasses for everyone." He then turned to Patrick and explained, "It will take a few moments to give you an honest answer, which you obviously deserve. We traveled forty days from Marseille. It is an average time when you sail from France. If you start from England with favorable winds, it might take you even less time."

"Did you see any ships loaded with grain there?"

"As a matter of fact, two schooners were emptying their locks. I met the captain of one of them, and he said they would be going back to New York once they cleared their load."

"You could say then that four-month is enough for a ship to make a round trip from here to Marseille and back."

"I don't think that it is that simple. It depends on when in the season you travel. There are times when safe travel is out of the question because of strong winds. Why are you so interested in grain shipment?"

"I am a farmer here. Some merchants buy all my grain production. Recently, they proposed that I buy grain from local farmers, and they will give me a good price for both my grain and anyone else's produce. I think that if they are buying so much, there must be a good profit in it."

"What about a war and the British?"

245

"I didn't come here to look for trouble or get shot. I came to the colonies to have a good, safe life for my family. During the war, you can also get shot by hiding under the table. On the other hand, you can make enough money to last you for a long, happy life once the war is over."

"Isn't it time now to handle the war first and join the Continental Army?" Kaz asked. "It looks like the British will be chasing you and your grain all over the Atlantic. If you don't settle the fight with the King first, there might be no ships with grain traveling to the old continent."

"You are right, Sir, but soldiers must eat. We have more farmers than soldiers here, and we all will be in trouble if we forget about food production and trade. The challenge is how to balance between the two." Patrick took a swig of beer and continued, "It is all complicated. I thought that if I had a chance to find out something firsthand, it would help me make up my mind."

"It looks like you are thinking about more than just selling your grain," Robert remarked.

"Yes, you are right. I am thinking about talking to some big farmers here like myself and buying a ship to transport grain ourselves. I think this would help the United States more than just shooting the British and selling grain to whoever shows up without checking profit margins."

"What do you grow here and where?" Kaz asked, thinking about his wheat production in Zazulińce.

"It is mostly wheat. I buy it from New York down to Virginia."

"It is a lot of grain. How do you transport it to the New York harbor?"

"Hudson River is the main artery. After Henry Hudson sailed it for the Dutch East India Company in 1607, they called it the North River. And then you have the South River, which we call Delaware. These two are the spine of the colonies. I am interested in any wheat along these two rivers. The grain trade went hot after a large price spike in 1745, and then the price doubled in 1750. Wheat production has been looking better ever since. Almost all plots of land along the Hudson are planted with wheat."

CHAPTER 9

The Battle of Brandywine (1777)

Neshaminy Falls

On August 29, sentries deployed by General Washington around his headquarters at Neshaminy Falls outside Philadelphia spotted a man around thirty in a strange uniform. He rode over and, using the combination of broken English and impeccable French, asked to see General Lafayette. The guards were not sure whether to bother the Marquis. So many strange people were vying for his attention, and the guards' job was to screen them, stopping any troublesome nuisance. Ultimately, they decided to send the word to Lafayette, who, to their surprise, ran down a few steps and greeted this strange visitor with open arms.

Kaz handed the reins to one of the guards and smiled. They started talking like old friends.

"How is France? How is Paris?" Lafayette asked.

"Not the same without you, but they manage somehow. Here: It is a letter from your wife, Marie Adrienne Francoise. It should explain everything," Kaz answered, handing Lafayette a pink envelope smelling lavender.

Lafayette sniffed the letter and said, "Now I know it all. Thank you, Kaz," and put it in his chest pocket. Twenty-year-old Marie-Joseph Paul Ives Roch Gilbert du Motier was twelve years younger than Kaz. Still, they both followed a similar career of wealthy European land-owning family aristocrats and shared a large circle of friends and acquaintances.

"I am glad to see you, Gilbert," Kaz said. "Tell me, have you left any British for me to fight, or am I too late?"

"We have our hands full. I am considering sailing back to France and lobbying King Louis for serious assistance to the cause of these brave patriots."

"Before you leave, would you mind bringing me to General Washington? Maybe I can be of some help here."

"Oh yes, let's go and find Washington. He will be glad to see you."

"How long have you been here? I heard that your family was not too happy with your trip."

"Yes, I had to avoid my uncle and the British, but I landed in Georgetown, Georgia, on June 13."

"I arrived in Marblehead near Boston on July 23. We should have sailed together," Kaz said. "How is General Washington's Army?"

"He has about eleven thousand poorly armed men with even worse clothes. They are all willing to fight, but they have little idea what war really means. We marched them through Philadelphia just last week on Sunday to boost morale in the city. They did their best to be presentable. We made them all wear green twigs in their hats to make them look uniform. Any soldier who would dare to miss the march expected 31 lashes at the first halting place. They did not step in time when marching, and not all carried their heads upright. They looked more like a hunting party than an army, but at least we have them here ready to follow orders. It is up to us to make them into a fighting force. One thing is certain; their cause is right, and they all wholeheartedly believe in it. They are fighting for their homesteads. It motivates people more than kings and queens," Lafayette explained.

"I am so glad you are here. We must start working these men into an army," Lafayette continued. "They have a lot of motivation and courage but little knowledge of the military. Usually, they are set up in two lines, with shorter ones in the first row. That's about all of their formation and overall tactics as of now."

"How do they treat you, a Frenchman?" Kaz asked.

"They were laughing at me first and telling jokes behind my back, but it all ended once the British showed up at the Chesapeake. They are great soldiers, and you can trust them with your life. They are lions, not chickens."

"I am here to do all I can to be of service to the Continental Army."

"What timing, Kaz. We were sitting here deciding where General Howe was with his British army after boarding his ships and sailing into the Atlantic. Only a week ago, we found out that he landed at

Chesapeake Bay, about 60 miles to the south of here. Then the dispatch came informing about 260 ships and 17,000 British Army. They are coming to Philadelphia. They will be here soon," continued Lafayette, visibly pleased to see Kaz.

As they walked across a large lawn, Kaz spotted a man near the whipping post riding a horse backward, dressed in his uniform, turned the wrong way outwards.

"What is the meaning of that?" Kaz asked and pointed out to the man.

"He was caught deserting and stealing a horse from Colonel Moylan's Regiment of Light Dragoons. He was sentenced to death, but General Washington's clemency got him this humiliating parade and a dishonorable discharge from the army," Lafayette explained. "If we decided to execute every horse thief and every kid who lost his nerve during battle, we would end up with no army and no support from the local population," Lafayette explained.

They walked over to a two-story stone house with a large maple tree to the left, with the branches gently rapping on the windowpanes of the first floor. Soon after, they stood before General Washington in his war room.

[Moland House, Washington's residence at Neshaminy Creek]

"You came at a critical moment, Count Pułaski. However, I cannot accept your services without the approval of Congress," Washington said. "I will write a letter of recommendation at once to John Hancock, the President of the Continental Congress."

"On my way here, it seemed to me that the British forces were pushing on your positions. I don't think they will wait for Congress to approve their attack," Kaz commented.

"We do not know yet exactly what they are planning, but we are ready for them here."

"Knowing the British, they will show up with their boats in the Delaware River and attack Philadelphia with their cannons," Kaz ventured a guess.

"Luckily, we've had the services of your countryman, Colonel Tadeusz Kościuszko. He came here and engineered a blockade of the river. If they could come up Delaware, we would be sitting ducks, and our members of Congress, rather than debate, would have to run for their lives. Luckily, we were able to block the river just in time."

"Where are they coming from then?"

"We just found out that over two hundred ships are standing between the capes of Chesapeake Bay, and their troops are marching up north. Sometimes, fighting is the easiest part of the war. Now, I am forced to wait, and you will also wait if you so wish."

"I would like to wait here so that we do not waste time once Congress makes the decision," Kaz proposed.

"You are welcome to stay with us, dear Count. We have started the deployment along Brandywine Creek so that we will be on the move soon."

Scouting

Pułaski camped near Washington's headquarters and rode up and down Brandywine scouting the position. He followed American scouts, and when they returned to base, he decided to continue reconnaissance further upstream. Weaving between the bushes and tall grasses, he noticed a movement on the opposite shore. He dismounted and found a small hill covered with high shrubs. It protected him from view and gave him a perfect vantage position to survey the area.

Upriver, he noticed a line of horseback riders crossing the waterway. Between large numbers of red coats, he recognized a few Hessian uniforms and their characteristic hats, which he knew from the streets and fields of Warszawa. One of the horses buckled, and the rider fell off, losing his hat. Kaz took a long twig and waited for the cap to float downstream toward him. In a few minutes, he held a Hessian hat with its gold front soaked with the Brandywine Creek water. It took Kaz a few more minutes to assess that the force crossing the creek was hundreds, if not more. They were not just a few scouts but combat regiments ready to deploy on the east side of the stream. Their plan was evident to Kaz. They wanted to attack the exposed right flank of the Continental Army.

Kaz withdrew carefully and hopped on his mount. He rode back full speed all the way, right in front of Washington's headquarters. There was a lot of commotion, with dispatchers and officers running up and down the front stairs. Luckily, Lafayette just stepped out and noticed Kaz.

"Gilbert!" Kaz shouted. "I must see General Washington at once. Your positions are compromised. You do not have time to wait."

"Let's see what we can do," Gilbert replied, knowing that Kaz would not waste a minute on unnecessary gossip. The Marquis waved his hand, asking Kaz to come up the front stairs. Together they rushed into Washington's war room.

"Here you are again. I have no news for you from Congress yet, dear Count," said Washington, looking from a table full of maps.

"This time, I have news for you, Sir. I was scouting the creek. You are in danger of losing your position. The British forded the creek and are moving on your right flank in force. You must act now."

"What is he talking about?" opposed Colonel Baylor, the 3rd Regiment of Continental Light Dragoons commander. "Our reconnaissance units just briefed me. We hold all positions. Not a mouse has crossed the creek."

[Brandywine Creek]

"I saw British soldiers crossing the creek with my own eyes," Pułaski retorted.

"Look across the river, and you will see where they are. I can see Hessian gold helmets glistening in the Sun every day," Colonel Moylan observed.

"Hessians, I know them well. They are born killers, but even they, attacking upfront, will not be able to penetrate your defenses here. They serve more as a decoy up front, attracting your attention away from their real plans of attack."

"Impossible. We have scouted the area up to Buffington's Ford, and our videttes saw nothing," Baylor insisted.

"And what is this?" asked Pułaski, producing the hat he had fished from the creek. "I saw them crossing upstream. You will have thousands of them here soon, and your right flank is exposed."

"Impossible," Colonel Baylor commented.

"It is not a possibility. It is a fact. I guess that General Howe left the Hessians in the center, shining their helmets at you with General Wilhelm von Knyphausen upfront while he took the main force and is crossing the creek as we are speaking. They will be ready to strike in hours.

"We will not live to see that I am right if you don't act now, General. You must act, or your army is lost, Sir."

Pułaski grabbed a pen and drew a map with the opposing fronts of the armies divided by the creek. He then drew a semicircle from the left wing of Howe's troops across the Brandywine River and into the right flank of Washington's troops. He took a dagger and nailed it to the map at the spot where Howe's troops would strike.

"Here is where they are aiming to stab you. It is a fatal blow. If they succeed, the only question is if they kill you here on the spot or hang you later."

Washington looked at the map and Pułaski. He moved his hand over the map and started tapping his fingers around the spot marked with the dagger. Suddenly, he stood upright and looked at Kaz, saying, "Count Pułaski, do what you can. Take my cavalry guard and Godspeed. These are the only troops now at my immediate disposal. If your assessment is correct, we have no time to rearrange the troops," Washington said. "We can argue your point later if we are still alive."

Kaz assembled Washington's guards and intercepted General Howe's forces. The British were organizing their columns when Kaz attacked them for the first time. They did not even know what happened when the first line started crumbling, charged with decisive ferocity and blinding speed. They stopped and regrouped, guarding their left flank. This time, Kaz struck from the river marshes using the trail he had found during his first reconnaissance.

These frantic attacks slowed the British enough to give Washington time to organize the withdrawal of his forces in good order. The battle lasted continuously for 11 hours. It was the second battle of the American Revolutionary War and the largest in scale. Although the British eventually won the combat, General Washington was able to break contact with the attackers and save his army to fight another day.

Kaz risked his life the first moment the situation demanded decisive action while some army officers were circulating between Congress and Washington without seeing the enemy. He showed extraordinary command by leading over 30 men in and out of trouble while raining death and confusion on the enemy. Congress was so impressed with Kaz's action that they approved John Hancock's recommendation, and Kaz was commissioned as a Brigadier General with the honorific title of "Commander of Horse."

Kaz won some friends and enemies with his courageous action. An Irish immigrant opposed him. Senior Colonel Stephen Moylan was in line to achieve the title of Brigadier General, but Congress granted the title to Kaz. On the other hand, he won the favors of Colonel Theodoric Bland of Virginia and his nephew, who later became the famous Light Horse, Harry Lee.

Pułaski Legion

Kaz had a few extended conversations with General Washington. Pułaski and Washington understood one another as landowners dedicated to defending their holdings and their countries with blood. Kaz wanted to make sure that Washington understood how he viewed the role of a horse in the organization of an army. According to Kaz, a successful army should use horses to their fullest potential. Men in the war had used mounted units for millennia. The Chagar Bazar tablets depicted Assyrian horsemen warriors of 1800 B.C. On a vast continental plate in America, the horse should play multiple roles in the army.

Kaz was impressed with General Washington's ability as commander-in-chief. He saw a man who could squeeze the maximum out of what he had at his disposal, always open to new information and able to make decisions under enormous pressure. With his experience of continuous warfare for five years, Kaz wanted to convey all his practical knowledge, which would benefit the Continental Army.

In the array of multiple possible cavalry tasks, most of the Continental officers treated horses as beasts of burden. They could pull wagons full of supplies or transport troops. They served as reconnaissance and dispatch units. They were used by officers so that they looked dashing during parades. Unfortunately, in Kaz's eyes, the most crucial element of what a horse could bring to the army was neglected. With the ratio of one cavalryman to fifteen infantries, the Continental Army ignored the advantage it could gain with more horse riders. The cavalry should be divided into logistic and combat functions. Stormtroopers bursting through enemy lines in the least expected places and possibly deciding the outcome of a battle should be ready to serve immediate tactical needs.

There was little understanding of the dramatic difference between horses bred for various roles. A domestic horse and a warhorse were so different that an untrained eye could distinguish between them. The difference ran much more profound than a cursory look. It took generations of breeding to produce a reliable warhorse. There was no quality place during the Revolutionary War where horses were bred for war in America. Kaz had to work with five, ten, and fifteen-year-old horses, which did not have the necessary basic training. They were not brought up from their early years with the veteran war horses. Still, Kaz knew that after a year of meticulous preparation, there would be a marked improvement in the quality of the Continental Army equine stock.

At times, Kaz was pacing around Washington's room as George was leafing through stacks of paperwork.

"Army is a blind mass of men," Kaz elaborated. "You must train them how to fight, but most of all, you must know when and where to fight. You need a group of soldiers who are your eyes and ears. They should be highly mobile, able to move in front and the back of your army at a moment's notice. They should lead the attack and protect the rear from any ambush or during the retreat. They should bring you all the information you need about the enemy. If there are any traps set for you, they should be first to discover them or be struck by them. They must know how to maneuver at great speed on and off the battlefield across vast terrain so that the enemy would be shocked, surprised, confused, and afraid, not knowing what to expect next. By utilizing the cavalry in such a way, the enemy should think you have more soldiers and supplies. They should be convinced that your soldiers never sleep, eat, or rest. They should think that your soldiers are ten feet tall and strong as a horse itself."

It looked like Kaz was the personification of this ideal cavalryman most of the time. He was constantly on the move. Even sitting in a chair, it looked like he was riding a horse.

One day, to demonstrate how vital speed was for effective cavalry tactics, Kaz brought a hammer and a piece of wood.

"Dear General. Let's take a simple test. Take this hammer and try to break this piece of wood by pressing on it with all your force," Kaz said.

George looked at Kaz, surprised. Reluctantly, he decided to try mostly not to discourage Kaz.

"Try harder, General. Nothing? Let me give it a try."

Kaz swung the hammer and quickly broke the board.

"You did not push into it. You hit it," George observed.

"Yes, exactly. Speed is the key: speed and shock. I surprised you by changing the rules, and I applied speed instead of slow movement. It is what I mean by effective cavalry stormtrooper attack. They should be your hammer, the combination of shock and speed."

Kaz was convinced that the Continental Army should be active through winter. During his talks with Washington, Kaz tried to explain his point of view, saying, "The less real power you have, the more you should try to create an appearance of strength, dedication, and resolve. If we want to win this war, we must not follow the British strategy and plans but create our own and force it on them. They have more men, money, ships, and time. We need to limit their resources. If we give them time to rest and resupply, the calculus is obvious; they will win.

"Instead of focusing on how to train their troops, where to deliver supplies, or how many extra units to procure, they should be forced to answer what we dictate on the ground. We should burn their quartermaster supplies, attack headquarters, destroy convoys, divide them by diversion, and show through facts that they operate on enemy territory and cannot trust or rely on anyone from the local population. They should not trust even one another, especially their intelligence. A well-run winter disruption campaign will reduce their preparedness for spring operations."

Washington agreed with Kaz's assessment but had to follow political reality. It meant that he had to plead with the Continental Congress and listen to their point of view, regardless of how impractical or disruptive it was at times.

Kaz argued, "Consider forming an independent cavalry unit, not subordinate to the demands of the infantry. They needed horses but could not use them to their full potential. I suggest that the unit answer directly to the Commander in Chief, which means to you. You have full operational awareness and would be able to use it best. It will help you better influence the space and time of engagement. You should not wait a minute if there is a need to strike."

Washington would listen patiently and intercede occasionally. He said, "I understand and appreciate your involvement and expertise. However, you must recognize that if I were to ignore Congress and do how I please, I would lose critical assistance sustaining the military. Be patient, Kaz, and we will eventually get the necessary support and approval."

"But when? Time is of the essence."

"It will happen in due course. Let us hope sooner rather than later."

Planning the organization of his cavalry unit, Kaz proposed his second in command. He knew that an able and experienced cavalry officer had arrived from Europe. He was Michael Kovats, a Hungarian hussar with service experience in the Prussian army.

[Michael Kovats de Fabriczy]

In 1777, after learning about the American Revolution, Kovats offered his sword to the American ambassador in France, Benjamin Franklin, writing in Latin:

Most Illustrious Sir:
Golden freedom cannot be purchased with yellow gold.

263

I, who have the honor to present this letter to your Excellency, am also following the call of the Fathers of the Land, as the pioneers of freedom always did. I am a free man and a Hungarian. As to my military status, I was trained in the Royal Prussian Army and raised from the lowest rank to the dignity of a Captain of the Hussars, not so much by luck and the mercy of chance than by most diligent self-discipline and the virtue of my arms. The dangers and the bloodshed of a great many campaigns taught me how to mold a soldier, and, when made, how to arm him and let him defend the dearest of the lands with his best ability under any conditions and developments of the war.

At last, awaiting your gracious answer, I have no wish greater than to leave forthwith, to be where I am needed most, to serve and die in everlasting obedience to Your Excellency and the Congress.

Most faithful unto death,

Bordeaux, January 13th, 1777. Michael Kovats de Fabriczy

P. S: As yet, I am unable to write fluently in French or English and had only the choice of writing either in German or Latin; for this I apologize to your Excellency.

On February 4, 1778, Kaz wrote a letter of recommendation to Washington stating:

"There is an officer now in this Country whose name is Kovats. I know him to have served with reputation in the Prussian service and assure Your Excellency that he is in every way equal to his undertaking."

Later, in another letter to Washington dated March 19, Kaz again recommended Kovats, writing, "I would propose, for my subaltern, an experienced officer, by name Kovats, formerly a Colonel and partisan in the Prussian service."

Time was passing by, and Kaz was getting desperate. And then, on 28 March 1778, he received long-awaited news. Congress commissioned Pułaski Legion, which followed a personal recommendation by Tadeusz Kościuszko's friend General Horatio Gates, the winner from Saratoga. Michael Kovats was named Colonel Commandant of the legion. Kaz also selected Major Julius de Montfort and Captain Jan Zieliński as his officers. Kaz secured appropriate advertisements in local newspapers. The selection of soldiers would include the deserters if approved by General Washington.

On April 6, Congress allotted $130 to Brigadier General Kazimierz Pułaski for each trained recruit. Each soldier in the cavalry or infantry unit would be provided with a rifle, a hat, a pair of trousers, a comb, two stockings, two pairs of boots, three pairs of shoes, and a cartouche or nameplate. Additionally, the cavalry soldiers were equipped with a lance, a couple of boots, a saddle, a halter, a brush, a curry comb, saddlebags, and a rope. The total amount to be dispensed in installments would be $50,000.

[Pułaski Cavalryman, Total War]

Kaz ordered Abraham Morrow sabers, made in Philadelphia. They had long, single-edged blades, handy when fighting a horse with their extended reach. Kaz knew them from Poland, where he saw and used them in action, although a Polish saber was the most popular in the Commonwealth. He selected excellent French Charleville muskets, Model 1776, shipped to Portsmouth, New Hampshire, early that year.

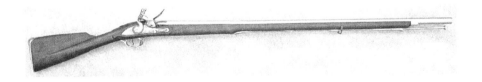

[Charleville 1776 muskets]

He also purchased some Hessian dragoon pistols, a large caliber weapon, much like the ones Hessians at Brandywine were using.

Effective 18 April 1778, Kaz was finally allowed to perform the task he had suggested to Washington in August of 1777. He began to organize and train an independent hussar regiment for the American army as a tactical strike force and not merely as infantry support. Kaz also started working on the first cavalry manual for the Continental Army, ensuring the uniformity of training for soldiers and horses. He described the techniques and exercises needed to train all aspects of cavalry tactics, from individual soldiers to platoons, squadrons, and regiments. The cavalrymen were taught how to form rows, lines, and columns as well as how to move, attack, and defend.

The recruiting of men began almost immediately, and by October 1778, the legion consisted of 330 officers and men. Kovats drilled these men according to the hussar tradition and tactics. They resembled their European counterparts in basic form, training, and organization. The soldiers of the Pułaski Legion were primarily French, German, and American, with a few Poles, Hungarians, Scots, and Irishmen.

CHAPTER 10

Winter at Valley Forge (1777)

Fight for Survival

After the defeat at Brandywine and the loss of Philadelphia, the Continental Congress decided to seize military activities. They used the winter months to prepare the Army for the campaign of 1778. Thousands of soldiers were dispatched to Valley Forge and simply hid in a forest. The conditions at Valley Forge were miserable. There were no facilities for them. The soldiers built everything from scratch. At the beginning of the winter camp, it was decided that soldiers would build wooden cabins out of freshly cut logs. They used mud to insulate the gaps between the logs and hew planks to cover the roofs with shingles. Kaz had to worry not only about his soldiers but also about horses.

Most soldiers came in ragged clothes, and over a quarter did not have shoes. Fortunately, December and January were not brutally cold. And then came February with blistering wind and snow. Without shoes, soldiers on duty had to return to the cabins after a few hours of service to warm up their feet or risk losing their toes to frostbite. More enterprising ones would wrap their feet with clothes and fashion soles out of tree bark, tied with lashings.

On 22 December 1777, just three days after they arrived at Valley Forge, Kaz went over to Washington to report on the status of his unit and especially the horses.

"It is tough for the soldiers here, but remember that a horse needs more than a man to survive," Kaz explained. "An average thousand-pound mount needs twenty pounds of hay a day. You can limit its ratio to ten pounds, but the horse will die if you cut it more. We could supplement their diet with oats, but it is also in short supply. I feel that the quartermasters forget about our horses. If it continues, we will have no horses left for spring."

"Yes, at times, I feel that this winter camp is the most difficult challenge for our army yet," Washington said.

"Our chances to winter here and improve the condition of the Army are bleak. The countryside is cleaned out of forage, and if we do not have adequate supplies, we will have fewer soldiers in spring than what we are bringing here now. It is a death trap," Kaz commented.

Washington agreed and said, "I am of a similar opinion, but we have run out of options. Here is the letter I am sending to Congress."

Henry Laurens, President of Congress, at York, Pa.
It is with infinite pain and concern that I transmit [to] Congress ...
Letters respecting the State of the Commissary's department. If these
matters are not exaggerated, I do not know from what cause this
alarming deficiency or rather total failure of Supplies arises; But
unless more Vigorous exertions and better regulations take place in
that line, and immediately, this Army must dissolve. I have done all in

my power by remonstrating, by writing to, by ordering the Commissaries on this Head... but without any good effect or obtaining more than a present scanty relief.

"We must find strength and motivation in our politicians and citizens to support the military. It is a test of the whole government system. Either we stand strong and true together, or we perish," Washington continued. "I must find a way to unite us all for our common cause."

[A log cabin at Valley Forge]

Initially, Kaz could not find enough men to build the stables, but around mid-January, when the cabins for most of his men were built, they began working on gazebos for horses. It was just in time before the February blast of cold weather. The worst enemies for them were diseases, hunger, and freezing temperatures. Many more died of illnesses and frostbite than of enemy fire.

Infantry Soldier

On the way from morning drills, Kaz noticed a human corpse lying on the ground between two fir trees. He jumped off his horse and examined the body closer. It was a teenage boy with a ragged shirt and no shoes. He lay on his back with his legs bent and knees pointing to the left. His left arm clutched his legs and pulled them towards his torso to preserve heat. His right arm was extended from the elbow up, pointing to the sky. His wide-open brown eyes were looking at the treetops and beyond. He seemed to be calling to someone above. Kaz touched his hand and realized that the boy was frozen solid.

Kaz jumped on his horse and galloped back to his regiment. Inquiring among the officers, he discovered the boy was sent to bring more logs for the cabins and did not return. His name was Jeffrey Johnson, and he joined the Army just before the Valley Forge. Kaz found Robert and told him to select a few men with shovels to give Jeff a proper burial.

"Robert, could you find out if he still has a mother, and could you write a letter to her on my behalf?" Kaz asked. "She deserves more than my broken English. I remember how I felt when I learned from my brother that my father had died and was buried in the steppes, far away from the family cemetery. It was a hard blow. Now, I think it was proper for my father to be buried there, and I would not move him even if I could. Jeffrey's mother deserves to know where her son is rested."

Kaz joined Robert and the soldiers dispatched to bury Jeffrey. The ground was frozen, and it took a while to dig up a grave. As they worked on breaking the icy crust, Kaz looked around and found a birch tree. He took a hatchet and started fashioning a cross. When one of the soldiers picked up Jeff's remains, Kaz glanced at the grave and said, "Stop, wait. It is not deep enough for a hero like Jeffrey. He needs proper six feet."

Kaz took a shovel and jumped into the hole. Robert grabbed the second shovel to push fresh dirt, falling back into the grave. Once Kaz was satisfied with the depth, he reached out with the shovel, and one of the soldiers pulled him up. They gently lowered Jeff's body to his eternal resting place. Kaz hammered the cross into the soft mound of fresh dirt. Robert carved Jeffrey's name on a birch plate.

Jeffrey Johnson
1662-1778
Soldier of the Continental
Army

Kaz lit a pine branch filled with sap and burned the letters on the freshly cut board. It charred the fresh wood making the letters black and visible against the white birch bark. They nailed the plate to the cross.

As the days moved on, Kaz noticed more bodies now and then. Finally, more than half of the soldiers at Valley Forge died of disease, frost, and starvation. Still, Washington and his men persevered, and 2,000 cabins were built within a month. The fourth-largest congregation of people in the colonies after Philadelphia, New York, and Boston was buzzing with activity.

David

David was pulling a heavy log through the thick brush. He was freezing and had nothing to eat for three days. The news was that Commissary William Buchanan, yet again, delivered little from the long list of needed supplies. There was no flour, bread, pork, salt beef, hams, veal, mutton, or fish. Farmers did not want to sell any cabbages, turnips, potatoes, lard, or molasses. They were complaining that Continental money was losing value so quickly that soon it would not be worth the printed paper. Some Tory farmers would tie Continental bills to their dogs' tails in a display of contempt. Still, the cabins had to be built, or soldiers would freeze.

David came barefoot to join the Army in September of last year. His preacher was giving fiery sermons about the need to defend the country from the King's greed. His friends joined before the harvest. Once the wheat was safely stocked in the barn, David kissed his Mother and walked for two days to register. Since then, he has learned how to march and shoot a musket. He was given some woolen cloth to wrap around his feet, but they were not enough to protect him from freezing when winter came. He worked as much as he could, but he had to keep his feet warm. One of his toes turned black. The older soldiers told him he should go to the hospital and cut off his toe. David was afraid of hospitals because so many died there.

With his bundled feet hurting him badly and strength leaving his young body, he slid, ripping his rags off his feet. The log fell on his left thigh, and David could not pull himself from underneath. Fortunately, soft snow falling on the ever-present mud cushioned the heavy impact, and David did not break any of his bones. Still, David could be doomed if someone did not show up to help him. He yelled "help" a few times, but nobody heard his pleas.

Luckily, Kaz was around riding through the forest and heard David. Soon, he found David wiggling under the heavy load. He jumped off his horse and lifted the tree trunk off David's leg. David was so exhausted that he did not move or say anything. Strength left his tired body, and he lost consciousness. Kaz dragged him over his saddle and rode towards his cabin. He called for Robert, and they carried the boy to Kaz's quarters. They wrapped David in a blanket and placed him by the fire.

"Fetch the doctor, Robert," Kaz said. "This boy won't make it; he needs help to survive."

When the doctor started examining David, he noticed the black toe and said, "He is emaciated and freezing. He would not have survived an hour if you hadn't found him. We must cut his pinky toe off before he wakes up. It makes no sense to wait."

The doctor opened his satchel and produced a knife, scissors, a bottle of alcohol, and some bandages. They laid the boy on the table, and the doctor proceeded with the operation. He disinfected the foot, cut the toe off, and cauterized the wound. Then, he wrapped the wound with clean bandages.

"Put him on my bed for now," Kaz said. "We shouldn't drag him around too much. Let him warm up and get some rest here."

"Poor boy, he gave his pinky toe to his new country. Hopefully, it will be enough," Robert said. Then, he turned to the doctor and said, "So much death and not a single enemy bullet. I hope we will survive the ordeal. The worst for me are the deceased with scarred faces full of ulcers and oozing puss. What are these ugly bumps on their faces with dents in the middle?"

"It is smallpox," the doctor answered.

"Oh, my God. It is what I thought, but I didn't even want to say it out loud. If it spreads, we might face another deadly enemy."

"Yes, sir. There are simply too many of us in a crowded place in miserable conditions to have a fighting chance against the red plague. This virus is more dangerous than the Loyalists."

"How many men can we lose to smallpox here at Valley Forge?" Robert inquired.

"With overcrowding, poor sanitary conditions, exhaustion, and malnutrition, I would venture over fifty percent, much more than on any battlefield. Don't forget that we still have great pox, also called syphilis, to worry about," the doctor continued.

"Is there anything we may do to stop the spread?" Kaz asked.

"We should inoculate all men if we can find enough antidote supplies. A big challenge remains, though. How can you convince a soldier to be cut with a knife and infected as a remedy? Some fear the inoculation more than death itself."

"Fear and ignorance are often as lethal as bullets. We cannot save these soldiers from smallpox if they do not get treated," Kaz said.

"It is yet another battle we must win, and Washington is doing all a man can do. He must find the supplies of serum and then fight men in Congress who are against inoculation," the doctor observed.

"What is the situation with the inoculations at this time?" Robert asked.

Currently, I inoculate new recruits daily. We calculate that we have more than half of the soldiers already treated. What about you? Did you have your inoculations?" the doctor asked.

"Not yet. I did not even have time to think about it," Kaz replied.

"I have a few doses in my satchel. We can do it now if you want," the doctor offered.

"Let us do it, Kaz. David had his toe removed. We should get smallpox treatments," Robert suggested.

"How long will it take?" Kaz asked.

"Just a moment. Let me get my scalpel ready," the doctor answered.

"Fine, let us do it. It would be silly to avoid British bullets only to be vanquished by a virus. What should we do, doc?" Kaz asked.

"Roll up your sleeve, sit down, and expect little pain," the doctor responded.

The doctor pulled the flasks with fibers soaked with infected pustular matter and alcohol, motioning to Kaz to get ready. As Kaz rolled up his sleeve and sat on a chair, the doctor disinfected the knife. With a practiced motion, he wiped Kaz's arm with a cotton swab soaked in alcohol and made a small incision on his arm. He placed a thread of the infected tissue into the wound and covered it with a cabbage leaf. Then, he completed the treatment by bandaging the wound.

"Did it hurt?" Robert asked as he rolled his sleeve and sat in his chair, ready for the procedure.

"I had worse," Kaz smiled, thinking about the numerous cuts, bruises, and heavy wounds he had experienced. "What now, doctor?" Kaz asked.

"Be careful about a week. If you do not get a high fever, you should be fine. I hope we will have enough soldiers following your lead and accepting the cure," the doctor observed.

"Did you remember to inoculate George Washington?" Robert asked.

"He does not need to be inoculated. He developed immunity to smallpox when he traveled with his half-brother Lawrence to the island of Barbados in the West Indies in 1751, where he was infected with the virus and was bedridden for months. Look at his face, and you will see the leftover scars. The same is with most of the British. They had serious bouts of smallpox on the islands, which gave the survivors immunity," the doctor continued.

"I heard that smallpox beat us in Quebec," Robert commented.

The doctor moved over to Robert's chair with his equipment and answered, "It killed more of us than the Loyalists did. Out of 1,900 Continental soldiers involved in the siege of Quebec, almost half were defeated by the virus. Then, we sent an additional 10,000 and lost 3,000 of them to smallpox. Smallpox canceled our dreams of the fourteenth colony in Canada."

The doctor deftly completed Robert's inoculation, closed his satchel, and said, "Gentlemen, I must run. Dying men are waiting for me. They do not want to leave us alone yet."

Robert rolled his sleeve over the bandage and said, "Thank you, doc. If the British only knew, they would kidnap you, and we would be finished here. In the meantime, keep up your good work."

"Death takes these boys before they can look the enemy in the eyes," said Kaz looking at David.

"Let's hope that this one will see his enemy," answered Robert, putting a few more logs into the fireplace. "Let's hope he will send some of them where he hasn't yet gone."

"Go find out who he is and who is looking for him. I will stay here," Kaz said.

Robert put his coat on and left the cabin. Kaz was sitting on his chair while David was still sleeping on his bed. Kaz stretched his legs and stared into the fire.

"I must find a way to reach local farmers and store owners. Otherwise, cold and starvation will win this war for the British," Kaz thought.

Kaz did not like the decision to winter the Army so close to the enemy without good prospects of keeping the soldiers fed and warm. This decision would cost the lives of countless patriots. Like the Bar Confederates, Continentals attracted the best of the best, the most motivated and willing to fight for their rights. He knew he needed more supplies and better shelter for every horse in his unit. He decided to spend much of his personal funds to dress and feed his regiment, but he did not have nearly enough to save the whole Army.

His sister Anna wrote to him that she could release some assets from their estates frozen by the Russians, but not near enough to what Kaz used to have at his disposal before the Bar Confederation. If not for the Russian control of Poland, Kaz could finance the needs of all his soldiers at Valley Forge. Unfortunately, his family sacrificed its wealth on the altar of the Commonwealth of Poland-Lithuania. Still, if he, his brothers, and mainly their father had not fought that hard, risking everything, he would probably never have gone to America.

As a Brigadier General, Kaz decided to fight every day to save as many soldiers as possible. Valley Forge was a battle that had to be won, or the war might be lost.

The door opened wide, and Robert walked in with a shirt and trousers in his hands. Pointing to the lying soldier, Robert said, "He is David Rogers from the local militia," and put the clothes on the bed by David. "He had already built his cabin with his dozen, but so many others were still working on their shelters. David did not have shoes, so he could not spend too much time in the cold, mud, and snow. Still, when he felt warm enough, he would go and help his friends. Today, he decided to bring some logs for Jonathan and Bart's cabin. He went into the woods, and they had not heard from him since. They looked carefully around, but nothing; he vanished into thin air."

David started stirring in Kaz's bed. When they looked at him, he opened his eyes and said, "Water, give me some water, please." David's eyes were burning with fever, but he looked much better. His face lost the white-bluish sheen of a man near death. His cheeks were burning red hot. Kaz got up, took some water from a bucket next to the door with a ladle, and went over to David.

"Do I know you?" David asked. "I am burning hot. I don't recognize your face."

"I am General Kazimierz Pułaski. You are in my cabin. Here. Have a sip of water," answered Kaz leaning over David.

David rushed to stand up at attention but only managed to raise his head and fell on the pillow, exhausted.

"Drink the water. You will salute me later. Now, I order you to get better. Rest and get your strength back," Kaz said.

"Yes, Sir, General, Sir," answered David and started drinking the water. Kaz circled between the bucket and David a few more times. When he went over to his bed again, he saw David sleeping soundly with a hint of a smile on his lips.

Next week, when Kaz was looking over some paperwork, the door to his cabin opened wide, and David came in with a bundle of firewood. He was proudly sporting regular cavalry boots and a black woolen jacket.

"Anything else, General, Sir? David asked.

"That will do. You may go to your cabin. I will fetch you if I need anything. How is your leg?"

"Couldn't be better, Sir. My feet don't hurt, and I can attend to all my duties. I never knew that you could be outside in winter and your feet would not hurt," said David smiling as he left the cabin.

Wigilia

For Kaz, his cousin Captain Jan Zieliński and other Poles in Kaz's Legion, December 24 had a special meaning. Every Polish household in Poland and worldwide prepares a traditional supper on that day. According to the Bible, Wigilia (the Vigil) is waiting for baby Jesus to be born. The family gets together and waits for the first star to appear on the horizon to start a carefully choreographed Christmas gathering. It begins with a breaking the bread ceremony, followed by dinner and caroling around a festooned Christmas tree. Wigilia usually ends with a Pasterka (the Shepherds), the midnight mass.

Opłatek, a Christmas wafer, is critical to the Wigilia breaking of the bread ceremony. It is a rectangular, thinly rolled biscuit around six by four inches made of wheat flour and water, like the altar bread, which in the form of round, approximately three-inch disks is served by Catholic priests during communion. It is embossed with images of the Virgin Mary, Jesus, the nativity scene, or the star of Bethlehem. It commemorates the last supper, where Jesus shared bread and wine with his disciples.

[Opłatek, Polish Christmas wafer]

Before the dinner begins, an opłatek is shared between the participants. Family members and guests each receive a piece of opłatek from the host of the Wigilia supper. The tradition is to split into pairs and offer opłatek to someone who wishes the partner all the best for the upcoming year and breaks a tiny piece with every wish. He then swallows a handful of little morsels to complete the ceremony. The participants go from person to person to make sure they share and break bread with everyone in pairs of two.

One must keep an opłatek so that only a tiny part is offered for the breaking. Some guests, especially children, might break off half of the provided piece on the first try; then, you have nothing to share with other guests. By doing it every year, you practice the eloquence of well-wishing. You listen to some around the table who have a gift for it and turn the well-wishing ceremony into an oratory art. Even the least spoken get better with it every year. A piece of the wafer is also given to domestic animals.

Polish soldiers at Valley Forge began getting ready for the Wigilia weeks ahead, planning to gather in Kaz's headquarters. They included Robert and Michael Kovats, who also contributed to the preparation. Jan went fishing while Robert found a Noble fir for a Christmas tree. At the same time, David and Jan were working on decorations. Food was scarce at Valley Forge, but for what was the Polish ingenuity. Jan Zieliński even made sauerkraut for the occasion. He found a twenty-pound oak barrel, packed it with chopped cabbage, added rock salt, and waited. After two weeks, the sauerkraut was ready. Kaz got a tablecloth from the nuns and brought hay, which he put under the tablecloth. As tradition dictated, they set up a table with an extra seat and a plate for an unexpected guest. Maybe even Jesus would come and enjoy the Wigilia taking the empty chair.

David was checking the sky for the first star when someone knocked at the door. Most of them recognized the visitor. He was a Polish military engineer working for the Continental Army, Colonel Tadeusz Kościuszko.

[Andrzej Tadeusz Bonawentura Kościuszko]

"Lord Brothers, I learned that there were Poles at Valley Forge. I came here knowing that you would celebrate Wigilia. I also knew you would save an extra seat for an unexpected guest. The problem is that there are two of us," Tadeusz Kościuszko said. He came together with his adjutant, Agrippa Hull, an African American free man assigned to Kościuszko by the Army.

"Of course, we have a saved seat, and we will also have one for your slave," Kaz answered.

"He is not a slave. He is a free man like you or me," Tad laughed.

"You both are welcome. As the saying goes, "Guest home, God home," answered Kaz, getting up. "I apologize for the 'slave' remark, Agrippa. It is so confusing here. I don't quite understand this notion of freedom for all and slavery for some at the same time."

Agrippa bowed and started shaking hands as all around the table came over to Tad and Agrippa, shaking their hands and giving them a bear hug. In no time, an extra seat and a plate were arranged for Agrippa, and everyone sat down around the table.

Tad took his seat and said, "You must explain to Agrippa that we Poles are not like your average white man here. He was concerned that you would not be pleased to have a black man around your table."

"Dear Agrippa," Jan answered. "None of us has any slaves. We will never have one. We are against slavery. We believe in freedom for all, no exceptions, period."

"Living in Poland, we experienced Tatar raids. They were capturing people for the slave markets of the Ottoman Empire. It is a long and painful story. Some families in Poland, especially in our Wild East, have family members missing due to these raids. Rest assured that here, under this roof and during this holy gathering, you are one of us celebrating the coming of our Lord Jesus," Kaz said.

Suddenly, David jumped up from his seat and ran to the door.

"Here, see, the first star. You said that everything would start when we see the first star!" David screamed excitedly. Everyone looked at Kaz, who took a platter of opłatek wafers and started passing them around the table. Since it was the first Wigilia for David, Michael, and Agrippa, they watched others and followed their example.

Kaz went over to Michael Kovats and started breaking pieces of his opłatek, saying, "All the best, my friend (crack). I am so glad we are here together, fighting for what is just. I wish you success with our lancers and patience with the quartermasters (crack). Stay safe and healthy (crack). I hope that one day you will return to a free Hungary and visit me at Zazulińce for a glass of mead (crack)," said Kaz, with each "crack" breaking a piece of Michael's opłatek. Then he gave Michael a long hug.

"I hope you will drink a glass of mead with me," Michael answered, knowing that Kaz had avoided alcohol.

"With you, I will, Michael."

"I wish you success with the cavalry (crack). I hope you will complete your cavalry manual for the Continental Army (crack). I trust that thousands of lancers will read it and train to your standards (crack). We have a long road ahead, but we should reach our goal with God's grace." Michael took a handful of opłatek pieces, which he had broken off Kaz's opłatek, and swallowed them.

Each participant took turns sharing the opłatek and wishing fortune and good health. Agrippa went over to David and said, "It is you and me who are born here and do it for the first time. I hope that our wishes will be met. I wish you the end of war and peace for all, David (crack)," Agrippa said.

"Thank you. I hope that I will see my mother and my priest. I will tell them about Wigilia. I am glad you are here, and we can share this meal. I wish you a long life and that everything you pray for will come true (crack). I pray that when this war is over, you will have a piece of land that you can call your own and that people will respect you for what you have done for this country of ours (crack)."

Agrippa looked at this young Continental and smiled. Then, they tried a hug, which Poles were sharing so easily. They both agreed they needed more practice to feel natural when hugging a man.

Kaz found Robert and had to wait until he finished breaking the opłatek with Jan. As Jan and Robert finished their exchange, Kaz stood in front of his friend.

"Robert, where have you dragged me here, so far away from Poland? When will we be done with this war? No matter. I wish you health, luck, and happiness (crack). I wish you could take me on my ship all the way to Scotland (crack). I wish we could both see your glens and all family and friends you left behind (crack). I wish we beat the British together (crack)," Kaz said while breaking little pieces off Robert's opłatek.

"Kaz, I thought it would be a year or two with your father, and I would be on my way home to Scotland. And here we are on the other side of the globe. How many years? Fight after fight, war after war. Imagine owning a ship and sailing from Poland to Scotland under the British nose. We don't pay them any tax. We ship Polish mead and vodka and bring our whisky in return. Stay strong, stay healthy, and make all your soldiers train to your level of expectation (crack). I wish that you will not be betrayed anymore (crack).

"Finally, I wish all your dreams come true (crack). Finally, make your wish, and it will come true. What would you like to happen for you?" asked Robert looking his friend in the eyes.

"My father is dead. I lost my lands. I wish I could go back to Poland and clear my name from the sin of regicide. I would like to see Zazulińce and my sisters. I would like to see Helena."

"Helena? I knew that there was a woman."

"She is more than just a woman."

"Is there anything more you want to tell me about her?"

"There is nothing more to say," said Kaz looking at the Christmas tree.

They felt an extra bond of friendship growing among them with every wish. It gave them hope, trust, and inner peace desperately needed during this cold and hungry winter of stubborn daily fight for survival through fatigue, pain, disease, and cold. It was an annual ritual for Poles, which they always welcomed and embraced, knowing how much it helped them grow the bond of national unity and strength. For Michael, David, and Agrippa, it was a new experience. They found it overwhelming. It gave them a boost of solidarity and fraternity, which they had never experienced at that level.

They all sat down around the table, appreciating the company, the abundance, and the variety of food, which they did not expect to see in this starving camp. Most of all, they appreciated the honesty and sincerity of the interactions.

"We have twelve dishes as tradition dictates," started Kaz. "Thank you all for whatever you had to do to bring the potatoes, cabbage, fish, and soups to this table. Tom and Michael joined together to have it all cooked and seasoned with spices I have not seen here in America yet. Enjoy."

They started with white borscht and potatoes. Fried fish and potatoes followed. Cabbage with peas was the next dish, followed by mushroom-filled pierogi. In the end, they enjoyed a cup of red beet borscht. Jan was incredibly proud to find lemon and garlic to spice the red borscht just right.

"Tad, why didn't you join us as your brother Józef did and fight as a Bar Confederate?" Jan asked Tad.

"It was a question of honor and the word I gave. I studied at Cadet Corp for the King at that time. We took an oath to fight for Poland and the King. Rather than fight you, I left for France and studied engineering as the situation developed. I thought that the time to fight would come. I did not want to break my oath."

"I know what you mean," Kaz commented. "I had the same problem when the Russians caught me at the beginning of our fight and forced me to swear that I would give up my arms. Once they let me go, I resumed the fight treating my oath to them as forced under duress and therefore invalid. It has bothered me ever since they humiliated me into breaking my word. Till today, it hangs over me like a dark cloud. They stabbed me deep to the core of who I am. I understand your dilemma, Tad."

"What happened at Ticonderoga?" Robert asked.

"Congress sent me to Fort Ticonderoga to do the surveys and decide how to improve the defenses. I suggested the construction of the battery at SugarLoaf, but the garrison commander, Brigadier General Arthur St. Clair, refused. He thought it was a waste of time and men," Tad answered.

"Would that battery not help stop the British army's advance when General John Burgoyne arrived in July 1777?" Robert inquired.

"Yes, it would have, but we were routed there and had to withdraw. Then, I was commissioned to delay the British advances. We fell trees, dammed rivers, and destroyed bridges. It slowed their supply train and gave us time to break contact with their Army."

"Funny how I did the similar work delaying the British at Brandywine," Kaz remarked. "I was doing everything possible to slow them down, and eventually, General Washington succeeded in breaking contact and losing our trail."

"So, I hear. General Washington told me once that he would not have to be worried about his back if only he had more Polish officers," Tad responded.

"I heard that they let you do what you wanted at Saratoga," Robert continued with his questions, happy that he had a chance to meet such an accomplished officer.

"Oh, Saratoga. Yes, we built quite a system. When the British showed up, they were sitting ducks. We covered them with our artillery fire and reduced their numerical advantage. In the end, General Burgoyne was left with no other option but to surrender to General Gates."

"You were lucky that General St. Clair was not there. We would have to run again," Agrippa remarked.

"How is it for you, Agrippa? There are not many blacks fighting for the Continentals," Michael asked.

[Agrippa Hull, Berkshire Museum]

"First, you have to be free to do as you wish. Then, you must trust that your fight makes sense. For me, I don't care. I fight for myself. I fight for my honor and my liberty. The British can offer me nothing but a bunch of lies. So, I fight with the Continentals."

"How is fighting with Tad?"

"He is great. I learned so much, especially about engineering. He also gave me hope that some whites are human beings, not hungry flesh-eating beasts. Some, especially down south, look at us and see an animal. It makes them cannibals who prey on other humans, I guess. I appreciate Tad's friendship," answered Agrippa, taking another serving of fish.

"I wonder how you could cope with his name. Kościuszko, it cannot get any worse than that," Robert joked.

"Yeah, I loved the way Tad handled it. Some wanted to address him as Colonel K. His response was, 'I can risk my life to fight for you. You can risk breaking your tongue and pronouncing my name, Kościuszko. After that, I saw many practicing his name. And you know what? They did it. It is surprising what you can do if you honestly try."

"What a story," David exclaimed. "I have to admit that I did not even think about trying, but now I will. Colonel Kościuszko, Kościuszko. You are right, Agrippa. It can break your tongue."

Everybody started laughing, but David continued practicing until he could pronounce it almost as well as Agrippa.

293

Jan produced a bottle of moonshine, which he had manufactured. He stood up and started pouring it for all the companions. He looked at Kaz and asked, "What shall we sing first?"

"What about 'Shepherds Arrived at Bethlehem'?" Kaz proposed. "Lead on, Jan."

They all started a song, which each Pole heard and sang from the time they could remember. Their strong, sonorous voices were raised when the time for refrain came.

Glory on the Highest,
Glory on the Highest
And peace on earth…

"I heard that you studied music and composed as well. Is it true, Colonel?" Michael asked Tad Kościuszko.

"Yes, I did," Tad answered. "It was in a different world, a different time. Let me see." Tad got up and moved over to the Christmas tree by the fireplace. He looked at the glowing logs and poked them with a long stick. Then, he started sadly and longingly:

Little baby Jesus
Lies in a manger
Cries from cold
His Mother could not afford a dress…

Agrippa joined Tad for the refrain. It looked like he must have heard this song many times before. His profoundly resonant bass harmonized with Tad's tenor. They all stepped into a somber mood, thinking about the dear ones left behind in the colonies and around the world. Kaz decided to change the melancholy atmosphere and asked, "Lord Brothers, what about 'Today in Bethlehem'?"

Today in Bethlehem
Today in Bethlehem
Happy tidings
Virgin Maiden, Virgin Maiden
Gave birth to a son
Glory on the Highest...

The caroling and merry-making continued late into the night. They all had to get up early for their duties, but no one wanted this sacred moment to end. Eventually, Tad and Agrippa rose first. They bid everyone farewell and mounted their destriers. Jan and Kaz went out to say their goodbyes. When they left, Jan went over to his mount and returned with a small leather sack.

"Check it out, cousin," said Jan untying the leather strap.

"What is it?" asked Kaz looking at something that resembled gunpowder. "It is too dark. I have no idea. I give up."

"This is my gold," Jan answered, smiling. "It is the sand from the Wisła riverbank in Mazowsze (Mazovia). It is our homeland soil. I took it with me on the road and had been carrying it all the time. Whenever I feel homesick, I grab this sack and put it behind my shirt, close to my heart."

"Thank you for sharing it with me. I might ask you to let me have it one day."

"Any time, any time, cousin. I hope we will see the banks of the Wisła and walk barefoot on the sand, feeling how it squeezes between our toes," Jan said. He took his sack back and gave his cousin a long hug. They both stopped for a while, thinking that they heard the voice of the boatmen carrying grain from Podole to Gdańsk, but they were mistaken. It was only the wind howling between the huts.

The rest of the revelers followed on foot to their respective cabins. The night was cold and windy, but the food and memories of the evening gave everyone a boost, which carried them over the dreariness and misery of winter at Valley Forge.

The Drills

General Charles Lee used to fight in Poland for King Stan. Since the Seven Year War between England and France, they had known each other. On 26 May 1772, as Kaz was escaping Częstochowa, Lee was promoted to lieutenant colonel of the Crown Army of Poland by King Stan. Lee was born in Darnhall, Cheshire, England, in 1732 and moved to America in 1773, where he bought an estate in western Virginia. When fighting in the American War of Independence broke out, Lee volunteered his services to the Patriot cause. With his military training and experience, he was hoping to get a commission as the Commander in Chief of the Continental Army but was passed over for General Washington, partly because Washington was a native-born American. Before the American Revolution, Lee fought for the British in the northeast and knew the Iroquois well. He married the daughter of the Mohawk chief.

When Artemas Ward resigned as second in command of the Continental Army, Lee assumed the position. Although second in command, Lee did not hesitate to criticize Washington and openly judge him as inferior. Among the challenges posed by the British, Washington had to protect his position among the Continentals and stay on top of intrigues within the newly minted American government.

As with the General Command of the Bar Confederation, Kaz was not a part of the infighting in the colonies, but he knew that among four cavalry commanders, Moylan was openly hostile to him. General Washington's cavalry consisted of 727 troopers and officers under four regimental commands, divided among colonels Moylan, Bland, Sheldon, and Baylor. Kaz often delegated over one thousand horse units to subordinates during his command in Poland. At times, Kaz led twenty thousand men, a body twice the size of the whole Continental Army. Kaz could not see the point of having as many officers in so small a cavalry, but the subtle politics of unwarlike men often eluded him. Apparently, General Washington agreed; in what came as a bitter surprise to the various colonels, Kaz was promoted to Brigadier General and outranked them all with the stroke of a pen.

During one of the meetings attended by the four cavalry commanders, Washington and Lee, the conversation focused on Kaz. Colonel Stephen Moylan was famous for first using the term the United States of America in a letter dated January 1776. As the commander of the Fourth Continental Light Dragoons and the secretary to General Washington, he did not appreciate the honest, blunt opinions Kaz shared concerning the poor organization of the American cavalry and regarded them as brash and impertinent.

Forgetting that he was also an immigrant who settled in Philadelphia in 1768, Moylan said, "I don't think that we need to sit here and listen to the comments of an officer who just stepped off a boat."

Lee raised his brows and observed, "Colonel, it would behoove you to pay more attention to what General Pułaski has to say. You might learn a great deal from him. Your reconnaissance of Brandywine would have cost us the Army if not for the intervention of the Count. Surely, it is better to learn from a friend in camp than an enemy in the field."

"It was not I, Sir, who penned Colonel Baylor's scouting reports, which were received too late and were misused once received. Be that as it may, the officer should learn English first, and only then would he be able to properly relate to the farmers who complain that he is robbing them blind in purchases and requisitions. Remember that we have only one-third of the population supporting us, with another third supporting the British and the last third on the fence looking for who will come out on top."

"We do not have time for political concerns. We must start winning this war now, or we can forget about politics," Lee responded.

"I don't think that General Pułaski is fit to lead the cavalry with all the demands put on it from the Army. A man such as he could not be entrusted with the clerical duties coincidental to logistics, security, reconnaissance, maintaining command and control over so vast a force as our proud Continental Cavalry," Moylan proffered.

Trying to steer his officers toward consensus, Washington smiled and suggested, "Maybe we should consider diversification and look at various roles played by horses, separating combat from logistical support."

Colonel George Baylor, commander of the 3rd Regiment of Light Dragoons, nodded and remarked, "I cannot deny that his skills are impressive, our General Pułaski. I have observed a marked improvement in the men since he took responsibility for their training. We should give him credit where credit is due."

General Charles Henry Lee looked at Moylan and said, "You might not know it, but I served as a colonel for the King of Poland once, years ago now. Even then, Count Pułaski had a reputation as a man you did not want riding against you. He made fools of more commanders than Colonel Moylan here might believe." He offered Moylan a good-natured smile to break some of the mounting tension at the table but received only an icy glance in return.

"Anyway," continued Lee, "it seems that we would be foolish to ignore such an officer when delegating command, sir." He offered a deferential nod to General Washington at the head of the table.

Moylan started shaking his head, smirked tartly, and said, "How can you compare some remote parts of Europe to the fight for freedom from tyranny against the British? We deal with the French and the Spanish while the Dutch and the Portuguese watch every move with actuarial interest."

Lee took a deep breath and responded in a measured, assertive tone, "Dear Colonel. It seems that you have a limited understanding of the totality of world politics. Let me enlighten you. Poland has about the same territory we have here, one million square kilometers, around 430 square miles. While we expanded from 2,000 in 1625 to 2 million citizens in 1775, Poland shrunk from 20 million to 12 million. The action is there. This population reduction is due to continuous foreign interests always pursuing the richness of Poland. Our war lasted four years while they have been fighting for over one hundred years.

"They are fighting because that 'remote' part of Europe, as you called it, is worth the fight. They are fighting over control of the most fertile lands in Europe. When they fight, prices of wheat and oats double and triple in France and England. I predict that the world will be fighting for that stretch of land for years to come, not because Poles do something right or wrong. They will fight there because it is a valuable piece of global property."

"I don't see how their wars relate to our war despite your lecture on the economy of wheat production. We must stay focused on what is ahead of us here rather than be distracted by some tales of fame and glory on the other side of the world. Besides, if they lose their crop production, we will gain. Some of us are already prospering by selling our wheat to France, Spain, Holland, and the West Indies. Aren't you one of them?" Moylan remarked.

"As second in command, I analyzed what General Pułaski could offer to our needs. First, our ambassador to France, Benjamin Franklin, admitted that he knew precious little about Poland, and only thanks to some sound advice in France he focused more on the Count. He was surprised and impressed with what he had learned. Most importantly, he realized that Europe did not end in England or France.

"Did you know General Pułaski experienced five years of continuous combat against overwhelming odds? He attacked four strategically critical fortresses. He fought four major battles in 1768, ten in 1769, four in 1770, and five in 1771, not counting dozens of minor skirmishes. He was heavily wounded at least five times."

"It would be nice if he won any of them," Moylan remarked, still unconvinced.

"He won most of them. He took Poland's most critical military and spiritual fortress and held it for three years until he was chased away by a smear campaign in 1772. We are lucky to have a commander of his caliber on our side. It is up to us to learn from him.

"I understand hurt pride, believe me. I know it is not easy for you all to accept his leadership and rank. It is not always easy for me to follow General Washington, but in the end, it is not about our personal preferences. We must unite and put our country's needs, which you so aptly called the United States of America, as our main priority.

"We can spread the blame for Brandywine's mistakes on whomever we want. Ultimately, he saved our skin there, and we either learn from it, or we lose looking for someone to take the responsibility but neglect the needed improvement of our command structure."

General Lee supported General Howe's recommendation that Kaz command his unit independently of every other General's individual needs for horses; instead, responding only to the commander-in-chief. Lee suggested a more significant force, but Congress approved only 68 cavalrymen and 200 infantries for the Pułaski Legion. Still, it was Kaz's command, and he could do what he deemed proper, needing only Washington's approval. His headquarters were in Baltimore, from which he traveled extensively.

General Charles Lee decided to observe one of Kaz's training sessions personally. The Legion was not at full strength yet, but the practice continued daily unabated.

Before the main exercise, Kaz and Mike demonstrated some individual drills to the cavalrymen. They started by charging one another and slapping the mounts with straw mats. They were provoking the horses to retaliate rather than obey the rider. Then, they rode in the middle of two rails spread twenty feet apart and stopped next to one another. On a horn signal, the horses started pushing each other sideways, trying to move the opponent into the rail, while the riders focused on protecting their inside legs from injury.

The following pattern was a tight double eight. Mike and Kaz followed the pattern simultaneously, with the eights forming an 88.

They were passing each other no more than three feet away on the inner curve of the circles. The pace of the workout increased steadily from a slow step to trot and gallop.

The last was the stop-and-go drill. It started with Mike and Kaz standing ten feet apart while a line of riders passed to the left, right, and between them, screaming and slapping their mounts with straw mats. The horses stood still as if oblivious to the mayhem around them. Suddenly, they both jumped into action and charged some of the riders, pushing them side to side, which ended with some riders falling off their mounts.

Eventually, Kaz ordered all cavalrymen to line up in a single file and stand on their saddles. It was a focusing exercise for the soldiers and their mounts. It required extraordinary balance and focus. When Kaz introduced this drill, most cavalrymen considered it impossible to master. Much to their surprise and delight, the impossible became an impressive routine with each day of practice.

[US Army Cavalry Drill, a 1911 postcard, eBay]

In today's main practice, Mike Kovats, Robert Burns, and Kaz's cousin Captain Jan Zieliński led the coordinated assault on enemy positions, which comprised three rows of straw targets, twenty in each row. The objective was to attack, feign panic, and disperse in apparent disarray, only to reappear from two directions to cut the enemy to pieces. It required impressive coordination between infantry and cavalry formations. The drill depended on timing and an ability to read and adapt to new orders at full gallop.

Kaz was signaling commands to the infantrymen and forty-four lancers. General Lee saw Kaz appear at the edge of the woods. A few cannons started blaring into the field. Kaz waved his arm and folded one of his cavalry wings like a bird. Squeezed infantry started pouring from underneath the wing, like the lava of mud sprinkled with the stars of bayonets. Like vultures, the troops charged, seeking death and destruction.

The speed of charge and timing of the maneuvers impressed General Lee. He felt for a moment that the Legion would wipe out the invisible enemy. He was bracing for war cries and gory glory. Instead, Kaz galloped over.

"I have only forty-four of them now. Congress allowed a maximum of sixty-eight. Imagine what we could do with five hundred. I would have blown the Hessians at Brandywine to smithereens with force like that. They would be able to give out one volley without a clear target, and that would be the end to their aura of invincibility."

"Kaz, I will remember this training forever. I had no idea that horses could move that fast in tight formations. Once you dispersed them and they started galloping to and fro, I thought it was all over. It looked like they messed up the signals. There was no way to bring them to order again. And then, how the heck did you pull it through? When the foot soldiers started running, and the lancers showed up at full speed, I thought they would simply trample poor fellows to death. Wow, if I were your enemy, I would die just looking at your maneuvers. It would make me dizzy and confused."

"Let's try this," Kaz proposed. He produced a burlap blanket and handed it to the General. "Hold it in your right hand extended like that, and do not let go no matter what," shouted Kaz, circling the General. He galloped one hundred feet away and turned his mount on a dime.

Kaz then charged at full speed, pulling his long lance out of nowhere and throwing it at the General. Lee felt beads of cold sweat dripping down his forehead and neck, but he held onto the burlap target. The lance hit the blanket two feet below the outstretched arm of the General and stuck in the ground, leaving the third of it still piercing the veil. Then, Kaz moved over even faster and closer. Suddenly his saber cut the burlap hardly a foot from the General's arm, and the lance fell to the ground. The General dropped his arm and shook his head. It was death waving at him. The blow was so quick and devastatingly accurate that the General couldn't react even if he tried.

Kaz returned thinking about his first clumsy attack at Captain Valery Riazin in Podole near Zazulińce and about Tom putting him through his awkward paces with the saber in an apple orchard. It was so long ago. Since then, so much has happened.

Kaz decided to take a detour through the countryside on the way to his headquarters. Riding leisurely, admiring the lush vegetation, he spotted a few blueberries hiding between small elliptical dark green leaves. Kaz came closer and saw a patch of low bushes covered with dark blueberries. He jumped off his horse and picked a few. Before he knew it, he was running from bush to bush, filling his hat. When he filled it to the brim, Kaz jumped on his mount and carried the trophy back to his cabin.

He rushed through the door and placed the hat on the table. Admiring his find, he called his orderly, screaming, "Witek! I mean, David! David report!"

David appeared in the doorway and looked surprised at the hat full of blueberries.

"Listen, David, can you find me a quart of raspberries and some heavy cream?" asked Kaz.

"I see what I can do, sir," David said, wondering where he would find the raspberries. The task turned out more straightforward than he expected. The first person he asked for the strange request was Sergeant Breen. William lived with a Native woman who happened to have some raspberries and cream in their cabin. David returned to Kaz's headquarters with two cups, one full of raspberries and one with cream.

Kaz looked at the cups with delight and exclaimed, "Thank you, David. You made my day. That will be all, thank you."

When David left, Kaz took raspberries with blueberries and placed them in the biggest bowl he could find. He poured the cream over them and gingerly mixed the contents. Sitting before his window with the bowl facing him, he smiled and admired the view. He closed his eyes and, clearly, heard Helena's laughter. He could swear that she was standing in the field of blueberries beaming at him worry-free as only she knew how.

Joe

One day just after sunset, Agrippa Hull visited Kaz unannounced. Rather than smiling and relaxing as Kaz remembered him from Wigilia, Agrippa seemed nervous and unsure of himself. He did not look Kaz in the eyes but was casting glances around the cabin and turning his head towards the door. Kaz was concerned that maybe he had some bad news regarding Tadeusz Kościuszko.

"There is no need to coat it," started Kaz. "Tell me what is on your mind. I can take it no matter how hard it seems." Agrippa smiled sheepishly and noticeably forced himself to look at Kaz.

"Come on, Agrippa," Kaz encouraged him. "Take a seat and relax. We are soldiers. We have seen a lot and heard even more. How hard can it be?" Agrippa sat by the fireplace sideways to Kaz. He looked at the glowing ambers, suddenly picked up the chair and turned it to face Kaz.

"It is not about me. There are things here that we do not talk about openly. They hang over us like a dark cloud, yet we pretend they don't exist." Agrippa stuttered," Let me tell you candidly what is on my mind."

"It is always the best way. No matter what it is, I promise I can handle the news," encouraged Kaz.

"You are recruiting soldiers to your Legion, and I know some of them are deserters and criminals."

"Yes, I have permission to look around and select whoever I deem fit, no matter his record," Kaz answered.

"There are mistakes, transgressions, and crimes. I understand. Still, there are things that no one here will forgive," Agrippa continued.

"What is on your mind, Agrippa? Let me have it."

"It is the issue of African Americans like me. Some of us are treated not like men but like property. I know you are against slavery, but would you go so far as to accept a runaway slave into your Legion?" Agrippa turned his head around to the left and right, relaxing his neck muscles. It seemed that the most challenging part of this conversation was behind him. He looked at Kaz and waited.

Kaz took a deep breath and started slowly, "Thank you for your trust. I can feel the unease between promises and the hard realities of life in the Colonies. They warned and even challenged me a few times because of my choice of men, who were questionable in some eyes. A man's record, nationality, religion, or skin color are superficial. I am interested in my soldier's spirit, ability, stamina, and motivation. I want to go to war with him, not sit and debate moral or ethical conundrums in a tavern for a few hours. It is a question of life and death, not someone's opinion or judgment."

"The person I have in mind will be a great soldier, but he is a fugitive slave."

"If you vouch for him, it is enough for me to meet him and decide then and there."

"I can call him here now. He is waiting in the bushes."

309

"OK, bring him in, and we will talk. It should not take me long to give you my answer."

Agrippa was back in a few minutes, accompanied by a medium-height, muscular man in his mid-twenties with a round face full of bumps and a deeply dark, ebony skin color. He was wearing an osnaburg shirt torn at the elbows and a pair of trousers, which have seen better days. Kaz looked at the man with surprise and asked, "Is your name Joe?"

"Yes, Sir," answered Joe, more surprised than Kaz. He did not dare to ask how Kaz happened to know his name. He started thinking that agreeing to come here was a big risk and a mistake.

Kaz went to his chest and reached for one of the shirts. He walked over to Joe and handed him the shirt saying, "You have had this shirt for quite a while. I don't think that anyone can repair it with a needle. It is time to throw it out and get a new shirt. Here, throw your old top in the fire and put this one on. Your shirt hardly covers your chest any longer."

Kaz remembered a poster he saw in Carlin's tailor shop in Boston. He was sure the man standing before him was the fugitive slave Joe from the pamphlet. He also remembered telling Robert, "If I met Joe, I would give him twenty dollars to stay away from his owner." True to his word, Kaz reached into his wallet and produced a twenty-dollar bill saying, "Here, Joe, buy yourself a set of clothes and take a bath."

Joe hesitatingly took the money, put it in his pocket, and started taking his osnaburg shirt off. With the shirt in his hand, he looked at Kaz, who nodded. Joe tossed his tattered rag into the fireplace. Kaz noticed a six-inch letter "s" burned into Joe's flesh on the left at his elbow's height as he was leaning over. He remembered that Joe's owner was Charles Smith.

"I want you to report to Sergeant Breen tomorrow at six p.m., dressed and washed."

Joe stood in the middle of the room, slightly bent, confused, and uncertain, still unable to understand what had just happened.

Kaz smiled reassuringly, saying, "Joe, I know that Agrippa will explain all details to you better than I could. I just want to let you know that I read your owner, Mr. Smith's letter looking for you when I was in Boston. It is how I guessed your name. As long as I am the commander of the Pulaski Legion, I will vouch for you and fight anyone who would harm any of my soldiers. I know that, like Agrippa, you have your reason to stand up and fight. Who you are and how you contacted me stays between us three."

Recruiting a group of dedicated fighters willing to put their lives on the line was a challenge involving many tough decisions. A successful commander had to be a judge of character, ready to make hard choices and then live or die by them. It was one such moment.

311

CHAPTER 11

Haudenosaunee Territories (1778)

The Role of Cavalry

After surviving the difficulties of the winter camp at Valley Forge and Trenton, besides training his troops to be an effective, combat-ready strike force, Kaz assumed a more active role of a Brigadier General within the structures of the military power. To form a clear picture of all aspects of the war, he needed better intelligence of both strategic and tactical demands of his unit's role in the broader context of the Continental Army.

For Kaz, making quick tactical decisions and using force on a limited scale came naturally after five years of constant fighting in Poland. He remembered how his first decisions at the Bar Confederation's beginning helped take the fight to the Russians. He could maneuver his troops over large terrain and stay a step ahead of the enemy. Even if he lost a battle, he could escape, regroup, and often strike where and when the Russians least expected. He was caught and humiliated only once early in his career by the enemy, and he remembered how devastating it was. This experience helped him assess the situation at Brandywine and save Washington with his troops, although most of the command did not quite understand the danger and were too slow to react in time.

He knew that success depended on dictating the terms of engagement to your enemy, having operational initiative, and acting quickly and decisively for a weaker side. If a stronger enemy had time to weigh all options and meticulously execute his plan, the outcome was obvious; the stronger would win. However, if you took time away from him and made him react to your actions instead of executing his plans, the outcome might be quite the opposite. Therefore, you had to do everything to frustrate your enemy's plans and make him react to your initiative. Ideally, rather than executing his plans, the stronger enemy should be surprised by the weaker side and forced to respond. Soon, overwhelmed with the unpredictable course of events, he would abandon his plan and wait for the more vulnerable side to act first. Eventually, he might relinquish the initiative and merely react to the weaker opponent's tactics. This way, the stronger might get tired, and his potential advantage might disappear. Wisely selecting when to withdraw and when to strike, the weaker but more mobile and proactive opponent would win.

Assuming the role of Commander of the Horse assigned to him by the Continental Congress, Kaz had to know all aspects of the fight to stay on top of the game. Unfortunately, he had little information on the bigger picture of the goals and overall strategy. He was unsure what the Continentals were trying to accomplish in all aspects of their current situation. He was similarly perplexed as to the goals of the Iroquois.

Within all his doubts and frustrations, one thing was clear: his respect and, yes, admiration for George Washington and his role in stubbornly moving ahead despite the odds. Kaz knew that as a consummate soldier, one had to understand oneself and his enemy to win. He studied the Russians and knew what they had to offer in the strategy and tactics of war. Within the boundaries of the tools Kaz controlled, he was not defeated on the battlefield. He lost through Catherine's political maneuvering, which was beyond his grasp. He was no match for her power in wielding propaganda and manipulating international courts. Eventually, Kaz lost, destroyed by the blame of regicide, which hit him like the assassin's poison.

Kaz wanted to assist Washington to the best of his ability. He understood that he did not have much to offer in the fight in the internal and international political arenas. But he was confident that his knowledge of warfare and battle skills could enormously benefit Washington.

For the Continentals, fighting the British was a prominent and easily defined goal. Fighting the Natives, however, was much more complicated and questionable. When the British were fighting the French in America a hundred years before, both countries used the Natives on their sides. Kaz knew that the Iroquois Confederacy was a large country to the west of the colonies acknowledged by Great Britain, but he knew little about them except a few platitudes. He knew they were great warriors, and most were fighting on the side of the British. He also knew that they produced much-needed food, furs, and horses. The winter camp would have been much more tolerable if he could have used the Iroquois supplies at Valley Forge.

Kaz thought that making enemies of the Natives was a strategic mistake. Their decision to assist the British was explained to him due to their primitive outlook on life. Most Continentals called them "savages," but some of the Iroquois nations were still siding with the revolutionary cause and engaged in peaceful trade. He already knew that the Iroquois comprised six nations. Two of the six did not support the British. How was it possible that they were divided among themselves? Suppose they were so primitive and obtuse as the Continentals disrespectfully regarded them. If true, such simple-minded people would not tolerate two opposite ways of looking at the Loyalists and the Continentals. Why would they tolerate such opposing commitments within their ranks? Was it possible to convince some of the four nations supporting the British to join the American cause?

To Kaz, the newly formed United States, in many ways, resembled Poland. Both were large countries in the middle of a vast landmass. Further east from the Polish borders you focused on, the less knowledge and understanding the Polish decision-makers in the capital had. Those sitting in Warszawa often did not even want to be bothered with the information brought from the country's eastern borderlands. Poland had experts on matters involving the West. The problem was that Poland was never attacked by Belgium, Holland, France, Spain, or Portugal. Kaz knew of no one in Poland who was an expert in the far reaches of Poland's east, for example, China.

Similarly, colonists occupied only a narrow strip of the continental landmass close to the ocean. Their attention was focused on the east coast and even further east on England beyond the ocean. All but a few intrepid adventurers and explorers ventured west to seek new challenges and opportunities.

Like in Poland, the center in Philadelphia wanted to avoid being bothered too much by the far reaches of the continent. They wanted the British to go away and let them be. They wanted the profits from their narrow strip of continental landmass without the potential hassle of daily conflicts with the Natives and administrative responsibilities.

Kaz remembered that Poland was surprised by a savage attack from the east in the 13th century, over 500 years ago. Although it happened in the distant past, every Pole remembered that attack as if it happened yesterday. In Kraków, Poland's capital, a bugler sounded the alarm in 1243 to signal the approach of Mongolian raiders led by General Subutai. As he was blaring the warning tune, a Mongolian archer shot him through the neck, killing him instantly and stopping the alarm. When in Kraków, Kaz was immediately reminded of the story when he heard a trumpeter playing this interrupted tune hourly from the tall tower of the St. Mary's Church overlooking the main city square.

What if there was a more significant Native force lurking in the belly of America that no one knew about yet? Kaz realized that talking to Congress or lead strategists about such matters was a waste of time. He could not even convince them about the obvious; that they should use the horse like it was used in Poland, i.e., a strong military power to win battles with speed and surprising maneuver and police vast areas of land. Many in Congress looked at the horse from the British perspective, a powerful nation living on an island and moving around the world in ships. The Brits had little use for horses like the Commonwealth of Poland-Lithuania used them over huge terrain in continental Europe. If Americans wanted to be a force here on this continent and not only a fleeting result of the British colonization, they had to understand the importance of horses and use them properly.

For the British coming from an island, any conquered terrain was just property to be exploited, nothing more. In the long run, such an attitude would not work for US nationals. Treating indigenous people inhabiting their country and the land beyond the colonies as existing outside the framework of society and culture as inferior savages would bring structural problems for the future. Looking at a country next to you, manipulated by the British to fight against you, as just a band of "savages" acting without any rationale was a primitive way to approach continental challenges. He noticed that the Continentals who spent some time with the Natives shared his outlook. However, the majority relied on newspapers, books, and hearsay as the basis for their opinions.

Kaz believed that the Continentals had to change how they thought of themselves and America. It was not divine providence that brought them to this land as a blessing to the uncivilized savages. They were the inhabitants of a large landmass with all its complexities, benefits, and threats. The United States needed to develop relationships with the Natives based on mutual respect, profit, and cooperation and not simplistically treat them only as savage enemies to be conquered and subjugated.

The British successfully used the Natives in this way now, but they had no intention of building long-term honest relationships. They were building a structure that would bring them immediate profits, and then they would depart, leaving some form of policing needed for the exploitation to continue bringing profits to the Crown. On the other hand, since they were determined to stay, the Continentals should look for ways to coexist with the Natives. They should approach the Natives more honestly or risk ongoing problems.

The other option was to eliminate the Natives as pests and savages, but this would be against the ideals of freedom for all, which both General Washington and Benjamin Franklin advocated.

Like the US with the Natives, Poles had a similar challenge with the Tatars and the Cossacks. The pressure of people living next to you and not building relationships with them causes countless problems.

In the 10th century, rather than fight the Christians, pagan Poles invited a Bohemian Catholic princess to marry Polish Prince Mieszko and peacefully accepted Christianity. They used the same strategy in the 14th century when they refused to fight pagan Lithuanians. Instead, they invited pagan Prince Jagiełło to marry a Polish Catholic princess, become a Polish King and convert Lithuania to Christianity.

A peaceful effort to convince the Lithuanians to join the Poles rather than fight them brought 500 years of power and prosperity to both nations. Kaz thought it would make more sense for the United States to unite with the Iroquois Confederacy instead of keeping two fronts open, which meant fighting the British and the Natives simultaneously. Besides, because the British tried to use the Natives on their side by promising them independence, it would only make sense to frustrate British plans and give the Iroquois a similar but more attractive counteroffer. It was frustrating that almost all Continentals were blind to Kaz's point of view.

Thank God for Washington, who was a man of vision, resolve, and perseverance. Kaz knew that if he were in Washington's place, he would have gone mad with the Continental Congress. George had a remarkable ability to stay focused and on target regardless of the odds. He acknowledged the dissent, persevered, and eventually moved the cause forward. He had the wisdom to present his argument; if opposed, he thought it was his duty to clarify and wait. Washington respected the body politics to a level unheard of in most courts of Europe. He had the potential to lead this new country to great heights. Kaz trusted and respected Washington. He followed his decisions even if, at times, he thought they were wrong.

Washington used to say, "Dear Kaz, I do not think we are ready for such revolutionary ideas. It might happen in due time. Now, we need to shake off the British and then work on improving our notion of freedom and hopefully extend it to all." At times Washington would just sit, listen to Kaz, and nod.

"We have a bigger enemy than a group of locals defending their homesteads," argued Kaz. "If the American idea of freedom is freedom for few, how can it be considered a general concept for all? I understand fighting with outsiders, like the British. I do not see how you can fight with the indigenous population and hope to build a

319

thriving society that respects high moral ground anchored in ethical standing.

"I can teach you how to use a horse, but I think you also need Polish experience in how to be inclusive. We have been successful in bringing others to our table for 800 years. Our problem now is that we disrespect what we have created, and many of us value our personal gains over the country's welfare. If it continues, we will lose our power base, others will rule over us, and the golden freedom we love so much will be gone."

For Kaz, Continentals were spending more effort explaining why they should hate the Natives rather than planning how to build mutually profitable relationships. Like the British, the Russians used the divide-and-conquer strategy. When Pułaski was scouting for support of the Bar Confederation in the Polish Wild East, the Russians sent their agents who promised the peasants and militant Cossacks freedom from Polish oppression only if they started killing the Poles. Russian scheming eventually evolved into mass murders of Polish landowners, priests, and Jews. At the end of this bloodletting, the Russians abused the Ukrainians with the cruelty and brutality not heard of when Poles were in control of the lands. The Russian objective was to divide Poland and conquer it piece by piece.

For the Americans, trying to unite with the Natives to fight the British made much sense to Kaz. He decided to find a way to learn more about the Iroquois and, if an opportunity presented itself, to swing at least one of the Iroquois nations his way.

After Valley Forge, Puławski's cavalry was deployed in New York and Pennsylvania to flank any British and Native attacks while working on the combat readiness of the Legion. They were policing vast terrain, ready to move fast and react quickly by bringing the fight to the Iroquois. Puławski was disgusted. The Continentals should do the opposite if only to frustrate British plans. He argued that the local tribes should be allies because they knew the terrain and had ample food supplies. If the Natives worked with the Continentals, the British would be severely weakened.

Kaz sought an opportunity to learn more about the Iroquois and contribute to eventual victory by convincing the Natives to join the Continentals in the fight against the British. He decided to wait for an opportunity to gain direct knowledge of the Natives and try his idea of bringing some of them to the Continental cause.

Casper

One day, Kaz noticed a few Native riders watching the training of his Legion. After the training, he called Sgt. William Breen, one of his cavalrymen. William had an honest speckled face and reddish curly hair sticking out from under his hat.

"We are supposed to fight the Natives, and yet they are watching us in plain sight," Kaz said, pointing to the native onlookers in the crowd that gathered to watch the training. "Shouldn't we be concerned?"

"No," William answered. "There are so many different tribes. Some are not our enemies. These are the Tuscarora. They do not attack us but rather benefit from the trade. I think they are here to sell their pelts."

"Do they live close to the Iroquois?"

"They are the Iroquois. The Iroquois are a confederation of six different tribes."

"Do you know their names?"

"They are the Mohawk, Oneida, Onondaga, Cayuga, Seneca, and Tuscarora.

"Can I talk to them?"

"We can try."

Kaz and William rode over to the group and addressed one wearing a dark brown broadcloth coat, deerskin leggings, and high boots. He seemed to be the leader of the group. He had a chain around his neck with what looked like the skull of a small animal and a red bandana around his forehead. He had a musket by his saddle and a blanket rolled up behind him. His broad shoulders and big biceps, which seemed to be trapped in the sleeves of his jacket, indicated a man of remarkable physical strength.

"It looks like you understand horses. I am impressed by how well you sit on your ride," Kaz said.

"We are horse people. I am surprised that a white man knows the horses the way you do," answered the Tuscarora looking Kaz straight in the eyes.

"I am not a white man from here. In my country, we are one with our horses. It looks to me that you are the same."

"You are the first white man who said that an Indian and a white man are the same.

Also, I never heard that a white chief would talk to a bunch of Indians."

"If I do not ask questions, how can I learn?"

"Learn? White men do not learn. They teach."

"Then, you are right. I must be different."

"Did you say that I was right? You must be a contrary man."

"What is a contrary man?"

"A man that does everything opposite."

"Maybe I am. Still, I want to learn as much as possible about this land."

"Ask."

"First, what is your name?"

"I am Casper."

[Tuscarora Chief, Casper Peters]

"I don't want to talk. I want to see it. Can I see these different nations? Where they live. How do they ride their horses? What do they feed them?"

"Why would you like to know what we feed our horses?"

"I noticed a nice sheen on your mount's horsehair. They must have a different diet than the horses I see around here."

Casper looked at Kaz with interest and a hint of respect, saying, "You are not like the other white men. I know a lot of English, Irish, French, or German, but none like you."

"I am not English and certainly not German," answered Kaz, looking back at his unit, which he had left behind. "I must go back to my troops. Can we meet some other time?" Kaz asked.

"Let us meet here at dawn in three days," Casper suggested.

"I will wait for you here at dawn, Casper," Kaz responded, turning around his mount. He rode away, thinking that Casper might be his way to reach the Natives. William seemed to know more about the Natives than anyone Kaz had talked with so far.

"Where did you learn so much about the Indians?" Kaz asked.

"I traveled too much and got in trouble too often. Sometimes, they got me in trouble, sometimes out of trouble," William replied.

"Did you travel west, deep into their territory?"

"Oh yes, that's where you can find the best pelts and sometimes even get some gold."

"So, you were a fur trader?"

"I would not call myself a trader. I was the one who brought furs to the traders, and they would pay me scraps for the trouble. I lost more than I gained."

"Did you learn any of their languages?"

325

"I did. But I also learned that most of the time, it is better to keep your mouth shut if you want to learn anything."

"If I wanted to shut up and learn about the Indians, can I count on you?"

"I am your man, General."

"Report to my tent tomorrow after morning drills. We will start my education."

"Aye, Sir," replied William with a broad smile.

The next day right after the drills, Kaz released his mount to his orderly and went to his tent. As he sat down to review some mail, which he wanted to go over with Robert later, he heard his orderly, David.

"General, Sir. Sergeant Breen is reporting as ordered. May he enter?" David asked.

"Let him in," Kaz answered through the canvas. "And bring us both some coffee."

"I am glad you are here, William. I have a lot of questions."

"Go ahead, Sir. I hope I will have some answers," William replied, standing at attention. Kaz pointed to one of the two chairs around a roughly hewn pine table in the tent.

"At ease, soldier. Take a seat, William. We have a lot to discuss," Kaz said, sitting opposite William.

"Let's start with the Iroquois. You said they had six nations. I remember Tuscarora and Seneca. What were the others?"

"Mohawk, Oneida, Onondaga, and Cayuga."

"Mohawk, Oneida, Onondaga, Cayuga," repeated Kaz. "Can you tell me more about them?"

"The Mohawk are called people of the flint country; Oneida, people of the standing stone; Onondaga, people of the hills; Cayuga, people of the Great Swamp; Seneca, people of the Great Hill; and Tuscarora, people of the Shirt."

"Where do they live?"

"They live all around us but mostly to the north and west of here. They stretch from around Albany to great Lake Erie and beyond."

Kaz started pacing around the tent. He stood over a chest, opened the lid, and produced a map. Stretching the map on the table before William, he asked, "Can you point to their territories on this map?"

William leaned over and studied the map saying, "This map does not cover all their territories, but it is a good start.

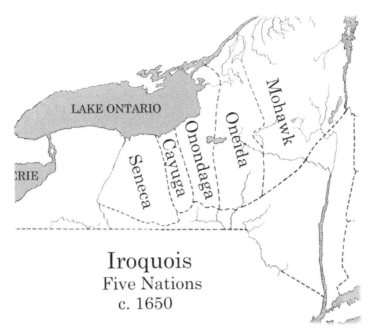

Iroquois
Five Nations
c. 1650

"Look at these lakes, Sir. These are Erie, Ontario, Seneca, and Lake George. The nations of the Iroquois Confederation, or Haudenosaunee as they call themselves, stretch from Lake Erie in the west through Lake Ontario and Lake George to the east. Seneca's lands extend from the eastern shores of Lake Erie eastwards. Then, we have Cayuga to the east of Seneca. After Cayuga, there are Onondaga and Oneida. Then, we have the Mohawk."

"Is it Iroquois or Haudeno something?"

"Iroquois is the name the French gave them. They call themselves the Haudenosaunee."

"And what about Tuscarora," Kaz reminded.

"You are right, Sir, Tuscarora. They live mostly in the Oneida lands."

"I thought that each had their own lands."

"Good point," William agreed. "The story goes that Tuscarora was not a part of the original Confederacy of the five nations. They lived way down south in North Carolina along the Roanoke and Pamlico rivers, but they were pushed by the British and started moving north. The Oneidas decided to give them quarters."

"So here we go from Lake Erie eastwards: Seneca, Cayuga, Tuscarora, Oneida, Onondaga, and Mohawk," repeated Kaz.

"Wow, no wonder you are the General. It took me over a year and some time as their prisoner to figure it out."

"Why would the Oneida give land to the Tuscarora?"

"Sometimes talking does more than fighting. Both nations use the Haudenosaunee language. Tuscarora wanted to tell their story, and Oneida listened. The story goes back to when the Tuscarora moved from around the great lakes down south. Then, the white settlers came. The Tuscarora traded with the whites getting metal tools and weapons for their food and pelts. The more whites came, the more trouble ensued. Then, there was the slave trade. Some whites started grabbing the Tuscarora and selling them at slave markets. They were sending them as far as the Caribbean Islands. It was too much for the Tuscarora, and wars began. Both sides were brutal and fought hard, but the Tuscarora eventually ran out of cannonballs and powder. The Tuscarora were rubbed out really well. Not many of them remained between the wars, slave trade, and the whites' diseases, like smallpox.

The Oneida gave them quarters, and so now, since 1722, we have six nations of the Confederacy."

"If they owe so much to the Haudenosaunee, why would the Tuscarora not fight with them on the British side?"

"I guess the Tuscarora know better than to trust King George. The British betrayed them many times. They also know that they are not strong enough to put up a winning fight against the whites. Believe me, they tried."

"Still, why would the Seneca or the Mohawk not make the Tuscarora join them to support the British?"

"The Confederacy is more than a simple power struggle. They have survived together for over 200 years without wars. They tell their children stories from their past before the Confederacy when they always fought one another. There was little happiness then but a lot of bloodletting, despair, and hatred. They do not want to go back to these dark times."

"It is a lot to take in, William. Why don't you tell me the key points again?" Kaz kept walking around the tent, stopping at times and repeating key phrases.

"Iroquois Confederacy, or Haudenosaunee, People of the Longhouse, as they call themselves," started William, "were also called the Iroquois League. Five Nations, or, from 1722, the Six Nations, are the confederation of Indian tribes across upper New York state, which during the 17th and 18th centuries played a strategic role in the struggle between the French and the British for mastery of the eastern coasts of North America."

After a few more lessons, Kaz had solid background knowledge of the Haudenosaunee Confederacy. The five original Iroquois nations were Mohawk (People of the Flint), Oneida (People of the Standing Stone), Onondaga (People of the Hills), Cayuga (People of the Great Swamp), and Seneca (People of the Great Hill). After Tuscarora (People of the Shirt) joined the original five, the Confederacy became known to the British as the Six Nations. It was recognized and accepted as such at Albany, New York, in 1722. Some claimed that they had been the world's oldest participatory democracy. Kaz was right. William seemed to know a lot and did not let his knowledge out, keeping to his current station in life, that of a Sergeant in the Continental Army.

The Trip

Casper sent word that the elders approved of Kaz's trip to the Haudenosaunee lands. He told William that everything was arranged for a trip and would like to meet Kaz. The following day, Kaz and Casper met after the afternoon drills. Kaz and William drove to the same cluster of trees where they had met Casper for the first time. It was an easily recognizable spot because one of the trees grew like a sentry to the rest. Its branches, covered with long needles, extended far from the trunk, creating a natural shelter where a rider could find protection from wind and rain. There were few trees like that around. It stood out for miles as a beacon or a messenger.

Casper did not look at Kaz or William. He leaned over and talked, focusing beyond the immediate surroundings, ready to act at a moment's notice for any challenge or threat.

"We will leave before dawn in two days," he said.

"How long will it take us to get there and back?" Kaz asked.

"We should be back in a week."

"Where are we going?"

"We are going to Sehgahunda, the valley of three falls in the Seneca lands."

Kaz nodded and motioned his horse towards his tent. There was nothing else to ask currently. It was time for action. Immediately, he started arranging for his absence. Kovats would be the only person who would know where Kaz was going. Kovats will resume command of the unit and focus on heavy drills so that no one in the Legion would have time or energy to overthink Kaz's absence.

Kaz showed up under the white pine tree at the designated time, right before sunrise. Casper was already there. He raised his right-hand chest high, ready to signal his horse to move. He looked past Kaz expanding his focus and attention on all signals near and far, being in sync with the surroundings. It was precisely how Kaz learned to behave on the road in Podole. They understood one another instantly.

"Here, it is a wampum belt," said Casper leaning over to Kaz and handing him a ten-inch-long belt of white beads with an intricate black pattern.

"This sign will protect you from any warrior in the Haudenosaunee territory. Keep it hidden, and do not show it to any white man. If you feel it necessary, show this belt to any warrior, and it will protect you from any harm. No one will ask you any questions. You will be free to do what is needed."

"Anything else I need to know?"

"We are on the trail pushing hard to cover a lot of distance. There will be no time to waste energy on anything else but the road ahead. In a day, we will reach a village where you will leave your horse and dress. You will get a new horse and a new set of clothes there. We will return to the same village where your horse and your uniform will be waiting for you on our way back. After a day's ride, you will be back with your regiment. Looking at your horse or your clothes, no one will notice that you covered a weeklong track over rough terrain," explained Casper and motioned his horse to move.

They set off with Kaz following Casper. In no time, Kaz realized that Casper was a seasoned warrior. He knew the battle started with moving your force away or toward an enemy, whether it took a second or a week. Every step of Casper's horse was measured and timed to exert the maximum effort needed to reach the destination on a strenuous track in the shortest time possible. Kaz knew what Casper was doing and was able to match his focus.

They moved incessantly through open fields and dense foliage. Casper did not hesitate even for a moment. At the time, he would turn into a thick brush only to find a faint trail along a small brook. He would wind around a hill or move straight up across the highest top, depending on the requirements of the terrain. The track was demanding and confusing to an untrained eye. Yet, it was evident that Casper knew exactly what to do.

At high noon, it became hot, with the Sun finding a way to bring the heat even between the trees. Eventually, the Sun began shining mainly on their faces. Casper slowed down or sped up depending on the terrain or the need for the horses to maintain their strength. Before sunset, they stopped by a creek where the horses had their water and some grass. Casper sat cross-legged, leaning at the tree trunk, and fell asleep. Kaz sat next to him and fell asleep as well. In maybe an hour, Casper woke Kaz up, and they mounted the horses. Kaz noticed that his horse was keeping up the pace but was not near the stamina of Casper's mount. He knew that trained horses would match their pace until total exhaustion.

They moved on through the night without easing the pace. After midnight, Casper lashed himself around the saddle and fell asleep while his horse followed along a mid-size river. Kaz did the same. His horse simply followed Casper's mount. At dawn, Kaz removed the lashing and continued after Casper. They swam across a wider river with the current that took them a quarter-mile off course. Once on the other side, they did not slow the pace. Kaz's horse was visibly weakened and could hardly keep pace. Casper did not even glance behind but slowed slightly and matched the ability of Kaz's mount.

Casper turned north between two hills along a faint path that led upward. Kaz sensed that they were getting closer to their destination. When they cleared a clump of ash trees, Kaz noticed the roofs of wooden cabins. Soon, they arrived at an approximately twelve feet high wooden palisade.

Casper approached two riders near the entrance while Kaz stood a few strides behind. After a brief exchange, one of the riders showed them the way to one of the houses. It was about a hundred feet long and twenty feet wide construction built of layers of elm bark on a frame of rafters and poles dug in the ground, bent at the top, and tied together to form a curved roof.

[Haudenosaunee longhouse, Alamy files]

335

Kaz counted about twenty longhouses arranged in a semicircle. He could see a few clouds of smoke coming out of some of them. They did not have chimneys but only openings in the roofs to release the smoke. Kaz could see the beds about two feet off the ground and a fire pit through a large open door in the middle of the mud floor.

A few people approached the visitors. Casper got off his horse and motioned to Kaz to dismount. Watching Casper, Kaz handed the reins of his horse to a young bare-chested boy with long, straight hair dressed in a leather belt, which was fastened around a piece of cloth extending between the boy's legs and hanging over the belt in front and the back. With the temperature over one hundred degrees, most men in the village enjoyed the Sun and did not wear any shirts.

Casper and Kaz went over to a clump of trees, which gave a welcome shade. Some women were waiting there for them with a few blankets. Casper took his shirt off and lay down under the tree. Kaz followed. Soon, both fell asleep. In three to four hours, they got up refreshed. The women came over with bundles of clothes.

"It is time to take a bath and change your clothes," Casper spoke for the first time since they left Kaz's headquarters. "Follow me."

They went down a descending meadow to a creek with crystal clear water about a hundred feet away. Casper took his clothes off and jumped right in the middle, stretching his arms and taking a slow, relaxing dive. Kaz again followed Casper. They rubbed their arms and legs in the water for a few refreshing minutes. Kaz felt that the bath helped him regain most of his lost energy.

They started dressing up when they left the stream and dried themselves with a cloth. Kaz had no problem wearing his leather leggings and a shirt, but putting on his shoes took him some time. Casper showed him how to use long leather laces to tie the moccasins around the leggings. The clothes felt soft and comfortable. The moccasins especially were a surprise; manufactured from deerskin, they weighed almost nothing but gave solid support. They were made from a continuous piece of leather from the front through the soles to the back of the shoe. The part around the toes was skillfully crimped and perfectly fitted Kaz's toes. The laces running across the bottom of the leggings protected the insides of the legs during long horse rides.

Kaz turned, bent, and squatted a few times to see how his new clothes would feel and if they would not limit his movements. He felt comfortable and not restrained in any way.

"Let us eat, drink and get on our way," Casper said.

They followed a resolute young woman dressed in a clean, modest, and tasteful manner. Her straight black hair was braided into two plaits decorated with red, black, and yellow beads. Similar beads were sowed into an intricate pattern on her knee-length leather dress cinched at the waist with a belt. Leggings made of the same material and decorated moccasins completed her attire. She took them to a long table between two longhouses. It was full of food, including meat, bread, beans, and corn. He noticed a rack filled with dried fish hanging down from the frame along the house wall opposite where he sat.

"It is strange that nobody welcomes us and tries to find out who I am," Kaz observed.

"They know who you are and know not to ask any questions. We are on the way to a Haudenosaunee business. They see that we are moving westward across, not along the valleys. It is not a usual trip within the boundaries of one Haudenosaunee nation but rather an international delegation. They also know that we are in a hurry and should not waste time on idle talking."

"I am surprised that at least a village elder or his representative hasn't shown up, and nobody is watching us."

"Oh, they are watching us. They have had their braves follow us for hours. Pay attention after we leave; I think you can spot our watchers if you focus. I am sure there will eventually be a song describing this visit."

Kaz sat down and looked at the food.

"Try our three sisters," Casper said.

"What are three sisters?"

"Here, they are corn, beans, and squash. They are gifts from our Creator."

Kaz liked corn on the cob and sweet beans seasoned with maple syrup. He also tried some deer meat and cornbread. Casper pointed to a clay bowl with soup. Kaz used a wooden spoon to sample some barley and pieces of meat in it. He took a few sips and tasted a hardy content full of animal fat. Just a few spoons were filling and would last a long time.

Once they had their share of food, they went to their mounts. They each were given a new horse. Kaz checked his saddle to make sure that it was tightened correctly. Yes, everything seemed perfect. He leaned over to the horse and introduced himself.

"It looks like we will be riding together, you and me," Kaz whispered. "Let's make sure that we both will do well."

He hugged the horse around the neck and gave him an apple, which he had taken from the food table for this occasion. He got into the saddle and waited, ready to move on. The mount was an intelligent creature, and they knew how to work in unison in no time. They left the village behind and moved on at a steady arduous tempo. The strength and stamina of both horses were perfectly matched. They were moving with surprising speed. The horses would increase the tempo to cover the rugged terrain quickly and then ease off at the descent when riding downhill. They took short breaks for water and food, sleeping in the saddle.

Onaquaga

The next day after dawn, they reached a small hill. Casper stopped and pointed to the river, winding its way through the forested hills below. Kaz could see a village extending on both banks.

"It is Onaquaga (now Windsor, NY) on the Susquehanna River," Casper explained.

[The valley of the Susquehanna River]

"It was originally home to Oneida. With the whites pushing us for over a hundred years, Onaquaga opened to other Haudenosaunee nations. Some Tuscarora came here chased from South Carolina and became the Sixth Nation of the Confederacy in 1722. Christian Indians have been living here since Reverend Gideon Hawley built his church. I would say there are around 500 people here at any given moment. They fish, plant corn, beans, and squash, and hunt. They also have some cattle around. It is a nice place to run a family. I hope it will stay this way."

"How many villages like the one we saw yesterday and this one here are there around in the Haudenosaunee lands?"

"I don't know exactly; fifty or more, I would say."

"Are there any Seneca or Mohawk here in Onaquaga?"

"Yes, they are here as well. After the 1768 Treaty of Fort Stanwix, Mohawks were forced north and west. A few settled here in Onaquaga, just west of the treaty line. There are also some Algonquian-speaking Lenape people," continued Casper jumping off his ride.

He waved at Kaz to follow him. He took his horse's bridle, pushed through some dense bushes, and started descending downhill. Soon, the riders reached a small creek where Casper, Kaz, and the horses enjoyed clean, fresh water. From this high vantage point, they observed the village sitting cross-legged by the bank. One could see groupings of longhouses and some stone structures on both sides of the river, patches of corn and beans with some fruit trees extended from the buildings to the forest. Here and there, they saw groups of cattle and horses fenced by the houses.

"We will drive through the village so that you will have a chance to see it up close. Joseph Brant is here with some of his Mohawk braves and the Royalists who serve under his command. You know that Joseph organized some raiding parties against the Continentals, but he allowed you free passage. Although we can pass, we do not want to look for trouble."

"Understood," Kaz replied.

"You will look and learn today. Tomorrow, you will have a chance to listen and talk."

Genesee River Gorge

Casper and Kaz were pushing on through the forest and numerous brooks, creeks, and rivers, with every step getting them closer to the Genesee River Valley. Eventually, Casper stopped at the top of a small hill.

"This is it, General. You are on your own now. Keep on riding straight east until you reach a descending clearing. Move down towards the trees. You will reach the river gorge, then make a right. Show your wampum, and they will bring you to your hosts. I will be waiting for you here, and we will ride back to your headquarters."

"Thank you, Casper," said Kaz. He leaned into his ride and resumed his track. There was no need for any conversation or empty talk. Kaz was by himself and was moving towards his destination with a clear mind.

Riding an undulating terrain, Kaz started slowly descending a vast meadow towards a forest of maple and ash trees. Suddenly, a hidden canyon with a deep gorge appeared and stunned him with its sheer beauty. A precipitous ravine cradled a shimmering ribbon of a river far below, over 500 feet deep. In front of him, at Kaz's eye level, a few majestic vultures and eagles were floating on warm air currents. He spotted a hawk much like the ones he would see up high in the sky in Podole. He never saw a bird of prey flying so close that he could see the hawk's eye scanning the terrain half a mile down. Suddenly, the hawk turned his beak down, folded its wings, and plunged into the abyss, disappearing under a vertical edge of a rock. Half a mile across the canyon's opposite side was a wall of white stone carved with horizontal lines and adorned with clumps of trees on top.

[The Canyon of the Genesee River]

Kaz squeezed his horse with his right heel slightly back and the toes of his left leg slightly forward. The horse turned northeast to the right and followed the ravine. The countryside was breathtakingly beautiful. The horse treaded among the roots of gigantic trees, which protruded from the ground embracing the bedrock. The Sun was glistening from above the ridge on the opposite side of the gorge, shooting golden shafts of light between the trees. Kaz noticed a deer looking straight at him from between the trees no more than a hundred feet away. He stopped and admired the spectacular view.

Everything around him seemed a perfect rendition of a fantastic dream describing the garden of Eden. In the perfect stillness of the moment, Kaz heard a faint hum. He motioned his horse towards the sound. With every step, it was getting louder. Kaz realized that it was the noise of rushing water. After a while, from atop, he saw a few gigantic boulders and the river winding around them. He followed the path high above the riverbed until he reached a vast meadow full of yellow, purple, and violet flowers.

And then, there it was, a veil of crystal-clear water falling a hundred feet from about a 200 feet wide ledge formed from horizontal plates of shale rock. It was one of the three waterfalls mentioned by Casper.

[Middle waterfall in the valley of the Genesee River]

Kaz became aware of a watchful presence, taking notice of a lone rider standing at the edge of the trees. He had an air of ageless curiosity; he remained as still as the trees that hid him, imperceptibly swaying with the breeze. Kaz reigned in his horse and raised a wampum belt in his right hand. Brandishing the colorful belt to the rider, Kaz gently spurred his mount closer. When he was about 30 feet distant, the rider turned his horse around and rode away through the trees. Kaz followed him at a respectful distance of 20 feet. After a short ride, they reached a clearing dominated by a tall white pine tree in its center. A few men were sitting cross-legged in the shade of the tree. The mounted brave stopped his horse, seemingly by thought, and motioned towards the group. Kaz got off his ride and handed the reins to the rider. Then, he approached the tree.

One of the sitting men got up and greeted Kaz. He had three eagle feathers pinned to the back of a red bandana around his head. He wore a white shirt, a black woolen coat, and a white and black bead necklace adorned by a large medallion. His leather leggings were fringed with four-five-inch-long leather strips.

"You are a white man who is not like a white man. You are here to listen and learn. Am I right?" Three Feathers asked.

"Yes, there is so much I do not know and do not understand."

"Sit with us."

Kaz took his place on the grass, sitting cross-legged in the circle of men.

"You are not like other white men, and still, they make you one of their war chiefs. How can you be their chief if you are not one of them?"

"The world is big with many nations and languages, yet war is the same wherever you go," Kaz answered.

He noticed that some men understood what he was saying while others had interpreters whispering to them from behind.

"So, you like war and follow it wherever you can find one," Three Feathers continued.

"I like peace, but war is on my way to peace."

"You are fighting for the Colonials, far away from your country and your people. Are you lost?"

"I follow my path wherever it takes me. I hope it will take me home one day, and I can sit under my tree like you are sitting here under your tree."

One from the circle of men who looked the oldest motioned to a young warrior across from him. The Young Warrior reached behind and produced a long pipe. He started packing it with tobacco. Kaz realized that it was a ceremonial ritual. The Young Warrior walked over to the Elder and handed him the pipe with a stick glowing hot red. The Elder lit the pipe. He seemed focused beyond this gathering. Smoke from the pipe was like a conduit transferring consciousness. He blew a puff of smoke in front of him and waved his hand to direct the smoke toward his forehead. Then, slowly and deliberately blew the smoke in four directions, passing the pipe to the next person in the circle. The one to the right of the Elder repeated the ceremony and passed the pipe along until it reached Three Feathers.

"Smoke a pipe with us, General," said Three Feathers, passing the pipe to Kaz.

346

Kaz took a long whiff and tried to follow the ceremonial steps. He blew some smoke out and motioned it over and around his head. He thought about how far he had traveled, and still, Kaz felt that he was just arm's length from Tom and his soldiers in Zazulińce. He saw his Tatars crouching around the fire in front of their tents. Some of the Cossacks smoked long pipes as the one Three Feathers handed him over. The Cossacks' heads, shaven up high with whisks of hair falling on their foreheads and over their eyes, made them look like some of the Native braves. Kaz blew a puff of smoke in four directions and sank deeper into his thoughts.

Rather than scouting the enemy for strengths and weaknesses, he focused on the valley of the Prądnik River north of Kraków. It was much smaller than this gorge, with a tiny brook and no waterfalls. Yet, he felt that spiritually, the two were connected. He sensed countless generations of men in their valleys across time and space. He realized that he came here to experience this emotion rather than fight the Revolutionary War with goals that, with every day, were more confusing and unclear. Instead of learning about the Senecas, Kaz discovered a part of himself, which he felt at times while riding the steppes of Podole, a deeper level of realization. He felt how his consciousness reached beyond everyday concerns, the worries of war, and the frustrations of winning or losing. Everything felt one to him. He perceived countless revolutions of the wheel of life as if he were watching the spindle of yarn.

He looked around, not knowing how long he was lost in his thoughts. The hosts patiently waited for him to regain his senses and return to them. Kaz slowly passed the pipe to the next man in the circle. The ceremony continued until the Elder received the pipe and handed it to the Young One.

"You came here to learn. Ask your questions," Three Feathers turned to Kaz.

"If you look for peace, why don't you turn to the Continentals and work a compromise?" Kaz asked.

"We tried. After dealing with the French and the Dutch, we worked with the King of England. Our chiefs even took a trip to London on their big boats for talks. All the pomp and glory of Great Britain and the King's pledges were just for show. The King was too weak to keep his assurances. Today, out of one enemy, we have two: King George and George Washington, the White Hair. They promise us things they cannot deliver. In the meantime, we are chased away from our hunting grounds. We are killed, and our crops are burned. The only thing the white men want from us now is to fight other white men for them and die. There is no talk of peace."

"And yet, you do it. You attack the Continentals for King George."

"We talked it over and decided that the King would win in the end. We cannot afford to side with the losing party. Besides, the Royals stick to their towns and forts. They do not venture into our lands. On the other hand, the Continentals send their hunting parties all the time. Then, they call it a peaceful settlement. Even if the White Hair tells them to stop, they do it anyway. When we complain about breaking the treaties, Washington always takes the settlers' side."

"Yet the Tuscarora decided to help the settlers."

"Yes, they did. Their pain with King George is so great that they cannot see through it. They lost their warriors. They lost their women and children; they lost their lands in the south. They were being kidnapped and sold as slaves. They do not see a way that would lead to any accommodations with the King."

When Kaz returned to the village with Casper, his uniform and boots were freshly washed and shined. His stirrup strap hookup was mended. The village elder greeted Kaz and handed him a blanket, smiling and showing with his hands that he should put it over his horse, under the saddle.

"This will last you," Casper said.

Kaz looked at the blanket carefully. He turned towards the village elder and bowed, saying, "thank you." In the corner of the blanket, Kaz noticed a subtle embroidered pattern. It was a five-inch-long array of squares and rectangles with an arrowhead or a tree in the middle, connected by a line.

"What is it?" Kaz asked.

"This is our sign. The symbol of the Haudenosaunee, our Confederacy," Casper answered.

[Flag of the Haudenosaunee]

"It is better you do not let anyone know you understand its meaning. It describes the five nations which started our union. Tuscarora joined later, so they are not here on our flag," Casper explained.

"What is this diamond in the middle?"

"It is a tree, the sign for the Onondaga."

"And the rest of it?"

"Each square represents a nation. So, the sign represents five nations from left to right, from the east to the west: Seneca, Cayuga, Onondaga, Oneida, and Mohawk."

"Why does the Onondaga have a tree?"

[A group of Eastern White Pines (pinus strobus)]

"It is the Tree of Peace, a white pine. It reminds us of Dekanawida. He was the Onondaga who traveled the nations and preached peace, friendship, and unity. His words were stronger than hatred and arrows. He brought the nations together."

"When did he die?"

"He never died. He lives as long as we remember him. He is as real as you and me. The roots of the White Pine Tree spread north, south, east, and west. You can always follow the roots to the source and take shelter under the tree of peace. Our chiefs sit beneath the tree and watch over the Great Peace."

Kaz felt that his scouting trip to the nations of the Haudenosaunee extended beyond lessons in geography, history, and geopolitical awareness. It reached deep into the ontology of human existence. The fight for individual, national, or ethnic identity seemed a meaningless squabble. The message of human uniqueness went beyond the importance of moral or existential dominance. His consciousness touched the primordial energy Kaz felt after the buffalo hunt in Podole. The Haudenosaunee circle of peace message seemed to extend beyond the immediate challenge of selecting the right side in the current conflict. Kaz came to the epiphany of spiritual growth. He understood that he reached beyond words in his search for answers.

He realized that he had been initiated into a higher level of awareness. From now on, he would carry within him an always present observer, a higher inner self witnessing his actions and the actions of everyone around him, including the living and the deceased. This internal identity was imminent, immovable, and always present. It reached beyond the concept of time and space. Kaz knew it existed before his birth and would continue after death. This enhanced state of awareness did not materialize because he met a few men under a tree by a river. The Great Peace Council was just a final drop in a stream of consciousness, which ebbed and flowed within Kaz since he could form his thoughts.

Sullivan Expedition (1779)

In December 1778, Kaz received a letter from Washington to join Major General John Sullivan in his extermination campaign against the Iroquois. Massacring the civilian population was against all of

Kaz's beliefs. With a heavy heart, he confronted General Washington and said, "You cannot build freedom and liberty by slaughtering the non-combatant population. Doing it will stain your otherwise pure intentions.

"Every woman and child killed in such brutal and premeditated fashion will burden your conscience. Murdering the weak and innocent while claiming the fight for honor and protection of freedom is a lie. Do you want to build a better new government or simply follow the example of Great Britain? Are you trying to outperform them in their cowardly tactics? Do not expect me to be an accomplice in such a deplorable act of slaughter. I cannot do it."

General Sullivan followed Washington's order to exterminate the "savages" in the Iroquois territory with morbid efficiency. He left Wyoming Valley in late June 1779 and arrived at Tioga, New York, on August 11. The biggest challenge for the 4,000 men who eventually joined him in this expedition was loading the barges with supplies. They were delayed for a month because of logistical nightmares. Once everything was in place, the barges with people, horses, cannons, and all needed supplies took off into the unknown.

Militarily, the braves were no match for this executionary outfit. General Sullivan tried to engage the Natives in a battle, but they were evading the Continentals with their superior scouting skills. When Sullivan scouts reported they spotted a village, his men would march overnight, hoping to surprise the Natives. Almost always, they found longhouses empty. Sometimes, they saw smoldering embers and kettles of corn on fire but no people.

On August 12, scouts reported 200-300 Natives in Chemung. Sullivan ordered an overnight march, but the village was deserted when they arrived. In a report, one of the officers wrote: "the village was beautiful, containing forty to fifty houses built of logs and frames." They burned the village on both sides of the river with the crops and winter food supplies.

The most significant engagement of the campaign was the battle of Newtown on August 29. Outnumbered and lacking arms and ammunition, the Natives had two options; surrender and be slaughtered or fight. Outflanked by Sullivan's troops, they were forced to engage Sullivan at the foot of a steep hill along the Chemung River. There were also some British units with the Natives, but Mohawk Chief Joseph Brandt was the Commander of the joint Iroquois-British forces. The Natives decided to fight to give time for the inhabitants of the two Cayuga towns of Nanticoke and Kanawaholla to flee.

[Monument at the field of battle in Newtown]

The Native braves lined the hill covered with pine and dense growth of shrub oak in a horseshoe pattern. The plan was to entice Sullivans' men to charge across the meadow and up the hill, exposing the Continentals to the flanking fire. Luckily, Sullivan's men discovered breastwork stations masked by bushes and grass and did not enter the trap. Instead, they placed their cannons up front and started bombing the Iroquois positions. They used their superior numbers to encircle the Native web. In a few hours of fighting, 1,000 Iroquois and Loyalists succumbed to 3,200 Continental soldiers. Once the artillery prep ended, and they reached the positions of the Iroquois-British forces, the Natives were gone. They escaped similarly to how General Washington disengaged the British army at Brandywine Creek.

Eventually, about 5,000 hungry and cold Natives converged on Fort Niagara, where the Niagara River flows into Lake Ontario. The British were surprised by the number of refugees. They were trying to find food for the migrants, but many died of starvation, cold, and diseases. Their death was a direct result of Sullivan's Expedition, which burned all winter food supplies of the Iroquois and chased them away from their homesteads. Most surviving Natives moved up north to Canada across the Niagara River, where they remain today. Their story was passed in an old oral fashion. In ceremonies held without white witnesses, the Seneca, Cayuga, Oneida, Onondaga, Mohawk, and Tuscarora pass it to their children.

Life across the Susquehanna River, which endured for centuries, was extinguished in a frenzy of mass killing. The 200-year-old

Haudenosaunee experiment of participative democracy was no more. With the barbaric vengeance of brutal invaders, yet another civilization was destroyed. It only remained for the conquerors to devise an excuse for their atrocities. Like in the case of Voltaire's effort to ridicule Poland, this was a minor concern to be addressed by the flagbearers of truth appointed by the Continentals. The Natives were reduced to blood-thirsty savages praying on defenseless women and children of peaceful settlers.

Kaz heard that the Susquehanna River unfurled the blood-colored banner carrying the record of Sullivans' attack along its banks across Pennsylvania and New York for a few days. Gone were newly converted Christian Natives, young children with their dreams and ambitions listening to their parents for lessons meant to protect them for the future. Their love and envy were extinguished like a candle flame.

A few callous executioners heard their cries. Some would undoubtedly wake up at night screaming while the ghosts of innocence would haunt them in their nightmarish dreams. But once they were gone, the traces of the genocide would forever disappear. A blanket of grass and bushes would cover burned houses. Eventually, during the Sullivan expedition, the Americans destroyed over forty native towns and burned over 160,000 bushels of corn.

CHAPTER 12
Savannah (1779)

The Southern Campaign

After three years of fighting the Patriots, King George III could not stop the rebellion in the colonies. The King planned to crush the rebellion at the source in the first years of the American Revolution. He captured New York in 1776 and the seat of the Continental Congress, Philadelphia, in 1778. George Washington avoided the destruction of his army by outmaneuvering and outlasting royalist forces.

The King's generals decided to change his strategy. They sent his troops south, planning to take Savannah in Georgia before making a victorious march back north, attracting the loyalists to their banner along the way. The King believed that most Continentals were loyal to the Crown, and only a few committed revolutionaries were his problem. He expected to trap the rebels between the army moving from the south and the forces in Canada, New York, and Pennsylvania.

In December 1778, the British, under Sir Archibald Campbell, KB, captured Savannah. Reinforced by General Augustine Prevost, determined loyalists marched north on Augusta, Georgia. The Continentals were fighting hard but could not stop the British assault.

In February 1779, General Washington called Kaz to his headquarters and said, "Dear Brigadier General. I need you to save my army again as you did at Brandywine. The British are moving their southern army north and a northern detachment south. The intention seems clear. They took Savannah and established themselves there in strength. If they were to come here, I would not have the force to stop them. I sent General Lincoln to organize a defense, but he failed to halt their advance with some loss. King George believed that if he could establish his forces in the southern colonies, the masses of the south would rise and crush the Patriot cause. The situation would seem to be critical, General.

[Thirteen colonies in 1775]

"I count that your Legion, which looked so impressive during the August parade, will be able to sow havoc and confuse the enemy while we recruit more militias to join General Lincoln. I fear I must again rely on you and your Legion to succeed in salvaging the situation. According to officers who grew up in the area, the terrain is conducive to cavalry. More in Congress are beginning to see the benefit of your knowledge and experience.

"We also hope that the French will come and join us actively. The British keep the bulk of the fleet at home. London feels unsafe without half the world's warships at anchor in the Thames estuary. The French are taking the opportunity to ravage the West Indies, leaving you and me with little to offer the men besides encouragement and the promise of eventual pay." General Washington sank into his seat and stared into the flames of the hearth in his war room.

"My men are eager, Sir," Kaz said. "And what I said earlier still holds. I am prepared to die, and so are my men if need be. We plan to hurry and slay the British and Hessians at the end of the line of march. For what it's worth, my men hold you to those promises of pay, Sir, but they aren't holding their breath waiting for it. There is an intuitive understanding in the camp that they will be paid when they secure victory. They have seen what stands in the way. They know what must be done, have the confidence to do it, and the pride to see it through no matter the cost."

Washington regained his characteristically alert posture and said, "Very well, General. I am glad I can still count on you in this dire hour of need. Our spies report that the British consider you the most dangerous of our commanders in the field. You bring a surprisingly new level of cavalry expertise thus far not observed on the battlefields of America. I know that your skill applied down south will markedly improve our chances of slowing down the British," Washington added, "It is a 600 miles trek to South Carolina. I will insist that the quartermaster outfit your troops with all necessary provisions."

On 19 March 1779, a day before their march south to Georgia, Kaz assembled his Legion in York Town. The quartermaster's office paid the legionnaires' wages for the first time. Kaz used his own money before to facilitate the purchase of arms and uniforms for his Legion despite late payments and constant fights with the accountants. However, he did not have the $29 per month required to cover the legionaries' salaries. It was the first pay in the men's threadbare pockets since the war had begun, and it had an impact. Though the American dollar was almost worthless, the printed note bespoke a mint in operation somewhere behind the lines. The army ran on half rations and righteous indignation for their arrogant enemy. It grew more organized and confident by the day that success in battle would bring back pay.

Kaz stood before his men, who had responded to his call and joined the Legion. Despite the hardships and challenges of demanding training, they remained faithful to the Cause and proved their commitment. He appreciated this group of Continentals who challenged mighty Britain, dared to form a government, and called themselves the United States of America. His troops believed they participated in the fight for something unique, a government that would give an average citizen freedom and justice. When told secondhand, not many thought that these men burned for the Cause; no one doubted it after speaking with one of them or seeing them fight or ride. The Brigadier General paced in front of his men with a grim smile. They already had a pride, nearing impetuosity, that Englishmen took decades to foster. The Coldstream Guard had over a century of battlefield honor to call upon in action. The Pulaski's Legion did not care for any of these obscure details of their opposition. They cared only for their horses, weapons, fellows, leaders, and nation newly born in war.

In the second line of infantry, Kaz noticed a new face. On a closer look, he recognized the man.

"Are you the father of Timothy?" Kaz asked.

"Yes, Sir, I am Fleck, Private Kevin Fleck, Sir."

"We met in Boston in Carlin's tailor shop. You were purchasing the first set of men's clothes for Timmy." The ranker stood at perfect attention and blinked madly in anxiety.

"Yes, I remember. You were asking about the wanted man poster for a fugitive slave."

"Indeed. How is Timothy these days?"

"He is home with his mother. I will join them once we get rid of these god-damned Redcoats!" It drew a cheer from the surrounding men and broadened the smile on Kaz's lips.

"How did you end up in my Legion?"

"I read your appeal in a newspaper. I told my wife I could not stay home if you came from Poland to fight for our freedom. It would make me nothing but a coward and a hypocrite." The cheers of his comrades bolstered the man's voice and gave his eye a fiery blaze.

"I am grateful for your trust, Private Kevin Fleck. As all you men know, King George has spies everywhere, and men like you, Private Kevin Fleck, keep the King up at night. Because a man like you, and all you men, cannot be broken!" Kaz stood up in the stirrups and let his voice boom over his men like a cannonade of grape. The men roared in response and nearly deafened Kaz, who stood at the center of it all. "Men who cannot be slowed! Cannot be reasoned with! Men who succor the innocent and dispatch the mercenary dogs sent to kill you to Hell!" The men roared still louder, some drawing sabers. "Sent to kill you, then to strangle your nation in its cradle! Will you have your children kneel and scrape to a king across the sea?" The men who had not drawn steel yet did so now and began to howl with rage at the thought of the consequence of defeat.

Kaz knew almost each of his men personally and remembered many of their individual stories. Stopping in front of each for a moment, he said, "You faced hunger, mud, cold, and disease, and here you stand! We march into the swamps to our south, where we will face heat, insects, and muck. There will be alligators, snakes, also mosquitoes bringing fever and malaria. The enemy, remember, will face these obstacles as well but will have inferior knowledge of the country. You terrify the swine who stand in your way. You are not men, but nightmare made real. You will be remembered for centuries

362

to come. Keep your powder and socks always dry." The men bellowed as a single body; some fired pistols into the air. Kaz was confident they were ready.

"Tomorrow, our infantry will start the trek to Charleston. The cavalry will follow shortly, and we will meet in South Carolina. You have free time until tomorrow. Enjoy the rest of the day, and have a good night's sleep. Company commanders report for warning orders. Dismissed."

He waved at his most trusted few who stayed behind; the rest filed in a loud but orderly column.

"Are you ready to give it all you have?" Kaz asked.

"We are ready, General. Now that they have paid us like real soldiers, we feel we can handle some real soldier's work," David said with a smile.

"Make sure you don't lose any more toes or don't start asking to borrow any of mine," Robert laughed.

"I have boots now," David replied, pointing to his shiny black cavalry boots. "Nothing can get to my feet."

"David is like Achilles, only rather than lose his heel, he lost his toe," Kovats added. "He is on the way to becoming a regular hero. I want to listen to the songs they will be singing about him in the taverns."

Robert raised his hand in the air looking for inspiration, and improvised,

> *Let's sing about David*
> *The nine-toed man*
> *Who fought the British*
> *Like no one can.*

Everybody, including Robert, agreed that it was an awful rhyme.

"There is no song yet, but we have money, so we can at least go to a tavern and try some beer," Robert suggested. "David, the hero, should pay the first round."

"David already sent his money to his mother," Kaz said. "The first round is on me. I invite you all to Philadelphia. We will entertain in style at the City Tavern. It is on the west side of Second Street between Walnut and Chestnut.

Michael laughed and said, "General, you drink more than water and coffee? Wow, that's a surprise. We must be doing something right, and how do you know about this tavern?"

When they arrived in Philadelphia, it turned out that the City Tavern was all booked for the day.

"Let us go to the Indian Queen at the southeast corner of Market and Fourth," Kaz suggested.

"I suspect you spend more time drinking than fighting, Kaz," Robert joked.

"General Lafayette told me about this place. They brought him here to have his wounds dressed after his first battle. He said he enjoyed the good care, excellent food, and beautiful female attendants," Kaz explained.

For the first time in a long while, they felt relieved and optimistic. A heavy burden of toiling from day to day to simply survive was lifted. They were not hungry, cold, or hurt. They began to believe that fortune smiled at them this time and that this ordeal might be over one day. They saw winged victory in their dreams, floating before them as they dozed in the saddle.

Charleston

Kaz moved his unit at a steady strenuous pace. For most Legionnaires, this was the first time they would apply their training in action. The foot soldiers were sent ahead with a plan that the lancers meet them around Charleston.

The more south they moved, the warmer it got. The Legionnaires remembered Kaz's words and tried to keep their powder and socks dry. However, they often had to march through rivers, with cartridges high above their heads but the boots deep in water and mud. Valley Forge was the best training for any encounter with soil. During winter, they walked in it, lost their shoes in it, tasted it, and crawled in it for months. This experience served them well during their trek down south.

Some of them started getting sick. They suffered from malaria and overall exhaustion. Around the end of April, David began vomiting.

He could hardly stay in his saddle or keep his food. With each passing day, his condition worsened. At the beginning of May, he was delirious. He would daydream. One could hear mainly two words through his parched lips: "water" and "mother."

One day he stopped talking. Kaz was in front scouting the terrain when he spotted a buffalo atop a hill on the horizon. It crested the summit and disappeared. When the Legion stopped for a few hours respite, Robert noticed that David had lashed himself to his horse and must have expired on the way. They took him off his mount and called Kaz.

He came over, and his face turned white. He started swinging his body back and forth, steadily bending his head low and then swinging it up high behind his torso. He hit his fist on his knee repeatedly and stared at David.

"I did not do it. I failed to keep my word. I did not help David to look his enemy in the eye."

"He had a soldier's concerns. His enemy was not a man, but loneliness, fear, and death," Robert added.

Kaz delayed David's demise when he dragged him out of the snow and mud at Valley Forge. This time, dressed in his lancer uniform, sporting the shiny cavalry boots, he had his eyes closed by Robert. He would not open them again. Where was the pastor whose sermons made David volunteer? Would he know? Would he deliver a homily? Would he at least pray over this perfect patriot? What of David's mother? He was that countless eon of souls who turned the idea of a few into the grim reality of daily toil. How many would follow David? Were we worthy of his sacrifice? How long would we remember? Would we be able to carry his burden and keep the hope alive? Barefoot and freezing, he went out to haul logs for his friends. Now in the heat of the southern Sun, he was stopped while struggling to bring aid to the unknown.

David sacrificed all he had for the idea of freedom and his new country, the United States of America. He had nothing else but his young life and the belief that fighting for a noble cause was worth his youthful dedication. He was not even blessed with a bullet but was dying for days in pain with his beautiful body sacrificed piece by piece. He did not have a chance to look his enemy in the eye on the battlefield. He was the salt of the nation, a nameless one who built the foundation. He was the skeleton that built the coral reef for the vibrant future enjoyed by millions. Without his steadfast commitment, there would be no hope for better days. He was the catalyst that materialized dreams and prophetic words.

And yet again, they started digging a grave. They knew that six feet were not enough. Kaz was hewing a plate while Robert was fashioning a cross. The plaque read:

> *Lancer David Rogers*
> *1760-1779*
> *The Continental Army*
> *Pulaski Legion*

In May 1779, they were in Charleston, South Carolina, and joined with the forces of General Benjamin Lincoln. After they exchanged pleasantries with the General, Kaz asked, "What is our situation here?"

"It is tough. The Brits established themselves in Savannah and then moved up north. We gave them all we got at Kettle Creek, but they got us back at Brier Creek, and here we are. They are moving on Charleston, and we don't have enough men to stop Campbell," General explained.

"Let's see what we can do," Kaz answered. "Can I have a few of your scouts and look around?"

"You are God sent. Do what you think is right to get you going. Local people here think mostly of surrender."

"There will be no surrender as long as I am alive," Kaz looked the General in the eyes. "I owe it to those who died helping me get this far." Kaz came back in a few hours and decided to counterattack immediately.

"We will give them all we have. You are right, General. If we don't stop them here, they will gain momentum, swing the locals their way, and start moving up north to wipe out General Washington. It will be here or nowhere."

General Lincoln looked at Kaz and observed with a gloomy grin, "It might be too late already. The citizens of Charleston are debating the surrender terms as we speak."

"Where? Let's ride."

Shortly, Kaz, with his cavalry, was in the middle of town. Kaz and Colonel John Laurens appeared before Governor John Rutledge and the Council, who was getting up on a stand to address the citizens on Main Street.

Kaz drove between the stand and the congregation and shouted, "We have ridden 600 miles from Philadelphia to fight the British here. You will have to fight us if you want to surrender!"

"But Sir, you have just arrived. You don't understand the situation; it's dire. I have a responsibility to the town; it would be folly to condemn the townsfolk. It's been months without any sign of help from Congress," the Governor said.

Kaz jumped off his mount and hopped on the riser next to the Governor with his saber drawn, declaring in a slow, measured tone, "I am that sign, and my men. We rode these many miles to give battle. Will you all tell me that you would refuse your soldiers?

General Moultrie, who was in command of South Carolina forces, joined Kaz and chimed in, "The hell with the British. We will not surrender. Lead on General. We will follow."

"That's better," shouted Kaz. "The hard part accomplished. What is left to do is to break this damned siege." He jumped on his mount and was gone.

Kaz planned to launch a daring surprise attack against overwhelming British forces under the command of General Prevost, who was leisurely waiting for the surrender of Charleston. Although audacious and risky, the plan had merit if executed precisely. It should demoralize the British and stop them from their advance northward. The infantry was supposed to lie in hiding while the cavalry would emerge, fake retreat, and lead the Loyalists into a trap.

Kaz appeared in front of his infantrymen and spoke, "Our country is counting on us. All those guys in Philadelphia and New York will be lost if we do not stop the British here. It is just a drill. Remember what we practiced at Trenton; there is nothing to it. We must stay focused and keep our nerves under control. Do not move until you get the signal."

The trap was set. As the cavalry was maneuvering at full speed under the hail of bullets, the infantrymen were hiding in the thicket with the rifles loaded, ready to shoot. The first line was so close to the charging lancers that they sprayed mud from under the hoofs on the infantry uniforms. The cavalry charged and, as planned, started retreating, faking panic. The British followed them as Kaz had predicted.

And then the worst happened. One of the foot soldiers watched as his friend got shot in front of him. When the cavalryman fell from his horse, his infantry friend hiding in ambush pulled a trigger. A volley of shots followed, and the British stopped their attack. They did not fall for the trap. They realized where Kaz's infantry was hiding and directed their superior firepower at the thicket.

The cavalry had just regrouped and charged the British but without the element of surprise and no flanking fire from the infantry. The first British volley hit Captain Jan Zielinski as he was slashing his way through a line of British infantry. Kaz rode over to him but could not keep him on his mount. He lowered Jan's limping body to the ground. Kaz looked at his face and noticed two parallel cuts on his cheek. The double slashes vaguely reminded him of the cuts on the revered face of the Black Madonna of Częstochowa. There was no time to do anything for Jan.

The British arranged the troops in three lines, which gave them an almost continuous line of fire. Kaz charged with a few of his men after the second volley. He pinned a red coat to the ground with his lance and drove along the British line slashing his way with short, deadly blows.

Michael Kovats fanned the other way and rained deadly blows in true Hungarian fashion on the first row. Some of his men were following him, but it was impossible to match Michael's speed and lethal accuracy. He penetrated the second row making the British drop their guns and run. Unfortunately, the third row had time to reload before he reached them. He was hit repeatedly in the shoulders and the chest. Michael fell killed in action with his saber in his hand.

The British gave the command to retreat. Kaz stood with the remaining few covered in sweat, mud, and blood when the shooting stopped. He lost almost half of his men, who dared to stop thousands.

This heroic attack of the Pułaski Legion forced General Prevost to retreat south across the Savannah River and regroup in Georgia. The determination and ferocity of Kaz's attack convinced Prevost that he might be expecting substantial numbers of new Continentals reinforcing Charleston. This single brave charge stifled King George's plan to attack the Americans from the south and finish the colonial rebellion with a victory march up north. Yet again, Kaz removed the imminent threat looming over General Washington, which gave him time to work his magic and strengthen the Continental Army.

Kaz set out looking for Colonel Kovats and Jan. He found Michael propped by a tree trunk with his saber in his hand, smiling. It looked like he would jump up to his feet and join Kaz. Sadly, red and black holes in his uniform told a different story. Michael kept his word given to Benjamin Franklin in one of his letters, which he finished writing in Latin, *Fidelissimus ad Mortem* (Most Faithful unto Death).

Kaz put his hand on Michael's face and pulled his lids down, closing the Hungarian brave's eyes forever. He whispered a well-known phrase, which Poles and Hungarians had repeated for centuries fighting like brothers on numerous battlefields, *"Lengyel, Magyar – két jó barát, együtt harcol, s issza borát."* Then, he repeated it in Polish, *"Polak, Węgier, dwa bratanki i do szabli, i do szklanki."* He stood slowly up and looked around for a piece of wood that he could use to fashion a plaque while Robert worked on a cross. Kaz said this time in English, "A Pole, a Hungarian, two brothers, both to the saber and the bottle."

They left him on a mound between two Sabal palmetto trees with a plaque:

> *Colonel Michael Kovats de Fabriczy*
>
> *1724-1779*
>
> *The Continental Army*
>
> *Pułaski Legion*

The eternal companion to Michael Kovats, who shared his burial place, was Captain Jan Zieliński. When they laid Jan to rest, Kaz took a leather sack with the sand from the Wisła River from his saddlebag. He opened it and sprinkled some over Jan's uniform. Then, he tied the rest carefully and placed it in Jan's hand.

In a rare moment of sincere openness, Kaz shared his deep feelings with the assembled and said, "Heroes don't die in the field of battle. They are waiting like the knights of King Łokietek in their cave near Kraków. We destroy a part of our identity when we forget about their sacrifice and courage. They are ready to give their lives again whenever we relive their stories. When we don't hold them in our hearts, we are diminished, fading into a grotesque minimum of individual egoist urges devoid of the latent potential for greatness and glory they carry.

"When we understand that our life starts with a dream, heroes are reborn. It takes compassion to find a place for them in our thoughts. They don't mind waiting until we ascend the level of humane awareness high enough to find room for them in our hearts. They do not get angry or jealous of our mundane priorities and concerns, which blind us from seeing the gift they offer.

"They carry an eternal blessing waiting to be discovered. Their life story is an opłatek, from which we can break a piece and relish the strength and honor it brings. You share their effort whenever you look at a palm tree and think about Michael and Jan. Their sacrifice is not lost if you are a torchbearer carrying their memory."

The British opponent in the battle, Brigade Major Skelly, paid Pułaski's Legion the highest of compliments describing it as "the best cavalry the rebels ever had."

Volunteers

Kaz turned his mount around and started riding on with his decimated Legion moving closely behind when he noticed a group of riders fanning out from the trees. Although they did not wear British uniforms, Kaz was unsure of their intentions. He decided to stop and confront them directly. At least fifty of them rode over to Kaz, forming a semi-circle enclosing Kaz's men. They were dressed better than a similar group would up north, but they did not look like a military unit. Still, Kaz did not like their posture and the flanking.

"Who are you? What do you want?" Kaz asked as his men were fanning on both his sides.

One of the men sporting a long, dense mane of grayish hair down to his neck, which framed his white wide-brimmed hat, replied, "We are here to fight with you, General. It looks like you brought great warriors, but many stayed in the woods. I am Boyd, James Boyd. Our families will make sure to tend to their graves."

"I don't have any uniforms for you."

"We don't need uniforms. We need the British to shoot at. It looks like you chased them back to Georgia and didn't leave any for us. Get us to the British, and we will be even. I heard you in Charleston and followed you all this time, thinking about your words. Before we had a chance to talk, you did more fighting than all of us here so far. Yes, I am a free man and will not be reduced to a serf by some guy in London."

Kaz looked at this group of local militias, which, like Polish szlachta, stood for their new country in the hour of need. They understood the risks, but they also knew that freedom could not defend itself. It needed blood to grow a deep root. The British had little chance to prevail with men like them in their way.

Letter to Congress

Although Kaz lost so many men, his attack was not in vain. It stopped the British in their tracks, and they withdrew to Savannah. Kaz was admitted into the leading counsel of southern American leaders. He disliked the slowly grinding bureaucratic wheels of Congress, where paperwork and accountants always trumped the needs of the military in the field. Here, he was much closer to the decision-makers who were not hindered by the political machinery as much as it happened in Philadelphia.

On August 19, Kaz sent a letter to the Continental Congress. He wrote that he was expecting $60,000 of his private funds to be transferred from Europe to his account in the United States. With this money secured, Kaz intended to cover all the expenses of his Legion and not wait for crumbs from the table released by army auditors. He knew this letter would infuriate some who wanted to keep every decision under their control, knowing that money had a powerful grip on any independent initiative.

For the first time in the New World, he felt his effort brought tangible results. His ideas were set in motion, and he was optimistic about the outcome of the southern campaign. The British were stopped in their tracks and were retreating. If they were stopped down south, it would be easier for Washington to operate up north. Kaz was given respect and attention from the counsel here. His plans were implemented without delay and were bringing visibly positive outcomes.

His idea of buying a ship and organizing a naval military unit, which would transport cavalry to the desired location, might yet be implemented. He had thought about it ever since his trip to Turkey. He wanted to use a ship to move lethal force to any place reachable by sea. He saw that he could organize an outfit to swing fortunes in war with a bit of luck and a lot of hard work. Maybe one day, he could sail it to Gdańsk and hit the Russians and Prussians from the place they would least expect.

In the meantime, here in the United States, a marine cavalry would serve as a balancing force deployed from the south to the north at a moment's notice. The key to its success would be investing in each soldier's quality and combat readiness. It would be a naval hussar unit working much like the invincible Polish cavalry of the 17th and 18th centuries, able to wipe out more numerous forces with superior equipment and training. The old question of quantity versus quality would again prove that a healthy, competent, well-equipped mobile soldier is worth ten times more than a hungry, barefooted, and poorly trained recruit.

French Fleet

More good news was that a French fleet was on its way to attack Savannah. On September 3, General Lincoln learned that Admiral Charles Hector Comte D'Estaing was sailing from the Caribbean. His orders were to sail upriver and attack Savannah before running out of supplies and before the winter storms hit the Atlantic.

Kaz decided to keep the operational initiative and push hard down south. General Lincoln understood and accepted his plan to Kaz's delight without delay, deciding to leave on September 11. When General Lincoln was about to cross the Savannah River, the borderline between South Carolina and Georgia, he chose the Pułaski Legion as his vanguard. Lincoln dispatched an officer ahead to secure the crossing at Zubly's Ferry and turned to Kaz, saying, "You are the best in scouting any terrain for soldiers and eventual traps. I need you on the other side of the Savannah River to prepare for our crossing. Let me know when and where we can cross."

Before Lincoln finished, Kaz was already on his horse. When he reached Zubly's Ferry, only one leaky canoe could carry three infantry soldiers or one cavalryman at a time.

[The Savannah River]

The cavalryman and his supplies took the whole canoe while the horse swam tied to the boat. Before the group in charge of securing the boats finished arguing why they did not have the vessels yet, five of the Pułaski's soldiers were on the other bank. Eventually, thirty cavalrymen led by Kaz's trusted adjutant Captain Paul Bentalou crossed the Savannah River and were in Georgia. After the heroic death of Captain Kovats, Paul was now Kaz's key confidant. Kaz followed Bentalou the next day with the whole Legion. They met near Savannah. Bentalou reported that he did not find any British forces on the way, which meant they all moved back to Savannah without leaving any sentries around.

The truth was that the British did spot Bentalou's unit and frantically started to prepare their defenses. General Prevost had no intention of giving up Savannah. He was a seasoned commander and used all the hands-on deck to repel the attack. Enslaved Africans toiled day and night, digging trenches and breastworks, reinforcing redoubts and barricades.

The Legion spent the night at the estate near Savannah. Kaz sent a dispatch to General Lincoln:

We are stationed around seven miles from Savannah in the house of widow Gibbons, located on the road to Ogeechee Ferry. We are trying to make contact with the French Admiral.

[Note: The note is in the Polish Museum of America in Chicago.]

In the morning, Pułaski's scouts spotted a rider in a French uniform. He turned out to be a dispatcher from Admiral D'Estaing, trying to establish contact with General Lincoln and carrying messages. Since the Admiral knew that Pułaski was somewhere around, the dispatcher also brought cordial greetings to Kaz.

Kaz wasted no time and rode to meet the Admiral. They talked about friends they had left in France. Then, the Admiral asked Kaz to lead his army toward Savannah.

"Shouldn't we wait for General Lincoln first?" Kaz asked. "He is on his way and should be here shortly."

The Admiral lifted his shoulders in a half-shrug and said, "I am pressed for time, dear Count. I am bringing 4,000 soldiers and little in the way of supplies. We fought long and hard in the West Indies and are barely prepared to tarry long here. I must leave before the storms close the Atlantic passage while my supplies last. Besides, I am fighting two enemies already: dysentery and scurvy. There is also a high risk of the British coming with their armada and effectively blocking me in the river. Let us proceed, and hopefully, General Lincoln will not miss the battle."

Admiral D'Estaing sent a messenger to General Prevost demanding the immediate surrender of the city on behalf of the King of France. In response, General Prevost asked for a 24-hour truce to discuss the Admiral's proposal with his counsel. The Admiral graciously agreed. General Prevost used the extra time to double his preparation of the defenses. He brought an additional 800 men under Colonel Maitland to reinforce his troops. In all, General Prevost had 3,200 men defending Savannah.

The Admiral was not idle during the truce either. He used the time to bring cannons from his ships and set them 1,000 feet from the British positions. He could not sail any closer to the city because the British scuttled some ships and blocked Comte D'Estaing's approach. When Prevost ultimately refused to surrender the town, D'Estaing started a five-day-long continuous bombardment.

Eventually, General Lincoln arrived, leading 1,000 men out of around 5,000 at his disposal at Charleston. Combined French and American forces of 5,000 were in place for the decisive assault. General Lincoln, Admiral D'Estaing, and Kaz started final preparations with a small group of trusted officers.

The Admiral looked at all assembled advisors and said, "Gentlemen, I don't have much time to spare. If we don't act promptly, you might lose the help of my ships and my men."

"The British are getting weaker day by day. The more we wait, the weaker they become," Lincoln replied.

"They are seasoned, well-equipped soldiers waiting to be reinforced from the ocean at any time. Time is working on their side," Admiral remarked.

Lincoln turned to Kaz and asked, "Kaz, how will you crack this nut?"

"We are evenly matched number-wise. To be confident in our strength, we should have at least three times more soldiers than the defenders, which we do not enjoy. They are well dug in and seem to have enough supplies. Our only chance is a bold and decisive move. We should break through, storm inside, and attack the city in force."

"James, show us the maps," said Lincoln pointing to Sergeant Major James Curry of the Charleston Grenadiers. All present leaned over the maps stretched on the table.

"Kaz, do you see any weak spots?" General Lincoln asked.

"Not really. The city is on an elevation backed by a river. There would be a good way to break through to the left by the marches, but they knew about it and built this redoubt. They call it Spring Hill Redoubt."

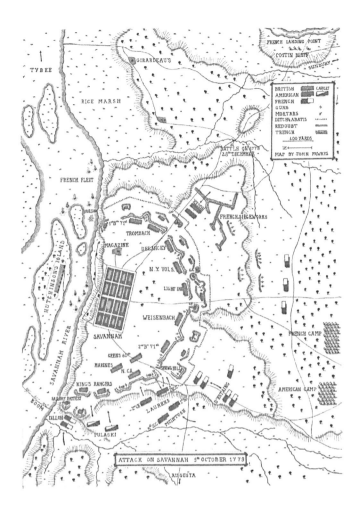

[The Siege of Savannah 1779]

"What then, gentlemen? We need action," the Admiral urged.

"We must force our way through and bring havoc to the city," General Lincoln observed. "The citizens are pushing General Prevost to surrender, but the old fox would not budge."

"What if," started Kaz pacing around the table. "We need to confuse them before our major assault. We have no choice but to attack that confounded Spring Hill Redoubt," continued Kaz jumping to the map and pointing to the mound on the left by the river. "This is our way in. We could sneak through the marshes under cover of darkness and fog and launch an all-out assault at dawn."

"Since I am insisting on the attack and I already challenged Prevost directly, I will lead the charge. I need you, my dear Lincoln, to create a diversion. Light this citadel up with numerous incursions. Make them move the troops away from the Spring Hill Redoubt if possible. Once I take the redoubt, General Pułaski will follow through with his cavalry. It should work. Agreed?"

"Agreed, my Admiral. Let's chase the old fox out of his den," General Lincoln echoed.

Attack

The line between a plan and its execution is rarely seamless. So it was at Savannah on 9 October 1779. The cover of darkness and fog was supposed to be an element of surprise, shielding the attackers from view. It turned out that it worked against the French and the Continentals. The units lost their way in the dark, trudging through muddy marshes and rice fields by the river. The allied French and American forces were not ready for an attack as planned by 4 o'clock but after 5:30 am. All units were deployed within 160 yards of the edge of the woods bordering Savannah. Rather than before dawn, they were ready to attack when the cover of darkness and fog was gone. The Sun illuminated white French uniforms as they marched in their tight attack formation, perfectly visible to the defenders hunkering in the Spring Hill Redoubt. With every step closer to the stronghold, they could hear more distinct tones of bagpipes.

The worst yet was the betrayal of Sergeant Major James Curry. Right after the war council, Curry deserted the Continentals and informed the British about the main points of the attack and its timing. General Prevost reacted by reinforcing the garrison of the Spring Hill Redoubt overnight with the grenadiers of the 60th Regiment, a battalion of Maitland's Highlanders, the 71st Regiment of Foot, and Fraser's Highlanders, who had distinguished themselves at Stono Ferry, and a company of marines, all commanded by Lieutenant Colonel John Maitland. They had their rifles trained on the attackers, ready to fire at a moment's notice, with bagpipers urging them on to battle. The surprised party was the French and the Continentals. The first volley had a devastating effect.

[French troops attacking the Spring Hill Redoubt]

The attackers reached Augusta Road, but wave after wave was cut to shreds. The British were shooting at them with massive fire advantage from an elevated position. They had two 18-pound guns firing directly at the approaching three columns. Two British galleys and a frigate directed their cannon fire at Augusta Road, adding to the carnage. Bodies filled trenches below the redoubt. Admiral D'Estaing was twice wounded.

Swedish Count Curt von Stedingk led the left attack column, reaching the last trench. In his journal, he wrote, "I had the pleasure of planting the American flag on the last trench, but the enemy renewed its attack, and our people were annihilated by cross-fire." Heavily maimed, he was forced to retreat with the last twenty of his men, who were all wounded.

[Final charge of General Pułaski, painting by Stanisław Kaczor Batowski]

Kaz positioned his Legion where Bull Street extended south of the city. When he heard that the Admiral was injured, he decided to take over the command. Leaving his units protected by a few hills under the command of Colonel Peter Horry, he rode over to the front of the remaining troops, followed by his adjutant, Captain Paul Bentalou, and Colonel John C. Cooper. John was particularly impressed with Kaz's military skills and expertise. He took every opportunity to study fencing and horsemanship with Kaz. He promised Kaz that one day a Cooper would pay a debt of honor and fight for Poland in her hour of need.

Suddenly, Kaz shouted, *"Jezus, Maryja!"* His horse buckled and stood up on his hind legs. Kaz noticed a red stain on the saddle as he glanced at the horse. He leaned over, and blood started streaming down his leg. It was shrapnel the size of a walnut, which hit Kaz on his right thigh. Yet again, Kaz was betrayed by someone he was supposed to trust. It was the final treachery. An American Sergeant General, James Curry, betrayed the cause, and Kaz paid the ultimate price.

Kaz sensed a presence far in the distance as he was losing consciousness. It was the feeling of primordial awareness. He leaned backward in his saddle, losing balance. He was observing his body from up high. His head tilted backward, and the Sun penetrated his eyes. Gravity pulled his body back to the left side of his mount. His limp spine bent grotesquely so that his head almost touched his horse's croup. Rather than raised with the hand firmly gripping the saber, his arm was jerked aimlessly by sudden moves of the frantic steed. His fingers were opened with the blade dangling hopelessly as if trying to urge Kaz to renew the attack. He started sliding to the left with his head lower than the saddle. He gazed upside down in astonishment through his wide-open eyes.

Sunrays dancing on his retina created a multicolor veil through which he noticed a buffalo grazing miles away upon the crest of a hill. He felt the base of his consciousness expanding far beyond Savannah. He sensed the same presence when encountering his first buffalo at Zazulińce sixteen years ago. It was extending through time and space from the kernel of consciousness, encompassing generations of men coming out of their valleys. Kaz watched them tossed by the waves of life from the ocean deep with the buffalo by his side.

THE END

APPENDIX

TO CHAPTER 3: Historical Background

As Poland grew in strength and wealth, her elites became affluent. It brought the vices of vanity, decadence, and pride. The most potent magnates in 18th century Poland knew their family was more prosperous and influential than a mere king. Indeed, the Crown revenue was less than the legendary wealth of the key Polish and Lithuanian magnates, who often plotted and took part in international intrigues to the detriment of the Crown. They lacked the foresight to imagine the unimaginable: that their game of thrones would bring an end to Poland as a country. Ultimately, they destroyed the golden goose, which laid the golden eggs for generations. They thought that the goose was so big that nobody would be able to destroy it. In the end, it was only a goose; the lions that were to protect her deteriorated into pigs, slaughtered one by one in the barbecue of history.

In 1697, Augustus II the Strong was elected as the King of Poland and, automatically, the Grand Duke of Lithuania. He was the Saxon Hercules able to break horseshoes with his bare hands. To become the King of Poland, he converted to Catholicism, much like the Lithuanian Jagiełło had done in 1386. He fathered 365 to 382 children. It was not nearly as much as Genghis Khan, credited with 1,000 to 2,000 offspring, but still an impressive number. His only legitimate child who followed him on the Polish throne deservedly earned the nickname Augustus III the Fat.

Before the election of 1764, rather than concentrate on what the voters would like, the candidates had to secure the resources needed for the election process. They used their private funds as well as the assets and connections of their family and friends. Since more was needed, the prospective candidates focused their campaigns on securing powerful, wealthy sponsors from other nations. The key here was to attract other countries and the families connected with them. Often wealthy families controlled more than one country, an accepted process in Europe. Polish families and kings also invested their funds to support candidates in other countries.

The best way to limit the influence of outsiders and preserve the integrity and continuity of Poland-Lithuania had been to secure the continuation of rule for the same family. Once a line expired, the free election process opened the door to foreign influence.

Deciding to allow a candidate from the Saxon House of Wettin to rule Poland in 1697 after he converted from Lutheran to Roman Catholic faith seemed a good option to most. Money from Prussia and Russia played a part as well. The Wettins represented an old family dating back to 1030 when they started ruling the Saxon Eastern March of the Holy Roman Empire. After the family was divided into two branches in 1485, the Albertine Branch ruled most of Saxony. Poles calculated that the Wettins might be a successful union with the west, much like the house of Jagiełło from Lithuania turned out to be a success in the east.

Augustus III, the last of the Saxon kings of Poland, was a significant setback. Rather than work on the affairs of the state, he focused his time on leisure, art, and entertainment. He failed to focus on maintaining the tradition of securing the future through hereditary continuity, which was the critical factor in the demise of his House of Wettin and Poland.

While the rulers of other countries were fighting for domination, Augustus III enjoyed his pleasant life in Dresden, rarely even visiting Warszawa. His rule resulted in the downfall of his own Saxon house of Wettin and the catastrophic election of Stanisław Anthony Poniatowski to the King of Poland in 1764 after Augustus' death.

The fight for the succession of the Polish Crown started in earnest on 5 October 1763, when Augustus III died, which began Interregnum, a period and process described by the constitution. When a king died, the Roman Catholic Primate of Poland assumed the duties of the Interrex and managed the election process. A series of national assemblies, called diets, were organized. First was the Convocation Diet, where the candidates were proposed, selected, and approved. It was followed by the Election Diet held at the Wola field near Warszawa. Once elected, the King officially signed the Pacta Conventa, a set of rules he swore to obey. Finally, the Interrex called for the crowning ceremony, and the newly elected King assumed the royal duties.

The oldest son of Augustus III, Frederick Christian, was destined to be a relatively strong candidate, but on 17 December 1763, he died of smallpox. His son was too young to run effectively, leaving his brothers as possible runners-up from the House of Wettin. Unfortunately, Augustus III had not secured enough funds and powerful connections before he died to guarantee the third Wettin on the Polish throne.

Another German paying close attention to the fate of the Polish Crown was Princess Sophie Friederike Auguste von Anhalt-Zerbst-Dornburg, born in 1729 in Stettin, Pomerania (now Szczecin, Poland). She took the election process much more seriously than Augustus III did. She managed to move to Russia, convert to Orthodox Christianity, kill her husband, Czar Peter III, and become the Empress of Russia while Augustus III was hunting, buying paintings, and listening to the music of Bach in Dresden.

Understanding the threat Poland posed to her ambitious plans of expanding Russia eastward, Catherine took the issue of Polish succession seriously. She invested enormous sums of money and her significant international connections to systematically build a successful coalition to influence the election process. She also picked a suitable candidate, Stanisław Poniatowski.

Before the election, Catherine wrote to King Frederick of Prussia on 17 October 1763, suggesting Stanisław Anthony Poniatowski as the candidate for the King of Poland. She reasoned that being the least popular of the contenders among the Polish nobility, she would easily manipulate him if he were to win the throne. Count Hermann Karl von Keyserling, Catherine's envoy to Poland, did not like Prince Adam Czartoryski, a candidate suggested by the House of Czartoryski. He wrote about the prince, "He is too smart, too rich, too much of a Pole, and would not serve as a Russian candidate; he dreams only to make Poland a reorganized state." On 11 April 1764, Russia and Prussia signed a secret pact mutually pledging to promote Anthony Poniatowski to the throne. It was followed almost 200 years later by the similarly infamous Ribbentrop Molotov pact, which started World War II in 1939.

The Interrex, Polish Roman Catholic primate Władysław Łubieński, chose the Convocation Diet for 7 May 1764 and the Election Diet for 27 August 1764. The diets brought large numbers of soldiers to Warszawa. Brightly colored uniforms indicated their loyalty to a specific party or a family. Troops filled the streets and courtyards. They loitered around the city, mainly congregating around diet chambers. Russian troops numbering 8,000 were brought under the pretense of safeguarding from any excesses of anarchy. There were even outlandish claims that the Russians were protecting the voters against the excesses of the Crown army.

Primate Łubieński was a member of the House of Czartoryski coterie, called the Familia (Family). Viable contenders were Carl Christian Joseph of the House of Wettin, Crown Hetman Jan Klemens Branicki, the Republican of the House of Potocki coterie, Prince Adam Kazimierz Czartoryski of the House of Czartoryski, and the least popular candidate Stanisław Anthony Poniatowski of the House of Czartoryski coterie.

During the actual election, there was only one candidate left standing. The rest had been "handled" by Empress Catherine. She held Carl Christian Joseph in his Courland palace in Mitawa at the coast of the Baltic Sea, so he could not attend the election. Prince Adam Czartoryski resigned under pressure from Catherine in favor of

Stanisław Anthony. The majority of szlachta was strongly anti-Russian and supported Branicki. If the election had been free without Russian meddling, Branicki would have won. Hetman Branicki was maneuvered out of his office and chased out of the country by a group led by primate Łubieński during the Convocation Diet.

As the only remaining candidate, Stanisław Anthony, the court Stolnik (officer) from the Grand Duchy of Lithuania, was unanimously elected. The House of Czartoryski invited Russian soldiers to "protect the election," but they did not bother to think about how they would send these soldiers back.

Previous elections celebrated Polish freedom and democracy, albeit not for all, but a million with the titles of szlachta were still eligible to vote. They would usually attend the election 50,000 to 100,000 strong and proud. The result of Russian scheming, enabled by the ambitious House of Czartoryski, who decided to bend the rules in their favor, was the main reason why only little over 5,000 voters were attending the election, surrounded beyond the election field of Wola by 8,000 Russian militaries. Most of the Commonwealth was disappointed with the deterioration of the electoral process. They were disgusted with the plotting and double talk. Disillusioned, many boycotted the 1764 election. In their wildest dreams, none of them expected that the result of this sham would be the end of the most serene republic, as they used to call the Commonwealth of Poland-Lithuania.

On 7 September 1764, Stanisław Anthony Poniatowski was elected King of Poland and the Grand Duke of Lithuania with the unanimous consent of a mere 5,584 votes. On 25 November 1764, Primate Władysław Łubieński crowned Poniatowski as King of Poland. Once elected and crowned, Stanisław Anthony changed his name to Stanisław II August, also known as King Stan.

The courts of France, Austria, and Turkey did not accept the election. They regarded King Stanisław II August Poniatowski as a pawn in the hands of Empress Catherine. It took enormous diplomatic effort and war with Turkey to change their minds.

King Stan swore to be a King of Poland, anointed to lead the largest country in Europe to greatness. Instead, his rule ended in 1795 when he signed documents that partitioned Poland, terminating her 800 years of political existence. He completed his life in humiliation as a pensioner of Empress Catherine in St. Petersburg. He preferred disgraceful retirement in the place of an honorable fight to preserve Poland's independence.

The election of 1764 was a depressing event, with various coteries using foreign aid to gain an advantage for their families, disregarding the Commonwealth's security. Short-sighted, rather than using foreign influences, they were manipulated by them to the ends they did not fully understand. Once Poland was attacked by her neighbors and eliminated from the political map of Europe in 1795, historians started writing not about what Poles were trying to accomplish but rather about what foreign powers decided to achieve through this catastrophic election. After all, losers do not count, and Poland lost.

Made in the USA
Middletown, DE
09 September 2023

37839443R00223